THE BURWASH EDITION OF THE COMPLETE
WORKS IN PROSE AND VERSE OF

RUDYARD KIPLING

VOLUME XIII

PUCK OF POOK'S HILL
REWARDS AND FAIRIES

The Collected Works Of

RUDYARD KIPLING

Puck Of Pook's Hill
Rewards And Fairies

BURWASH

AMS PRESS

NEW YORK

This is a numbered set, of which this is number . . .

Reprinted from a copy in the collection of the
Harvard University Libraries
From the edition of 1941, Garden City
First AMS EDITION published 1970
Manufactured in the United States of America

With permission of the estate of Rudyard Kipling,
Doubleday and Company, Inc., and Macmillan and Company, Ltd.

International Standard Book Number:
complete set: 0-404-03740-2
volume 13: 0-404-03753-4

Library of Congress Catalog Card Number: 75-120920

AMS PRESS, INC.
NEW YORK, N. Y. 10003

CONTENTS

PUCK OF POOK'S HILL

CONTENTS

xiii

PUCK OF POOK'S HILL

Puck of Pook's Hill was first published in 1906

WELAND'S SWORD

PUCK'S SONG

See you the dimpled track that runs
  All hollow through the wheat?
O that was where they hauled the guns
  That smote King Philip's fleet!

See you our little mill that clacks,
  So busy by the brook?
She has ground her corn and paid her tax
  Ever since Domesday Book.

See you our stilly woods of oak,
  And the dread ditch beside?
O that was where the Saxons broke,
  On the day that Harold died!

See you the windy levels spread
  About the gates of Rye?
O that was where the Northmen fled,
  When Alfred's ships came by!

See you our pastures wide and lone,
  Where the red oxen browse?
O there was a City thronged and known,
  Ere London boasted a house!

And see you, after rain, the trace
  Of mound and ditch and wall?
O that was a Legion's camping-place,
  When Caesar sailed from Gaul!

PUCK OF POOK'S HILL

And see you marks that show and fade,
  Like shadows on the Downs?
O they are the lines the Flint Men made,
  To guard their wondrous towns!

Trackway and Camp and City lost,
  Salt Marsh where now is corn;
Old Wars, old Peace, old Arts that cease,
  And so was England born!

She is not any common Earth,
  Water or Wood or Air,
But Merlin's Isle of Gramarye,
  Where you and I will fare.

WELAND'S SWORD

THE CHILDREN were at the Theatre, acting to Three Cows as much as they could remember of *Midsummer Night's Dream*. Their father had made them a small play out of the big Shakespeare one, and they had rehearsed it with him and with their mother till they could say it by heart. They began where Nick Bottom the weaver comes out of the bushes with a donkey's head on his shoulders, and finds Titania Queen of the Fairies asleep. Then they skipped to the part where Bottom asks three little fairies to scratch his head and bring him honey, and they ended where he falls asleep in Titania's arms. Dan was Puck and Nick Bottom, as well as all three Fairies. He wore a pointy-eared cloth cap for Puck, and a paper donkey's head out of a Christmas cracker—but it tore if you were not careful—for Bottom. Una was Titania, with a wreath of columbines and a foxglove wand.

The Theatre lay in a meadow called the Long Slip. A little mill-stream, carrying water to a mill two or three fields away, bent round one corner of it, and in the middle of the bend lay a large old Fairy Ring of darkened grass, which was the stage. The mill-stream banks, overgrown with willow, hazel, and guelder-rose, made convenient places to wait in till your turn came; and a grown-up who had seen it said that Shakespeare himself could not have imagined a more suitable setting for his play. They were not, of course, allowed to act on Midsummer Night itself, but they went down after tea on Midsummer Eve, when the shadows were growing, and they took their supper—hard-boiled eggs, Bath Oliver biscuits, and salt in an envelope—with them. Three Cows had been milked and were grazing steadily with a tearing noise that one could hear all down the meadow; and the noise of the Mill at work sounded like bare feet running on hard ground. A cuckoo sat on a gate-post singing his broken June tune, 'cuckoo-cuk,' while a busy kingfisher crossed from the mill-stream to the brook which ran on the other side of the meadow. Everything else was a sort of thick, sleepy stillness smelling of meadow-sweet and dry grass.

Their play went beautifully. Dan remembered all his parts—Puck, Bottom, and the three Fairies—and Una never forgot a word of Titania—not even the difficult piece where she tells the Fairies how to feed Bottom with 'apricocks, green figs, and dewberries,' and all the lines end in 'ies.' They were both so pleased that they acted it three times over from beginning to end before they sat down in the unthistly centre of the Ring to eat eggs and Bath Olivers. This was when they heard a whistle among the alders on the bank, and they jumped.

The bushes parted. In the very spot where Dan had stood as Puck they saw a small, brown, broad-shouldered, pointy-eared person with a snub nose, slanting blue eyes, and a grin that ran right across his freckled face. He shaded his forehead as though he were watching Quince, Snout, Bottom, and the others rehearsing *Pyramus and Thisbe*, and, in a voice as deep as Three Cows asking to be milked, he began:—

> '*What hempen homespuns have we swaggering here,*
> *So near the cradle of the fairy Queen?*'

He stopped, hollowed one hand round his ear, and, with a wicked twinkle in his eye, went on:—

6

WELAND'S SWORD

'What, a play toward? I'll be an auditor;
An actor, too, perhaps, if I see cause.'

The children looked and gasped. The small thing—he was
no taller than Dan's shoulder—stepped quietly into the Ring.

'I'm rather out of practice,' said he; 'but that's the way my
part ought to be played.'

Still the children stared at him—from his dark-blue cap,
like a big columbine flower, to his bare, hairy feet. At last
he laughed.

'Please don't look like that. It isn't *my* fault. What else
could you expect?' he said.

'We didn't expect any one,' Dan answered slowly. 'This is
our field.'

'Is it?' said their visitor, sitting down. 'Then what on
Human Earth made you act *Midsummer Night's Dream* three
times over, *on* Midsummer Eve, *in* the middle of a Ring, and
under—right *under* one of my oldest hills in Old England?
Pook's Hill—Puck's Hill—Puck's Hill—Pook's Hill! It's as
plain as the nose on my face.'

He pointed to the bare, fern-covered slope of Pook's Hill
that runs up from the far side of the mill-stream to a dark
wood. Beyond that wood the ground rises and rises for five
hundred feet, till at last you climb out on the bare top of
Beacon Hill, to look over the Pevensey Levels and the Channel and half the naked South Downs.

'By Oak, Ash, and Thorn!' he cried, still laughing. 'If this
had happened a few hundred years ago you'd have had all
the People of the Hills out like bees in June!'

'We didn't know it was wrong,' said Dan.

'Wrong!' The little fellow shook with laughter. 'Indeed, it
isn't wrong. You've done something that Kings and Knights

7

and Scholars in old days would have given their crowns and
spurs and books to find out. If Merlin himself had helped
you, you couldn't have managed better! You've broken the
Hills—you've broken the Hills! It hasn't happened in a thousand years.'

'We—we didn't mean to,' said Una.

'Of course you didn't! That's just why you did it. Unluckily
the Hills are empty now, and all the People of the Hills are
gone. I'm the only one left. I'm Puck, the oldest Old Thing
in England, very much at your service if—if you care to have
anything to do with me. If you don't, of course you've only
to say so, and I'll go.'

He looked at the children, and the children looked at him
for quite half a minute. His eyes did not twinkle any more.
They were very kind, and there was the beginning of a good
smile on his lips.

Una put out her hand. 'Don't go,' she said. 'We like you.'

'Have a Bath Oliver,' said Dan, and he passed over the
squashy envelope with the eggs.

'By Oak, Ash, and Thorn,' cried Puck, taking off his blue
cap, 'I like you too. Sprinkle a plenty salt on the biscuit,
Dan, and I'll eat it with you. That'll show you the sort of
person *I* am. Some of us'—he went on, with his mouth full—
'couldn't abide Salt, or Horseshoes over a door, or Mountain-
ash berries, or Running Water, or Cold Iron, or the sound of
Church Bells. But I'm Puck!'

He brushed the crumbs carefully from his doublet and
shook hands.

'We always said, Dan and I,' Una stammered, 'that if it
ever happened we'd know ex-actly what to do; but—but now
it seems all different somehow.'

'She means meeting a fairy,' said Dan. '*I* never believed in
'em—not after I was six, anyhow.'

8

'I did,' said Una. 'At least, I sort of half believed till we learned "Farewell, Rewards." Do you know "Farewell, Rewards and Fairies"?'

'Do you mean this?' said Puck. He threw his big head back and began at the second line:—

> *'Good housewives now may say,*
> *For now foul sluts in dairies*
> *Do fare as well as they;*
> *And though they sweep their hearths no less*

('Join in, Una!')

> *Than maids were wont to do,*
> *Yet who of late for cleanliness*
> *Finds sixpence in her shoe?'*

The echoes flapped all along the flat meadow.

'Of course I know it,' he said.

'And then there's the verse about the Rings,' said Dan. 'When I was little it always made me feel unhappy in my inside.'

'"Witness those rings and roundelays," do you mean?' boomed Puck, with a voice like a great church organ.

> *'Of theirs which yet remain,*
> *Were footed in Queen Mary's days*
> *On many a grassy plain,*
> *But since of late Elizabeth,*
> *And, later, James came in,*
> *Are never seen on any heath*
> *As when the time hath been.'*

'It's some time since I heard that sung, but there's no good beating about the bush: it's true. The People of the Hills have all left. I saw them come into Old England and I saw them go. Giants, trolls, kelpies, brownies, goblins, imps; wood, tree, mound, and water spirits; heath-people, hill-watchers, treasure-guards, good people, little people, pish-ogues, leprechauns, night-riders, pixies, nixies, gnomes, and the rest—gone, all gone! I came into England with Oak, Ash, and Thorn, and when Oak, Ash, and Thorn are gone I shall go too.'

Dan looked round the meadow—at Una's Oak by the lower gate; at the line of ash trees that overhang Otter Pool where the mill-stream spills over when the Mill does not need it; and at the gnarled old white-thorn where Three Cows scratched their necks.

'It's all right,' he said; and added, 'I'm planting a lot of acorns this autumn too.'

'Then aren't you most awfully old?' said Una.

'Not old—fairly long-lived, as folk say hereabouts. Let me see—my friends used to set my dish of cream for me o' nights when Stonehenge was new. Yes, before the Flint Men made the Dewpond under Chanctonbury Ring.'

Una clasped her hands, cried 'Oh!' and nodded her head.

'She's thought a plan,' Dan explained. 'She always does like that when she thinks a plan.'

'I was thinking—suppose we saved some of our porridge and put it in the attic for you? They'd notice if we left it in the nursery.'

'Schoolroom,' said Dan quickly, and Una flushed, because they had made a solemn treaty that summer not to call the schoolroom the nursery any more.

'Bless your heart o' gold!' said Puck. 'You'll make a fine considering wench some market-day. I really don't want you to put out a bowl for me; but if ever I need a bite, be sure I'll tell you.'

He stretched himself at length on the dry grass, and the children stretched out beside him, their bare legs waving happily in the air. They felt they could not be afraid of him any more than of their particular friend old Hobden the hedger. He did not bother them with grown-up questions, or laugh at the donkey's head, but lay and smiled to himself in the most sensible way.

'Have you a knife on you?' he said at last.

Dan handed over his big one-bladed outdoor knife, and Puck began to carve out a piece of turf from the centre of the Ring.

'What's that for—magic?' said Una, as he pressed up the square of chocolate loam that cut like so much cheese.

'One of my little magics,' he answered, and cut another. 'You see, I can't let you into the hills because the People of the Hills have gone; but if you care to take seizin from me, I may be able to show you something out of the common here on Human Earth. You certainly deserve it.'

'What's taking seizin?' said Dan cautiously.

'It's an old custom the people had when they bought and sold land. They used to cut out a clod and hand it over to the buyer, and you weren't lawfully seized of your land—it didn't really belong to you—till the other fellow had actually given you a piece of it—like this.' He held out the turves.

'But it's our own meadow,' said Dan, drawing back. 'Are you going to magic it away?'

Puck laughed. 'I know it's your meadow, but there's a great deal more in it than you or your father ever guessed. Try!'

He turned his eyes on Una.

'I'll do it,' she said. Dan followed her example at once.

'Now are you two lawfully seized and possessed of all Old England,' began Puck, in a sing-song voice. 'By right of Oak, Ash, and Thorn are you free to come and go and look and

know where I shall show or best you please. You shall see
What you shall see and you shall hear What you shall hear,
though It shall have happened three thousand year; and you
shall know neither Doubt nor Fear. Fast! Hold fast all I
give you.'

The children shut their eyes, but nothing happened.

'Well?' said Una, disappointedly opening them. 'I thought
there would be dragons.'

' "Though It shall have happened three thousand year," '
said Puck, and counted on his fingers. 'No; I'm afraid there
were no dragons three thousand years ago.'

'But there hasn't happened anything at all,' said Dan.

'Wait awhile,' said Puck. 'You don't grow an oak in a year
—and Old England's older than twenty oaks. Let's sit down
again and think. *I* can do that for a century at a time.'

'Ah, but you're a fairy,' said Dan.

'Have you ever heard me say that word yet?' said Puck
quickly.

'No. You talk about "the People of the Hills," but you
never say "fairies," ' said Una. 'I was wondering at that. Don't
you like it?'

'How would you like to be called "mortal" or "human
being" all the time?' said Puck; 'or "son of Adam" or "daughter of Eve"?'

'I shouldn't like it at all,' said Dan. 'That's how the Djinns
and Afrits talk in the *Arabian Nights.*'

'And that's how *I* feel about saying—that word that I don't
say. Besides, what you call *them* are made-up things the
People of the Hills have never heard of—little buzzflies with
butterfly wings and gauze petticoats, and shiny stars in their
hair, and a wand like a school-teacher's cane for punishing
bad boys and rewarding good ones. *I* know 'em!'

'We don't mean that sort,' said Dan. 'We hate 'em too.'

'Exactly,' said Puck. 'Can you wonder that the People of the Hills don't care to be confused with that painty-winged, wand-waving, sugar-and-shake-your-head set of impostors? Butterfly wings, indeed! I've seen Sir Huon and a troop of his people setting off from Tintagel Castle for Hy-Brasil in the teeth of a sou'-westerly gale, with the spray flying all over the Castle, and the Horses of the Hills wild with fright. Out they'd go in a lull, screaming like gulls, and back they'd be driven five good miles inland before they could come head to wind again. Butterfly wings! It was Magic—Magic as black as Merlin could make it, and the whole sea was green fire and white foam with singing mermaids in it. And the Horses of the Hills picked their way from one wave to another by the lightning flashes! *That* was how it was in the old days!'

'Splendid,' said Dan, but Una shuddered.

'I'm glad they're gone, then; but what made the People of the Hills go away?' Una asked.

'Different things. I'll tell you one of them some day—the thing that made the biggest flit of any,' said Puck. 'But they didn't all flit at once. They dropped off, one by one, through the centuries. Most of them were foreigners who couldn't stand our climate. *They* flitted early.'

'How early?' said Dan.

'A couple of thousand years or more. The fact is they began as Gods. The Phoenicians brought some over when they came to buy tin; and the Gauls, and the Jutes, and the Danes, and the Frisians, and the Angles brought more when they landed. They were always landing in those days, or being driven back to their ships, and they always brought their Gods with them. England is a bad country for Gods. Now, *I* began as I mean to go on. A bowl of porridge, a dish of milk, and a little quiet fun with the country folk in the lanes was enough for me then, as it is now. I belong here, you see, and I have been mixed up with people all my days. But most of the others insisted on being Gods, and having temples, and altars, and priests, and sacrifices of their own.'

'People burned in wicker baskets?' said Dan. 'Like Miss Blake tells us about?'

'All sorts of sacrifices,' said Puck. 'If it wasn't men, it was horses, or cattle, or pigs, or metheglin—that's a sticky, sweet sort of beer. *I* never liked it. They were a stiff-necked, extravagant set of idols, the Old Things. But what was the result? Men don't like being sacrificed at the best of times; they don't even like sacrificing their farm-horses. After a while, men simply left the Old Things alone, and the roofs of their temples fell in, and the Old Things had to scuttle out and pick up a living as they could. Some of them took to hanging about trees, and hiding in graves and groaning o' nights. If they groaned loud enough and long enough they might frighten a poor countryman into sacrificing a hen, or leaving a pound of butter for them. I remember one Goddess called Belisama. She became a common wet water-spirit somewhere in Lancashire. And there were hundreds of other friends of mine. First they were Gods. Then they were People of the Hills, and then they flitted to other places because they couldn't get on with the English for one reason or another. There was only one Old Thing, I remember, who honestly worked for his living after he came down in the world. He was called Weland, and he was a smith to some Gods. I've forgotten their names, but he used to make them swords and spears. I think he claimed kin with Thor of the Scandinavians.'

'*Heroes of Asgard* Thor?' said Una. She had been reading the book.

'Perhaps,' answered Puck. 'None the less, when bad times came, he didn't beg or steal. He worked; and I was lucky enough to be able to do him a good turn.'

'Tell us about it,' said Dan. 'I think I like hearing of Old Things.'

They rearranged themselves comfortably, each chewing a grass stem. Puck propped himself on one strong arm and went on:—

'Let's think! I met Weland first on a November afternoon in a sleet storm, on Pevensey Level——'

'Pevensey? Over the hill, you mean?' Dan pointed south.

'Yes; but it was all marsh in those days, right up to Horse-bridge and Hydeneye. I was on Beacon Hill—they called it Brunanburgh then—when I saw the pale flame that burning thatch makes, and I went down to look. Some pirates—I think they must have been Peofn's men—were burning a village on the Levels, and Weland's image—a big, black wooden thing with amber beads round its neck—lay in the bows of a black thirty-two-oar galley that they had just beached. Bitter cold it was! There were icicles hanging from her deck and the oars were glazed over with ice, and there was ice on Weland's lips. When he saw me he began a long chant in his own tongue, telling me how he was going to rule England, and how I should smell the smoke of his altars from Lincolnshire to the Isle of Wight. *I* didn't care! I'd seen too many Gods charging into Old England to be upset about it. I let him sing himself out while his men were burning the village, and then I said (I don't know what put it into my head), "Smith of the Gods," I said, "the time comes when I shall meet you plying your trade for hire by the wayside." '

'What did Weland say?' said Una. 'Was he angry?'

'He called me names and rolled his eyes, and I went away to wake up the people inland. But the pirates conquered the country, and for centuries Weland was a most important God. He had temples everywhere—from Lincolnshire to the Isle of Wight, as he said—and his sacrifices were simply scandalous. To do him justice, he preferred horses to men; but men *or* horses, I knew that presently he'd have to come down in the world—like the other Old Things. I gave him lots of time— I gave him about a thousand years—and at the end of 'em I went into one of his temples near Andover to see how he prospered. There was his altar, and there was his image, and there were his priests, and there were the congregation, and everybody seemed quite happy, except Weland and the priests. In the old days the congregation were unhappy until the priests had chosen their sacrifices; and so would *you* have been. When the service began a priest rushed out, dragged a man up to the altar, pretended to hit him on the head with a little gilt axe, and the man fell down and pretended to die. Then everybody shouted: "A sacrifice to Weland! A sacrifice to Weland!" '

'And the man wasn't really dead?' said Una.

'Not a bit. All as much pretence as a dolls' tea-party. Then they brought out a splendid white horse, and the priest cut some hair from its mane and tail and burned it on the altar, shouting, "A sacrifice!" That counted the same as if a man and a horse had been killed. I saw poor Weland's face through the smoke, and I couldn't help laughing. He looked so disgusted and so hungry, and all he had to satisfy himself was a horrid smell of burning hair. Just a dolls' tea-party!

'I judged it better not to say anything then ('twouldn't have been fair), and the next time I came to Andover, a few hundred years later, Weland and his temple were gone, and there was a Christian bishop in a church there. None of the People of the Hills could tell me anything about him, and I supposed that he had left England.' Puck turned, lay on his other elbow, and thought for a long time.

'Let's see,' he said at last. 'It must have been some few years later—a year or two before the Conquest, I think—that I came back to Pook's Hill here, and one evening I heard old Hobden talking about Weland's Ford.'

'If you mean old Hobden the hedger, he's only seventy-two. He told me so himself,' said Dan. 'He's an intimate friend of ours.'

'You're quite right,' Puck replied. 'I meant old Hobden's ninth great-grandfather. He was a free man and burned charcoal hereabouts. I've known the family, father and son, so long that I get confused sometimes. Hob of the Dene was my Hobden's name, and he lived at the Forge cottage. Of course, I pricked up my ears when I heard Weland mentioned, and I scuttled through the woods to the Ford just beyond Bog Wood yonder.' He jerked his head westward, where the valley narrows between wooded hills and steep hop-fields.

'Why, that's Willingford Bridge,' said Una. 'We go there for walks often. There's a kingfisher there.'

'It was Weland's Ford then, dearie. A road led down to it from the Beacon on the top of the hill—a shocking bad road it was—and all the hillside was thick, thick oak-forest, with deer in it. There was no trace of Weland, but presently I saw a fat old farmer riding down from the Beacon under the greenwood tree. His horse had cast a shoe in the clay, and when he came to the Ford he dismounted, took a penny out of his purse, laid it on a stone, tied the old horse to an oak, and called out: "Smith, Smith, here is work for you!" Then he sat down and went to sleep. You can imagine how *I* felt when I saw a white-bearded, bent old blacksmith in a leather apron creep out from behind the oak and begin to shoe the horse. It was Weland himself. I was so astonished that I jumped out and said: "What on Human Earth are you doing here, Weland?" '

'Poor Weland!' sighed Una.

'He pushed his long hair back from his forehead (he didn't recognise me at first). Then he said: "*You* ought to know. You foretold it, Old Thing. I'm shoeing horses for hire. I'm not even Weland now," he said. "They call me Wayland-Smith." '

'Poor chap!' said Dan. 'What did you say?'

'What could I say? He looked up, with the horse's foot on his lap, and he said, smiling, "I remember the time when I wouldn't have accepted this old bag of bones as a sacrifice, and now I'm glad enough to shoe him for a penny."

' "Isn't there any way for you to get back to Valhalla, or wherever you come from?" I said.

' "I'm afraid not," he said, rasping away at the hoof. He had a wonderful touch with horses. The old beast was whinnying on his shoulder. "You may remember that I was not a gentle God in my Day and my Time and my Power. I shall never be released till some human being truly wishes me well."

' "Surely," said I, "the farmer can't do less than that. You're shoeing the horse all round for him."

' "Yes," said he, "and my nails will hold a shoe from one full moon to the next. But farmers and Weald clay," said he, "are both uncommon cold and sour."

'Would you believe it, that when that farmer woke and found his horse shod he rode away without one word of thanks? I was so angry that I wheeled his horse right round and walked him back three miles to the Beacon, just to teach the old sinner politeness.'

'Were you invisible?' said Una. Puck nodded gravely.

'The Beacon was always laid in those days ready to light, in case the French landed at Pevensey; and I walked the horse about and about it that lee-long summer night. The farmer thought he was bewitched—well, he *was*, of course— and he began to pray and shout. *I* didn't care! I was as good a Christian as he any fair-day in the County; and about four o'clock in the morning a young novice came along from the monastery that used to stand on the top of Beacon Hill.'

'What's a novice?' said Dan.

'It really means a man who is beginning to be a monk, but in those days people sent their sons to a monastery just the same as a school. This young fellow had been to a monastery in France for a few months every year, and he was finishing his studies in the monastery close to his home here. Hugh was his name, and he had got up to go fishing hereabouts. His people owned all this valley. Hugh heard the farmer shouting, and asked him what in the world he meant. The old man spun him a wonderful tale about fairies and goblins and witches; and I *know* he hadn't seen a thing except rabbits and red deer all that night. (The People of the Hills are like otters —they don't show except when they choose.) But the novice wasn't a fool. He looked down at the horse's feet, and saw the new shoes fastened as only Weland knew how to fasten 'em. (Weland had a way of turning down the nails that folks called the Smith's Clinch.)

' "H'm!" said the novice. "Where did you get your horse shod?"

'The farmer wouldn't tell him at first, because the priests never liked their people to have any dealings with the Old Things. At last he confessed that the Smith had done it. "What did you pay him?" said the novice. "Penny," said the farmer very sulkily. "That's less than a Christian would have charged," said the novice. "I hope you threw a 'Thank you' into the bargain." "No," said the farmer; "Wayland-Smith's a heathen." "Heathen or no heathen," said the novice, "you took his help, and where you get help there you must give thanks." "What?" said the farmer—he was in a furious temper because I was walking the old horse in circles all this time—"What, you young jackanapes?" said he. "Then by your reasoning I ought to say 'Thank you' to Satan if he helped me?" "Don't roll about up there splitting reasons with me," said the novice. "Come back to the Ford and thank the Smith, or you'll be sorry."

'Back the farmer had to go. I led the horse, though no one saw me, and the novice walked beside us, his gown swishing through the shiny dew and his fishing-rod across his shoulders, spear-wise. When we reached the Ford again—it was five o'clock and misty still under the oaks—the farmer simply wouldn't say "Thank you." He said he'd tell the Abbot that the novice wanted him to worship heathen Gods. Then Hugh the novice lost his temper. He just cried, "Out!" put his arm under the farmer's fat leg, and heaved him from his saddle on to the turf, and before he could rise he caught him by the back of the neck and shook him like a rat till the farmer growled, "Thank you, Wayland-Smith."

'Did Weland see all this?' said Dan.

'Oh yes, and he shouted his old war-cry when the farmer thudded on to the ground. He was delighted. Then the novice turned to the oak tree and said, "Ho, Smith of the Gods! I am ashamed of this rude farmer; but for all you have done in kindness and charity to him and to others of our people, I thank you and wish you well." Then he picked up his fishing-rod—it looked more like a tall spear than ever—and tramped off down your valley.'

'And what did poor Weland do?' said Una.

'He laughed and he cried with joy, because he had been released at last, and could go away. But he was an honest Old Thing. He had worked for his living and he paid his debts before he left. "I shall give that novice a gift," said Weland. "A gift that shall do him good the wide world over and Old England after him. Blow up my fire, Old Thing, while I get the iron for my last task." Then he made a sword—a dark-grey, wavy-lined sword—and I blew the fire while he hammered. By Oak, Ash, and Thorn, I tell you, Weland was a Smith of the Gods! He cooled that sword in running water twice, and the third time he cooled it in the evening dew, and he laid it out in the moonlight and said Runes (that's charms) over it, and he carved Runes of Prophecy on the blade. "Old Thing," he said to me, wiping his forehead, "this is the best blade that Weland ever made. Even the user will never know how good it is. Come to the monastery."

'We went to the dormitory where the monks slept, we saw the novice fast asleep in his cot, and Weland put the sword into his hand, and I remember the young fellow gripped it in his sleep. Then Weland strode as far as he dared into the Chapel and threw down all his shoeing-tools—his hammers, and pincers, and rasps—to show that he had done with them for ever. It sounded like suits of armour falling, and the sleepy monks ran in, for they thought the monastery had been attacked by the French. The novice came first of all, waving his new sword and shouting Saxon battle-cries. When they saw the shoeing-tools they were very bewildered, till the novice asked leave to speak, and told what he had done to the farmer, and what he had said to Wayland-Smith, and how, though the dormitory light was burning, he had found the wonderful Rune-carved sword in his cot.

'The Abbot shook his head at first, and then he laughed

and said to the novice: "Son Hugh, it needed no sign from a heathen God to show me that you will never be a monk. Take your sword, and keep your sword, and go with your sword, and be as gentle as you are strong and courteous. We will hang up the Smith's tools before the Altar," he said, "because, whatever the Smith of the Gods may have been in the old days, we know that he worked honestly for his living and made gifts to Mother Church." Then they went to bed again, all except the novice, and he sat up in the garth playing with his sword. Then Weland said to me by the stables: "Farewell, Old Thing; you had the right of it. You saw me come to England, and you see me go. Farewell!"

'With that he strode down the hill to the corner of the Great Woods—Woods Corner, you call it now—to the very place where he had first landed—and I heard him moving through the thickets towards Horsebridge for a little, and then he was gone. That was how it happened. I saw it.'

Both children drew a long breath.

'But what happened to Hugh the novice?' said Una.

'And the sword?' said Dan.

Puck looked down the meadow that lay all quiet and cool in the shadow of Pook's Hill. A corncrake jarred in a hayfield near by, and the small trouts of the brook began to jump. A big white moth flew unsteadily from the alders and flapped round the children's heads, and the least little haze of water-mist rose from the brook.

'Do you really want to know?' Puck said.

'We do,' cried the children. 'Awfully!'

'Very good. I promised you that you shall see What you shall see, and you shall hear What you shall hear, though It shall have happened three thousand year; but just now it seems to me that, unless you go back to the house, people will be looking for you. I'll walk with you as far as the gate.'

'Will you be here when we come again?' they asked.

'Surely, sure-ly,' said Puck. 'I've been here some time already. One minute first, please.'

He gave them each three leaves—one of Oak, one of Ash, and one of Thorn.

'Bite these,' said he. 'Otherwise you might be talking at home of what you've seen and heard, and—if I know human beings—they'd send for the doctor. Bite!'

They bit hard, and found themselves walking side by side to the lower gate. Their father was leaning over it.

'And how did your play go?' he asked.

'Oh, splendidly,' said Dan. 'Only afterwards, I think, we went to sleep. It was very hot and quiet. Don't you remember, Una?'

Una shook her head and said nothing.

'I see,' said her father.

> 'Late—late in the evening Kilmeny came home,
> For Kilmeny had been she could not tell where,
> And Kilmeny had seen what she could not declare.

But why are you chewing leaves at your time of life, daughter? For fun?'

'No. It was for something, but I can't azactly remember,' said Una.

And neither of them could till——

A TREE SONG

Of all the trees that grow so fair,
  Old England to adorn,
Greater are none beneath the Sun,
  Than Oak, and Ash, and Thorn.
Sing Oak, and Ash, and Thorn, good Sirs
  (All of a Midsummer morn)!
Surely we sing no little thing,
  In Oak, and Ash, and Thorn!

Oak of the Clay lived many a day,
  Or ever Aeneas began;
Ash of the Loam was a lady at home,
  When Brut was an outlaw man;
Thorn of the Down saw New Troy Town
  (From which was London born);
Witness hereby the ancientry
  Of Oak, and Ash, and Thorn!

Yew that is old in churchyard mould,
  He breedeth a mighty bow;
Alder for shoes do wise men choose,
  And beech for cups also.
But when ye have killed, and your bowl is spilled,
  And your shoes are clean outworn,
Back ye must speed for all that ye need,
  To Oak, and Ash, and Thorn!

Ellum she hateth mankind, and waiteth
  Till every gust be laid,

PUCK OF POOK'S HILL

To drop a limb on the head of him
  That anyway trusts her shade:
But whether a lad be sober or sad,
  Or mellow with ale from the horn,
He will take no wrong when he lieth along
  'Neath Oak, and Ash, and Thorn!

Oh, do not tell the Priest our plight,
  Or he would call it a sin;
But—we have been out in the woods all night,
  A-conjuring Summer in!
And we bring you news by word of mouth—
  Good news for cattle and corn—
Now is the Sun come up from the South,
  With Oak, and Ash, and Thorn!

Sing Oak, and Ash, and Thorn, good Sirs
  (All of a Midsummer morn)!
England shall bide till Judgment Tide,
  By Oak, and Ash, and Thorn!

YOUNG MEN AT THE MANOR

YOUNG MEN AT THE MANOR

THEY WERE FISHING, a few days later, in the bed of the brook that for centuries had cut deep into the soft valley soil. The trees closing overhead made long tunnels through which the sunshine worked in blobs and patches. Down in the tunnels were bars of sand and gravel, old roots and trunks covered with moss or painted red by the irony water; foxgloves growing lean and pale towards the light; clumps of fern and thirsty shy flowers who could not live away from moisture and shade. In the pools you could see the wave thrown up by the trouts as they charged hither and yon, and the pools were joined to each other—except in flood-time, when all was one brown rush—by sheets of thin broken water that poured themselves chuckling round the darkness of the next bend.

This was one of the children's most secret hunting-grounds, and their particular friend, old Hobden the hedger, had shown them how to use it. Except for the click of a rod hitting a low willow, or a switch and tussle among the young ash-leaves as a line hung up for the minute, nobody in the hot pasture could have guessed what game was going on among the trouts below the banks.

'We've got half-a-dozen,' said Dan, after a warm, wet hour. 'I vote we go up to Stone Bay and try Long Pool.'

Una nodded—most of her talk was by nods—and they crept from the gloom of the tunnels towards the tiny weir that turns the brook into the mill-stream. Here the banks are low and bare, and the glare of the afternoon sun on the Long Pool below the weir makes your eyes ache.

When they were in the open they nearly fell down with astonishment. A huge grey horse, whose tail-hairs crinkled the glassy water, was drinking in the pool, and the ripples about his muzzle flashed like melted gold. On his back sat an old, white-haired man dressed in a loose glimmery gown of chain-mail. He was bare-headed, and a nut-shaped iron helmet hung at his saddle-bow. His reins were of red leather five or six inches deep, scalloped at the edges, and his high padded saddle with its red girths was held fore and aft by a red leather breastband and crupper.

'Look!' said Una, as though Dan were not staring his very eyes out. 'It's like the picture in your room—"Sir Isumbras at the Ford." '

The rider turned towards them, and his thin, long face was just as sweet and gentle as that of the knight who carries the children in that picture.

'They should be here now, Sir Richard,' said Puck's deep voice among the willow-herb.

'They are here,' the knight said, and he smiled at Dan with the string of trouts in his hand. 'There seems no great change in boys since mine fished this water.'

'If your horse has drunk, we shall be more at ease in the Ring,' said Puck; and he nodded to the children as though he had never magicked away their memories a week before.

The great horse turned and hoisted himself into the pasture with a kick and a scramble that tore the clods down rattling.

'Your pardon!' said Sir Richard to Dan. 'When these lands were mine, I never loved that mounted men should cross the brook except by the paved ford. But my Swallow here was thirsty, and I wished to meet you.'

'We're very glad you've come, sir,' said Dan. 'It doesn't matter in the least about the banks.'

He trotted across the pasture on the sword side of the

mighty horse, and it was a mighty iron-handled sword that
swung from Sir Richard's belt. Una walked behind with Puck.
She remembered everything now.

'I'm sorry about the Leaves,' he said, 'but it would never
have done if you had gone home and told, would it?'

'I s'pose not,' Una answered. 'But you said that all the
fair—People of the Hills had left England.'

'So they have; but I told you that you should come and go
and look and know, didn't I? The knight isn't a fairy. He's Sir
Richard Dalyngridge, a very old friend of mine. He came
over with William the Conqueror, and he wants to see you
particularly.'

'What for?' said Una.

'On account of your great wisdom and learning,' Puck
replied, without a twinkle.

'Us?' said Una. 'Why, I don't know my Nine Times—not
to say it dodging, and Dan makes the most *awful* mess of
fractions. He can't mean *us!*'

'Una!' Dan called back. 'Sir Richard says he is going to
tell what happened to Weland's sword. He's got it. Isn't it
splendid?'

'Nay—nay,' said Sir Richard, dismounting as they reached
the Ring, in the bend of the mill-stream bank. 'It is you that
must tell me, for I hear the youngest child in our England
to-day is as wise as our wisest clerk.' He slipped the bit out
of Swallow's mouth, dropped the ruby-red reins over his
head, and the wise horse moved off to graze.

Sir Richard (they noticed he limped a little) unslung his
great sword.

'That's it,' Dan whispered to Una.

'This is the sword that Brother Hugh had from Wayland-
Smith,' Sir Richard said. 'Once he gave it me, but I would
not take it; but at the last it became mine after such a fight

as never christened man fought. See!' He half drew it from its
sheath and turned it before them. On either side just below
the handle, where the Runic letters shivered as though they
were alive, were two deep gouges in the dull, deadly steel.
'Now, what Thing made those?' said he. 'I know not, but
you, perhaps, can say.'

'Tell them all the tale, Sir Richard,' said Puck. 'It concerns
their land somewhat.'

'Yes, from the very beginning,' Una pleaded, for the knight's
good face and the smile on it more than ever reminded her
of 'Sir Isumbras at the Ford.'

They settled down to listen, Sir Richard bareheaded to
the sunshine, dandling the sword in both hands, while the
grey horse cropped outside the Ring, and the helmet on
the saddle-bow clinged softly each time he jerked his head.

'From the beginning, then,' Sir Richard said, 'since it concerns your land, I will tell the tale. When our Duke came
out of Normandy to take his England, great knights (have
ye heard?) came and strove hard to serve the Duke, because
he promised them lands here, and small knights followed
the great ones. My folk in Normandy were poor; but a great
knight, Engerrard of the Eagle—Engenulf De Aquila—who
was kin to my father, followed the Earl of Mortain, who
followed William the Duke, and I followed De Aquila. Yes,
with thirty men-at-arms out of my father's house and a new
sword, I set out to conquer England three days after I was
made knight. I did not then know that England would conquer me. We went up to Santlache with the rest—a very
great host of us.'

'Does that mean the Battle of Hastings—Ten Sixty-Six?'
Una whispered, and Puck nodded, so as not to interrupt.

'At Santlache, over the hill yonder'—he pointed south-
eastward towards Fairlight—'we found Harold's men. We

fought. At the day's end they ran. My men went with De Aquila's to chase and plunder, and in that chase Engerrard of the Eagle was slain, and his son Gilbert took his banner and his men forward. This I did not know till after, for Swallow here was cut in the flank, so I stayed to wash the wound at a brook by a thorn. There a single Saxon cried out to me in French, and we fought together. I should have known his voice, but we fought together. For a long time neither had any advantage, till by pure ill-fortune his foot slipped and his sword flew from his hand. Now I had but newly been made knight, and wished, above all, to be courteous and fameworthy, so I forbore to strike and bade him get his sword again. "A plague on my sword," said he. "It has lost me my first fight. You have spared my life. Take my sword." He held it out to me, but as I stretched my hand the sword groaned like a stricken man, and I leaped back crying, "Sorcery!"

(The children looked at the sword as though it might speak again.)

'Suddenly a clump of Saxons ran out upon me and, seeing a Norman alone, would have killed me, but my Saxon cried out that I was his prisoner, and beat them off. Thus, see you, he saved my life. He put me on my horse and led me through the woods ten long miles to this valley.'

'To here, d'you mean?' said Una.

'To this very valley. We came in by the Lower Ford under the King's Hill yonder'—he pointed eastward where the valley widens.

'And was that Saxon Hugh the novice?' Dan asked.

'Yes, and more than that. He had been for three years at the monastery at Bec by Rouen, where'—Sir Richard chuckled —'the Abbot Herluin would not suffer me to remain.'

'Why wouldn't he?' said Dan.

'Because I rode my horse into the refectory, when the
scholars were at meat, to show the Saxon boys we Normans
were not afraid of an Abbot. It was that very Saxon Hugh
tempted me to do it, and we had not met since that day.
I thought I knew his voice even inside my helmet, and, for
all that our Lords fought, we each rejoiced we had not slain
the other. He walked by my side, and he told me how a
heathen God, as he believed, had given him his sword,
but he said he had never heard it sing before. I remember
I warned him to beware of sorcery and quick enchantments.'
Sir Richard smiled to himself. 'I was very young—very young!

'When we came to his house here we had almost forgotten
that we had been at blows. It was near midnight, and the
Great Hall was full of men and women waiting news. There
I first saw his sister, the Lady Aelueva, of whom he had spoken
to us in France. She cried out fiercely at me, and would have
had me hanged in that hour, but her brother said that I had
spared his life—he said not how he saved mine from the
Saxons—and that our Duke had won the day; and even
while they wrangled over my poor body, of a sudden he fell
down in a swoon from his wounds.

' "This is *thy* fault," said the Lady Aelueva to me, and
she kneeled above him and called for wine and cloths.

' "If I had known," I answered, "he should have ridden
and I walked. But he set me on my horse; he made no complaint; he walked beside me and spoke merrily throughout.
I pray I have done him no harm."

' "Thou hast need to pray," she said, catching up her under-
lip. "If he dies, thou shalt hang."

'They bore off Hugh to his chamber; but three tall men
of the house bound me and set me under the beam of the
Great Hall with a rope round my neck. The end of the rope

34

they flung over the beam, and they sat them down by the fire
to wait word whether Hugh lived or died. They cracked nuts
with their knife-hilts the while.'

'And how did you feel?' said Dan.

'Very weary; but I did heartily pray for my school-mate
Hugh his health. About noon I heard horses in the valley,
and the three men loosed my ropes and fled out, and De
Aquila's men rode up. Gilbert De Aquila came with them,
for it was his boast that, like his father, he forgot no man that
served him. He was little, like his father, but terrible, with a
nose like an eagle's nose and yellow eyes like an eagle. He
rode tall war-horses—roans, which he bred himself—and he
could never abide to be helped into the saddle. He saw the
rope hanging from the beam and laughed, and his men
laughed, for I was too stiff to rise.

' "This is poor entertainment for a Norman knight," he
said, 'but, such as it is, let us be grateful. Show me, boy, to
whom thou owest most, and we will pay them out of hand."

'What did he mean? To kill 'em?' said Dan.

'Assuredly. But I looked at the Lady Aelueva where she
stood among her maids, and her brother beside her. De
Aquila's men had driven them all into the Great Hall.'

'Was she pretty?' said Una.

'In all my long life I have never seen woman fit to strew
rushes before my Lady Aelueva,' the knight replied, quite
simply and quietly. 'As I looked at her I thought I might
save her and her house by a jest.

' "Seeing that I came somewhat hastily and without warning," said I to De Aquila, "I have no fault to find with the
courtesy that these Saxons have shown me." But my voice
shook. It is—it was not good to jest with that little man.

'All were silent awhile, till De Aquila laughed. "Look,

men—a miracle," said he. "The fight is scarce sped, my father is not yet buried, and here we find our youngest knight already set down in his Manor, while his Saxons—ye can see it in their fat faces—have paid him homage and service! By the Saints," he said, rubbing his nose, "I never thought England would be so easy won! Surely I can do no less than give the lad what he has taken. This Manor shall be thine, boy," he said, "till I come again, or till thou art slain. Now, mount, men, and ride. We follow our Duke into Kent to make him King of England."

'He drew me with him to the door while they brought his horse—a lean roan, taller than my Swallow here, but not so well girthed.

' "Hark to me," he said, fretting with his great war-gloves. "I have given thee this Manor, which is a Saxon hornets' nest, and I think thou wilt be slain in a month—as my father was slain. Yet if thou canst keep the roof on the hall, the thatch on the barn, and the plough in the furrow till I come back, thou shalt hold the Manor from me; for the Duke has promised our Earl Mortain all the lands by Pevensey, and Mortain will give me of them what he would have given my father. God knows if thou or I shall live till England is won; but remember, boy, that here and now fighting is foolishness and"—he reached for the reins—"craft and cunning is all."

' "Alas, I have no cunning," said I.

' "Not yet," said he, hopping abroad, foot in stirrup, and poking his horse in the belly with his toe. "Not yet, but I think thou hast a good teacher. Farewell! Hold the Manor and live. Lose the Manor and hang," he said, and spurred out, his shield-straps squeaking behind him.

'So, children, here was I, little more than a boy, and Santlache fight not two days old, left alone with my thirty men-at-arms, in a land I knew not, among a people whose tongue I could not speak, to hold down the land which I had taken from them.'

'And that was here at home?' said Una.

'Yes, here. See! From the Upper Ford, Weland's Ford, to the Lower Ford, by the Belle Allée, west and east it ran half a league. From the Beacon of Brunanburgh behind us here, south and north it ran a full league—and all the woods were full of broken men from Santlache, Saxon thieves, Norman plunderers, robbers, and deer-stealers. A hornets' nest indeed!

'When De Aquila had gone, Hugh would have thanked me for saving their lives; but the Lady Aelueva said that I had done it only for the sake of receiving the Manor.

' "How could I know that De Aquila would give it me?" I said. "If I had told him I had spent my night in your halter he would have burned the place twice over by now."

' "If any man had put *my* neck in a rope," she said, "I would have seen his house burned thrice over before *I* would have made terms."

' "But it was a woman," I said; and I laughed, and she wept and said that I mocked her in her captivity.

' "Lady," said I, "there is no captive in this valley except one, and he is not a Saxon."

'At this she cried that I was a Norman thief, who came with false, sweet words, having intended from the first to turn her out in the fields to beg her bread. Into the fields! She had never seen the face of war!

'I was angry, and answered, "This much at least I can disprove, for I swear"—and on my sword-hilt I swore it in that place—"I swear I will never set foot in the Great Hall till the Lady Aelueva herself shall summon me there."

'She went away, saying nothing, and I walked out, and

Hugh limped after me, whistling dolorously (that is a custom of the English), and we came upon the three Saxons that
had bound me. They were now bound by my men-at-arms, and
behind them stood some fifty stark and sullen churls of the
House and the Manor, waiting to see what should fall. We
heard De Aquila's trumpets blow thin through the woods
Kentward.

' "Shall we hang these?" said my men.

' "Then my churls will fight," said Hugh, beneath his
breath; but I bade him ask the three what mercy they hoped
for.

' "None," said they all. "She bade us hang thee if our
master died. And we would have hanged thee. There is no
more to it."

'As I stood doubting, a woman ran down from the oak
wood above the King's Hill yonder, and cried out that some
Normans were driving off the swine there.

' "Norman or Saxon," said I, "we must beat them back, or
they will rob us every day. Out at them with any arms ye
have!" So I loosed those three carles and we ran together, my
men-at-arms and the Saxons with bills and axes which they
had hidden in the thatch of their huts, and Hugh led them.
Half-way up the King's Hill we found a false fellow from
Picardy—a sutler that sold wine in the Duke's camp—with a
dead knight's shield on his arm, a stolen horse under him,
and some ten or twelve wastrels at his tail, all cutting and
slashing at the pigs. We beat them off, and saved our pork.
One hundred and seventy pigs we saved in that great battle.'
Sir Richard laughed.

'That, then, was our first work together, and I bade Hugh
tell his folk that so would I deal with any man, knight or
churl, Norman or Saxon, who stole as much as one egg from
our valley. Said he to me, riding home: "Thou hast gone

38

far to conquer England this evening." I answered: "England
must be thine and mine, then. Help me, Hugh, to deal aright
with these people. Make them to know that if they slay me
De Aquila will surely send to slay them, and he will put a
worse man in my place." "That may well be true," said he,
and gave me his hand. "Better the devil we know than the
devil we know not, till we can pack you Normans home."
And so, too, said his Saxons; and they laughed as we drove the
pigs down-hill. But I think some of them, even then, began
not to hate me.'

'I like Brother Hugh,' said Una softly.

'Beyond question he was the most perfect, courteous, valiant, tender, and wise knight that ever drew breath,' said Sir
Richard, caressing the sword. 'He hung up his sword—this
sword—on the wall of the Great Hall, because he said it was
fairly mine, and never he took it down till De Aquila returned, as I shall presently show. For three months his men
and mine guarded the valley, till all robbers and night-walk-
ers learned there was nothing to get from us save hard tack
and a hanging. Side by side we fought against all who came—
thrice a week sometimes we fought—against thieves and landless knights looking for good manors. Then we were in some
peace, and I made shift by Hugh's help to govern the valley—
for all this valley of yours was my Manor—as a knight should.
I kept the roof on the hall and the thatch on the barn,
but . . . the English are a bold people. His Saxons would
laugh and jest with Hugh, and Hugh with them, and—this
was marvellous to me—if even the meanest of them said that
such and such a thing was the Custom of the Manor, then
straightway would Hugh and such old men of the Manor as
might be near forsake everything else to debate the matter—
I have seen them stop the Mill with the corn half ground—
and if the custom or usage were proven to be as it was said,

why, that was the end of it, even though it were flat against
Hugh, his wish and command. Wonderful!'

'Aye,' said Puck, breaking in for the first time. 'The Custom of Old England was here before your Norman knights
came, and it outlasted them, though they fought against it
cruel.'

'Not I,' said Sir Richard. 'I let the Saxons go their stubborn
way, but when my own men-at-arms, Normans not six months
in England, stood up and told me what was the custom of the
country, *then* I was angry. Ah, good days! Ah, wonderful
people! And I loved them all.'

The knight lifted his arms as though he would hug the
whole dear valley, and Swallow, hearing the chink of his
chain-mail, looked up and whinnied softly.

'At last,' he went on, 'after a year of striving and contriving
and some little driving, De Aquila came to the valley, alone
and without warning. I saw him first at the Lower Ford, with
a swineherd's brat on his saddle-bow.

' "There is no need for thee to give any account of thy
stewardship," said he. "I have it all from the child here."
And he told me how the young thing had stopped his tall
horse at the Ford, by waving of a branch, and crying that
the way was barred. "And if one bold, bare babe be enough
to guard the Ford in these days, thou hast done well," said
he, and puffed and wiped his head.

'He pinched the child's cheek, and looked at our cattle
in the flat by the river.

' "Both fat," said he, rubbing his nose. "This is craft and
cunning such as I love. What did I tell thee when I rode
away, boy?"

' "Hold the Manor or hang," said I. I had never forgotten it.

' "True. And thou hast held." He clambered from his

saddle and with his sword's point cut out a turf from the bank and gave it me where I kneeled.'

Dan looked at Una, and Una looked at Dan.

'That's seizin,' said Puck, in a whisper.

' "Now thou art lawfully seized of the Manor, Sir Richard," said he—'twas the first time he ever called me that—"thou and thy heirs for ever. This must serve till the King's clerks write out thy title on a parchment. England is all ours—if we can hold it."

' "What service shall I pay?" I asked, and I remember I was proud beyond words.

' "Knight's fee, boy, knight's fee!" said he, hopping round his horse on one foot. (Have I said he was little, and could not endure to be helped to his saddle?) "Six mounted men or twelve archers thou shalt send me whenever I call for them, and—where got you that corn?" said he, for it was near harvest, and our corn stood well. "I have never seen such bright straw. Send me three bags of the same seed yearly, and furthermore, in memory of our last meeting—with the rope round thy neck—entertain me and my men for two days of each year in the Great Hall of thy Manor."

' "Alas!" said I, "then my Manor is already forfeit. I am under vow not to enter the Great Hall." And I told him what I had sworn to the Lady Aelueva.'

'And hadn't you ever been into the house since?' said Una.

'Never,' Sir Richard answered, smiling. 'I had made me a little hut of wood up the hill, and there I did justice and slept. . . . De Aquila wheeled aside, and his shield shook on his back. "No matter, boy," said he. "I will remit the homage for a year." '

'He meant Sir Richard needn't give him dinner there the first year,' Puck explained.

'De Aquila stayed with me in the hut, and Hugh, who

could read and write and cast accounts, showed him the Roll
of the Manor, in which were written all the names of our
fields and men, and he asked a thousand questions touching
the land, the timber, the grazing, the Mill, and the fish-ponds,
and the worth of every man in the valley. But never he
named the Lady Aelueva's name, nor went he near the Great
Hall. By night he drank with us in the hut. Yes, he sat
on the straw like an eagle ruffled in her feathers, his yellow
eyes rolling above the cup, and he pounced in his talk like
an eagle, swooping from one thing to another, but always
binding fast. Yes; he would lie still awhile, and then rustle in
the straw, and speak sometimes as though he were King William himself, and anon he would speak in parables and tales,
and if at once we saw not his meaning he would yerk us in
the ribs with his scabbarded sword.

'"Look you, boys," said he, "I am born out of my due time.
Five hundred years ago I would have made all England such
an England as neither Dane, Saxon, nor Norman should have
conquered. Five hundred years hence I should have been such
a counsellor to Kings as the world hath never dreamed of. 'Tis
all here," said he, tapping his big head, "but it hath no play
in this black age. Now Hugh here is a better man than thou
art, Richard." He had made his voice harsh and croaking,
like a raven's.

'"Truth," said I. "But for Hugh, his help and patience and
long-suffering, I could never have kept the Manor."

'"Nor thy life either," said De Aquila. "Hugh has saved
thee not once, but a hundred times. Be still, Hugh!" he said.
"Dost thou know, Richard, why Hugh slept, and why he still
sleeps, among thy Norman men-at-arms?"

'"To be near me," said I, for I thought this was truth.

'"Fool!" said De Aquila. "It is because his Saxons have

begged him to rise against thee, and to sweep every Norman
out of the valley. No matter how I know. It is truth. Therefore Hugh hath made himself an hostage for thy life, well
knowing that if any harm befell thee from his Saxons thy
Normans would slay him without remedy. And this his Saxons know. Is it true, Hugh?"

' "In some sort," said Hugh shamefacedly; "at least, it
was true half a year ago. My Saxons would not harm Richard
now—I think they know him—but I judged it best to make
sure."

'Look, children, what that man had done—and I had
never guessed it! Night after night had he lain down among
my men-at-arms, knowing that if one Saxon had lifted knife
against me, his life would have answered for mine.

' "Yes," said De Aquila. "And he is a swordless man." He
pointed to Hugh's belt, for Hugh had put away his sword—
did I tell you?—the day after it flew from his hand at Santlache. He carried only the short knife and the long-bow.
"Swordless and landless art thou, Hugh; and they call thee
kin to Earl Godwin." (Hugh was indeed of Godwin's blood.)
"The Manor that was thine is given to this boy and to his
children for ever. Sit up and beg, for he can turn thee out
like a dog, Hugh."

'Hugh said nothing, but I heard his teeth grind, and I bade
De Aquila, my own overlord, hold his peace, or I would
stuff his words down his throat. Then De Aquila laughed till
the tears ran down his face.

' "I warned the King," said he, "what would come of giving England to us Norman thieves. Here art thou, Richard,
less than two days confirmed in thy Manor, and already thou
hast risen against thy overlord. What shall we do to him,
Sir Hugh?"

' "I am a swordless man," said Hugh. "Do not jest with me," and he laid his head on his knees and groaned.

' "The greater fool thou," said De Aquila, and all his voice changed; "for I have given thee the Manor of Dallington up the hill this half-hour since," and he yerked at Hugh with his scabbard across the straw.

' "To me?" said Hugh. "I am a Saxon, and, except that I love Richard here, I have not sworn fealty to any Norman."

' "In God's good time, which because of my sins I shall not live to see, there will be neither Saxon nor Norman in England," said De Aquila. "If I know men, thou art more faithful unsworn than a score of Normans I could name. Take Dallington, and join Sir Richard to fight me to-morrow, if it please thee!"

' "Nay," said Hugh. "I am no child. Where I take a gift, there I render service"; and he put his hands between De Aquila's, and swore to be faithful, and, as I remember, I kissed him, and De Aquila kissed us both.

'We sat afterwards outside the hut while the sun rose, and De Aquila marked our churls going to their work in the fields, and talked of holy things, and how we should govern our Manors in time to come, and of hunting and of horse-breeding, and of the King's wisdom and unwisdom; for he spoke to us as though we were in all sorts now his brothers. Anon a churl stole up to me—he was one of the three I had not hanged a year ago—and he bellowed—which is the Saxon for whispering—that the Lady Aelueva would speak to me at the Great House. She walked abroad daily in the Manor, and it was her custom to send me word whither she went, that I might set an archer or two behind and in front to guard her. Very often I myself lay up in the woods and watched on her also.

'I went swiftly, and as I passed the great door it opened

from within, and there stood my Lady Aelueva, and she said to me: "Sir Richard, will it please you enter your Great Hall?" Then she wept, but we were alone.'

The knight was silent for a long time, his face turned across the valley, smiling.

'Oh, well done!' said Una, and clapped her hands very softly. 'She was sorry, and she said so.'

'Aye, she was sorry, and she said so,' said Sir Richard, coming back with a little start. 'Very soon—but *he* said it was two full hours later—De Aquila rode to the door, with his shield new scoured (Hugh had cleansed it), and demanded entertainment, and called me a false knight, that would starve his overlord to death. Then Hugh cried out that no man should work in the valley that day, and our Saxons blew horns, and set about feasting and drinking, and running of races, and dancing and singing; and De Aquila climbed upon a horse-block and spoke to them in what he swore was good Saxon, but no man understood it. At night we feasted in the Great Hall, and when the harpers and the singers were gone we four sat late at the high table. As I remember, it was a warm night with a full moon, and De Aquila bade Hugh take down his sword from the wall again, for the honour of the Manor of Dallington, and Hugh took it gladly enough. Dust lay on the hilt, for I saw him blow it off.

'She and I sat talking a little apart, and at first we thought the harpers had come back, for the Great Hall was filled with a rushing noise of music. De Aquila leaped up; but there was only the moonlight fretty on the floor.

' "Hearken!" said Hugh. "It is my sword," and as he belted it on the music ceased.

' "Over Gods, forbid that I should ever belt blade like that," said De Aquila. "What does it foretell?"

' "The Gods that made it may know. Last time it spoke

was at Hastings, when I lost all my lands. Belike it sings now that I have new lands and am a man again," said Hugh.

He loosed the blade a little and drove it back happily into the sheath, and the sword answered him low and crooningly, as—as a woman would speak to a man, her head on his shoulder.

'Now that was the second time in all my life I heard this Sword sing.' . . .

'Look!' said Una. 'There's Mother coming down the Long Slip. What will she say to Sir Richard? She can't help seeing him.'

'And Puck can't magic us this time,' said Dan.

'Are you sure?' said Puck; and he leaned forward and whispered to Sir Richard, who, smiling, bowed his head.

'But what befell the sword and my brother Hugh I will tell on another time,' said he, rising. 'Ohé, Swallow!'

The great horse cantered up from the far end of the meadow, close to Mother.

They heard Mother say: 'Children, Gleason's old horse has broken into the meadow again. Where did he get through?'

'Just below Stone Bay,' said Dan. 'He tore down simple flobs of the bank! We noticed it just now. And we've caught no end of fish. We've been at it all the afternoon.'

And they honestly believed that they had. They never noticed the Oak, Ash, and Thorn leaves that Puck had slyly thrown into their laps.

SIR RICHARD'S SONG

I followed my Duke ere I was a lover,
*   To take from England fief and fee;*
But now this game is the other way over—
*   But now England hath taken me!*

I had my horse, my shield and banner,
*   And a boy's heart, so whole and free;*
But now I sing in another manner—
*   But now England hath taken me!*

As for my Father in his tower,
*   Asking news of my ship at sea;*
He will remember his own hour—
*   Tell him England hath taken me!*

As for my Mother in her bower,
*   That rules my Father so cunningly;*
She will remember a maiden's power—
*   Tell her England hath taken me!*

As for my Brother in Rouen city,
*   A nimble and naughty page is he;*
But he will come to suffer and pity—
*   Tell him England hath taken me!*

As for my little Sister waiting
*   In the pleasant orchards of Normandie;*
Tell her youth is the time for mating—
*   Tell her England hath taken me!*

47

PUCK OF POOK'S HILL

As for my Comrades in camp and highway,
   That lift their eyebrows scornfully;
Tell them their way is not my way—
   Tell them England hath taken me!

Kings and Princes and Barons famèd,
   Knights and Captains in your degree;
Hear me a little before I am blamèd—
   Seeing England hath taken me!

Howso great man's strength be reckoned,
   There are two things he cannot flee;
Love is the first, and Death is the second—
   And Love, in England, hath taken me!

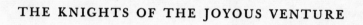

THE KNIGHTS OF THE JOYOUS VENTURE

HARP SONG OF THE DANE WOMEN

What is a woman that you forsake her,
And the hearth-fire and the home-acre,
To go with the old grey Widow-maker?

She has no house to lay a guest in—
But one chill bed for all to rest in,
That the pale suns and the stray bergs nest in.

She has no strong white arms to fold you,
But the ten-times-fingering weed to hold you
Bound on the rocks where the tide has rolled you.

Yet, when the signs of summer thicken,
And the ice breaks, and the birch-buds quicken,
Yearly you turn from our side, and sicken—

Sicken again for the shouts and the slaughters,—
And steal away to the lapping waters,
And look at your ship in her winter quarters.

You forget our mirth, and talk at the tables,
The kine in the shed and the horse in the stables—
To pitch her sides and go over her cables!

Then you drive out where the storm-clouds swallow:
And the sound of your oar-blades falling hollow
Is all we have left through the months to follow.

Ah, what is Woman that you forsake her,
And the hearth-fire and the home-acre,
To go with the old grey Widow-maker?

THE KNIGHTS OF THE JOYOUS VENTURE

IT WAS TOO HOT to run about in the open, so Dan asked their friend, old Hobden, to take their own dinghy from the pond and put her on the brook at the bottom of the garden. Her painted name was the *Daisy*, but for exploring expeditions she was the *Golden Hind* or the *Long Serpent*, or some such suitable name. Dan hiked and howked with a boat-hook (the brook was too narrow for sculls), and Una punted with a piece of hop-pole. When they came to a very shallow place (the *Golden Hind* drew quite three inches of water) they disembarked and scuffled her over the gravel by her tow-rope, and when they reached the overgrown banks beyond the garden they pulled themselves up-stream by the low branches.

That day they intended to discover the North Cape like 'Othere, the old sea-captain,' in the book of verses which Una had brought with her; but on account of the heat they changed it to a voyage up the Amazon and the sources of the Nile. Even on the shaded water the air was hot and heavy with drowsy scents, while outside, through breaks in the trees, the sunshine burned the pasture like fire. The kingfisher was asleep on his watching-branch, and the blackbirds scarcely took the trouble to dive into the next bush. Dragon-flies wheeling and clashing were the only things at work, except the moor-hens and a big Red Admiral, who flapped down out of the sunshine for a drink.

When they reached Otter Pool the *Golden Hind* grounded comfortably on a shallow, and they lay beneath a roof of close green, watching the water trickle over the flood-gates down the mossy brick chute from the mill-stream to the brook. A big trout—the children knew him well—rolled head and shoulders at some fly that sailed round the bend, while, once in just so often, the brook rose a fraction of an inch against all the wet pebbles, and they watched the slow draw and shiver of a breath of air through the tree-tops. Then the little voices of the slipping water began again.

'It's like the shadows talking, isn't it?' said Una. She had given up trying to read. Dan lay over the bows, trailing his hands in the current. They heard feet on the gravel-bar that runs half across the pool and saw Sir Richard Dalyngridge standing over them.

'Was yours a dangerous voyage?' he asked, smiling.

'She bumped a lot, sir,' said Dan. 'There's hardly any water this summer.'

'Ah, the brook was deeper and wider when my children played at Danish pirates. Are you pirate-folk?'

'Oh no. We gave up being pirates years ago,' explained Una. 'We're nearly always explorers now. Sailing round the world, you know.'

'Round?' said Sir Richard. He sat him in the comfortable crotch of an old ash-root on the bank. 'How can it be round?'

'Wasn't it in your books?' Dan suggested. He had been doing geography at his last lesson.

'I can neither write nor read,' he replied. 'Canst *thou* read, child?'

'Yes,' said Dan, 'barring the very long words.'

'Wonderful! Read to me, that I may hear for myself.'

Dan flushed, but opened the book and began—gabbling a little—at 'The Discoverer of the North Cape.'

THE KNIGHTS OF THE JOYOUS VENTURE

'Othere, the old sea-captain,
Who dwelt in Helgoland,
To King Alfred, the lover of truth,
Brought a snow-white walrus-tooth,
Which he held in his brown right hand.'

'But—but—this I know! This is an old song! This I have
heard sung! This is a miracle,' Sir Richard interrupted. 'Nay,
do not stop!' He leaned forward, and the shadows of the leaves
slipped and slid upon his chain-mail.

' "I ploughed the land with horses,
But my heart was ill at ease,
For the old sea-faring men
Came to me now and then
With their sagas of the seas." '

His hand fell on the hilt of the great sword. 'This is truth,'
he cried, 'for so did it happen to me,' and he beat time de-
lightedly to the tramp of verse after verse.

' "And now the land," said Othere,
"Bent southward suddenly,
And I followed the curving shore,
And ever southward bore
Into a nameless sea." '

'A nameless sea!' he repeated. 'So did I—so did Hugh and I.'
'Where did you go? Tell us,' said Una.
'Wait. Let me hear all first.' So Dan read to the poem's very
end.

'Good,' said the knight. 'That is Othere's tale—even as I have heard the men in the Dane ships sing it. Not in those same valiant words, but something like to them.'

'Have you ever explored North?' Dan shut the book.

'Nay. My venture was South. Farther South than any man has fared, Hugh and I went down with Witta and his heathen.' He jerked the tall sword forward, and leaned on it with both hands; but his eyes looked long past them.

'I thought you always lived here,' said Una timidly.

'Yes; while my Lady Aelueva lived. But she died. She died. Then, my eldest son being a man, I asked De Aquila's leave that he should hold the Manor while I went on some journey or pilgrimage—to forget. De Aquila, whom the Second William had made Warden of Pevensey in Earl Mortain's place, was very old then, but still he rode his tall roan horses, and in the saddle he looked like a little white falcon. When Hugh, at Dallington over yonder, heard what I did, he sent for my second son, whom being unmarried he had ever looked upon as his own child, and, by De Aquila's leave, gave him the Manor of Dallington to hold till he should return. Then Hugh came with me.'

'When did this happen?' said Dan.

'That I can answer to the very day, for as we rode with De Aquila by Pevensey—have I said that he was Lord of Pevensey and of the Honour of the Eagle?—to the Bordeaux ship that fetched him his wines yearly out of France, a Marsh man ran to us crying that he had seen a great black goat which bore on his back the body of the King, and that the goat had spoken to him. On that same day Red William our King, the Conqueror's son, died of a secret arrow while he hunted in a forest. "This is a cross matter," said De Aquila, "to meet on the threshold of a journey. If Red William be dead I may have to fight for my lands. Wait a little."

56

THE KNIGHTS OF THE JOYOUS VENTURE

'My Lady being dead, I cared nothing for signs and omens, nor Hugh either. We took that wine-ship to go to Bordeaux; but the wind failed while we were yet in sight of Pevensey, a thick mist hid us, and we drifted with the tide along the cliffs to the west. Our company was, for the most part, merchants returning to France, and we were laden with wool and there were three couple of tall hunting-dogs chained to the rail. Their master was a knight of Artois. His name I never learned, but his shield bore gold pieces on a red ground, and he limped, much as I do, from a wound which he had got in his youth at Mantes siege. He served the Duke of Burgundy against the Moors in Spain, and was returning to that war with his dogs. He sang us strange Moorish songs that first night, and half persuaded us to go with him. I was on pilgrimage to forget— which is what no pilgrimage brings. I think I would have gone, but . . .

'Look you how the life and fortune of man changes! Towards morning a Dane ship, rowing silently, struck against us in the mist, and while we rolled hither and yon Hugh, leaning over the rail, fell outboard. I leaped after him, and we two tumbled aboard the Dane, and were caught and bound ere we could rise. Our own ship was swallowed up in the mist. I judge the Knight of the Gold Pieces muzzled his dogs with his cloak, lest they should give tongue and betray the merchants, for I heard their baying suddenly stop.

'We lay bound among the benches till morning, when the Danes dragged us to the high deck by the steering-place, and their captain—Witta, he was called—turned us over with his foot. Bracelets of gold from elbow to armpit he wore, and his red hair was long as a woman's, and came down in plaited locks on his shoulder. He was stout, with bowed legs and long arms. He spoiled us of all we had, but when he laid hand on Hugh's sword and saw the runes on the blade hastily he thrust it back.

Yet his covetousness overcame him and he tried again and
again, and the third time the Sword sang loud and angrily, so
that the rowers leaned on their oars to listen. Here they all
spoke together, screaming like gulls, and a Yellow Man, such
as I have never seen, came to the high deck and cut our bonds.
He was yellow—not from sickness, but by nature—yellow as
honey, and his eyes stood endwise in his head.'

'How do you mean?' said Una, her chin on her hand.

'Thus,' said Sir Richard. He put a finger to the corner of
each eye, and pushed it up till his eyes narrowed to slits.

'Why, you look just like a Chinaman!' cried Dan. 'Was the
man a Chinaman?'

'I know not what that may be. Witta had found him half
dead among ice on the shores of Muscovy. *We* thought he was
a devil. He crawled before us and brought food in a silver dish
which these sea-wolves had robbed from some rich abbey, and
Witta with his own hands gave us wine. He spoke a little in
French, a little in South Saxon, and much in the Northman's
tongue. We asked him to set us ashore, promising to pay him
better ransom than he would get price if he sold us to the
Moors—as once befell a knight of my acquaintance sailing
from Flushing.'

' "Not by my father Guthrum's head," said he. "The Gods
sent ye into my ship for a luck-offering."

'At this I quaked, for I knew it was still the Danes' custom to
sacrifice captives to their Gods for fair weather.

' "A plague on thy four long bones!" said Hugh. "What
profit canst thou make of poor old pilgrims that can neither
work nor fight?"

' "Gods forbid I should fight against thee, poor Pilgrim with
the Singing Sword," said he. "Come with us and be poor no
more. Thy teeth are far apart, which is a sure sign thou wilt
travel and grow rich."

' "What if we will not come?" said Hugh.

' "Swim to England or France," said Witta. "We are midway between the two. Unless ye choose to drown yourselves no hair of your head will be harmed here aboard. We think ye bring us luck, and I myself know the runes on that Sword are good." He turned and bade them hoist sail.

'Hereafter all made way for us as we walked about the ship, and the ship was full of wonders.'

'What was she like?' said Dan.

'Long, low, and narrow, bearing one mast with a red sail, and rowed by fifteen oars a side,' the knight answered. 'At her bows was a deck under which men might lie, and at her stern another shut off by a painted door from the rowers' benches. Here Hugh and I slept, with Witta and the Yellow Man, upon tapestries as soft as wool. I remember'—he laughed to himself —'when first we entered there a loud voice cried, "Out swords! Out swords! Kill, kill!" Seeing us start Witta laughed, and showed us it was but a great-beaked grey bird with a red tail. He sat her on his shoulder, and she called for bread and wine hoarsely, and prayed him to kiss her. Yet she was no more than a silly bird. But—ye knew this?' He looked at their smiling faces.

'We weren't laughing at you,' said Una. 'That must have been a parrot. It's just what Pollies do.'

'So we learned later. But here is another marvel. The Yellow Man, whose name was Kitai, had with him a brown box. In the box was a blue bowl with red marks upon the rim, and within the bowl, hanging from a fine thread, was a piece of iron no thicker than that grass stem, and as long, maybe, as my spur, but straight. In this iron, said Witta, abode an Evil Spirit which Kitai, the Yellow Man, had brought by Art Magic out of his own country that lay three years' journey southward. The Evil Spirit strove day and night to return to his country, and therefore, look you, the iron needle pointed continually to the South.'

'South?' said Dan suddenly, and put his hand into his pocket.

'With my own eyes I saw it. Every day and all day long, though the ship rolled, though the sun and the moon and the stars were hid, this blind Spirit in the iron knew whither it would go, and strained to the South. Witta called it the Wise Iron, because it showed him his way across the unknowable seas.' Again Sir Richard looked keenly at the children. 'How think ye? Was it sorcery?'

'Was it anything like this?' Dan fished out his old brass pocket-compass, that generally lived with his knife and key-ring. 'The glass has got cracked, but the needle waggles all right, sir.'

The knight drew a long breath of wonder. 'Yes, yes! The Wise Iron shook and swung in just this fashion. Now it is still. Now it points to the South.'

'North,' said Dan.

'Nay, South! There is the South,' said Sir Richard. Then they both laughed, for naturally when one end of a straight compass-needle points to the North, the other must point to the South.

'Té,' said Sir Richard, clicking his tongue. 'There can be no sorcery if a child carries it. Wherefore does it point South— or North?'

'Father says that nobody knows,' said Una.

Sir Richard looked relieved. 'Then it may still be magic. It was magic to *us*. And so we voyaged. When the wind served we hoisted sail, and lay all up along the windward rail, our shields on our backs to break the spray. When it failed, they rowed with long oars; the Yellow Man sat by the Wise Iron, and Witta steered. At first I feared the great white-flowering waves,

but as I saw how wisely Witta led his ship among them I grew
bolder. Hugh liked it well from the first. My skill is not upon
the water; and rocks and whirlpools such as we saw by the
West Isles of France, where an oar caught on a rock and broke,
are much against my stomach. We sailed South across a stormy
sea, where by moonlight, between clouds, we saw a Flanders
ship roll clean over and sink. Again, though Hugh laboured
with Witta all night, I lay under the deck with the Talking
Bird, and cared not whether I lived or died. There is a sickness
of the sea which for three days is pure death! When we next
saw land Witta said it was Spain, and we stood out to sea. That
coast was full of ships busy in the Duke's war against the Moors,
and we feared to be hanged by the Duke's men or sold into
slavery by the Moors. So we put into a small harbour which
Witta knew. At night men came down with loaded mules, and
Witta exchanged amber out of the North against little wedges
of iron and packets of beads in earthen pots. The pots he put
under the decks, and the wedges of iron he laid on the bottom
of the ship after he had cast out the stones and shingle which
till then had been our ballast. Wine, too, he bought for lumps
of sweet-smelling grey amber—a little morsel no bigger than a
thumb-nail purchased a cask of wine. But I speak like a
merchant.'

'No, no! Tell us what you had to eat,' cried Dan.

'Meat dried in the sun, and dried fish and ground beans,
Witta took in; and corded frails of a certain sweet, soft fruit,
which the Moors use, which is like paste of figs, but with thin,
long stones. Aha! Dates is the name.

' "Now," said Witta, when the ship was loaded, "I counsel
you strangers to pray to your Gods, for, from here on, our
road is No Man's road." He and his men killed a black goat
for sacrifice on the bows; and the Yellow Man brought out a

small, smiling image of dull-green stone and burned incense before it. Hugh and I commended ourselves to God, and Saint Barnabas, and Our Lady of the Assumption, who was specially dear to my Lady. We were not young, but I think no shame to say whenas we drove out of that secret harbour at sunrise over a still sea, we two rejoiced and sang as did the knights of old when they followed our great Duke to England. Yet was our leader an heathen pirate; all our proud fleet but one galley perilously overloaded; for guidance we leaned on a pagan sorcerer; and our port was beyond the world's end. Witta told us that his father Guthrum had once in his life rowed along the shores of Africa to a land where naked men sold gold for iron and beads. There had he bought much gold, and no few elephants' teeth, and thither by help of the Wise Iron would Witta go. Witta feared nothing—except to be poor.

' "My father told me," said Witta, "that a great Shoal runs three days' sail out from that land, and south of the shoal lies a Forest which grows in the sea. South and east of the Forest my father came to a place where the men hid gold in their hair; but all that country, he said, was full of Devils who lived in trees, and tore folk limb from limb. How think ye?"

' "Gold or no gold," said Hugh, fingering his sword, "it is a joyous venture. Have at these Devils of thine, Witta!"

' "Venture!" said Witta sourly. "I am only a poor sea-thief. I do not set my life adrift on a plank for joy, or the venture. Once I beach ship again at Stavanger, and feel the wife's arms round my neck, I'll seek no more ventures. A ship is heavier care than a wife or cattle."

'He leaped down among the rowers, chiding them for their little strength and their great stomachs. Yet Witta was a wolf in fight, and a very fox in cunning.

'We were driven South by a storm, and for three days and

three nights he took the stern-oar, and threddled the longship through the sea. When it rose beyond measure he brake a pot of whale's oil upon the water, which wonderfully smoothed it, and in that anointed patch he turned her head to the wind and threw out oars at the end of a rope, to make, he said, an anchor at which we lay rolling sorely, but dry. This craft his father Guthrum had shown him. He knew, too, all the Leech-Book of Bald, who was a wise doctor, and he knew the Ship-Book of Hlaf the Woman, who robbed Egypt. He knew all the care of a ship.

'After the storm we saw a mountain whose top was covered with snow and pierced the clouds. The grasses under this mountain, boiled and eaten, are a good cure for soreness of the gums and swelled ankles. We lay there eight days, till men in skins threw stones at us. When the heat increased Witta spread a cloth on bent sticks above the rowers, for the wind failed between the Island of the Mountain and the shore of Africa, which is east of it. That shore is sandy, and we rowed along it within three bowshots. Here we saw whales, and fish in the shape of shields, but longer than our ship. Some slept, some opened their mouths at us, and some danced on the hot waters. The water was hot to the hand, and the sky was hidden by hot, grey mists, out of which blew a fine dust that whitened our hair and beards of a morning. Here, too, were fish that flew in the air like birds. They would fall on the laps of the rowers, and when we went ashore we would roast and eat them.'

The knight paused to see if the children doubted him, but they only nodded and said, 'Go on.'

'The yellow land lay on our left, the grey sea on our right. Knight though I was, I pulled my oar amongst the rowers. I caught seaweed and dried it, and stuffed it between the pots of beads lest they should break. Knighthood is for the land. At sea, look you, a man is but a spurless rider on a bridleless horse. I learned to make strong knots in ropes—yes, and to join two ropes end to end, so that even Witta could scarcely see where they had been married. But Hugh had tenfold more sea-cunning than I. Witta gave him charge of the rowers of the left side. Thorkild of Borkum, a man with a broken nose, that wore a Norman steel cap, had the rowers of the right, and each side rowed and sang against the other. They saw that no man was idle. Truly, as Hugh said, and Witta would laugh at him, a ship is all more care than a Manor.

'How? Thus. There was water to fetch from the shore when we could find it, as well as wild fruit and grasses, and sand for scrubbing of the decks and benches to keep them sweet. Also we hauled the ship out on low islands and emptied all her gear, even to the iron wedges, and burned off the weed, that had grown on her, with torches of rush, and smoked below the decks with rushes dampened in salt water, as Hlaf the Woman orders in her Ship-Book. Once when we were thus stripped, and the ship lay propped on her keel, the bird cried, "Out swords!" as though she saw an enemy. Witta vowed he would wring her neck.'

'Poor Polly! Did he?' said Una.

'Nay. She was the ship's bird. She could call all the rowers by name. . . . Those were good days—for a wifeless man—with Witta and his heathen—beyond the world's end. . . . After many weeks we came on the great Shoal which stretched, as Witta's father had said, far out to sea. We skirted it till we were giddy with the sight and dizzy with the sound of bars and breakers, and when we reached land again we found a naked black people dwelling among woods, who for one wedge of iron loaded us with fruits and grasses and eggs. Witta scratched his head at them in sign he would buy gold. They had no gold, but they understood the sign (all the gold-traders hide their gold in their thick hair), for they pointed along the coast. They beat, too, on their chests with their clenched hands, and that, if we had known it, was an evil sign.'

'What did it mean?' said Dan.

'Patience. Ye shall hear. We followed the coast eastward sixteen days (counting time by sword-cuts on the helm-rail) till we came to the Forest in the Sea. Trees grew there out of mud, arched upon lean and high roots, and many muddy waterways ran all-whither into darkness, under the trees. Here we lost the sun. We followed the winding channels between the trees, and where we could not row we laid hold of the crusted roots and hauled ourselves along. The water was foul, and great glittering flies tormented us. Morning and evening a blue mist covered the mud, which bred fevers. Four of our rowers sickened, and were bound to their benches, lest they should leap overboard and be eaten by the monsters of the mud. The Yellow Man lay sick beside the Wise Iron, rolling his head and talking in his own tongue. Only the Bird throve. She sat on Witta's shoulder and screamed in that noisome, silent darkness. Yes; I think it was the silence we most feared.'

He paused to listen to the comfortable home noises of the brook.

'When we had lost count of time among those black gullies and swashes we heard, as it were, a drum beat far off, and following it we broke into a broad, brown river by a hut in a clearing among fields of pumpkins. We thanked God to see the sun again. The people of the village gave the good welcome, and Witta scratched his head at them (for gold), and showed them our iron and beads. They ran to the bank—we were still in the ship—and pointed to our swords and bows, for always when near shore we lay armed. Soon they fetched store of gold in bars and in dust from their huts, and some great blackened elephants' teeth. These they piled on the bank, as though to tempt us, and made signs of dealing blows in battle, and pointed up to the tree-tops, and to the forest behind. Their captain or chief sorcerer then beat on his chest with his fists, and gnashed his teeth.

'Said Thorkild of Borkum: "Do they mean we must fight for all this gear?" and he half drew sword.

' "Nay," said Hugh. "I think they ask us to league against some enemy."

' "I like this not," said Witta, of a sudden. "Back into mid-stream."

'So we did, and sat still all, watching the black folk and the gold they piled on the bank. Again we heard drums beat in the forest, and the people fled to their huts, leaving the gold unguarded.

'Then Hugh, at the bows, pointed without speech, and we saw a great Devil come out of the forest. He shaded his brows with his hand, and moistened his pink tongue between his lips—thus.'

'A Devil!' said Dan, delightfully horrified.

'Yea. Taller than a man; covered with reddish hair. When he had well regarded our ship, he beat on his chest with his fists till it sounded like rolling drums, and came to the bank swinging all his body between his long arms, and gnashed his teeth at us. Hugh loosed arrow, and pierced him through the throat. He fell roaring, and three other Devils ran out of the forest and hauled him into a tall tree out of sight. Anon they cast down the blood-stained arrow, and lamented together among the leaves. Witta saw the gold on the bank; he was loath to leave it. "Sirs," said he (no man had spoken till then), "yonder is what we have come so far and so painfully to find, laid out to our very hand. Let us row in while these Devils bewail themselves, and at least bear off what we may."

'Bold as a wolf, cunning as a fox was Witta! He set four archers on the fore-deck to shoot the Devils if they should leap from the tree, which was close to the bank. He manned ten oars a side, and bade them watch his hand to row in or back out, and so coaxed he them toward the bank. But none would set foot ashore, though the gold was within ten paces. No man is hasty to his hanging! They whimpered at their oars like beaten hounds, and Witta bit his fingers for rage.

'Said Hugh of a sudden, "Hark!" At first we thought it was the buzzing of the glittering flies on the water; but it grew loud and fierce, so that all men heard.'

'What?' said Dan and Una.

'It was the Sword.' Sir Richard patted the smooth hilt. 'It sang as a Dane sings before battle. "I go," said Hugh, and he leaped from the bows and fell among the gold. I was afraid to my four bones' marrow, but for shame's sake I followed, and Thorkild of Borkum leaped after me. None other came. "Blame me not," cried Witta behind us, "I must abide by my ship." We three had no time to blame or praise. We stooped to the gold and threw it back over our shoulders, one hand on our swords and one eye on the tree, which nigh overhung us.

'I know not how the Devils leaped down, or how the fight began. I heard Hugh cry: "Out! out!" as though he were at Santlache again; I saw Thorkild's steel cap smitten off his head by a great hairy hand, and I felt an arrow from the ship whistle past my ear. They say that till Witta took his sword to the rowers he could not bring his ship inshore; and each one of the four archers said afterwards that he alone had pierced the Devil that fought me. I do not know. I went to it in my mail-shirt, which saved my skin. With long-sword and belt-dagger I fought for the life against a Devil whose very feet were hands, and who whirled me back and forth like a dead branch. He had me by the waist, my arms to my side, when an arrow from the ship pierced him between the shoulders, and he loosened grip. I passed my sword twice through him, and he crutched himself away between his long arms, coughing and moaning. Next, as I remember, I saw Thorkild of Borkum, bareheaded and smiling, leaping up and down before a Devil that leaped and gnashed his teeth. Then Hugh passed, his sword shifted to his left hand, and I wondered why I had not known that Hugh was a lefthanded man; and thereafter I remembered nothing till I felt spray on my face, and we were in sunshine on the open sea. That was twenty days after.'

'What had happened? Did Hugh die?' the children asked.

'Never was such a fight fought by christened man,' said Sir Richard. 'An arrow from the ship had saved me from my Devil, and Thorkild of Borkum had given back before his Devil, till the bowmen on the ship could shoot it all full of arrows from near by; but Hugh's Devil was cunning, and had kept behind trees, where no arrow could reach. Body to body there, by stark strength of sword and hand, had Hugh slain him, and, dying, the Thing had clenched his teeth on the sword. Judge what teeth they were!'

Sir Richard turned the sword again that the children might see the two great chiselled gouges on either side of the blade.

'Those same teeth met in Hugh's right arm and side,' Sir Richard went on. 'I? Oh, I had no more than a broken foot and a fever. Thorkild's ear was bitten, but Hugh's arm and side clean withered away. I saw him where he lay along, sucking a fruit in his left hand. His flesh was wasted off his bones, his hair was patched with white, and his hand was blue-veined like a woman's. He put his left arm round my neck and whispered, "Take my sword. It has been thine since Hastings, O my brother, but I can never hold hilt again." We lay there on the high deck talking of Santlache, and, I think, of every day since Santlache, and it came so that we both wept. I was weak, and he little more than a shadow.

' "Nay—nay," said Witta, at the helm-rail. "Gold is a good right arm to any man. Look—look at the gold!" He bade Thorkild show us the gold and the elephants' teeth, as though we had been children. He had brought away all the gold on the bank, and twice as much more, that the people of the village gave him for slaying the Devils. They worshipped us as Gods, Thorkild told me: it was one of their old women healed up Hugh's poor arm.'

'How much gold did you get?' asked Dan.

'How can I say? Where we came out with wedges of iron under the rowers' feet we returned with wedges of gold hidden beneath planks. There was dust of gold in packages where we slept and along the side, and crosswise under the benches we lashed the blackened elephants' teeth.

' "I had sooner have my right arm," said Hugh, when he had seen all.

' "Ahai! That was my fault," said Witta. "I should have taken ransom and landed you in France when first you came aboard, ten months ago."

' "It is over-late now," said Hugh, laughing.

'Witta plucked at his long shoulder-lock. "But think!" said he. "If I had let ye go—which I swear I would never have done, for I love ye more than brothers—if I had let ye go, by now ye might have been horribly slain by some mere Moor in the Duke of Burgundy's war, or ye might have been murdered by land-thieves, or ye might have died of the plague at an inn. Think of this and do not blame me over-much, Hugh. See! I will only take a half of the gold."

' "I blame thee not at all, Witta," said Hugh. "It was a joyous venture, and we thirty-five here have done what never men have done. If I live till England, I will build me a stout keep over Dallington out of my share."

' "I will buy cattle and amber and warm red cloth for the wife," said Witta, "and I will hold all the land at the head of Stavanger Fiord. Many will fight for me now. But first we must turn North, and with this honest treasure aboard I pray we meet no pirate ships."

'We did not laugh. We were careful. We were afraid lest we should lose one grain of our gold, for which we had fought Devils.

' "Where is the Sorcerer?" said I, for Witta was looking at the Wise Iron in the box, and I could not see the Yellow Man.

' "He has gone to his own country," said he. "He rose up in the night while we were beating out of that forest in the mud, and said that he could see it behind the trees. He leaped out on to the mud, and did not answer when we called; so we called no more. He left the Wise Iron, which is all that I care for—and see, the Spirit still points to the South."

'We were troubled for fear that the Wise Iron should fail us now that its Yellow Man had gone, and when we saw the Spirit still served us we grew afraid of too strong winds, and of shoals, and of careless leaping fish, and of all the people on all the shores where we landed.'

'Why?' said Dan.

'Because of the gold—because of our gold. Gold changes men altogether. Thorkild of Borkum did not change. He laughed at Witta for his fears, and at us for our counselling Witta to furl sail when the ship pitched at all.

' "Better be drowned out of hand," said Thorkild of Borkum, "than go tied to a deck-load of yellow dust."

'He was a landless man, and had been slave to some King in the East. He would have beaten out the gold into deep bands to put round the oars, and round the prow.

'Yet, though he vexed himself for the gold, Witta waited upon Hugh like a woman, lending him his shoulder when the ship rolled, and tying of ropes from side to side that Hugh might hold by them. But for Hugh, he said—and so did all his men—they would never have won the gold. I remember Witta made a little, thin gold ring for our Bird to swing in.

'Three months we rowed and sailed and went ashore for fruits or to clean the ship. When we saw wild horsemen, riding among sand-dunes, flourishing spears, we knew we were on the Moors' coast, and stood over north to Spain; and a strong south-west wind bore us in ten days to a coast of high red rocks, where we heard a hunting-horn blow among the yellow gorse and knew it was England.

' "Now find ye Pevensey yourselves," said Witta. "I love not these narrow ship-filled seas."

'He set the dried, salted head of the Devil, which Hugh had killed, high on our prow, and all boats fled from us. Yet, for our gold's sake, we were more afraid than they. We crept along the coast by night till we came to the chalk cliffs, and so east to Pevensey. Witta would not come ashore with us, though Hugh promised him wine at Dallington enough to swim in. He was on fire to see his wife, and ran into the Marsh after sunset, and there he left us and our share of gold, and backed out on the same tide. He made no promise; he swore no oath; he looked for no thanks; but to Hugh, an armless man, and to me, an old cripple whom he could have flung into the sea, he passed over wedge upon wedge, packet upon packet of gold and dust of gold, and only ceased when we would take no more. As he stooped from the rail to bid us farewell he stripped off his right-arm bracelets and put them all on Hugh's left, and he kissed Hugh on the cheek. I think when Thorkild of Borkum bade the rowers give way we were near weeping. It is true that Witta was an heathen and a pirate; true it is he held us by force many months in his ship, but I loved that bow-legged, blue-eyed man for his great boldness, his cunning, his skill, and, beyond all, for his simplicity.'

'Did he get home all right?' said Dan.

'I never knew. We saw him hoist sail under the moon-track and stand away. I have prayed that he found his wife and the children.'

'And what did you do?'

'We waited on the Marsh till the day. Then I sat by the gold, all tied in an old sail, while Hugh went to Pevensey, and De Aquila sent us horses.'

Sir Richard crossed hands on his sword-hilt, and stared down-stream through the soft warm shadows.

'A whole shipload of gold!' said Una, looking at the little *Golden Hind*. 'But I'm glad I didn't see the Devils.'

'I don't believe they were Devils,' Dan whispered back.

'Eh?' said Sir Richard. 'Witta's father warned him they were unquestionable Devils. One must believe one's father, and not one's children. What were my Devils, then?'

Dan flushed all over. 'I—I only thought,' he stammered; 'I've got a book called *The Gorilla Hunters*—it's a continuation of *Coral Island*, sir—and it says there that the gorillas (they're big monkeys, you know) were always chewing iron up.'

'Not always,' said Una. 'Only twice.' They had been reading *The Gorilla Hunters* in the orchard.

'Well, anyhow, they always drummed on their chests, like

Sir Richard's did, before they went for people. And they built houses in trees, too.'

'Ha!' Sir Richard opened his eyes. 'Houses like flat nests did our Devils make, where their imps lay and looked at us. I did not see them (I was sick after the fight), but Witta told me, and, lo, ye know it also? Wonderful! Were our Devils only nest-building apes? Is there no sorcery left in the world?'

'I don't know,' answered Dan uncomfortably. 'I've seen a man take rabbits out of a hat, and he told us we could see how he did it, if we watched hard. And we did.'

'But we didn't,' said Una, sighing. 'Oh! there's Puck!'

The little fellow, brown and smiling, peered between two stems of an ash, nodded, and slid down the bank into the cool beside them.

'No sorcery, Sir Richard?' he laughed, and blew on a full dandelion-head he had picked.

'They tell me that Witta's Wise Iron was a toy. The boy carries such an iron with him. They tell me our Devils were apes, called gorillas!' said Sir Richard indignantly.

'That is the sorcery of books,' said Puck. 'I warned thee they were wise children. All people can be wise by reading of books.'

'But are the books true?' Sir Richard frowned. 'I like not all this reading and writing.'

'Ye-es,' said Puck, holding the naked dandelion-head at arm's length. 'But if we hang all fellows who write falsely, why did De Aquila not begin with Gilbert the Clerk? *He* was false enough.'

'Poor false Gilbert. Yet, in his fashion, he was bold,' said Sir Richard.

'What did he do?' said Dan.

'He wrote,' said Sir Richard. 'Is the tale meet for children, think you?' He looked at Puck; but 'Tell us! Tell us!' cried Dan and Una together.

73

THORKILD'S SONG

There's no wind along these seas,
  Out oars for Stavanger!
  Forward all for Stavanger!
So we must wake the white-ash breeze,
  Let fall for Stavanger!
  A long pull for Stavanger!

Oh, hear the benches creak and strain!
  (A long pull for Stavanger!)
She thinks she smells the Northland rain!
  (A long pull for Stavanger!)

She thinks she smells the Northland snow,
And she's as glad as we to go.

She thinks she smells the Northland rime,
And the dear dark nights of winter-time.

Her very bolts are sick for shore,
And we—we want it ten times more!

So all you Gods that love brave men,
Send us a three-reef gale again!

Send us a gale, and watch us come,
With close-cropped canvas slashing home!

But—there's no wind on all these seas.
  A long pull for Stavanger!
So we must wake the white-ash breeze,
  A long pull for Stavanger!

OLD MEN AT PEVENSEY

OLD MEN AT PEVENSEY

'IT HAS NOUGHT TO DO with apes or Devils,' Sir Richard went on, in an undertone. 'It concerns De Aquila, than whom there was never bolder nor craftier, nor more hardy knight born. And remember he was an old, old man at that time.'

'When?' said Dan.

'When we came back from sailing with Witta.'

'What did you do with your gold?' said Dan.

'Have patience. Link by link is chain-mail made. I will tell all in its place. We bore the gold to Pevensey on horseback— three loads of it—and then up to the north chamber, above the Great Hall of Pevensey Castle, where De Aquila lay in winter. He sat on his bed like a little white falcon, turning his head swiftly from one to the other as we told our tale. Jehan the Crab, an old sour man-at-arms, guarded the stairway, but De Aquila bade him wait at the stair-foot, and let down both leather curtains over the door. It was Jehan whom De Aquila had sent to us with the horses, and only Jehan had loaded the gold. When our story was told, De Aquila gave us the news of England, for we were as men waked from a year-long sleep. The Red King was dead—slain (ye remember?) the day we set sail—and Henry, his younger brother, had made himself King of England over the head of Robert of Normandy. This was the very thing that the Red King had done to Robert when our Great William died. Then Robert of Normandy, mad, as De Aquila said, at twice missing of this kingdom, had sent an army against England, which army had been well beaten back to their ships at Portsmouth. A little earlier, and Witta's ship would have rowed through them.

' "And now," said De Aquila, "half the great Barons of the North and West are out against the King between Salisbury and Shrewsbury, and half the other half wait to see which way the game shall go. They say Henry is overly English for their stomachs, because he hath married an English wife and she hath coaxed him to give back their old laws to our Saxons. (Better ride a horse on the bit he knows, *I* say!) But that is only a cloak to their falsehood." He cracked his finger on the table where the wine was spilt, and thus he spoke:—

' "William crammed us Norman barons full of good English acres after Santlache. *I* had my share too," he said, and clapped Hugh on the shoulder; "but I warned him—I warned him before Odo rebelled—that he should have bidden the Barons give up their lands and lordships in Normandy if they would be English lords. Now they are all but princes both in England and Normandy—trencher-fed hounds, with a foot in one trough and both eyes on the other! Robert of Normandy has sent them word that if they do not fight for him in England he will sack and harry out their lands in Normandy. Therefore Clare has risen, FitzOsborne has risen, Montgomery has risen—whom our First William made an English Earl. Even D'Arcy is out with his men, whose father I remember a little hedge-sparrow knight near by Caen. If Henry wins, the Barons can still flee to Normandy, where Robert will welcome them. If Henry loses, Robert, he says, will give them more lands in England. Oh, a pest—a pest on Normandy, for she will be our England's curse this many a long year!"

' "Amen," said Hugh. "But will the war come our ways, think you?"

' "Not from the North," said De Aquila. "But the sea is

always open. If the Barons gain the upper hand Robert will send another army into England for sure, and this time I think he will land here—where his father, the Conqueror, landed. Ye have brought your pigs to a pretty market! Half England alight, and gold enough on the ground"—he stamped on the bars beneath the table—"to set every sword in Christendom fighting."

' "What is to do?" said Hugh. "I have no keep at Dallington; and if we buried it, whom could we trust?"

' "Me," said De Aquila. "Pevensey walls are strong. No man but Jehan, who is my dog, knows what is between them." He drew a curtain by the shot-window and showed us the shaft of a well in the thickness of the wall.

' "I made it for a drinking-well," he said, "but we found salt water, and it rises and falls with the tide. Hark!" We heard the water whistle and blow at the bottom. "Will it serve?" said he.

' "Needs must," said Hugh. "Our lives are in thy hands." So we lowered all the gold down except one small chest of it by De Aquila's bed, which we kept as much for his delight in its weight and colour as for any of our needs.

'In the morning, ere we rode to our Manors, he said: "I do not say farewell; because ye will return and bide here. Not for love nor for sorrow, but to be with the gold. Have a care," he said, laughing, "lest I use it to make myself Pope. Trust me not, but return!" '

Sir Richard paused and smiled sadly.

'In seven days, then, we returned from our Manors—from the Manors which had been ours.'

'And were the children quite well?' said Una.

'My sons were young. Land and governance belong by right to young men.' Sir Richard was talking to himself. 'It

would have broken their hearts if we had taken back our
Manors. They made us great welcome, but we could see—
Hugh and I could see—that our day was done. I was a cripple
and he a one-armed man. No!' He shook his head. 'And therefore'—he raised his voice—'we rode back to Pevensey.'

'I'm sorry,' said Una, for the knight seemed very sorrowful.

'Little maid, it all passed long ago. They were young; we
were old. We let them rule the Manors. "Aha!" cried De
Aquila from his shot-window, when we dismounted. "Back
again to earth, old foxes?" but when we were in his chamber
above the Hall he puts his arms about us and says, "Welcome,
ghosts! Welcome, poor ghosts!" . . . Thus it fell out that we
were rich beyond belief, and lonely. And lonely!'

'What did you do?' said Dan.

'We watched for Robert of Normandy,' said the knight.
'De Aquila was like Witta. He suffered no idleness. In fair
weather we would ride along between Bexlei on the one side,
to Cuckmere on the other—sometimes with hawk, sometimes
with hound (there are stout hares both on the Marsh and
the Downland), but always with an eye to the sea, for fear of
fleets from Normandy. In foul weather he would walk on the
top of his tower, frowning against the rain—peering here and
pointing there. It always vexed him to think how Witta's ship
had come and gone without his knowledge. When the wind
ceased and ships anchored, to the wharf's edge he would go
and, leaning on his sword among the stinking fish, would call
to the mariners for their news from France. His other eye he
kept landward for word of Henry's war against the Barons.

'Many brought him news—jongleurs, harpers, pedlars, sut-
lers, priests, and the like; and, though he was secret enough
in small things, yet, if their news misliked him, then, regarding neither time nor place nor people, he would curse our

King Henry for a fool or a babe. I have heard him cry aloud
by the fishing-boats: "If I were King of England I would do
thus and thus"; and when I rode out to see that the warning-
beacons were laid and dry, he hath often called to me from
the shot-window: "Look to it, Richard! Do not copy our blind
King, but see with thine own eyes and feel with thine own
hands." I do not think he knew any sort of fear. And so we
lived at Pevensey, in the little chamber above the Hall.

'One foul night came word that a messenger of the King
waited below. We were chilled after a long riding in the fog
towards Bexlei, which is an easy place for ships to land. De
Aquila sent word the man might either eat with us or wait
till we had fed. Anon Jehan, at the stair-head, cried that he
had called for horse, and was gone. "Pest on him!" said De
Aquila. "I have more to do than to shiver in the Great Hall
for every gadling the King sends. Left he no word?"

' "None," said Jehan, "except"—he had been with De Aquila
at Santlache—"except he said that if an old dog could not
learn new tricks it was time to sweep out the kennel."

' "Oho!" said De Aquila, rubbing his nose, "to whom did
he say that?"

' "To his beard, chiefly, but some to his horse's flank as he
was girthing up. I followed him out," said Jehan the Crab.

' "What was his shield-mark?"

' "Gold horseshoes on black," said the Crab.

' "That is one of Fulke's men," said De Aquila.'

Puck broke in very gently, 'Gold horseshoes on black is *not*
the Fulkes' shield. The Fulkes' arms are——'

The knight waved one hand statelily.

'Thou knowest that evil man's true name,' he replied, 'but
I have chosen to call him Fulke because I promised him I
would not tell the story of his wickedness so that any man

might guess it. I have changed *all* the names in my tale. His children's children may be still alive.'

'True—true,' said Puck, smiling softly. 'It is knightly to keep faith—even after a thousand years.'

Sir Richard bowed a little and went on:—

' "Gold horseshoes on black?" said De Aquila. "I had heard Fulke had joined the Barons, but if this is true our King must be of the upper hand. No matter, all Fulkes are faithless. Still, I would not have sent the man away empty."

' "He fed," said Jehan. "Gilbert the Clerk fetched him meat and wine from the kitchens. He ate at Gilbert's table."

'This Gilbert was a clerk from Battle Abbey, who kept the accounts of the Manor of Pevensey. He was tall and pale-coloured, and carried those new-fashioned beads for counting of prayers. They were large brown nuts or seeds, and hanging from his girdle with his pen and ink-horn they clashed when he walked. His place was in the great fireplace. There was his table of accounts, and there he lay o' nights. He feared the hounds in the Hall that came nosing after bones or to sleep on the warm ashes, and would slash at them with his beads— like a woman. When De Aquila sat in Hall to do justice, take fines, or grant lands, Gilbert would so write it in the Manor-roll. But it was none of his work to feed our guests, or to let them depart without his lord's knowledge.

'Said De Aquila, after Jehan was gone down the stair: "Hugh, hast thou ever told my Gilbert thou canst read Latin hand-of-write?"

' "No," said Hugh. "He is no friend to me, or to Odo my hound either." "No matter," said De Aquila. "Let him never know thou canst tell one letter from its fellow, and"—here he yerked us in the ribs with his scabbard—"watch him, both of ye. There be devils in Africa, as I have heard, but by the

Saints, there be greater devils in Pevensey!" And that was all
he would say.

'It chanced, some small while afterwards, a Norman man-
at-arms would wed a Saxon wench of the Manor, and Gilbert
(we had watched him well since De Aquila spoke) doubted
whether her folk were free or slave. Since De Aquila would
give them a field of good land, if she were free, the matter
came up at the justice in Great Hall before De Aquila. First
the wench's father spoke; then her mother; then all together,
till the Hall rang and the hounds bayed. De Aquila held up
his hands. "Write her free," he called to Gilbert by the
fireplace. "A' God's Name, write her free, before she deafens
me! Yes, yes," he said to the wench that was on her knees at
him; "thou art Cerdic's sister, and own cousin to the Lady of
Mercia, if thou wilt be silent. In fifty years there will be neither
Norman nor Saxon, but all English," said he, "and *these* are
the men that do our work!" He clapped the man-at-arms that
was Jehan's nephew on the shoulder, and kissed the wench,
and fretted with his feet among the rushes to show it was
finished. (The Great Hall is always bitter cold.) I stood at his
side; Hugh was behind Gilbert in the fireplace making to play
with wise rough Odo. He signed to De Aquila, who bade
Gilbert measure the new field for the new couple. Out then
runs our Gilbert between man and maid, his beads clashing
at his waist, and the Hall being empty, we three sit by the fire.

'Said Hugh, leaning down to the hearth-stones, "I saw this
stone move under Gilbert's foot when Odo snuffed at it.
Look!" De Aquila digged in the ashes with his sword; the
stone tilted; beneath it lay a parchment folden, and the
writing atop was: "Words spoken against the King by our Lord
of Pevensey—the second part."

'Here was set out (Hugh read it us whispering) every jest

De Aquila had made to us touching the King; every time he had called out to me from the shot-window, and every time he had said what he would do if he were King of England. Yes, day by day had his daily speech, which he never stinted, been set down by Gilbert, tricked out and twisted from its true meaning, yet withal so cunningly that none could deny who knew him that De Aquila had in some sort spoken those words. Ye see?'

Dan and Una nodded.

'Yes,' said Una gravely. 'It isn't what you say so much. It's what you mean when you say it. Like calling Dan a beast in fun. Only grown-ups don't always understand.'

' "He hath done this day by day before our very face?" said De Aquila.

' "Nay, hour by hour," said Hugh. "When De Aquila spoke even now, in the Hall, of Saxons and Normans, I saw Gilbert write on a parchment, which he kept beside the Manor-roll, that De Aquila said soon there would be no Normans left in England if his men-at-arms did their work aright."

' "Bones of the Saints!" said De Aquila. "What avail is honour or a sword against a pen? Where did Gilbert hide that writing? He shall eat it."

' "In his breast when he ran out," said Hugh. "Which made me look to see where he kept his finished stuff. When Odo scratched at this stone here, I saw his face change. So I was sure."

' "He is bold," said De Aquila. "Do him justice. In his own fashion, my Gilbert is bold."

' "Overbold," said Hugh. "Hearken here," and he read: "Upon the Feast of St. Agatha, our Lord of Pevensey, lying in his upper chamber, being clothed in his second fur gown reversed with rabbit——"

' "Pest on him! He is not my tire-woman!" said De Aquila, and Hugh and I laughed.

' "Reversed with rabbit, seeing a fog over the marshes, did wake Sir Richard Dalyngridge, his drunken cup-mate" (here they laughed at me) "and said, 'Peer out, old fox, for God is on the Duke of Normandy's side.' "

' "So did I. It was a black fog. Robert could have landed ten thousand men, and we none the wiser. Does he tell how we were out all day riding the Marsh, and how I near perished in a quicksand, and coughed like a sick ewe for ten days after?" cried De Aquila.

' "No," said Hugh. "But here is the prayer of Gilbert himself to his master Fulke."

' "Ah," said De Aquila. "Well I knew it was Fulke. What is the price of my blood?"

' "Gilbert prayeth that when our Lord of Pevensey is stripped of his lands on this evidence which Gilbert hath, with fear and pains, collected——"

' "Fear and pains is a true word," said De Aquila, and sucked in his cheeks. "But how excellent a weapon is a pen! I must learn it."

' "He prays that Fulke will advance him from his present service to that honour in the Church which Fulke promised him. And lest Fulke should forget, he has written below, 'To be Sacristan of Battle.' "

'At this De Aquila whistled. "A man who can plot against one lord can plot against another. When I am stripped of my lands Fulke will whip off my Gilbert's foolish head. None the less Battle needs a new Sacristan. They tell me the Abbot Henry keeps no sort of rule there."

' "Let the Abbot wait," said Hugh. "It is our heads and our lands that are in danger. This parchment is the second part of the tale. The first has gone to Fulke, and so to the King, who will hold us traitors."

' "Assuredly," said De Aquila. "Fulke's man took the first part that evening when Gilbert fed him, and our King is so beset by his brother and his Barons (small blame, too!) that he is mad with mistrust. Fulke has his ear, and pours poison into it. Presently the King gives him my land and yours. This is old," and he leaned back and yawned.

' "And thou wilt surrender Pevensey without word or blow?" said Hugh. "We Saxons will fight your King then. I will go warn my nephew at Dallington. Give me a horse!"

' "Give thee a toy and a rattle," said De Aquila. "Put back the parchment, and rake over the ashes. If Fulke is given my Pevensey, which is England's gate, what will he do with it? He is Norman at heart, and his heart is in Normandy, where he can kill peasants at his pleasure. He will open England's gate to our sleepy Robert, as Odo and Mortain tried to do, and then there will be another landing and another Santlache. Therefore I cannot give up Pevensey."

' "Good!" said we two.

' "Ah, but wait! If my King be made, on Gilbert's evidence, to mistrust me, he will send his men against me here, and while we fight, England's gate is left unguarded. Who will be the first to come through thereby? Even Robert of Normandy. Therefore I cannot fight my King." He nursed his sword—thus.

' "This is saying and unsaying like a Norman," said Hugh. "What of our Manors?"

' "I do not think for myself," said De Aquila, "nor for our King, nor for your lands. I think for England, for whom neither King nor Baron thinks. I am not Norman, Sir Richard, nor Saxon, Sir Hugh. English am I."

' "Saxon, Norman, or English," said Hugh, "our lives are thine, however the game goes. When do we hang Gilbert?"

' "Never," said De Aquila. "Who knows, he may yet be Sacristan of Battle, for, to do him justice, he is a good writer. Dead men make dumb witnesses. Wait."

' "But the King may give Pevensey to Fulke. And our Manors go with it," said I. "Shall we tell our sons?"

' "No. The King will not wake up a hornets' nest in the South till he has smoked out the bees in the North. He may hold me a traitor; but at least he sees I am not fighting against him; and every day that I lie still is so much gain to him while he fights the Barons. If he were wise he would wait till that war were over before he made new enemies. But I think Fulke will play upon him to send for me, and if I do not obey the summons, that will, to Henry's mind, be proof of my treason. But mere talk, such as Gilbert sends, is no proof nowadays. We Barons follow the Church, and, like Anselm, we speak what we please. Let us go about our day's dealings, and say naught to Gilbert."

' "Then we do nothing?" said Hugh.

' "We wait," said De Aquila. "I am old, but still I find that the most grievous work I know."

'And so we found it, but in the end De Aquila was right.

'A little later in the year, armed men rode over the hill, the Golden Horseshoes flying behind the King's banner. Said De Aquila, at the window of our chamber: "How did I tell you? Here comes Fulke himself to spy out his new lands which our King hath promised him if he can bring proof of my treason."

' "How dost thou know?" said Hugh.

' "Because that is what I would do if I were Fulke, but *I* should have brought more men. My roan horse to your old shoes," said he, "Fulke brings me the King's Summons to leave Pevensey and join the war." He sucked in his cheeks and drummed on the edge of the well-shaft, where the water sounded all hollow.

' "Shall we go?" said I.

' "Go! At this time of year? Stark madness," said he. "Take *me* from Pevensey to fisk and flyte through fern and forest, and in three days Robert's keels would be lying on Pevensey mud with ten thousand men! Who would stop them—Fulke?"

'The horns blew without, and anon Fulke cried the King's Summons at the great door, that De Aquila with all men and horse should join the King's camp at Salisbury.

' "How did I tell you?" said De Aquila. "There are twenty Barons 'twixt here and Salisbury could give King Henry good land service, but he has been worked upon by Fulke to send South and call me—*me!*—off the Gate of England, when his enemies stand about to batter it in. See that Fulke's men lie in the big south barn," said he. "Give them drink, and when Fulke has eaten we will drink in my chamber. The Great Hall is too cold for old bones."

'As soon as he was off-horse Fulke went to the chapel with Gilbert to give thanks for his safe coming, and when he had eaten—he was a fat man, and rolled his eyes greedily at our good roast Sussex wheatears—we led him to the little upper chamber, whither Gilbert had already gone with the Manor-roll. I remember when Fulke heard the tide blow and whistle in the shaft he leaped back, and his long down-turned stirrup-shoes caught in the rushes and he stumbled, so that Jehan behind him found it easy to knock his head against the wall.'

'Did you know it was going to happen?' said Dan.

'Assuredly,' said Sir Richard, with a sweet smile. 'I put my foot on his sword and plucked away his dagger, but he knew not whether it was day or night for awhile. He lay rolling his eyes and bubbling with his mouth, and Jehan roped him like a calf. He was cased all in that new-fangled armour which we call lizard-mail. Not rings like my hauberk here'—Sir Richard tapped his chest—'but little pieces of dagger-proof steel overlapping on stout leather. We stripped it off (no need to spoil good harness by wetting it), and in the neck-piece De Aquila found the same folden piece of parchment which we had put back under the hearth-stone.

'At this Gilbert would have run out. I laid my hand on his shoulder. It sufficed. He fell to trembling and praying on his beads.

' "Gilbert," said De Aquila, "here be more notable sayings and doing of our Lord of Pevensey for thee to write down. Take pen and ink-horn, Gilbert. We cannot all be Sacristans of Battle."

'Said Fulke from the floor, "Ye have bound a King's messenger. Pevensey shall burn for this."

' "Maybe. I have seen it besieged once," said De Aquila, "but heart up, Fulke. I promise thee that thou shalt be hanged in the middle of the flames at the end of that siege, if I have to share my last loaf with thee; and that is more than Odo would have done when we starved out him and Mortain."

'Then Fulke sat up and looked long and cunningly at De Aquila.

' "By the Saints," said he, "why didst thou not say thou wast on the Duke Robert's side at the first?"

' "Am I?" said De Aquila.

'Fulke laughed and said, "No man who serves King Henry dare do this much to his messenger. When didst thou come over to the Duke? Let me up and we can smooth it out together." And he smiled and becked and winked.

' "Yes, we will smooth it out," said De Aquila. He nodded to me, and Jehan and I heaved up Fulke—he was a heavy man—and lowered him into the shaft by a rope, not so as to stand on our gold, but dangling by his shoulders a little above. It was turn of ebb, and the water came to his knees. He said nothing, but shivered somewhat.

'Then Jehan of a sudden beat down Gilbert's wrist with his sheathed dagger. "Stop!" he said. "He swallows his beads."

' "Poison, belike," said De Aquila. "It is good for men who know too much. I have carried it these thirty years. Give me!"

'Then Gilbert wept and howled. De Aquila ran the beads through his fingers. The last one—I have said they were large nuts—opened in two halves on a pin, and there was a small folded parchment within. On it was written: *The Old Dog goes to Salisbury to be beaten. I have his Kennel. Come quickly.*

' "This is worse than poison," said De Aquila very softly, and sucked in his cheeks. Then Gilbert grovelled in the rushes, and told us all he knew. The letter, as we guessed, was from Fulke to the Duke (and not the first that had passed between them); Fulke had given it to Gilbert in the chapel, and Gilbert thought to have taken it by morning to a certain fishing-boat at the' wharf, which trafficked between Pevensey and the French shore. Gilbert was a false fellow, but he found time between his quakings and shakings to swear that the master of the boat knew nothing of the matter.

' "He hath called me shaved-head," said Gilbert, "and he hath thrown haddock-guts at me; but for all that, he is no traitor."

' "I will have no clerk of mine mishandled or miscalled," said De Aquila. "That seaman shall be whipped at his own mast. Write me first a letter, and thou shalt bear it, with the order for the whipping, to-morrow to the boat."

'At this Gilbert would have kissed De Aquila's hand—he

had not hoped to live until the morning—and when he trembled less he wrote a letter as from Fulke to the Duke, saying that the Kennel, which signified Pevensey, was shut, and that the Old Dog (which was De Aquila) sat outside it, and, moreover, that all had been betrayed.

' "Write to any man that all is betrayed," said De Aquila, "and even the Pope himself would sleep uneasily. Eh, Jehan? If one told thee all was betrayed, what wouldst thou do?"

' "I would run away," said Jehan. "It might be true."

' "Well said," quoth De Aquila. "Write, Gilbert, that Montgomery, the great Earl, hath made his peace with the King, and that little D'Arcy, whom I hate, hath been hanged by the heels. We will give Robert full measure to chew upon. Write also that Fulke himself is sick to death of a dropsy."

' "Nay!" cried Fulke, hanging in the well-shaft. "Drown me out of hand, but do not make a jest of me."

' "Jest? I?" said De Aquila. "I am but fighting for life and lands with a pen, as thou hast shown me, Fulke."

'Then Fulke groaned, for he was cold, and, "Let me confess," said he.

' "Now this is right neighbourly," said De Aquila, leaning over the shaft. "Thou hast read my sayings and doings—or at least the first part of them—and thou art minded to repay me with thy own doings and sayings. Take pen and ink-horn, Gilbert. Here is work that will not irk thee."

' "Let my men go without hurt, and I will confess my treason against the King," said Fulke.

' "Now, why has he grown so tender of his men of a sudden?" said Hugh to me; for Fulke had no name for mercy to his men. Plunder he gave them, but pity, none.

' "Té! Té!" said De Aquila. "Thy treason was all confessed long ago by Gilbert. It would be enough to hang Montgomery himself."

' "Nay; but spare my men," said Fulke; and we heard him splash like a fish in a pond, for the tide was rising.

' "All in good time," said De Aquila. "The night is young; the wine is old; and we need only the merry tale. Begin the story of thy life since when thou wast a lad at Tours. Tell it nimbly!"

' "Ye shame me to my soul," said Fulke.

' "Then I have done what neither King nor Duke could do," said De Aquila. "But begin, and forget nothing."

' "Send thy man away," said Fulke.

' "That much can I do," said De Aquila. "But, remember, I am like the Danes' King. I cannot turn the tide."

' "How long will it rise?" said Fulke, and splashed anew.

' "For three hours," said De Aquila. "Time to tell all thy good deeds. Begin, and, Gilbert,—I have heard thou art somewhat careless—do not twist his words from their true meaning."

'So—fear of death in the dark being upon him—Fulke began, and Gilbert, not knowing what his fate might be, wrote it word by word. I have heard many tales, but never heard I aught to match the tale of Fulke his black life, as Fulke told it hollowly, hanging in the shaft.'

'Was it bad?' said Dan, awestruck.

'Beyond belief,' Sir Richard answered. 'None the less, there was that in it which forced even Gilbert to laugh. We three laughed till we ached. At one place his teeth so chattered that we could not well hear, and we reached him down a cup of wine. Then he warmed to it, and smoothly set out all his shifts, malices, and treacheries, his extreme boldnesses (he was desperate bold); his retreats, shufflings, and counterfeitings (he was also inconceivably a coward); his lack of gear and honour; his despair at their loss; his remedies, and well-coloured contrivances. Yes, he waved the filthy rags of his life before us, as though they had been some proud banner. When he ceased, we saw by torches that the tide stood at the corners of his mouth, and he breathed strongly through his nose.

'We had him out, and rubbed him; we wrapped him in a cloak, and gave him wine, and we leaned and looked upon him, the while he drank. He was shivering, but shameless.

'Of a sudden we heard Jehan at the stairway wake, but a boy pushed past him, and stood before us, the Hall-rushes in his hair, all slubbered with sleep. "My father! My father! I dreamed of treachery," he cried, and babbled thickly.

' "There is no treachery here," said Fulke. "Go!" and the boy turned, even then not fully awake, and Jehan led him by the hand to the Great Hall.

' "Thy only son!" said De Aquila. "Why didst thou bring the child here?"

' "He is my heir. I dared not trust him to my brother," said Fulke, and now he was ashamed. De Aquila said nothing, but sat weighing a wine-cup in his two hands—thus. Anon, Fulke touched him on the knee.

' "Let the boy escape to Normandy," said he, "and do with me at thy pleasure. Yea, hang me to-morrow, with my letter to Robert round my neck, but let the boy go."

' "Be still," said De Aquila. "I think for England."

'So we waited what our Lord of Pevensey should devise; and the sweat ran down Fulke's forehead.

'At last said De Aquila: "I am too old to judge, or to trust any man. I do not covet thy lands, as thou hast coveted mine; and whether thou art any better or any worse than any other black Angevin thief, it is for thy King to find out. Therefore, go back to thy King, Fulke."

' "And thou wilt say nothing of what has passed?" said Fulke.

' "Why should I? Thy son will stay with me. If the King

calls me again to leave Pevensey, which I must guard against England's enemies; if the King sends his men against me for a traitor; or if I hear that the King in his bed thinks any evil of me or my two knights, thy son will be hanged from out this window, Fulke." '

'But it hadn't anything to do with his son,' cried Una, startled.

'How could we have hanged Fulke?' said Sir Richard. 'We needed him to make our peace with the King. He would have betrayed half England for the boy's sake. Of that we were sure.'

'I don't understand,' said Una. 'But I think it was simply awful.'

'So did not Fulke. He was well pleased.'

'What? Because his son was going to be killed?'

'Nay. Because De Aquila had shown him how he might save the boy's life and his own lands and honours. "I will do it," he said. "I swear I will do it. I will tell the King thou art no traitor, but the most excellent, valiant, and perfect of us all. Yes, I will save thee."

'De Aquila looked still into the bottom of the cup, rolling the wine-dregs to and fro.

' "Ay," he said. "If I had a son, I would, I think, save him. But do not by any means tell me how thou wilt go about it."

' "Nay, nay," said Fulke, nodding his bald head wisely. "That is my secret. But rest at ease, De Aquila, no hair of thy head nor rood of thy land shall be forfeited," and he smiled like one planning great good deeds.

' "And henceforward," said De Aquila, "I counsel thee to serve one master—not two."

' "What?" said Fulke. "Can I work no more honest trading between the two sides these troublous times?"

' "Serve Robert or the King—England or Normandy," said De Aquila. "I care not which it is, but make thy choice here and now."

' "The King, then," said Fulke, "for I see he is better served than Robert. Shall I swear it?"

' "No need," said De Aquila, and he laid his hand on the parchments which Gilbert had written. "It shall be some part of my Gilbert's penance to copy out the savoury tale of thy life, till we have made ten, twenty, an hundred, maybe, copies. How many cattle, think you, would the Bishop of Tours give for that tale? Or thy brother? Or the Monks of Blois? Minstrels will turn it into songs which thy own Saxon serfs shall sing behind their plough-stilts, and men-at-arms riding through thy Norman towns. From here to Rome, Fulke, men will make very merry over that tale, and how Fulke told it, hanging in a well, like a drowned puppy. This shall be thy punishment, if ever I find thee double-dealing with thy King any more. Meantime, the parchments stay here with thy son. Him I will return to thee when thou hast made my peace with the King. The parchments never."

'Fulke hid his face and groaned.

' "Bones of the Saints!" said De Aquila, laughing. "The pen cuts deep. I could never have fetched that grunt out of thee with any sword."

' "But so long as I do not anger thee, my tale will be secret?" said Fulke.

' "Just so long. Does that comfort thee, Fulke?" said De Aquila.

' "What other comfort have ye left me?" he said, and of a sudden he wept hopelessly like a child, dropping his face on his knees.'

'Poor Fulke!' said Una.

'I pitied him also,' said Sir Richard.

' "After the spur, corn," said De Aquila, and he threw Fulke three wedges of gold that he had taken from our little chest by the bedplace.

' "If I had known this," said Fulke, catching his breath, "I would never have lifted hand against Pevensey. Only lack of this yellow stuff has made me so unlucky in my dealings."

'It was dawn then, and they stirred in the Great Hall below. We sent down Fulke's mail to be scoured, and when he rode away at noon under his own and the King's banner very splendid and stately did he show. He smoothed his long beard, and called his son to his stirrup and kissed him. De Aquila rode with him as far as the New Mill landward. We thought the night had been all a dream.'

'But did he make it right with the King?' Dan asked. 'About your not being traitors, I mean?'

Sir Richard smiled. 'The King sent no second summons to Pevensey, nor did he ask why De Aquila had not obeyed the first. Yes, that was Fulke's work. I know not how he did it, but it was well and swiftly done.'

'Then you didn't do anything to his son?' said Una.

'The boy? Oh, he was an imp! He turned the keep doors out of dortoirs while we had him. He sang foul songs, learned in the Barons' camps—poor fool; he set the hounds fighting in Hall; he lit the rushes to drive out, as he said, the fleas; he drew his dagger on Jehan, who threw him down the stairway for it; and he rode his horse through crops and among sheep. But when we had beaten him, and showed him wolf and deer, he followed us old men like a young, eager hound, and called us "uncle." His father came the summer's end to take him away, but the boy had no lust to go, because of the otter-hunting, and he stayed on till the fox-hunting. I gave him a bittern's claw to bring him good luck at shooting. An imp, if ever there was!'

'And what happened to Gilbert?' said Dan.

'Not even a whipping. De Aquila said he would sooner a clerk, however false, that knew the Manor-roll than a fool, however true, that must be taught his work afresh. Moreover, after that night I think Gilbert loved as much as he feared De Aquila. At least he would not leave us—not even when Vivian, the King's Clerk, would have made him Sacristan of Battle Abbey. A false fellow, but, in his fashion, bold.'

'Did Robert ever land in Pevensey after all?' Dan went on.

'We guarded the coast too well while Henry was fighting his Barons; and three or four years later, when England had peace, Henry crossed to Normandy and showed his brother some work at Tenchebrai that cured Robert of fighting. Many of Henry's men sailed from Pevensey to that war. Fulke came, I remember, and we all four lay in the little chamber once again, and drank together. De Aquila was right. One should not judge men. Fulke was merry. Yes, always merry—with a catch in his breath.'

'And what did you do afterwards?' said Una.

We talked together of times past. That is all men can do when they grow old, little maid.'

The bell for tea rang faintly across the meadows. Dan lay in the bows of the *Golden Hind*; Una in the stern, the book of verses open in her lap, was reading from 'The Slave's Dream':—

> '*Again, in the mist and shadow of sleep,*
> *He saw his native land.*'

'I don't know when you began that,' said Dan sleepily.

On the middle thwart of the boat, beside Una's sun-bonnet, lay an Oak leaf, an Ash leaf, and a Thorn leaf, that must have dropped down from the trees above; and the brook gig-gled as though it had just seen some joke.

THE RUNES ON WELAND'S SWORD

A Smith makes me
To betray my Man
In my first fight.

To gather Gold
At the world's end
I am sent.

The Gold I gather
Comes into England
Out of deep Water.

Like a shining Fish
Then it descends
Into deep Water.

It is not given
For goods or gear,
But for The Thing.

The Gold I gather
A King covets
For an ill use.

The Gold I gather
Is drawn up
Out of deep Water.

PUCK OF POOK'S HILL

Like a shining Fish
Then it descends
Into deep Water.

It is not given
For goods or gear,
But for The Thing.

A CENTURION OF THE THIRTIETH

Cities and Thrones and Powers
 Stand in Time's eye,
Almost as long as flowers,
 Which daily die:
But, as new buds put forth
 To glad new men,
Out of the spent and unconsidered Earth,
 The Cities rise again.

This season's Daffodil,
 She never hears
What change, what chance, what chill,
 Cut down last year's:
But with bold countenance,
 And knowledge small,
Esteems her seven days' continuance
 To be perpetual.

So Time that is o'er-kind
 To all that be,
Ordains us e'en as blind,
 As bold as she:
That in our very death,
 And burial sure,
Shadow to shadow, well persuaded, saith,
 'See how our works endure!'

A CENTURION OF THE THIRTIETH

DAN HAD COME TO GRIEF over his Latin, and was kept in; so
Una went alone to Far Wood. Dan's big catapult and the
lead bullets that Hobden had made for him were hidden in
an old hollow beech-stub on the west of the wood. They had
named the place out of the verse in *Lays of Ancient Rome*:—

> *From lordly Volaterrae,*
> *Where scowls the far-famed hold*
> *Piled by the hands of giants*
> *For Godlike Kings of old.*

They were the 'Godlike Kings,' and when old Hobden
piled some comfortable brushwood between the big, wooden
knees of Volaterrae, they called him 'Hands of Giants.'

Una slipped through their private gap in the fence, and sat
still awhile, scowling as scowlily and lordlily as she knew
how; for Volaterrae is an important watch-tower that juts out
of Far Wood just as Far Wood juts out of the hillside. Pook's
Hill lay below her and all the turns of the brook as it wan-
ders out of the Willingford Woods, between hop-gardens, to
old Hobden's cottage at the Forge. The sou'-west wind (there
is always a wind by Volaterrae) blew from the bare ridge where
Cherry Clack Windmill stands.

Now wind prowling through woods sounds like exciting
things going to happen, and that is why on blowy days you
stand up in Volaterrae and shout bits of the *Lays* to suit its
noises.

Una took Dan's catapult from its secret place, and made ready to meet Lars Porsena's army stealing through the wind-whitened aspens by the brook. A gust boomed up the valley, and Una chanted sorrowfully:—

> 'Verbenna down to Ostia
> Hath wasted all the plain;
> Astur hath stormed Janiculum,
> And the stout guards are slain.'

But the wind, not charging fair to the wood, started aside and shook a single oak in Gleason's pasture. Here it made itself all small and crouched among the grasses, waving the tips of them as a cat waves the tip of her tail before she springs.

'Now welcome—welcome, Sextus,' sang Una, loading the catapult—

> 'Now welcome to thy home!
> Why dost thou stay, and turn away?
> Here lies the road to Rome.'

She fired into the face of the lull, to wake up the cowardly wind, and heard a grunt from behind a thorn in the pasture.

'Oh, my Winkie!' she said aloud, and that was something she had picked up from Dan. 'I b'lieve I've tickled up a Gleason cow.'

'You little painted beast!' a voice cried. 'I'll teach you to sling your masters!'

She looked down most cautiously, and saw a young man covered with hoopy bronze armour all glowing among the late broom. But what Una admired beyond all was his great

bronze helmet with a red horse-tail that flicked in the wind.
She could hear the long hairs rasp on his shimmery shoulder-
plates.

'What does the Faun mean,' he said, half aloud to himself,
'by telling me that the Painted People have changed?' He
caught sight of Una's yellow head. 'Have you seen a painted
lead-slinger?' he called.

'No-o,' said Una. 'But if you've seen a bullet——'

'Seen?' cried the man. 'It passed within a hair's-breadth of
my ear.'

'Well, that was me. I'm most awfully sorry.'

'Didn't the Faun tell you I was coming?' He smiled.

'Not if you mean Puck. I thought you were a Gleason cow.
I—I didn't know you were a—a—— What are you?'

He laughed outright, showing a set of splendid teeth. His
face and eyes were dark, and his eyebrows met above his big
nose in one bushy black bar.

'They call me Parnesius. I have been a Centurion of the
Seventh Cohort of the Thirtieth Legion—the Ulpia Victrix.
Did you sling that bullet?'

'I did. I was using Dan's catapult,' said Una.

'Catapults!' said he. 'I ought to know something about
them. Show me!'

He leaped the rough fence with a rattle of spear, shield, and
armour, and hoisted himself into Volaterrae as quickly as a
shadow.

'A sling on a forked stick. *I* understand!' he cried, and
pulled at the elastic. 'But what wonderful beast yields this
stretching leather?'

'It's laccy—elastic. You put the bullet into that loop, and
then you pull hard.'

The man pulled, and hit himself square on his thumb-nail.

'Each to his own weapon,' he said gravely, handing it back. 'I am better with the bigger machine, little maiden. But it's a pretty toy. A wolf would laugh at it. Aren't you afraid of wolves?'

'There aren't any,' said Una.

'Never believe it! A wolf's like a Winged Hat. He comes when he isn't expected. Don't they hunt wolves here?'

'We don't hunt,' said Una, remembering what she had heard from grown-ups. 'We preserve—pheasants. Do you know them?'

'I ought to,' said the young man, smiling again, and he imitated the cry of the cock-pheasant so perfectly that a bird answered out of the wood.

'What a big painted clucking fool is a pheasant!' he said. 'Just like some Romans!'

'But you're a Roman yourself, aren't you?' said Una.

'Ye-es and no. I'm one of a good few thousands who have never seen Rome except in a picture. My people have lived at Vectis for generations. Vectis—that island West yonder that you can see from so far in clear weather.'

'Do you mean the Isle of Wight? It lifts up just before rain, and you see it from the Downs.'

'Very likely. Our villa's on the south edge of the Island, by the Broken Cliffs. Most of it is three hundred years old, but the cow-stables, where our first ancestor lived, must be a hundred years older. Oh, quite that, because the founder of our family had his land given him by Agricola at the Settlement. It's not a bad little place for its size. In springtime violets grow down to the very beach. I've gathered seaweeds for myself and violets for my Mother many a time with our old nurse.'

'Was your nurse a—a Romaness too?'

'No, a Numidian. Gods be good to her! A dear, fat, brown thing with a tongue like a cow-bell. She was a free woman. By the way, are you free, maiden?'

'Oh, quite,' said Una. 'At least, till tea-time; and in summer our governess doesn't say much if we're late.'

The young man laughed again—a proper understanding laugh.

'I see,' said he. 'That accounts for your being in the wood. *We* hid among the cliffs.'

'Did *you* have a governess, then?'

'Did we not? A Greek, too. She had a way of clutching her dress when she hunted us among the gorse-bushes that made us laugh. Then she'd say she'd get us whipped. She never did, though, bless her! Aglaia was a thorough sportswoman, for all her learning.'

'But what lessons did you do—when—when you were little?'

'Ancient history, the Classics, arithmetic, and so on,' he answered. 'My sister and I were thickheads, but my two brothers (I'm the middle one) like those things, and, of course, Mother was clever enough for any six. She was nearly as tall as I am, and she looked like the new statue on the Western Road—the Demeter of the Baskets, you know. And funny! Roma Dea! How Mother could make us laugh!'

'What at?'

'Little jokes and sayings that every family has. Don't you know?'

'I know *we* have, but I didn't know other people had them too,' said Una. 'Tell me about all your family, please.'

'Good families are very much alike. Mother would sit spinning of evenings while Aglaia read in her corner, and Father did accounts, and we four romped about the passages. When

our noise grew too loud the Pater would say, "Less tumult!
Less tumult! Have you never heard of a Father's right over
his children? He can slay them, my loves—slay them dead,
and the Gods highly approve of the action!" Then Mother
would prim up her dear mouth over the wheel and answer:
"H'm! I'm afraid there can't be much of the Roman Father
about you!" Then the Pater would roll up his accounts, and
say, "I'll show you!" and then—then, he'd be worse than
any of us!'

'Fathers can—if they like,' said Una, her eyes dancing.

'Didn't I say all good families are very much the same?'

'What did you do in summer?' said Una. 'Play about, like
us?'

'Yes, and we visited our friends. There are no wolves in
Vectis. We had many friends, and as many ponies as we
wished.'

'It must have been lovely,' said Una. 'I hope it lasted for
ever.'

'Not quite, little maid. When I was about sixteen or seventeen, the Father felt gouty, and we all went to the Waters.'

'What waters?'

'At Aquae Sulis. Every one goes there. You ought to get
your Father to take you some day.'

'But where? I don't know,' said Una.

The young man looked astonished for a moment. 'Aquae
Sulis,' he repeated. 'The best baths in Britain. Just as good,
I'm told, as Rome. All the old gluttons sit in hot water, and
talk scandal and politics. And the Generals come through the
streets with their guards behind them; and the magistrates
come in their chairs with their stiff guards behind them; and
you meet fortune-tellers, and goldsmiths, and merchants, and
philosophers, and feather-sellers, and ultra-Roman Britons,
and ultra-British Romans, and tame tribesmen pretending to

be civilised, and Jew lecturers, and—oh, everybody interesting. We young people, of course, took no interest in politics. We had not the gout. There were many of our age like us. We did not find life sad.

'But while we were enjoying ourselves without thinking, my sister met the son of a magistrate in the West—and a year afterwards she was married to him. My young brother, who was always interested in plants and roots, met the First Doctor of a Legion from the City of the Legions, and he decided that he would be an Army doctor. I do not think it is a profession for a well-born man, but then—I'm not my brother. He went to Rome to study medicine, and now he's First Doctor of a Legion in Egypt—at Antinoë, I think, but I have not heard from him for some time.

'My eldest brother came across a Greek philosopher, and told my Father that he intended to settle down on the estate as a farmer and a philosopher. You see,'—the young man's eyes twinkled—'his philosopher was a long-haired one!'

'I thought philosophers were bald,' said Una.

'Not all. She was very pretty. I don't blame him. Nothing could have suited me better than my eldest brother's doing this, for I was only too keen to join the Army. I had always feared I should have to stay at home and look after the estate while my brother took *this*.'

He rapped on his great glistening shield that never seemed to be in his way.

'So we were well contented—we young people—and we rode back to Clausentum along the Wood Road very quietly. But when we reached home, Aglaia, our governess, saw what had come to us. I remember her at the door, the torch over her head, watching us climb the cliff-path from the boat. "Aie! Aie!" she said. "Children you went away. Men and a woman you return!" Then she kissed Mother, and Mother wept. Thus our visit to the Waters settled our fates for each of us, maiden.'

He rose to his feet and listened, leaning on the shield-rim.

'I think that's Dan—my brother,' said Una.

'Yes; and the Faun is with him,' he replied, as Dan with Puck stumbled through the copse.

'We should have come sooner,' Puck called, 'but the beauties of your native tongue, O Parnesius, have enthralled this young citizen.'

Parnesius looked bewildered, even when Una explained.

'Dan said the plural of "dominus" was "dominoes," and when Miss Blake said it wasn't he said he supposed it was "backgammon," and so he had to write it out twice—for cheek, you know.'

Dan had climbed into Volaterrae, hot and panting.

'I've run nearly all the way,' he gasped, 'and then Puck met me. How do you do, sir?'

'I am in good health,' Parnesius answered. 'See! I have tried to bend the bow of Ulysses, but——' He held up his thumb.

'I'm sorry. You must have pulled off too soon,' said Dan. 'But Puck said you were telling Una a story.'

'Continue, O Parnesius,' said Puck, who had perched himself on a dead branch above them. 'I will be chorus. Has he puzzled you much, Una?'

'Not a bit, except—I didn't know where Ak—Ak something was,' she answered.

'Oh, Aquae Sulis. That's Bath, where the buns come from. Let the hero tell his own tale.'

Parnesius pretended to thrust his spear at Puck's legs, but Puck reached down, caught at the horse-tail plume, and pulled off the tall helmet.

'Thanks, jester,' said Parnesius, shaking his curly dark head. 'That is cooler. Now hang it up for me. . . .

'I was telling your sister how I joined the Army,' he said to Dan.

'Did you have to pass an Exam?' Dan asked eagerly.

'No. I went to my Father, and said I should like to enter the Dacian Horse (I had seen some at Aquae Sulis); but he said I had better begin service in a regular Legion from Rome. Now, like many of our youngsters, I was not too fond of anything Roman. The Roman-born officers and magistrates looked down on us British-born as though we were barbarians. I told my Father so.

' "I know they do," he said; "but remember, after all, we are the people of the Old Stock, and our duty is to the Empire."

' "To which Empire?" I asked. "We split the Eagle before I was born."

' "What thieves' talk is that?" said my Father. He hated slang.

' "Well, sir," I said, "we've one Emperor in Rome, and I don't know how many Emperors the outlying Provinces have set up from time to time. Which am I to follow?"

' "Gratian," said he. "At least he's a sportsman."

' "He's all that," I said. "Hasn't he turned himself into a raw-beef-eating Scythian?"

' "Where did you hear of it?" said the Pater.

' "At Aquae Sulis," I said. It was perfectly true. This precious Emperor Gratian of ours had a bodyguard of fur-cloaked Scythians, and he was so crazy about them that he dressed like them. In Rome of all places in the world! It was as bad as if my own Father had painted himself blue!

' "No matter for the clothes," said the Pater. "They are

only the fringe of the trouble. It began before your time or mine. Rome has forsaken her Gods, and must be punished. The great war with the Painted People broke out in the very year the temples of our Gods were destroyed. We beat the Painted People in the very year our temples were rebuilt. Go back further still." . . . He went back to the time of Diocletian; and to listen to him you would have thought Eternal Rome herself was on the edge of destruction, just because a few people had become a little large-minded.

'*I* knew nothing about it. Aglaia never taught us the history of our own country. She was so full of her ancient Greeks.

' "There is no hope for Rome," said the Pater, at last. "She has forsaken her Gods, but if the Gods forgive *us* here, we may save Britain. To do that, we must keep the Painted People back. Therefore, I tell you, Parnesius, as a Father, that if your heart is set on service, your place is among men on the Wall—and not with women among the cities." '

'What Wall?' asked Dan and Una at once.

'Father meant the one we call Hadrian's Wall. I'll tell you about it later. It was built long ago, across North Britain, to keep out the Painted People—Picts, you call them. Father had fought in the great Pict War that lasted more than twenty years, and he knew what fighting meant. Theodosius, one of our great Generals, had chased the little beasts back far into the North before I was born. Down at Vectis, of course, we never troubled our heads about them. But when my Father spoke as he did, I kissed his hand, and waited for orders. We British-born Romans know what is due to our parents.'

'If I kissed my Father's hand, he'd laugh,' said Dan.

'Customs change; but if you do not obey your Father, the Gods remember it. You may be quite sure of *that*.

'After our talk, seeing I was in earnest, the Pater sent me

over to Clausentum to learn my foot-drill in a barrack full of foreign Auxiliaries—as unwashed and unshaved a mob of mixed barbarians as ever scrubbed a breastplate. It was your stick in their stomachs and your shield in their faces to push them into any sort of formation. When I had learned my work the Instructor gave me a handful—and they were a handful!—of Gauls and Iberians to polish up till they were sent to their stations up-country. I did my best, and one night a villa in the suburbs caught fire, and I had my handful out and at work before any of the other troops. I noticed a quiet-looking man on the lawn, leaning on a stick. He watched us passing buckets from the pond, and at last he said to me: "Who are you?"

' "A probationer, waiting for a command," I answered. *I* didn't know who he was from Deucalion!

' "Born in Britain?" he said.

' "Yes, if you were born in Spain," I said, for he neighed his words like an Iberian mule.

' "And what might you call yourself when you are at home?" he said, laughing.

' "That depends," I answered; "sometimes one thing and sometimes another. But now I'm busy."

'He said no more till we had saved the family Gods (they were respectable householders), and then he grunted across the laurels: "Listen, young sometimes-one-thing-and-some-times-another. In future call yourself Centurion of the Seventh Cohort of the Thirtieth, the Ulpia Victrix. That will help me to remember you. Your Father and a few other people call me Maximus."

'He tossed me the polished stick he was leaning on, and went away. You might have knocked me down with it!'

'Who was he?' said Dan.

'Maximus himself, our great General! *The* General of Britain who had been Theodosius's right hand in the Pict War! Not only had he given me my Centurion's stick direct, but three steps in a good Legion as well! A new man generally begins in the Tenth Cohort of his Legion, and works up.'

'And were you pleased?' said Una.

'Very. I thought Maximus had chosen me for my good looks and fine style in marching, but, when I went home, the Pater told me he had served under Maximus in the great Pict War, and had asked him to befriend me.'

'A child you were!' said Puck, from above.

'I was,' said Parnesius. 'Don't begrudge it me, Faun. Afterwards—the Gods know I put aside the games!' And Puck nodded, brown chin on brown hand, his big eyes still.

'The night before I left we sacrificed to our ancestors—the usual little Home Sacrifice—but I never prayed so earnestly to all the Good Shades, and then I went with my Father by boat to Regnum, and across the chalk eastwards to Anderida yonder.'

'Regnum? Anderida?' The children turned their faces to Puck.

'Regnum's Chichester,' he said, pointing towards Cherry Clack, and—he threw his arm South behind him—'Anderida's Pevensey.'

'Pevensey again!' said Dan. 'Where Weland landed?'

'Weland and a few others,' said Puck. 'Pevensey isn't young—even compared to me!'

'The headquarters of the Thirtieth lay at Anderida in summer, but my own Cohort, the Seventh, was on the Wall up North. Maximus was inspecting Auxiliaries—the Abulci, I think—at Anderida, and we stayed with him, for he and my

Father were very old friends. I was only there ten days when I was ordered to go up with thirty men to my Cohort.' He laughed merrily. 'A man never forgets his first march. I was happier than any Emperor when I led my handful through the North Gate of the Camp, and we saluted the guard and the Altar of Victory there.'

'How? How?' said Dan and Una.

Parnesius smiled, and stood up, flashing in his armour.

'So!' said he; and he moved slowly through the beautiful movements of the Roman Salute, that ends with a hollow clang of the shield coming into its place between the shoulders.

'Hail' said Puck. 'That sets one thinking!'

'We went out fully armed,' said Parnesius, sitting down; 'but as soon as the road entered the Great Forest, my men expected the pack-horses to hang their shields on. "No!" I said; "you can dress like women in Anderida, but while you're with me you will carry your own weapons and armour."

' "But it's hot," said one of them, "and we haven't a doctor. Suppose we get sunstroke, or a fever?"

' "Then die," I said, "and a good riddance to Rome! Up shield—up spears, and tighten your footwear!"

' "Don't think yourself Emperor of Britain already," a fellow shouted. I knocked him over with the butt of my spear, and explained to these Roman-born Romans that, if there were any further trouble, we should go on with one man short. And, by the Light of the Sun, I meant it too! My raw Gauls at Clausentum had never treated me so.

'Then, quietly as a cloud, Maximus rode out of the fern (my Father behind him), and reined up across the road. He wore the Purple, as though he were already Emperor; his leggings were of white buckskin laced with gold.

'My men dropped like—like partridges.

'He said nothing for some time, only looked, with his eyes puckered. Then he crooked his forefinger, and my men walked —crawled, I mean—to one side.

' "Stand in the sun, children," he said, and they formed up on the hard road.

' "What would you have done," he said to me, "if I had not been here?"

' "I should have killed that man," I answered.

' "Kill him now," he said. "He will not move a limb."

' "No," I said. "You've taken my men out of my command. I should only be your butcher if I killed him now." Do you see what I meant?' Parnesius turned to Dan.

'Yes,' said Dan. 'It wouldn't have been fair, somehow.'

'That was what I thought,' said Parnesius. 'But Maximus frowned. "You'll never be an Emperor," he said. "Not even a General will you be."

'I was silent, but my Father seemed pleased.

' "I came here to see the last of you," he said.

' "You have seen it," said Maximus. "I shall never need your son any more. He will live and he will die an officer of a Legion—and he might have been Prefect of one of my Provinces. Now eat and drink with us," he said. "Your men will wait till you have finished."

'My miserable thirty stood like wine-skins glistening in the hot sun, and Maximus led us to where his people had set a meal. Himself he mixed the wine.

' "A year from now," he said, "you will remember that you have sat with the Emperor of Britain—and Gaul."

' "Yes," said the Pater, "you can drive two mules—Gaul and Britain."

' "Five years hence you will remember that you have drunk" —he passed me the cup and there was blue borage in it— "with the Emperor of Rome!"

' "No; you can't drive three mules. They will tear you in pieces," said my Father.

' "And you on the Wall, among the heather, will weep because your notion of justice was more to you than the favour of the Emperor of Rome."

'I sat quite still. One does not answer a General who wears the Purple.

' "I am not angry with you," he went on; "I owe too much to your Father——"

' "You owe me nothing but advice that you never took," said the Pater.

' "——to be unjust to any of your family. Indeed, I say you may make a good Tribune, but, so far as I am concerned, on the Wall you will live, and on the Wall you will die," said Maximus.

' "Very like," said my Father. "But we shall have the Picts *and* their friends breaking through before long. You cannot move all troops out of Britain to make you Emperor, and expect the North to sit quiet."

' "I follow my destiny," said Maximus.

' "Follow it, then," said my Father, pulling up a fern root; "and die as Theodosius died."

' "Ah!" said Maximus. "My old General was killed because he served the Empire too well. *I* may be killed, but not for that reason," and he smiled a little pale grey smile that made my blood run cold.

' "Then I had better follow my destiny," I said, "and take my men to the Wall."

'He looked at me a long time, and bowed his head slanting like a Spaniard. "Follow it, boy," he said. That was all. I was only too glad to get away, though I had many messages for home. I found my men standing as they had been put—they had not even shifted their feet in the dust, and off I marched, still feeling that terrific smile like an east wind up my back. I never halted them till sunset, and'—he turned about and looked at Pook's Hill below him—'then I halted yonder.' He pointed to the broken, bracken-covered shoulder of the Forge Hill behind old Hobden's cottage.

'There? Why, that's only the old Forge—where they made iron once,' said Dan.

'Very good stuff it was too,' said Parnesius calmly. 'We mended three shoulder-straps here and had a spear-head riveted. The Forge was rented from the Government by a one-eyed smith from Carthage. I remember we called him Cyclops. He sold me a beaver-skin rug for my sister's room.'

'But it couldn't have been here,' Dan insisted.

'But it was! From the Altar of Victory at Anderida to the First Forge in the Forest here is twelve miles seven hundred paces. It is all in the Road Book. A man doesn't forget his first march. I think I could tell you every station between this and——' He leaned forward, but his eye was caught by the setting sun.

It had come down to the top of Cherry Clack Hill, and the light poured in between the tree-trunks so that you could see red and gold and black deep into the heart of Far Wood; and Parnesius in his armour shone as though he had been afire.

'Wait!' he said, lifting a hand, and the sunlight jinked on his glass bracelet. 'Wait! I pray to Mithras!'

He rose and stretched his arms westward, with deep, splendid-sounding words.

Then Puck began to sing too, in a voice like bells tolling, and as he sang he slipped from Volaterrae to the ground, and beckoned the children to follow. They obeyed; it seemed as though the voices were pushing them along; and through the

goldy-brown light on the beech leaves they walked, while
Puck between them chanted something like this:—

> 'Cur mundus militat sub vana gloria
> Cujus prosperitas est transitoria?
> Tam cito labitur ejus potentia
> Quam vasa figuli quae sunt fragilia.'

They found themselves at the little locked gates of the
wood.

> 'Quo Caesar abiit celsus imperio?
> Vel Dives splendidus totus in prandio?
> Dic ubi Tullius——'

Still singing, he took Dan's hand and wheeled him round
to face Una as she came out of the gate. It shut behind her,
at the same time as Puck threw the memory-magicking Oak,
Ash, and Thorn leaves over their heads.

'Well, you *are* jolly late,' said Una. 'Couldn't you get away
before?'

'I did,' said Dan. 'I got away in lots of time, but—but I
didn't know it was so late. Where've you been?'

'In Volaterrae—waiting for you.'

'Sorry,' said Dan. 'It was all that beastly Latin.'

A BRITISH-ROMAN SONG

(A.D. 406)

My father's father saw it not,
*   And I, belike, shall never come*
To look on that so-holy spot—
*   The very Rome—*

Crowned by all Time, all Art, all Might,
*   The equal work of Gods and Man,*
City beneath whose oldest height—
*   The Race began!*

Soon to send forth again a brood,
*   Unshakeable, we pray, that clings*
To Rome's thrice-hammered hardihood—
*   In arduous things.*

Strong heart with triple armour bound,
*   Beat strongly, for Thy life-blood runs,*
Age after Age, the Empire round—
*   In us Thy Sons,*

Who, distant from the Seven Hills,
*   Loving and serving much, require*
Thee—Thee to guard 'gainst home-born ills
*   The Imperial Fire!*

ON THE GREAT WALL

ON THE GREAT WALL

'When I left Rome for Lalage's sake
* By the Legions' Road to Rimini,*
She vowed her heart was mine to take
* With me and my shield to Rimini—*
*   (Till the Eagles flew from Rimini!)*
*   And I've tramped Britain, and I've tramped Gaul,*
*   And the Pontic shore where the snow-flakes fall*
*   As white as the neck of Lalage—*
*   (As cold as the heart of Lalage!)*
*   And I've lost Britain, and I've lost Gaul,'*

(the voice seemed very cheerful about it),

*   'And I've lost Rome, and, worst of all,*
*   I've lost Lalage!'*

They were standing by the gate to Far Wood when they heard this song. Without a word they hurried to their private gap and wriggled through the hedge almost atop of a jay that was feeding from Puck's hand.

'Gently!' said Puck. 'What are you looking for?'

'Parnesius, of course,' Dan answered. 'We've only just remembered yesterday. It isn't fair.'

Puck chuckled as he rose. 'I'm sorry, but children who spend the afternoon with me and a Roman Centurion need a little settling dose of Magic before they go to tea with their governess. Ohé, Parnesius!' he called.

'Here, Faun!' came the answer from Volaterrae. They could see the shimmer of bronze armour in the beech-crotch, and the friendly flash of the great shield uplifted.

'I have driven out the Britons.' Parnesius laughed like a boy. 'I occupy their high forts. But Rome is merciful! You may come up.' And up they three all scrambled.

'What was the song you were singing just now?' said Una, as soon as she had settled herself.

'That? Oh, *Rimini*. It's one of the tunes that are always being born somewhere in the Empire. They run like a pestilence for six months or a year, till another one pleases the Legions, and then they march to *that*.'

'Tell them about the marching, Parnesius. Few people nowadays walk from end to end of this country,' said Puck.

'The greater their loss. I know nothing better than the Long March when your feet are hardened. You begin after the mists have risen, and you end, perhaps, an hour after sundown.'

'And what do you have to eat?' Dan asked promptly.

'Fat bacon, beans, and bread, and whatever wine happens to be in the rest-houses. But soldiers are born grumblers. Their very first day out, my men complained of our waterground British corn. They said it wasn't so filling as the rough stuff that is ground in the Roman ox-mills. However, they had to fetch and eat it.'

'Fetch it? Where from?' said Una.

'From that newly-invented water-mill below the Forge.'

'That's Forge Mill—*our* Mill!' Una looked at Puck.

'Yes; yours,' Puck put in. 'How old did you think it was?'

'I don't know. Didn't Sir Richard Dalyngridge talk about it?'

'He did, and it was old in his day,' Puck answered. 'Hundreds of years old.'

'It was new in mine,' said Parnesius. 'My men looked at the flour in their helmets as though it had been a nest of adders. They did it to try my patience. But I—addressed them, and we became friends. To tell the truth, they taught me the Roman Step. You see, I'd only served with quick-marching Auxiliaries. A Legion's pace is altogether different. It is a long, slow stride, that never varies from sunrise to sunset. "Rome's Race—Rome's Pace," as the proverb says. Twenty-four miles in eight hours, neither more nor less. Head and spear up, shield on your back, cuirass-collar open one hand's-breadth—and that's how you take the Eagles through Britain.'

'And did you meet any adventures?' said Dan.

'There are no adventures South the Wall,' said Parnesius. 'The worst thing that happened me was having to appear before a magistrate up North, where a wandering philosopher had jeered at the Eagles. I was able to show that the old man had deliberately blocked our road; and the magistrate told him, out of his own Book, I believe, that, whatever his Gods might be, he should pay proper respect to Caesar.'

'What did you do?' said Dan.

'Went on. Why should *I* care for such things, my business being to reach my station? It took me twenty days.

'Of course, the farther North you go the emptier are the roads. At last you fetch clear of the forests and climb bare hills, where wolves howl in the ruins of our cities that have been. No more pretty girls; no more jolly magistrates who knew your Father when he was young, and invite you to stay with them; no news at the temples and way-stations except bad news of wild beasts. There's where you meet hunters, and trappers for the Circuses, prodding along chained bears and muzzled wolves. Your pony shies at them, and your men laugh.

'The houses change from gardened villas to shut forts with watch-towers of grey stone, and great stone-walled sheepfolds, guarded by armed Britons of the North Shore. In the naked hills beyond the naked houses, where the shadows of the clouds play like cavalry charging, you see puffs of black smoke from the mines. The hard road goes on and on—and the wind sings through your helmet-plume—past altars to Legions and Generals forgotten, and broken statues of Gods and Heroes, and thousands of graves where the mountain foxes and hares peep at you. Red-hot in summer, freezing in winter, is that big, purple heather country of broken stone.

'Just when you think you are at the world's end, you see a smoke from East to West as far as the eye can turn, and then, under it, also as far as the eye can stretch, houses and temples, shops and theatres, barracks and granaries, trickling along like dice behind—always behind—one long, low, rising and falling, and hiding and showing line of towers. And that is the Wall!'

'Ah!' said the children, taking breath.

'You may well,' said Parnesius. 'Old men who have followed the Eagles since boyhood say nothing in the Empire is more wonderful than first sight of the Wall!'

'Is it just *a* Wall? Like the one round the kitchen-garden?' said Dan.

'No, no! It is *the* Wall. Along the top are towers with guard-houses, small towers, between. Even on the narrowest part of it three men with shields can walk abreast, from guard-house to guard-house. A little curtain wall, no higher than a man's neck, runs along the top of the thick wall, so that from a distance you see the helmets of the sentries sliding back and forth like beads. Thirty feet high is the Wall, and on the Picts' side, the North, is a ditch, strewn with blades of old swords and spear-heads set in wood, and tyres of wheels joined by chains. The Little People come there to steal iron for their arrow-heads.

'But the Wall itself is not more wonderful than the town behind it. Long ago there were great ramparts and ditches on the South side, and no one was allowed to build there. Now the ramparts are partly pulled down and built over, from end to end of the Wall; making a thin town eighty miles long. Think of it! One roaring, rioting, cock-fighting, wolf-baiting, horse-racing town, from Ituna on the West to Sege-dunum on the cold eastern beach! On one side heather, woods and ruins where Picts hide, and on the other, a vast town—long like a snake, and wicked like a snake. Yes, a snake bask-ing beside a warm wall!

'My Cohort, I was told, lay at Hunno, where the Great North Road runs through the Wall into the Province of Valentia.' Parnesius laughed scornfully. 'The Province of Valentia! We followed the road, therefore, into Hunno town, and stood astonished. The place was a fair—a fair of peoples from every corner of the Empire. Some were racing horses: some sat in wine-shops: some watched dogs baiting bears, and many gathered in a ditch to see cocks fight. A boy not much older than myself, but I could see he was an officer, reined up before me and asked what I wanted.

' "My station," I said, and showed him my shield.' Parnesius held up his broad shield with its three X's like letters on a beer-cask.

' "Lucky omen!" said he. "Your Cohort's the next tower to us, but they're all at the cock-fight. This is a happy place. Come and wet the Eagles." He meant to offer me a drink.

' "When I've handed over my men," I said. I felt angry and ashamed.

' "Oh, you'll soon outgrow that sort of nonsense," he answered. "But don't let me interfere with your hopes. Go on to the Statue of Roma Dea. You can't miss it. The main road into Valentia!" and he laughed and rode off. I could see the statue not a quarter of a mile away, and there I went. At some time or other the Great North Road ran under it into Valentia; but the far end had been blocked up because of the Picts, and on the plaster a man had scratched, "Finish!" It was like marching into a cave. We grounded spears together, my little thirty, and it echoed in the barrel of the arch, but none came. There was a door at one side painted with our number. We prowled in, and I found a cook asleep, and ordered him to give us food. Then I climbed to the top of the Wall, and looked out over the Pict country, and I—thought,' said Parnesius. 'The bricked-up arch with "Finish!" on the plaster was what shook me, for I was not much more than a boy.'

'What a shame!' said Una. 'But did you feel happy after you'd had a good——' Dan stopped her with a nudge.

'Happy?' said Parnesius. 'When the men of the Cohort I was to command came back unhelmeted from the cock-fight, their birds under their arms, and asked me who I was? No, I was not happy; but I made my new Cohort unhappy too. . . . I wrote my Mother I was happy, but, oh, my friends'—he stretched arms over bare knees—'I would not wish my worst enemy to suffer as I suffered through my first months on the Wall. Remember this: among the officers was scarcely one, except myself (and I thought I had lost the favour of Maximus, my General), scarcely one who had not done something of wrong or folly. Either he had killed a man, or taken money, or insulted the magistrates, or blasphemed the Gods, and so had been sent to the Wall as a hiding-place from shame or fear. And the men were as the officers. Remember, also, that the Wall was manned by every breed and race in the Empire. No two towers spoke the same tongue, or worshipped the same Gods. In one thing only we were all equal. No matter what arms we had used before we came to the Wall, *on* the Wall we were all archers, like the Scythians. The Pict cannot run away from the arrow, or crawl under it. He is a bowman himself. *He* knows!'

'I suppose you were fighting Picts all the time,' said Dan.

'Picts seldom fight. I never saw a fighting Pict for half a year. The tame Picts told us they had all gone North.'

'What is a tame Pict?' said Dan.

'A Pict—there were many such—who speaks a few words of our tongue, and slips across the Wall to sell ponies and wolf-hounds. Without a horse and a dog, *and* a friend, man would perish. The Gods gave me all three, and there is no gift like friendship. Remember this'—Parnesius turned to Dan—'when you become a young man. For your fate will turn on the first true friend you make.'

'He means,' said Puck, grinning, 'that if you try to make yourself a decent chap when you're young, you'll make rather decent friends when you grow up. If you're a beast, you'll have beastly friends. Listen to the Pious Parnesius on Friendship!'

'I am not pious,' Parnesius answered, 'but I know what goodness means; and my friend, though he was without hope, was ten thousand times better than I. Stop laughing, Faun!'

'Oh, Youth Eternal and All-believing,' cried Puck, as he rocked on the branch above. 'Tell them about your Pertinax.'

'He was that friend the Gods sent me—the boy who spoke to me when I first came. Little older than myself, commanding the Augusta Victoria Cohort on the tower next to us and the Numidians. In virtue he was far my superior.'

'Then why was he on the Wall?' Una asked quickly. 'They'd all done something bad. You said so yourself.'

'He was the nephew, his father had died, of a great rich man in Gaul who was not always kind to his mother. When Pertinax grew up, he discovered this, and so his uncle shipped him off, by trickery and force, to the Wall. We came to know each other at a ceremony in our Temple—in the dark. It was the Bull-Killing,' Parnesius explained to Puck.

'*I* see,' said Puck, and turned to the children. 'That's something you wouldn't quite understand. Parnesius means he met Pertinax in church.'

'Yes—in the Cave we first met, and we were both raised to the Degree of Gryphons together.' Parnesius lifted his hand towards his neck for an instant. 'He had been on the Wall two years, and knew the Picts well. He taught me first how to take Heather.'

'What's that?' said Dan.

'Going out hunting in the Pict country with a tame Pict. You are quite safe so long as you are his guest, and wear a sprig of heather where it can be seen. If you went alone you would surely be killed, if you were not smothered first in the bogs. Only the Picts know their way about those black and hidden bogs. Old Allo, the one-eyed, withered little Pict from whom we bought our ponies, was our special friend. At first we went only to escape from the terrible town, and to talk together about our homes. Then he showed us how to hunt wolves and those great red deer with horns like Jewish candle-sticks. The Roman-born officers rather looked down on us for doing this, but we preferred the heather to their amusements. Believe me'—Parnesius turned again to Dan—'a boy is safe from all things that really harm when he is astride a pony or after a deer. Do you remember, O Faun,'—he turned to Puck

—'the little altar I built to the Sylvan Pan by the pine-forest beyond the brook?'

'Which? The stone one with the line from Xenophon?' said Puck, in quite a new voice.

'No! What do *I* know of Xenophon? That was Pertinax—after he had shot his first mountain-hare with an arrow—by chance! Mine I made of round pebbles in memory of my first bear. It took me one happy day to build.' Parnesius faced the children quickly.

'And that was how we lived on the Wall for two years—a little scuffling with the Picts, and a great deal of hunting with old Allo in the Pict country. He called us his children some-times, and we were fond of him and his barbarians, though we never let them paint us Pict-fashion. The marks endure till you die.'

'How's it done?' said Dan. 'Anything like tattooing?'

'They prick the skin till the blood runs, and rub in col-oured juices. Allo was painted blue, green, and red from his forehead to his ankles. He said it was part of his religion. He told us about his religion (Pertinax was always interested in such things), and as we came to know him well, he told us what was happening in Britain behind the Wall. Many things took place behind us in those days. And by the Light of the Sun,' said Parnesius earnestly, 'there was not much that those little people did not know! He told me when Maximus crossed over to Gaul, after he had made himself Emperor of Britain, and what troops and emigrants he had taken with him. We did not get the news on the Wall till fifteen days later. He told me what troops Maximus was taking out of Britain every month to help him to conquer Gaul; and I always found the numbers were as he said. Wonderful! And I tell another strange thing!'

He jointed his hands across his knees, and leaned his head on the curve of the shield behind him.

'Late in the summer, when the first frosts begin and the Picts kill their bees, we three rode out after wolf with some new hounds. Rutilianus, our General, had given us ten days' leave, and we had pushed beyond the Second Wall—beyond the Province of Valentia—into the higher hills, where there are not even any of old Rome's ruins. We killed a she-wolf before noon, and while Allo was skinning her he looked up and said to me, 'When you are Captain of the Wall, my child, you won't be able to do this any more!"

'I might as well have been made Prefect of Lower Gaul, so I laughed and said, "Wait till I am Captain." "No, don't wait," said Allo. "Take my advice and go home—both of you." "We have no homes," said Pertinax. "You know that as well as we do. We're finished men—thumbs down against both of us. Only men without hope would risk their necks on your ponies." The old man laughed one of those short Pict laughs—like a fox barking on a frosty night. "I'm fond of you two," he said. "Besides, I've taught you what little you know about hunting. Take my advice and go home."

' "We can't," I said. "I'm out of favour with my General, for one thing; and for another, Pertinax has an uncle."

' "I don't know about his uncle," said Allo, "but the trouble with you, Parnesius, is that your General thinks well of you."

' "Roma Dea!" said Pertinax, sitting up. 'What can you guess what Maximus thinks, you old horse-coper?"

'Just then (you know how near the brutes creep when one is eating?) a great dog-wolf jumped out behind us, and away our rested hounds tore after him, with us at their tails. He ran us far out of any country we'd ever heard of, straight as an arrow till sunset, towards the sunset. We came at last to long capes stretching into winding waters, and on a grey

beach below us we saw ships drawn up. Forty-seven we counted
—not Roman galleys but the raven-winged ships from the
North where Rome does not rule. Men moved in the ships,
and the sun flashed on their helmets—winged helmets of the
red-haired men from the North where Rome does not rule.
We watched, and we counted, and we wondered, for though
we had heard rumours concerning these Winged Hats, as the
Picts called them, never before had we looked upon them.

' "Come away! come away!" said Allo. "My Heather won't
protect you here. We shall all be killed!" His legs trembled
like his voice. Back we went—back across the heather under
the moon, till it was nearly morning, and our poor beasts
stumbled on some ruins.

'When we woke, very stiff and cold, Allo was mixing the
meal and water. One does not light fires in the Pict country
except near a village. The little men are always signalling to
each other with smokes, and a strange smoke brings them out
buzzing like bees. They can sting, too!

' "What we saw last night was a trading-station," said Allo.
"Nothing but a trading-station."

' "I do not like lies on an empty stomach," said Pertinax.
"I suppose" (he had eyes like an eagle's)—"I suppose *that*
is a trading-station also?" He pointed to a smoke far off on
a hill-top, ascending in what we call the Picts' Call:—Puff—
double-puff: double-puff—puff! They make it by raising and
dropping a wet hide on a fire.

' "No" said Allo, pushing the platter back into the bag.
"That is for you and me. Your fate is fixed. Come."

'We came. When one takes Heather, one must obey one's
Pict—but that wretched smoke was twenty miles distant, well
over on the East coast, and the day was as hot as a bath.

' "Whatever happens," said Allo, while our ponies grunted
along, "I want you to remember me."

' "I shall not forget," said Pertinax. "You have cheated me out of my breakfast."

' "What is a handful of crushed oats to a Roman?" he said. Then he laughed his laugh that was not a laugh. "What would *you* do if *you* were a handful of oats being crushed between the upper and lower stones of a mill?"

' "I'm Pertinax, not a riddle-guesser," said Pertinax.

' "You're a fool," said Allo. "Your Gods and my Gods are threatened by strange Gods, and all you can do is to laugh."

' "Threatened men live long," I said.

' "I pray the Gods that may be true," he said. "But I ask you again not to forget me."

'We climbed the last hot hill and looked out on the eastern sea, three or four miles off. There was a small sailing-galley of the North Gaul pattern at anchor; her landing-plank down and her sail half up; and below us, alone in a hollow, holding his pony, sat Maximus, Emperor of Britain! He was dressed like a hunter, and he leaned on his little stick; but I knew that back as far as I could see it, and I told Pertinax.

' "You're madder than Allo!" he said. "It must be the sun!"

'Maximus never stirred till we stood before him. Then he looked me up and down, and said: "Hungry again? It seems to be my destiny to feed you whenever we meet. I have food here. Allo shall cook it."

' "No," said Allo. "A Prince in his own land does not wait on wandering Emperors. I feed my two children without asking your leave." He began to blow up the ashes.

' "I was wrong," said Pertinax. "We are all mad. Speak up, O Madman called Emperor!"

'Maximus smiled his terrible tight-lipped smile, but two years on the Wall do not make a man afraid of mere looks. So I was not afraid.

' "I meant you, Parnesius, to live and die a Centurion of

the Wall," said Maximus. "But it seems from these"—he fumbled in his breast—"you can think as well as draw." He pulled out a roll of letters I had written to my people, full of drawings of Picts, and bears, and men I had met on the Wall. Mother and my sister always liked my pictures.

'He handed me one that I had called "Maximus's Soldiers." It showed a row of fat wine-skins, and our old Doctor of the Hunno hospital snuffing at them. Each time that Maximus had taken troops out of Britain to help him to conquer Gaul, he used to send the garrisons more wine—to keep them quiet, I suppose. On the Wall, we always called a wine-skin a "Maximus." Oh, yes; and I had drawn them in Imperial helmets.

' "Not long since," he went on, "men's names were sent up to Caesar for smaller jokes than this."

' "True, Caesar," said Pertinax; "but you forget that was before I, your friend's friend, became such a good spear-thrower."

'He did not actually point his hunting-spear at Maximus, but balanced it on his palm—so!

' "I was speaking of time past," said Maximus, never fluttering an eyelid. "Nowadays one is only too pleased to find boys who can think for themselves, *and* their friends." He nodded at Pertinax. "Your Father lent me the letters, Parnesius, so you run no risk from me."

' "None whatever," said Pertinax, and rubbed the spear-point on his sleeve.

' "I have been forced to reduce the garrisons in Britain, because I need troops in Gaul. Now I come to take troops from the Wall itself," said he.

' "I wish you joy of us," said Pertinax. "We're the last sweepings of the Empire—the men without hope. Myself, I'd sooner trust condemned criminals."

' "You think so?" he said, quite seriously. "But it will only

141

be till I win Gaul. One must always risk one's life, or one's soul, or one's peace—or some little thing."

'Allo passed round the fire with the sizzling deer's meat. He served us two first.

' "Ah!" said Maximus, waiting his turn. "I perceive you are in your own country. Well, you deserve it. They tell me you have quite a following among the Picts, Parnesius."

' "I have hunted with them," I said. "Maybe I have a few friends among the heather."

' "He is the only armoured man of you all who understands us," said Allo, and he began a long speech about our virtues, and how we had saved one of his grandchildren from a wolf the year before.'

'Had you?' said Una.

'Yes; but that was neither here nor there. The little green man orated like a—like Cicero. He made us out to be magnificent fellows. Maximus never took his eyes off our faces.

' "Enough," he said. "I have heard Allo on you. I wish to hear you on the Picts."

'I told him as much as I knew, and Pertinax helped me out. There is never harm in a Pict if you but take the trouble to find out what he wants. Their real grievance against us came from our burning their heather. The whole garrison of the Wall moved out twice a year, and solemnly burned the heather for ten miles North. Rutilianus, our General, called it clearing the country. The Picts, of course, scampered away, and all we did was to destroy their bee-bloom in the summer, and ruin their sheep-food in the spring.

' "True, quite true," said Allo. "How can we make our holy heather-wine, if you burn our bee-pasture?"

'We talked long, Maximus asking keen questions that

showed he knew much and had thought more about the Picts. He said presently to me: "If I gave you the old Province of Valentia to govern, could you keep the Picts contented till I won Gaul? Stand away, so that you do not see Allo's face; and speak your own thoughts."

' "No," I said. "You cannot remake that Province. The Picts have been free too long."

' "Leave them their village councils, and let them furnish their own soldiers," he said. "You, I am sure, would hold the reins very lightly."

' "Even then, no," I said. "At least not now. They have been too oppressed by us to trust anything with a Roman name for years and years."

'I heard old Allo behind me mutter: "Good child!"

' "Then what do you recommend," said Maximus, "to keep the North quiet till I win Gaul?"

' "Leave the Picts alone," I said. "Stop the heather-burning at once, and—they are improvident little animals—send them a shipload or two of corn now and then."

' "Their own men must distribute it—not some cheating Greek accountant," said Pertinax.

' "Yes, and allow them to come to our hospitals when they are sick," I said.

' "Surely they would die first," said Maximus.

' "Not if Parnesius brought them in," said Allo. "I could show you twenty wolf-bitten, bear-clawed Picts within twenty miles of here. But Parnesius must stay with them in hospital, else they would go mad with fear."

' "*I* see," said Maximus. "Like everything else in the world, it is one man's work. You, I think, are that one man."

' "Pertinax and I are one," I said.

' "As you please, so long as you work. Now, Allo, you know

that I mean your people no harm. Leave us to talk together,"
said Maximus.

' "No need!" said Allo. "I am the corn between the upper
and lower millstones. I must know what the lower millstone
means to do. These boys have spoken the truth as far as they
know it. I, a Prince, will tell you the rest. I am troubled about
the Men of the North." He squatted like a hare in the
heather, and looked over his shoulder.

' "I also," said Maximus, "or I should not be here."

' "Listen," said Allo. "Long and long ago the Winged
Hats"—he meant the Northmen—"came to our beaches and
said, 'Rome falls! Push her down!' We fought you. You sent
men. We were beaten. After that we said to the Winged Hats,
'You are liars! Make our men alive that Rome killed, and we
will believe you.' They went away ashamed. Now they come
back bold, and they tell the old tale, which we begin to believe—that Rome falls!"

' "Give me three years' peace on the Wall," cried Maximus,
"and I will show you and all the ravens how they lie!"

' "Ah, I wish it too! I wish to save what is left of the corn
from the millstones. But you shoot us Picts when we come to
borrow a little iron from the Iron Ditch; you burn our
heather, which is all our crop; you trouble us with your great
catapults. Then you hide behind the Wall, and scorch us with
Greek fire. How can I keep my young men from listening to
the Winged Hats—in winter especially, when we are hungry?
My young men will say, 'Rome can neither fight nor rule.
She is taking her men out of Britain. The Winged Hats will
help us to push down the Wall. Let us show them the secret
roads across the bogs.' Do *I* want that? No!" He spat like an
adder. "*I* would keep the secrets of my people though I were
burned alive. My two children here have spoken truth. Leave

us Picts alone. Comfort us, and cherish us, and feed us from far off—with the hand behind your back. Parnesius understands us. Let *him* have rule on the Wall, and I will hold my young men quiet for"—he ticked it off on his fingers—"one year easily: the next year not so easily: the third year, perhaps! See, I give you three years. If then you do not show us that Rome is strong in men and terrible in arms, the Winged Hats, I tell you, will sweep down the Wall from either sea till they meet in the middle, and you will go. *I* shall not grieve over that, but well I know tribe never helps tribe except for one price. We Picts will go too. The Winged Hats will grind us to this!" He tossed a handful of dust in the air.

' "Oh, Roma Dea!" said Maximus, half aloud. "It is always one man's work—always and everywhere!"

' "And one man's life," said Allo. "You are Emperor, but not a God. You may die."

' "I have thought of that too," said he. "Very good. If this wind holds, I shall be at the East end of the Wall by morning. To-morrow, then, I shall see you two when I inspect, and I will make you Captains of the Wall for this work."

' "One instant, Caesar," said Pertinax. "All men have their price. I am not bought yet."

' "Do *you* also begin to bargain so early?" said Maximus. "Well?"

' "Give me justice against my uncle Icenus, the Duumvir of Divio in Gaul," he said.

' "Only a life? I thought it would be money or an office. Certainly you shall have him. Write his name on these tablets —on the red side; the other is for the living!" And Maximus held out his tablets.

' "He is of no use to me dead," said Pertinax. "My mother

is a widow. I am far off. I am not sure he pays her all her dowry."

' "No matter. My arm is reasonably long. We will look through your uncle's accounts in due time. Now, farewell till to-morrow, O Captains of the Wall!"

'We saw him grow small across the heather as he walked to the galley. There were Picts, scores, each side of him, hidden behind stones. He never looked left or right. He sailed away southerly, full spread before the evening breeze, and when we had watched him out to sea, we were silent. We understood that Earth bred few men like to this man.

'Presently Allo brought the ponies and held them for us to mount—a thing he had never done before.

' "Wait awhile," said Pertinax, and he made a little altar of cut turf, and strewed heather-bloom atop, and laid upon it a letter from a girl in Gaul.

' "What do you do, O my friend?" I said.

' "I sacrifice to my dead youth," he answered, and, when the flames had consumed the letter, he ground them out with his heel. Then we rode back to that Wall of which we were to be Captains.'

Parnesius stopped. The children sat still, not even asking if that were all the tale. Puck beckoned, and pointed the way out of the wood. 'Sorry,' he whispered, 'but you must go now.'

'We haven't made him angry, have we?' said Una. 'He looks so far off, and—and—thinky.'

'Bless your heart, no. Wait till to-morrow. It won't be long. Remember, you've been playing *Lays of Ancient Rome*.'

And as soon as they had scrambled through their gap where Oak, Ash, and Thorn grew, that was all they remembered.

A SONG TO MITHRAS

Mithras, God of the Morning, our trumpets waken the Wall!
'Rome is above the Nations, but Thou art over all!'
Now as the names are answered, and the guards are marched
    away,
Mithras, also a soldier, give us strength for the day!

Mithras, God of the Noontide, the heather swims in the heat,
Our helmets scorch our foreheads, our sandals burn our feet.
Now in the ungirt hour; now ere we blink and drowse,
Mithras, also a soldier, keep us true to our vows!

Mithras, God of the Sunset, low on the Western main,
Thou descending immortal, immortal to rise again!
Now when the watch is ended, now when the wine is drawn,
Mithras, also a soldier, keep us pure till the dawn!

Mithras, God of the Midnight, here where the great bull dies,
Look on Thy children in darkness. Oh, take our sacrifice!
Many roads Thou hast fashioned: all of them lead to the
    Light!
Mithras, also a soldier, teach us to die aright!

THE WINGED HATS

THE WINGED HATS

THE NEXT DAY happened to be what they called a Wild Afternoon. Father and Mother went out to pay calls; Miss Blake
went for a ride on her bicycle, and they were left all alone till
eight o'clock.

When they had seen their dear parents and their dear pre-
ceptress politely off the premises they got a cabbage-leaf full
of raspberries from the gardener, and a Wild Tea from Ellen.
They ate the raspberries to prevent their squashing, and they
meant to divide the cabbage-leaf with Three Cows down at the
Theatre, but they came across a dead hedgehog which they
simply *had* to bury, and the leaf was too useful to waste.

Then they went on to the Forge and found old Hobden the
hedger at home with his son, the Bee Boy, who is not quite
right in his head, but who can pick up swarms of bees in his
naked hands; and the Bee Boy told them the rhyme about the
slow-worm:—

> *'If I had eyes as I could see,*
> *No mortal man would trouble me.'*

They all had tea together by the hives, and Hobden said
the loaf-cake which Ellen had given them was almost as good
as what his wife used to make, and he showed them how to
set a wire at the right height for hares. They knew about rabbits already.

Then they climbed up Long Ditch into the lower end of

Far Wood. This is sadder and darker than the Volaterrae end because of an old marlpit full of black water, where weepy, hairy moss hangs round the stumps of the willows and alders. But the birds come to perch on the dead branches, and Hobden says that the bitter willow-water is a sort of medicine for sick animals.

They sat down on a felled oak-trunk in the shadows of the beech undergrowth, and were looping the wires Hobden had given them, when they saw Parnesius.

'How quietly you came!' said Una, moving up to make room. 'Where's Puck?'

'The Faun and I have disputed whether it is better that I should tell you all my tale, or leave it untold,' he replied.

'I only said that if he told it as it happened you wouldn't understand it,' said Puck, jumping up like a squirrel from behind the log.

'I don't understand all of it,' said Una, 'but I like hearing about the little Picts.'

'What *I* can't understand,' said Dan, 'is how Maximus knew all about the Picts when he was over in Gaul.'

'He who makes himself Emperor anywhere must know everything, everywhere,' said Parnesius. 'We had this much from Maximus's mouth after the Games.'

'Games? What games?' said Dan.

Parnesius stretched his arm out stiffly, thumb pointed to the ground. 'Gladiators! *That* sort of game,' he said. 'There were two days' Games in his honour when he landed all unexpected at Segedunum on the East end of the Wall. Yes, the day after we had met him we held two days' Games; but I think the greatest risk was run, not by the poor wretches on the sand, but by Maximus. In the old days the Legions kept silence before their Emperor. So did not we! You could hear the solid roar run West along the Wall as his chair was carried rocking through the crowds. The garrison beat round him—clamouring, clowning, asking for pay, for change of quarters, for anything that came into their wild heads. That chair was like a little boat among waves, dipping and falling, but always rising again after one had shut the eyes.' Parnesius shivered.

'Were they angry with him?' said Dan.

'No more angry than wolves in a cage when their trainer walks among them. If he had turned his back an instant, or for an instant had ceased to hold their eyes, there would have been another Emperor made on the Wall that hour. Was it not so, Faun?'

'So it was. So it always will be,' said Puck.

'Late in the evening his messenger came for us, and we followed to the Temple of Victory, where he lodged with Rutilianus, the General of the Wall. I had hardly seen the General before, but he always gave me leave when I wished to take Heather. He was a great glutton, and kept five Asian cooks, and he came of a family that believed in oracles. We could smell his good dinner when we entered, but the tables were empty. He lay snorting on a couch. Maximus sat apart among long rolls of accounts. Then the doors were shut.

' "These are your men," said Maximus to the General, who propped his eye-corners open with his gouty fingers, and stared at us like a fish.

' "I shall know them again, Caesar," said Rutilianus.

' "Very good," said Maximus. "Now hear! You are not to move man or shield on the Wall except as these boys shall tell you. You will do nothing, except eat, without their permission. They are the head and arms. You are the belly!"

' "As Caesar pleases," the old man grunted. "If my pay and profits are not cut, you may make my Ancestors' Oracle my master. Rome has been! Rome has been!" Then he turned on his side to sleep.

' "He has it," said Maximus. "We will get to what *I* need."

'He unrolled full copies of the number of men and supplies on the Wall—down to the sick that very day in Hunno Hospital. Oh, but I groaned when his pen marked off detachment after detachment of our best—of our least worthless men! He took two towers of our Scythians, two of our North British Auxiliaries, two Numidian cohorts, the Dacians all, and half the Belgians. It was like an eagle pecking a carcass.

' "And now, how many catapults have you?" He turned up a new list, but Pertinax laid his open hand there.

' "No, Caesar," said he. "Do not tempt the Gods too far. Take men, or engines, but not both; else we refuse." '

'Engines?' said Una.

'The catapults of the Wall—huge things forty feet high to the head—firing nets of raw stone or forged bolts. Nothing can stand against them. He left us our catapults at last, but he took a Caesar's half of our men without pity. We were a shell when he rolled up the lists!

' "Hail, Caesar! We, about to die, salute you!" said Pertinax, laughing. "If any enemy even leans against the Wall now, it will tumble."

' "Give me the three years Allo spoke of," he answered, "and you shall have twenty thousand men of your own choosing up here. But now it is a gamble—a game played against the Gods, and the stakes are Britain, Gaul, and perhaps Rome. You play on my side?"

' "We will play, Caesar," I said, for I had never met a man like this man.

' "Good. To-morrow," said he, "I proclaim you Captains of the Wall before the troops."

'So we went into the moonlight, where they were cleaning the ground after the Games. We saw great Roma Dea atop of the Wall, the frost on her helmet, and her spear pointed towards the North Star. We saw the twinkle of night-fires all along the guard-towers, and the line of the black catapults growing smaller and smaller in the distance. All these things we knew till we were weary; but that night they seemed very strange to us, because the next day we knew we were to be their masters.

'The men took the news well; but when Maximus went away with half our strength, and we had to spread ourselves into the emptied towers, and the townspeople complained that trade would be ruined, and the autumn gales blew—it was dark days for us two. Here Pertinax was more than my right hand. Being born and bred among the great country-houses in Gaul, he knew the proper words to address to all—from Roman-born Centurions to those dogs of the Third—the Libyans. And he spoke to each as though that man were as high-minded as himself. Now *I* saw so strongly what things were needed to be done, that I forgot things are only accomplished by means of men. That was a mistake.

'I feared nothing from the Picts, at least for that year, but Allo warned me that the Winged Hats would soon come in from the sea at each end of the Wall to prove to the Picts how weak we were. So I made ready in haste, and none too soon. I shifted our best men to the ends of the Wall, and set up screened catapults by the beach. The Winged Hats would drive in before the snow-squalls—ten or twenty boats at a time—on Segedunum or Ituna, according as the wind blew.

'Now a ship coming in to land men must furl her sail. If you wait till you see her men gather up the sail's foot, your catapults can jerk a net of loose stones (bolts only cut through the cloth) into the bag of it. Then she turns over, and the sea makes everything clean again. A few men may come ashore, but very few. . . . It was not hard work, except the waiting on the beach in blowing sand and snow. And that was how we dealt with the Winged Hats that winter.

'Early in the spring, when the East winds blow like skinning-knives, they gathered again off Segedunum with many ships. Allo told me they would never rest till they had taken a tower in open fight. Certainly they fought in the open. We dealt with them thoroughly through a long day: and when all was finished, one man dived clear of the wreckage of his ship, and swam towards shore. I waited, and a wave tumbled him at my feet.

'As I stooped, I saw he wore such a medal as I wear.' Parnesius raised his hand to his neck. 'Therefore, when he could speak, I addressed him a certain Question which can only be answered in a certain manner. He answered with the necessary Word—the Word that belongs to the Degree of Gryphons in the science of Mithras my God. I put my shield over him till he could stand up. You see I am not short, but he was a head taller than I. He said: "What now?" I said: "At your pleasure, my brother, to stay or go."

'He looked out across the surf. There remained one ship unhurt, beyond range of our catapults. I checked the catapults and he waved her in. She came as a hound comes to a master. When she was yet a hundred paces from the beach, he flung back his hair, and swam out. They hauled him in, and went away. I knew that those who worship Mithras are many and of all races, so I did not think much more upon the matter.

'A month later I saw Allo with his horses—by the Temple of Pan, O Faun—and he gave me a great necklace of gold studded with coral.

'At first I thought it was a bribe from some tradesman in the town—meant for old Rutilianus. "Nay," said Allo. "This is a gift from Amal, that Winged Hat whom you saved on the beach. He says you are a Man."

'"He is a Man, too. Tell him I can wear his gift," I answered.

'"Oh, Amal is a young fool; but, speaking as sensible men, your Emperor is doing such great things in Gaul that the Winged Hats are anxious to be his friends, or, better still, the friends of his servants. They think you and Pertinax could lead them to victories." Allo looked at me like a one-eyed raven.

'"Allo," I said, "you are the corn between the two mill-stones. Be content if they grind evenly, and don't thrust your hand between them."

'"I?" said Allo. "I hate Rome and the Winged Hats equally; but if the Winged Hats thought that some day you and Pertinax might join them against Maximus, they would leave you in peace while you considered. Time is what we need— you and I and Maximus. Let me carry a pleasant message back to the Winged Hats—something for them to make a council over. We barbarians are all alike. We sit up half the night to discuss anything a Roman says. Eh?"

'"We have no men. We must fight with words," said Pertinax. "Leave it to Allo and me."

'So Allo carried word back to the Winged Hats that we would not fight them if they did not fight us; and they (I think they were a little tired of losing men in the sea) agreed to a sort of truce. I believe Allo, who being a horse-dealer loved lies, also told them we might some day rise against Maximus as Maximus had risen against Rome.

'Indeed, they permitted the corn-ships which I sent to the

Picts to pass North that season without harm. Therefore the Picts were well fed that winter, and since they were in some sort my children, I was glad of it. We had only two thousand men on the Wall, and I wrote many times to Maximus and begged—prayed—him to send me only one cohort of my old North British troops. He could not spare them. He needed them to win more victories in Gaul.

'Then came news that he had defeated and slain the Emperor Gratian, and thinking he must now be secure, I wrote again for men. He answered: *"You will learn that I have at last settled accounts with the pup Gratian. There was no need that he should have died, but he became confused and lost his head, which is a bad thing to befall any Emperor. Tell your Father I am content to drive two mules only; for unless my old General's son thinks himself destined to destroy me, I shall rest Emperor of Gaul and Britain, and then you, my two children, will presently get all the men you need. Just now I can spare none."*'

'What did he mean by his General's son?' said Dan.

'He meant Theodosius Emperor of Rome, who was the son of Theodosius the General under whom Maximus had fought in the old Pict War. The two men never loved each other, and when Gratian made the younger Theodosius Emperor of the East (at least, so I've heard), Maximus carried on the war to the second generation. It was his fate, and it was his fall. But Theodosius the Emperor is a good man. As I know.' Parnesius was silent for a moment and then continued.

'I wrote back to Maximus that, though we had peace on the Wall, I should be happier with a few more men and some new catapults. He answered: *"You must live a little longer under the shadow of my victories, till I can see what young Theodosius intends. He may welcome me as a brother-*

*Emperor, or he may be preparing an army. In either case I
cannot spare men just now."* '

'But he was always saying that,' cried Una.

'It was true. He did not make excuses; but thanks, as he said,
to the news of his victories, we had no trouble on the Wall
for a long, long time. The Picts grew fat as their own sheep
among the heather, and as many of my men as lived were well
exercised in their weapons. Yes, the Wall looked strong. For
myself, I knew how weak we were. I knew that if even a false
rumour of any defeat to Maximus broke loose among the
Winged Hats, they might come down in earnest, and then—the
Wall must go! For the Picts I never cared, but in those years
I learned something of the strength of the Winged Hats. They
increased their strength every day, but I could not increase my
men. Maximus had emptied Britain behind us, and I felt myself to be a man with a rotten stick standing before a broken
fence to turn bulls.

'Thus, my friends, we lived on the Wall, waiting—waiting—
waiting for the men that Maximus never sent.

'Presently he wrote that he was preparing an army against
Theodosius. He wrote—and Pertinax read it over my shoulder
in our quarters: *"Tell your Father that my destiny orders me
to drive three mules or be torn in pieces by them. I hope within
a year to finish with Theodosius, son of Theodosius, once and
for all. Then you shall have Britain to rule, and Pertinax, if
he chooses, Gaul. To-day I wish strongly you were with me to
beat my Auxiliaries into shape. Do not, I pray you, believe
any rumour of my sickness. I have a little evil in my old body
which I shall cure by riding swiftly into Rome."*

'Said Pertinax: "It is finished with Maximus. He writes as a
man without hope. I, a man without hope, can see this. What
does he add at the bottom of the roll? *'Tell Pertinax I have*

met his late Uncle, the Duumvir of Divio, and that he ac-
counted to me quite truthfully for all his Mother's monies. I
have sent her with a fitting escort, for she is the mother of a
hero, to Nicaea, where the climate is warm.'

' "That is proof," said Pertinax. "Nicaea is not far by sea
from Rome. A woman there could take ship and fly to Rome
in time of war. Yes, Maximus foresees his death, and is ful-
filling his promises one by one. But I am glad my uncle met
him." '

' "You think blackly to-day?" I asked.

' "I think truth. The Gods weary of the play we have played
against them. Theodosius will destroy Maximus. It is finished!"

' "Will you write him that?" I said.

' "See what I shall write," he answered, and he took pen
and wrote a letter cheerful as the light of day, tender as a
woman's and full of jests. Even I, reading over his shoulder,
took comfort from it till—I saw his face!

' "And now," he said, sealing it, "we be two dead men, my
brother. Let us go to the Temple."

'We prayed awhile to Mithras, where we had many times
prayed before. After that, we lived day by day among evil
rumours till winter came again.

'It happened one morning that we rode to the East shore,
and found on the beach a fair-haired man, half frozen, bound
to some broken planks. Turning him over, we saw by his belt-
buckle that he was a Goth of an Eastern Legion. Suddenly he
opened his eyes and cried loudly, "He is dead! The letters
were with me, but the Winged Hats sank the ship." So saying,
he died between our hands.

'We asked not who was dead. We knew! We raced before
the driving snow to Hunno, thinking perhaps Allo might be
there. We found him already at our stables, and he saw by our
faces what we had heard.

' "It was in a tent by the sea," he stammered. "He was be-headed by Theodosius. He sent a letter to you, written while he waited to be slain. The Winged Hats met the ship and took it. The news is running through the heather like fire. Blame me not! I cannot hold back my young men any more."

' "I would we could say as much for our men," said Pertinax, laughing. "But, Gods be praised, they cannot run away."

' "What do you do?" said Allo. "I bring an order—a message—from the Winged Hats that you join them with your men, and march South to plunder Britain."

' "It grieves me," said Pertinax, "but we are stationed here to stop that thing."

' "If I carry back such an answer they will kill me," said Allo. "I always promised the Winged Hats that you would rise when Maximus fell. I—I did not think he could fall."

' "Alas! my poor barbarian," said Pertinax, still laughing. "Well, you have sold us too many good ponies to be thrown back to your friends. We will make you a prisoner, although you are an ambassador."

' "Yes, that will be best," said Allo, holding out a halter. We bound him lightly, for he was an old man.

' "Presently the Winged Hats may come to look for you, and that will give us more time. See how the habit of playing for time sticks to a man!" said Pertinax, as he tied the rope.

' "No," I said. "Time may help. If Maximus wrote us a letter while he was a prisoner, Theodosius must have sent the ship that brought it. If he can send ships, he can send men."

' "How will that profit us?" said Pertinax. "We serve Maximus, not Theodosius. Even if by some miracle of the Gods Theodosius down South sent and saved the Wall, we could not expect more than the death Maximus died."

' "It concerns us to defend the Wall, no matter what Emperor dies, or makes die," I said.

' "That is worthy of your brother the philosopher," said Pertinax. "Myself I am without hope, so I do not say solemn and stupid things! Rouse the Wall!"

'We armed the Wall from end to end; we told the officers that there was a rumour of Maximus's death which might bring down the Winged Hats, but we were sure, even if it were true, that Theodosius, for the sake of Britain, would send us help. Therefore, we must stand fast. . . . My friends, it is above all things strange to see how men bear ill news! Often the strongest till then become the weakest, while the weakest, as it were, reach up and steal strength from the Gods. So it was with us. Yet my Pertinax by his jests and his courtesy and his labours had put heart and training into our poor numbers during the past years—more than I should have thought possible. Even our Libyan Cohort—the Third—stood up in their padded cuirasses and did not whimper.

'In three days came seven chiefs and elders of the Winged Hats. Among them was that tall young man, Amal, whom I had met on the beach, and he smiled when he saw my necklace. We made them welcome, for they were ambassadors. We showed them Allo, alive but bound. They thought we had killed him, and I saw it would not have vexed them if we had. Allo saw it too, and it vexed him. Then in our quarters at Hunno we came to council.

'They said that Rome was falling, and that we must join them. They offered me all South Britain to govern after they had taken a tribute out of it.

'I answered, "Patience. This Wall is not weighed off like plunder. Give me proof that my General is dead."

' "Nay," said one elder, "prove to us that he lives"; and another said cunningly, "What will you give us if we read you his last words?"

' "We are not merchants to bargain," cried Amal. "Moreover, I owe this man my life. He shall have his proof." He threw across to me a letter (well I knew the seal) from Maximus.

' "We took this out of the ship we sank," he cried. "I cannot read, but I know one sign, at least, which makes me believe." He showed me a dark stain on the outer roll that my heavy heart perceived was the valiant blood of Maximus.

' "Read!" said Amal. "Read, and then let us hear whose servants you are!"

'Said Pertinax, very softly, after he had looked through it: "I will read it all. Listen, barbarians!" He read that which I have carried next my heart ever since.'

Parnesius drew from his neck a folded and spotted piece of parchment, and began in a hushed voice:—

' "*To Parnesius and Pertinax, the not unworthy Captains of the Wall, from Maximus, once Emperor of Gaul and Britain, now prisoner waiting death by the sea in the camp of Theodosius—Greeting and Good-bye!*"

' "Enough," said young Amal; "there is your proof! You must join us now!"

'Pertinax looked long and silently at him, till that fair man blushed like a girl. Then read Pertinax:—

' "*I have joyfully done much evil in my life to those who have wished me evil, but if ever I did any evil to you two I repent, and I ask your forgiveness. The three mules which I strove to drive have torn me in pieces as your Father prophesied. The naked swords wait at the tent door to give me the death I gave to Gratian. Therefore I, your General and your Emperor, send you free and honourable dismissal from my service, which you entered; not for money or office, but, as it makes me warm to believe, because you loved me!*"

' "By the Light of the Sun," Amal broke in. "This was in some sort a Man! We may have been mistaken in his servants!"

'And Pertinax read on: *"You gave me the time for which I asked. If I have failed to use it, do not lament. We have gambled very splendidly against the Gods, but they hold weighted dice, and I must pay the forfeit. Remember, I have been; but Rome is; and Rome will be. Tell Pertinax his Mother is in safety at Nicaea, and her monies are in charge of the Prefect at Antipolis. Make my remembrances to your Father and to your Mother, whose friendship was great gain to me. Give also to my little Picts and to the Winged Hats such messages as their thick heads can understand. I would have sent you three Legions this very day if all had gone aright. Do not forget me. We have worked together. Farewell! Farewell! Farewell!"*

'Now, that was my Emperor's last letter.' (The children heard the parchment crackle as Parnesius returned it to its place.)

' "I was mistaken," said Amal. "The servants of such a man will sell nothing except over the sword. I am glad of it." He held out his hand to me.

' "But Maximus has given you your dismissal," said an elder. "You are certainly free to serve—or to rule—whom you please. Join—do not follow—join us!"

' "We thank you," said Pertinax. "But Maximus tells us to give you such messages as—pardon me, but I use his words—your thick heads can understand." He pointed through the door to the foot of a catapult wound up.

' "We understand," said an elder. "The Wall must be won at a price?"

' "It grieves me," said Pertinax, laughing, "but so it must be won," and he gave them of our best Southern wine.

'They drank, and wiped their yellow beards in silence till they rose to go.

'Said Amal, stretching himself (for they were barbarians): "We be a goodly company; I wonder what the ravens and the dogfish will make of some of us before this snow melts."

' "Think rather what Theodosius may send," I answered; and though they laughed, I saw that my chance shot troubled them.

'Only old Allo lingered behind a little.

' "You see," he said, winking and blinking, "I am no more than their dog. When I have shown their men the secret short ways across our bogs, they will kick me like one."

' "Then I should not be in haste to show them those ways," said Pertinax, "till I was sure that Rome could not save the Wall."

' "You think so? Woe is me!" said the old man. "I only wanted peace for my people," and he went out stumbling through the snow behind the tall Winged Hats.

'In this fashion then, slowly, a day at a time, which is very bad for doubting troops, the War came upon us. At first the Winged Hats swept in from the sea as they had done before, and there we met them as before—with the catapults; and they sickened of it. Yet for a long time they would not trust their duck-legs on land, and I think, when it came to revealing the secrets of the tribe, the little Picts were afraid or ashamed to show them all the roads across the heather. I had this from a Pict prisoner. They were as much our spies as our enemies, for the Winged Hats oppressed them, and took their winter stores. Ah, foolish Little People!

'Then the Winged Hats began to roll us up from each end of the Wall. I sent runners Southward to see what the news might be in Britain, but the wolves were very bold that winter, among the deserted stations where the troops had once been, and none came back. We had trouble, too, with the forage for the ponies along the Wall. I kept ten, and so did Pertinax. We lived and slept in the saddle, riding east or west, and we ate our worn-out ponies. The people of the town also made us some trouble till I gathered them all in one quarter behind Hunno. We broke down the Wall on either side of it to make as it were a citadel. Our men fought better in close order.

'By the end of the second month we were deep in the War as a man is deep in a snowdrift, or in a dream. I think we fought in our sleep. At least I know I have gone on the Wall and come off again, remembering nothing between, though my throat was harsh with giving orders, and my sword, I could see, had been used.

'The Winged Hats fought like wolves—all in a pack. Where they had suffered most, there they charged in most hotly. This was hard for the defenders, but it held them from sweeping on into Britain.

'In those days Pertinax and I wrote on the plaster of the bricked archway into Valentia the names of the towers, and the days on which they fell one by one. We wished for some record.

'And the fighting? The fight was always hottest to left and right of the great statue of Roma Dea, near to Rutilianus's house. By the Light of the Sun, that old fat man, whom we had not considered at all, grew young again among the trumpets! I remember he said his sword was an oracle! "Let us consult the Oracle," he would say, and put the handle against his ear, and shake his head wisely. "And *this* day is allowed Rutilianus to live," he would say, and, tucking up his cloak, he would puff and pant and fight well. Oh, there were jests in plenty on the Wall to take the place of food!

'We endured for two months and seventeen days—always being pressed from three sides into a smaller space. Several times Allo sent in word that help was at hand. We did not believe it, but it cheered our men.

'The end came not with shoutings of joy, but, like the rest, as in a dream. The Winged Hats suddenly left us in peace for one night and the next day; which is too long for spent men. We slept at first lightly, expecting to be roused, and then like logs, each where he lay. May you never need such sleep! When I waked our towers were full of strange, armed men, who watched us snoring. I roused Pertinax, and we leaped up together.

' "What?" said a young man in clean armour. "Do you fight against Theodosius? Look!"

'North we looked over the red snow. No Winged Hats were there. South we looked over the white snow, and behold there were the Eagles of two strong Legions encamped. East and west we saw flame and fighting, but by Hunno all was still.

' "Trouble no more," said the young man. "Rome's arm is long. Where are the Captains of the Wall?"

'We said we were those men.

' "But you are old and grey-haired," he cried. "Maximus said that they were boys."

' "Yes, that was true some years ago," said Pertinax. "What is our fate to be, you fine and well-fed child?"

' "I am called Ambrosius, a secretary of the Emperor," he answered. "Show me a certain letter which Maximus wrote from a tent at Aquileia, and perhaps I will believe."

'I took it from my breast, and when he had read it he saluted us, saying: "Your fate is in your own hands. If you choose to serve Theodosius, he will give you a Legion. If it suits you to go to your homes, we will give you a Triumph."

' "I would like better a bath, wine, food, razors, soaps, oils, and scents," said Pertinax, laughing.

' "Oh, I see you are a boy," said Ambrosius. "And you?" turning to me.

' "We bear no ill-will against Theodosius, but in War——"
I began.

' "In War it is as it is in Love," said Pertinax. "Whether
she be good or bad, one gives one's best once, to one only.
That given, there remains no second worth giving or taking."

' "That is true," said Ambrosius. "I was with Maximus before he died. He warned Theodosius that you would never
serve him, and frankly I say I am sorry for my Emperor."

' "He has Rome to console him," said Pertinax. "I ask you
of your kindness to let us go to our homes and get this smell
out of our nostrils."

'None the less they gave us a Triumph!'

'It was well earned,' said Puck, throwing some leaves into
the still water of the marlpit. The black, oily circles spread
dizzily as the children watched them.

'I want to know, oh, ever so many things,' said Dan. 'What
happened to old Allo? Did the Winged Hats ever come back?
And what did Amal do?'

'And what happened to the fat old General with the five
cooks?' said Una. 'And what did your Mother say when you
came home? . . .'

'She'd say you're settin' too long over this old pit, so late as
'tis already,' said old Hobden's voice behind them. 'Hst!' he
whispered.

He stood still, for not twenty paces away a magnificent dog-
fox sat on his haunches and looked at the children as though
he were an old friend of theirs.

'Oh, Mus' Reynolds, Mus' Reynolds!' said Hobden under
his breath. 'If I knowed all was inside your head, I'd know
something wuth knowin'. Mus' Dan an' Miss Una, come along
o' me while I lock up my liddle hen-house.'

A PICT SONG

Rome never looks where she treads,
　　Always her heavy hooves fall
On our stomachs, our hearts or our heads;
　　And Rome never heeds when we bawl.
Her sentries pass on—that is all,
　　And we gather behind them in hordes,
And plot to reconquer the Wall,
　　With only our tongues for our swords.

We are the Little Folk—we!
　　Too little to love or to hate.
Leave us alone and you'll see
　　How we can drag down the Great!
We are the worm in the wood!
　　We are the rot at the root!
We are the germ in the blood!
　　We are the thorn in the foot!

Mistletoe killing an oak—
　　Rats gnawing cables in two—
Moths making holes in a cloak—
　　How they must love what they do!
Yes,—and we Little Folk too,
　　We are as busy as they—
Working our works out of view—
　　Watch, and you'll see it some day!

No, indeed! We are not strong,
　　But we know Peoples that are.

Yes, and we'll guide them along,
To smash and destroy you in War!
We shall be slaves just the same?
Yes, we have always been slaves,
But you—you will die of the shame,
And then we shall dance on your graves!

We are the Little Folk, we, etc.

HAL O' THE DRAFT

Prophets have honour all over the Earth,
  Except in the village where they were born,
Where such as knew them boys from birth
  Nature-ally hold 'em in scorn.

When Prophets are naughty and young and vain,
  They make a won'erful grievance of it;
(You can see by their writings how they complain),
  But Oh, 'tis won'erful good for the Prophet!

There's nothing Nineveh Town can give
  (Nor being swallowed by whales between),
Makes up for the place where a man's folk live,
  That don't care nothing what he has been.
He might ha' been that, or he might ha' been this,
But they love and they hate him for what he is.

HAL O' THE DRAFT

A RAINY AFTERNOON drove Dan and Una over to play pirates in
the Little Mill. If you don't mind rats on the rafters and oats
in your shoes, the mill-attic, with its trap-doors and inscrip-
tions on beams about floods and sweethearts, is a splendid
place. It is lighted by a foot-square window, called Duck Window, that looks across to Little Lindens Farm, and the spot
where Jack Cade was killed.

When they had climbed the attic ladder (they called it 'the
mainmast tree,' out of the ballad of Sir Andrew Barton, and
Dan 'swarved it with might and main,' as the ballad says) they
saw a man sitting on Duck Window-sill. He was dressed in a
plum-coloured doublet and tight plum-coloured hose, and he
drew busily in a red-edged book.

'Sit ye! Sit ye!' Puck cried from a rafter overhead. 'See what
it is to be beautiful! Sir Harry Dawe—pardon, Hal—says I am
the very image of a head for a gargoyle.'

The man laughed and raised his dark velvet cap to the children, and his grizzled hair bristled out in a stormy fringe. He
was old—forty at least—but his eyes were young, with funny
little wrinkles all round them. A satchel of embroidered
leather hung from his broad belt, which looked interesting.

'May we see?' said Una, coming forward.

'Surely—sure-ly!' he said, moving up on the window-seat,
and returned to his work with a silver-pointed pencil. Puck
sat as though the grin were fixed for ever on his broad face,
while they watched the quick, certain fingers that copied it.

Presently the man took a reed pen from his satchel, and trimmed it with a little ivory knife, carved in the semblance of a fish.

'Oh, what a beauty!' cried Dan.

' 'Ware fingers! That blade is perilous sharp. I made it myself of the best Low Country cross-bow steel. And so, too, this fish. When his back-fin travels to his tail—so—he swallows up the blade, even as the whale swallowed Gaffer Jonah. . . . Yes, and that's my ink-horn. I made the four silver saints round it. Press Barnabas's head. It opens, and then——' He dipped the trimmed pen, and with careful boldness began to put in the essential lines of Puck's rugged face, that had been but faintly revealed by the silver-point.

The children gasped, for it fairly leaped from the page.

As he worked, and the rain fell on the tiles, he talked—now clearly, now muttering, now breaking off to frown or smile at his work. He told them he was born at Little Lindens Farm, and his father used to beat him for drawing things instead of doing things, till an old priest called Father Roger, who drew illuminated letters in rich people's books, coaxed the parents to let him take the boy as a sort of painter's apprentice. Then he went with Father Roger to Oxford, where he cleaned plates and carried cloaks and shoes for the scholars of a College called Merton.

'Didn't you hate that?' said Dan after a great many other questions.

'I never thought on't. Half Oxford was building new colleges or beautifying the old, and she had called to her aid the master-craftsmen of all Christendie—kings in their trade and honoured of Kings. I knew them. I worked for them: that was enough. No wonder——' He stopped and laughed.

'You became a great man, Hal,' said Puck.

'They said so, Robin. Even Bramante said so.'

'Why? What did you do?' Dan asked.

The artist looked at him queerly. 'Things in stone and such, up and down England. You would not have heard of 'em. To come nearer home, I re-builded this little St. Barnabas' church of ours. It cost me more trouble and sorrow than aught I've touched in my life. But 'twas a sound lesson.'

'Um,' said Dan. 'We've had lessons this morning.'

'I'll not afflict ye, lad,' said Hal, while Puck roared. 'Only 'tis strange to think how that little church was re-built, re-roofed, and made glorious, thanks to some few godly Sussex ironmasters, a Bristow sailor lad, a proud ass called Hal o' the Draft because, d'you see, he was always drawing and drafting; and'—he dragged the words slowly—'*and* a Scotch pirate.'

'Pirate?' said Dan. He wriggled like a hooked fish.

'Even that Andrew Barton you were singing of on the stair just now.' He dipped again in the ink-well, and held his breath over a sweeping line, as though he had forgotten everything else.

'Pirates don't build churches, do they?' said Dan. 'Or *do* they?'

'They help mightily,' Hal laughed. 'But you were at your lessons this morn, Jack Scholar.'

'Oh, pirates aren't lessons. It was only Bruce and his silly old spider,' said Una. 'Why did Sir Andrew Barton help you?'

'I question if he ever knew it,' said Hal, twinkling. 'Robin, how a' mischief's name am I to tell these innocents what comes of sinful pride?'

'Oh, we know all about *that*,' said Una pertly. 'If you get too beany—that's cheeky—you get sat upon, of course.'

Hal considered a moment, pen in air, and Puck said some long words.

'Aha! that was my case too,' he cried. 'Beany—you say—but certainly I did not conduct myself well. I was proud of—of such things as porches—a Galilee porch at Lincoln for choice —proud of one Torrigiano's arm on my shoulder, proud of my knighthood when I made the gilt scroll-work for the *Sovereign*—our King's ship. But Father Roger sitting in Merton College Library he did not forget me. At the top of my pride, when I and no other should have builded the porch at Lincoln, he laid it on me with a terrible forefinger to go back to my Sussex clays and re-build, at my own charges, my own church, where us Dawes have been buried for six generations. "Out! Son of my Art!" said he. "Fight the Devil at home ere you call yourself a man and a craftsman." And I quaked, and I went. . . . How's yon, Robin?' He flourished the finished sketch before Puck.

'Me! Me past peradventure,' said Puck, smirking like a man at a mirror. 'Ah, see! The rain has took off! I hate housen in daylight.'

'Whoop! Holiday!' cried Hal, leaping up. 'Who's for my Little Lindens? We can talk there.'

They tumbled downstairs, and turned past the dripping willows by the sunny mill-dam.

'Body o' me,' said Hal, staring at the hop-garden, where the hops were just ready to blossom. 'What are these? Vines? No, not vines, and they twine the wrong way to beans.' He began to draw in his ready book.

'Hops. New since your day,' said Puck. 'They're an herb of Mars, and their flowers dried flavour ale. We say—

> *'Turkeys, Heresy, Hops, and Beer*
> *Came into England all in one year.'*

'Heresy I know. I've seen Hops—God be praised for their beauty! What is your Turkis?'

The children laughed. They knew the Lindens turkeys, and as soon as they reached Lindens orchard on the hill the full flock charged at them.

Out came Hal's book at once. 'Hoity-toity!' he cried. 'Here's Pride in purple feathers! Here's wrathy contempt and the Pomps of the Flesh! How d'you call *them*?'

'Turkeys! Turkeys!' the children shouted, as the old gobbler raved and flamed against Hal's plum-coloured hose.

' 'Save Your Magnificence!' he said. 'I've drafted two good new things to-day.' And he doffed his cap to the bubbling bird.

Then they walked through the grass to the knoll where Little Lindens stands. The old farmhouse, weather-tiled to the ground, took almost the colour of a blood-ruby in the afternoon light. The pigeons pecked at the mortar in the chimney-stacks; the bees that had lived under the tiles since it was built filled the hot August air with their booming; and the smell of the box-tree by the dairy-window mixed with the smell of earth after rain, bread after baking, and a tickle of wood-smoke.

The farmer's wife came to the door, baby on arm, shaded her brows against the sun, stooped to pluck a sprig of rosemary, and turned down the orchard. The old spaniel in his barrel barked once or twice to show he was in charge of the empty house. Puck clicked back the garden-gate.

'D'you marvel that I love it?' said Hal, in a whisper. 'What can town folk know of the nature of housen—or land?'

They perched themselves arow on the old hacked oak bench in Lindens garden, looking across the valley of the brook at the fern-covered dimples and hollows of the Forge behind

Hobden's cottage. The old man was cutting a faggot in his garden by the hives. It was quite a second after his chopper fell that the chump of the blow reached their lazy ears.

'Eh—yeh!' said Hal. 'I mind when where that old gaffer stands was Nether Forge—Master John Collins's foundry. Many a night has his big trip-hammer shook me in my bed here. *Boom-bitty! Boom-bitty!* If the wind was east, I could hear Master Tom Collins's forge at Stockens answering his brother, *Boom-oop! Boom-oop!* and midway between, Sir John Pelham's sledge-hammers at Brightling would strike in like a pack o' scholars, and *"Hic-haec-hoc"* they'd say, *"Hic-haec-hoc,"* till I fell asleep. Yes. The valley was as full o' forges and fineries as a May shaw o' cuckoos. All gone to grass now!'

'What did they make?' said Dan.

'Guns for the King's ships—and for others. Serpentines and cannon mostly. When the guns were cast, down would come the King's Officers, and take our plough-oxen to haul them to the coast. Look! Here's one of the first and finest craftsmen of the Sea!'

He fluttered back a page of his book, and showed them a young man's head. Underneath was written: 'Sebastianus.'

'He came down with a King's Order on Master John Collins for twenty serpentines (wicked little cannon they be!) to furnish a venture of ships. I drafted him thus sitting by our fire telling Mother of the new lands he'd find the far side the world. And he found them, too! There's a nose to cleave through unknown seas! Cabot was his name—a Bristol lad—half a foreigner. I set a heap by him. He helped me to my church-building.'

'I thought that was Sir Andrew Barton,' said Dan.

'Ay, but foundations before roofs,' Hal answered. 'Sebastian first put me in the way of it. I had come down here, not to

serve God as a craftsman should, but to show my people how
great a craftsman I was. They cared not, and it served me
right, one split straw for my craft or my greatness. What a
murrain call had I, they said, to mell with old St. Barnabas'?
Ruinous the church had been since the Black Death, and
ruinous she should remain; and I could hang myself in my
new scaffold-ropes! Gentle and simple, high and low—the
Hayes, the Fowles, the Fenners, the Collinses—they were all
in a tale against me. Only Sir John Pelham up yonder at
Brightling bade me heart-up and go on. Yet how could I? Did
I ask Master Collins for his timber-tug to haul beams? The
oxen had gone to Lewes after lime. Did he promise me a set
of iron cramps or ties for the roof? They never came to hand,
or else they were spaulty or cracked. So with everything. Nothing said, but naught done except I stood by them, and then
done amiss. I thought the countryside was fair bewitched.'

'It was, sure-ly,' said Puck, knees under chin. 'Did you never
suspect ary one?'

'Not till Sebastian came for his guns, and John Collins
played him the same dog's tricks as he'd played me with my
ironwork. Week in, week out, two of three serpentines would
be flawed in the casting, and only fit, they said, to be re-
melted. Then John Collins would shake his head, and vow he
could pass no cannon for the King's service that were not perfect. Saints! How Sebastian stormed! *I* know, for we sat on this
bench sharing our sorrows inter-common.

'When Sebastian had fumed away six weeks at Lindens and
gotten just six serpentines, Dirk Brenzett, Master of the *Cygnet*
hoy, sends me word that the block of stone he was fetching me
from France for our new font he'd hove overboard to lighten
his ship, chased by Andrew Barton up to Rye Port.'

'Ah! The pirate!' said Dan.

'Yes. And while I am tearing my hair over this, Ticehurst Will, my best mason, comes to me shaking, and vowing that the Devil, horned, tailed, and chained, has run out on him from the church-tower, and the men would work there no more. So I took 'em off the foundations, which we were strengthening, and went into the Bell Tavern for a cup of ale. Says Master John Collins: "Have it your own way, lad; but if I was you, I'd take the sinnification o' the sign, and leave old Barnabas' church alone!" And they all wagged their sinful heads, and agreed. Less afraid of the Devil than of me—as I saw later.

'When I brought my sweet news to Lindens, Sebastian was limewashing the kitchen-beams for Mother. He loved her like a son.

' "Cheer up, lad," he says. "God's where He was. Only you and I chance to be pure pute asses. We've been tricked, Hal, and more shame to me, a sailor, that I did not guess it before! You must leave your belfry alone, forsooth, because the Devil is adrift there; and I cannot get my serpentines because John Collins cannot cast them aright. Meantime Andrew Barton hawks off the Port of Rye. And why? To take those very serpentines which poor Cabot must whistle for; the said serpentines, I'll wager my share of new continents, being now hid away in St. Barnabas' church-tower. Clear as the Irish coast at noon-day!"

' "They'd sure never dare to do it," I said; "and, for another thing, selling cannon to the King's enemies is black treason—hanging and fine."

' "It is sure, large profit. Men'll dare any gallows for that. I have been a trader myself," says he. "We must be upsides with 'em for the honour of Bristol."

'Then he hatched a plot, sitting on the limewash bucket.

We gave out to ride o' Tuesday to London and made a show of taking farewells of our friends—especially of Master John Collins. But at Wadhurst Woods we turned; rode home to the water-meadows; hid our horses in a willow-tot at the foot of the glebe, and, come night, stole a-tiptoe uphill to Barnabas' church again. A thick mist, and a moon striking through.

'I had no sooner locked the tower-door behind us than over goes Sebastian full length in the dark.

' "Pest!" he says. "Step high and feel low, Hal. I've stumbled over guns before."

'I groped, and one by one—the tower was pitchy dark—I counted the lither barrels of twenty serpentines laid out on pease straw. No conceal at all!

' "There's two demi-cannon my end," says Sebastian, slapping metal. "They'll be for Andrew Barton's lower deck. Honest—honest John Collins! So this is his warehouse, his arsenal, his armoury! Now see you why your pokings and pryings have raised the Devil in Sussex? You've hindered John's lawful trade for months," and he laughed where he lay.

'A clay-cold tower is no fireside at midnight, so we climbed the belfry stairs, and there Sebastian trips over a cow-hide with its horns and tail.

' "Aha! Your Devil has left his doublet! Does it become me, Hal?" He draws it on and capers in the slits of window-moon-light—won'erful devilish-like. Then he sits on the stairs, rapping with his tail on a board, and his back-aspect was dreader than his front, and a howlet lit in, and screeched at the horns of him.

' "If you'd keep out the Devil, shut the door," he whispered. "And that's another false proverb, Hal, for I can hear your tower-door opening."

' "I locked it. Who a-plague has another key, then?" I said.

' "All the congregation, to judge by their feet," he says, and peers into the blackness. "Still! Still, Hal! Hear 'em grunt! That's more o' my serpentines, I'll be bound. One—two—three—four they bear in! Faith, Andrew equips himself like an Admiral! Twenty-four serpentines in all!"

'As if it had been an echo, we heard John Collins's voice come up all hollow: "Twenty-four serpentines and two demi-cannon. That's the full tally for Sir Andrew Barton."

' "Courtesy costs naught," whispers Sebastian. "Shall I drop my dagger on his head?"

' "They go over to Rye o' Thursday in the wool-wains, hid under the wool-packs. Dirk Brenzett meets them at Udimore, as before," says John.

' "Lord! What a worn, handsmooth trade it is!" says Sebastian. "I lay we are the sole two babes in the village that have not our lawful share in the venture."

'There was a full score folk below, talking like all Roberts-bridge Market. We counted them by voice.

'Master John Collins pipes: "The guns for the French carrack must lie here next month. Will, when does your young fool" (me, so please you!) "come back from Lunnon?"

' "No odds," I heard Ticehurst Will answer. "Lay 'em just where you've a mind, Mus' Collins. We're all too afraid o' the Devil to mell with the tower now." And the long knave laughed.

' "Ah! 'tis easy enow for you to raise the Devil, Will," says another—Ralph Hobden of the Forge.

' "Aaa-men!" roars Sebastian, and ere I could hold him, he leaps down the stairs—won'erful devilish-like—howling no bounds. He had scarce time to lay out for the nearest than they ran. Saints, how they ran! We heard them pound on the door of the Bell Tavern, and then we ran too.

' "What's next?" says Sebastian, looping up his cow-tail as he leaped the briars. "I've broke honest John's face."

' "Ride to Sir John Pelham's," I said. "He is the only one that ever stood by me."

'We rode to Brightling, and past Sir John's lodges, where the keepers would have shot at us for deer-stealers, and we had Sir John down into his Justice's chair, and when we had told him our tale and showed him the cow-hide which Sebastian wore still girt about him, he laughed till the tears ran.

' "Wel-a-well!" he says. "I'll see justice done before daylight. What's your complaint? Master Collins is my old friend."

' "He's none of mine," I cried. "When I think how he and his likes have baulked and dozened and cozened me at every turn over the church"—and I choked at the thought.

' "Ah, but ye see now they needed it for another use," says he smoothly.

' "So they did my serpentines," Sebastian cries. "I should be half across the Western Ocean by now if my guns had been ready. But they're sold to a Scotch pirate by your old friend."

' "Where's your proof?" says Sir John, stroking his beard.

' "I broke my shins over them not an hour since, and I heard John give order where they were to be taken," says Sebastian.

' "Words! Words only," says Sir John. "Master Collins is somewhat of a liar at best."

'He carried it so gravely that, for the moment, I thought he was dipped in this secret traffick too, and that there was not an honest ironmaster in Sussex.

' "Name o' Reason!" says Sebastian, and raps with his cow-tail on the table, "whose guns are they, then?"

' "Yours, manifestly," says Sir John. "You come with the King's Order for 'em, and Master Collins casts them in his foundry. If he chooses to bring them up from Nether Forge and lay 'em out in the church-tower, why, they are e'en so much the nearer to the main road and you are saved a day's hauling. What a coil to make of a mere act of neighbourly kindness, lad!"

' "I fear I have requited him very scurvily," says Sebastian, looking at his knuckles. "But what of the demi-cannon? I could do with 'em well, but *they* are not in the King's Order."

' "Kindness—loving-kindness," says Sir John. "Questionless, in his zeal for the King and his love for you, John adds those two cannon as a gift. 'Tis plain as this coming daylight, ye stockfish!"

' "So it is," says Sebastian. "Oh, Sir John, Sir John, why did you never use the sea? You are lost ashore." And he looked on him with great love.

' "I do my best in my station." Sir John strokes his beard again and rolls forth his deep drumming Justice's voice thus: "But—suffer me!—you two lads, on some midnight frolic into which I probe not, roystering around the taverns, surprise Master Collins at his"—he thinks a moment—"at his good deeds done by stealth. Ye surprise him, I say, cruelly."

' "Truth, Sir John. If you had seen him run!" says Sebastian.

' "On this you ride breakneck to me with a tale of pirates, and wool-wains, and cow-hides, which, though it hath moved my mirth as a man, offendeth my reason as a magistrate. So I will e'en accompany you back to the tower with, perhaps, some few of my own people, and three-four wagons, and I'll be your warrant that Master John Collins will freely give you your guns and your demi-cannon, Master Sebastian." He breaks into his proper voice: "I warned the old tod and his neighbours long ago that they'd come to trouble with their side-sellings and bye-dealings; but we cannot have half Sussex hanged for a little gun-running. Are ye content, lads?"

' "I'd commit any treason for two demi-cannon," said Sebastian, and rubs his hands.

' "Ye have just compounded with rank treason-felony for the same bribe," says Sir John. "Wherefore to horse, and get the guns." '

'But Master Collins meant the guns for Sir Andrew Barton all along, didn't he?' said Dan.

'Questionless, that he did,' said Hal. 'But he lost them. We poured into the village on the red edge of dawn, Sir John horsed, in half-armour, his pennon flying; behind him thirty stout Brightling knaves, five abreast; behind them four woolwains, and behind them four trumpets to triumph over the jest, blowing: *Our King went forth to Normandie.* When we halted and rolled the ringing guns out of the tower, 'twas for all the world like Friar Roger's picture of the French siege in the Queen's Missal-book.'

'And what did we—I mean, what did our village do?' said Dan.

'Oh! Bore it nobly—nobly,' cried Hal. 'Though they had tricked me, I was proud of them. They came out of their housen, looked at that little army as though it had been a post, and went their shut-mouthed way. Never a sign! Never a word! They'd ha' perished sooner than let Brightling overcrow us. Even that villain, Ticehurst Will, coming out of the Bell for his morning ale, he all but runs under Sir John's horse.

' " 'Ware, Sirrah Devil!" cries Sir John, reining back.

' "Oh!" says Will. "Market-day, is it? And all the bullocks from Brightling here?"

'I spared him his belting for that—the brazen knave!

'But John Collins was our masterpiece! He happened alongstreet (his jaw tied up where Sebastian had clouted him) when we were trundling the first demi-cannon through the lych-gate.

'"I reckon you'll find her middlin' heavy," he says. "If you've a mind to pay, I'll loan ye my timber-tug. She won't lie easy on ary wool-wain."

'That was the one time I ever saw Sebastian taken flat aback. He opened and shut his mouth, fishy-like.

'"No offence," says Master John. "You've got her reasonable good cheap. I thought ye might not grudge me a groat if I helped move her." Ah, he was a masterpiece! They say that morning's work cost our John two hundred pounds, and he never winked an eyelid, not even when he saw the guns all carted off to Lewes.'

'Neither then nor later?' said Puck.

'Once. 'Twas after he gave St. Barnabas' the new chime of bells. (Oh, there was nothing the Collinses, or the Hayes, or the Fowles, or the Fenners would not do for the church then! "Ask and have" was their song). We had rung 'em in, and he was in the tower with Black Nick Fowle, that gave us our rood-screen. The old man pinches the bell-rope one hand and scratches his neck with t'other. "Sooner she was pulling yon clapper than my neck," he says. That was all! That was Sussex—seely Sussex for everlastin'!'

'And what happened after?' said Una.

'I went back into England,' said Hal slowly. 'I'd had my lesson against pride. But they tell me I left St. Barnabas' a jewel—justabout a jewel! Wel-a-well! 'Twas done for and among my own people, and—Father Roger was right—I never knew such trouble or such triumph since. That's the nature o' things. A dear—dear land.' He dropped his chin on his chest.

'There's your Father at the Forge. What's he talking to old

Hobden about?' said Puck, opening his hand with three leaves in it.

Dan looked towards the cottage.

'Oh, I know. It's that old oak lying across the brook. Pater always wants it grubbed.'

In the still valley they could hear old Hobden's deep tones.

'Have it *as* you've a mind to,' he was saying. 'But the vivers of her roots they hold the bank together. If you grub her out, the bank she'll all come tearin' down, an' next floods the brook'll swarve up. But have it *as* you've a mind. The Mistuss she sets a heap by the ferns on her trunk.'

'Oh! I'll think it over,' said the Pater.

Una laughed a little bubbling chuckle.

'What's Devil's in *that* belfry?' said Hal, with a lazy laugh. 'That should be a Hobden by his voice.'

'Why, the oak is the regular bridge for all the rabbits between the Three Acre and our meadow. The best place for wires on the farm, Hobden says. He's got two there now,' Una answered. '*He* won't ever let it be grubbed!'

'Ah, Sussex! Seely Sussex for everlastin',' murmured Hal; and the next moment their Father's voice calling across to Little Lindens broke the spell as little St. Barnabas' clock struck five.

A SMUGGLERS' SONG

If you wake at midnight, and hear a horse's feet,
Don't go drawing back the blind, or looking in the street,
Them that asks no questions isn't told a lie.
Watch the wall, my darling, while the Gentlemen go by!

>   *Five-and-twenty ponies,*
>   *Trotting through the dark—*
>   *Brandy for the Parson,*
>   *'Baccy for the Clerk;*
>   *Laces for a lady; letters for a spy,*

And watch the wall, my darling, while the Gentlemen go by!

Running round the woodlump if you chance to find
Little barrels, roped and tarred, all full of brandy-wine;
Don't you shout to come and look, nor take 'em for your play!
Put the brishwood back again,—and they'll be gone next day!

If you see the stable-door setting open wide;
If you see a tired horse lying down inside;
If your mother mends a coat cut about and tore;
If the lining's wet and warm—don't you ask no more!

If you meet King George's men, dressed in blue and red,
You be careful what you say, and mindful what is said.
If they call you 'pretty maid,' and chuck you 'neath the chin,
Don't you tell where no one is, nor yet where no one's been!

PUCK OF POOK'S HILL

Knocks and footsteps round the house—whistles after dark—
You've no call for running out till the house-dogs bark.
Trusty's *here, and* Pincher's *here, and see how dumb they lie—*
They *don't fret to follow when the Gentlemen go by!*

If you do as you've been told, likely there's a chance
You'll be give a dainty doll, all the way from France,
With a cap of Valenciennes, and a velvet hood—
A present from the Gentlemen, along o' being good!

> *Five-and-twenty ponies,*
> *Trotting through the dark—*
> *Brandy for the Parson,*
> *'Baccy for the Clerk.*

Them that asks no questions isn't told a lie—
Watch the wall, my darling, while the Gentlemen go by!

'DYMCHURCH FLIT'

THE BEE BOY'S SONG

Bees! Bees! Hark to your bees!
'Hide from your neighbours as much as you please,
But all that has happened, to *us* you must tell,
Or else we will give you no honey to sell!'

> *A Maiden in her glory,*
> *Upon her wedding-day,*
> *Must tell her Bees the story,*
> *Or else they'll fly away.*
> *Fly away—die away—*
> *Dwindle down and leave you!*
> *But if you don't deceive your Bees,*
> *Your Bees will not deceive you.*

> *Marriage, birth or buryin',*
> *News across the seas,*
> *All you're sad or merry in,*
> *You must tell the Bees.*
> *Tell 'em coming in an' out,*
> *Where the Fanners fan,*
> *'Cause the Bees are justabout*
> *As curious as a man!*

> *Don't you wait where trees are,*
> *When the lightnings play;*
> *Nor don't you hate where Bees are,*
> *Or else they'll pine away.*

PUCK OF POOK'S HILL

Pine away—dwine away—
Anything to leave you!
But if you never grieve your Bees,
Your Bees'll never grieve you!

'DYMCHURCH FLIT'

JUST AT DUSK, a soft September rain began to fall on the hop-pickers. The mothers wheeled the bouncing perambulators out of the gardens; bins were put away, and tally-books made up. The young couples strolled home, two to each umbrella, and the single men walked behind them laughing. Dan and Una, who had been picking after their lessons, marched off to roast potatoes at the oast-house, where old Hobden, with Blue-eyed Bess, his lurcher dog, lived all the month through, drying the hops.

They settled themselves, as usual, on the sack-strewn cot in front of the fires, and, when Hobden drew up the shutter, stared, as usual, at the flameless bed of coals spouting its heat up the dark well of the old-fashioned roundel. Slowly he cracked off a few fresh pieces of coal, packed them, with fingers that never flinched, exactly where they would do most good; slowly he reached behind him till Dan tilted the potatoes into his iron scoop of a hand; carefully he arranged them round the fire, and then stood for a moment, black against the glare. As he closed the shutter, the oast-house seemed dark before the day's end, and he lit the candle in the lanthorn. The children liked all these things because they knew them so well.

The Bee Boy, Hobden's son, who is not quite right in his head, though he can do anything with bees, slipped in like a shadow. They only guessed it when Bess's stump-tail wagged against them.

A big voice began singing outside in the drizzle:—

*'Old Mother Laidinwool had nigh twelve months been dead,
She heard the hops were doin' well, and then popped up her
     head.'*

'There can't be two people made to holler like that!' cried
old Hobden, wheeling round.

*'For, says she, "The boys I've picked with when I was young
     and fair,
They're bound to be at hoppin', and I'm——" '*

A man showed at the doorway.

'Well, well! They do say hoppin' 'll draw the very deadest,
and now I belieft 'em. You, Tom? Tom Shoesmith?' Hobden
lowered his lanthorn.

'You're a hem of a time makin' your mind to it, Ralph!'
The stranger strode in—three full inches taller than Hobden,
a grey-whiskered, brown-faced giant with clear blue eyes. They
shook hands, and the children could hear the hard palms rasp
together.

'You ain't lost none o' your grip,' said Hobden. 'Was it thirty
or forty year back you broke my head at Peasmarsh Fair?'

'Only thirty, an' no odds 'tween us regardin' heads, neither.
You had it back at me with a hop-pole. How did we get home
that night? Swimmin'?'

'Same way the pheasant come into Gubbs's pocket—by a
little luck an' a deal o' conjurin'.' Old Hobden laughed in his
deep chest.

'I see you've not forgot your way about the woods. D'ye
do any o' *this* still?' The stranger pretended to look along
a gun.

Hobden answered with a quick movement of the hand as
though he were pegging down a rabbit-wire.

'No. *That*'s all that's left me now. Age she must as Age she can. An' what's your news since all these years?'

> '*Oh, I've bin to Plymouth, I've bin to Dover—*
> *I've bin ramblin', boys, the wide world over,*'

the man answered cheerily. 'I reckon I know as much of Old England as most.' He turned towards the children and winked boldly.

'I lay they told you a sight o' lies, then. I've been into England fur as Wiltsheer once. I was cheated proper over a pair of hedgin'-gloves,' said Hobden.

'There's fancy-talkin' everywhere. *You*'ve cleaved to your own parts pretty middlin' close, Ralph.'

'Can't shift an old tree 'thout it dyin',' Hobden chuckled. 'An' I be no more anxious to die than you look to be to help me with my hops to-night.'

The great man leaned against the brickwork of the roundel, and swung his arms abroad. 'Hire me!' was all he said, and they stumped upstairs laughing.

The children heard their shovels rasp on the cloth where the yellow hops lie drying above the fires, and all the oast-house filled with the sweet, sleepy smell as they were turned.

'Who is it?' Una whispered to the Bee Boy.

'Dunno, no more'n you—if *you* dunno,' said he, and smiled.

The voices on the drying-floor talked and chuckled together, and the heavy footsteps moved back and forth. Presently a hop-pocket dropped through the press-hole overhead, and stiffened and fattened as they shovelled it full. 'Clank!' went the press, and rammed the loose stuff into tight cake.

'Gentle!' they heard Hobden cry. 'You'll bust her crop if you lay on so. You be as careless as Gleason's bull, Tom. Come an' sit by the fires. She'll do now.'

They came down, and as Hobden opened the shutter to see if the potatoes were done Tom Shoesmith said to the children, 'Put a plenty salt on 'em. That'll show you the sort o' man *I* be.' Again he winked, and again the Bee Boy laughed and Una stared at Dan.

'*I* know what sort o' man you be,' old Hobden grunted, groping for the potatoes round the fire.

'Do ye?' Tom went on behind his back. 'Some of us can't abide Horseshoes, or Church Bells, or Running Water; an', talkin' o' runnin' water'—he turned to Hobden, who was backing out of the roundel—'d'you mind the great floods at Robertsbridge, when the miller's man was drowned in the street?'

'Middlin' well.' Old Hobden let himself down on the coals by the fire-door. 'I was courtin' my woman on the Marsh that year. Carter to Mus' Plum I was, gettin' ten shillin's week. Mine was a Marsh woman.'

'Won'erful odd-gates place—Romney Marsh,' said Tom Shoesmith. 'I've heard say the world's divided like into Europe, Ashy, Afriky, Ameriky, Australy, an' Romney Marsh.'

'The Marsh folk think so,' said Hobden. 'I had a hem o' trouble to get my woman to leave it.'

'Where did she come out of? I've forgot, Ralph.'

'Dymchurch under the Wall,' Hobden answered, a potato in his hand.

'Then she'd be a Pett—or a Whitgift, would she?'

'Whitgift.' Hobden broke open the potato and ate it with the curious neatness of men who make most of their meals in the blowy open. 'She growed to be quite reasonable-like after livin' in the Weald awhile, but our first twenty year or two she was odd-fashioned, no bounds. And she was a won'erful hand with bees.' He cut away a little piece of potato and threw it out to the door.

'Ah! I've heard say the Whitgifts could see further through a millstone than most,' said Shoesmith. 'Did she, now?'

'She was honest-innocent of any nigromancin',' said Hobden. 'Only she'd read signs and sinnifications out o' birds flyin', stars fallin', bees hivin', and such. An' she'd lie awake—listenin' for calls, she said.'

'That don't prove naught,' said Tom. 'All Marsh folk has been smugglers since time everlastin'. 'Twould be in her blood to listen out o' nights.'

'Nature-ally,' old Hobden replied, smiling. 'I mind when there was smugglin' a sight nearer us than what the Marsh be. But that wasn't my woman's trouble. 'Twas a passel o' no-sense talk'—he dropped his voice—'about Pharisees.'

'Yes. I've heard Marsh men belief in 'em.' Tom looked straight at the wide-eyed children beside Bess.

'Pharisees,' cried Una. 'Fairies? Oh, *I* see!'

'People o' the Hills,' said the Bee Boy, throwing half of his potato towards the door.

'There you be!' said Hobden, pointing at him. 'My boy he has her eyes and her out-gate senses. That's what *she* called 'em!'

'And what did you think of it all?'

'Um—um,' Hobden rumbled. 'A man that uses fields an' shaws after dark as much as I've done, he don't go out of his road excep' for keepers.'

'But settin' that aside?' said Tom coaxingly. 'I saw ye throw the Good Piece out-at-doors just now. Do ye believe or—*do* ye?'

'There was a great black eye to that tater,' said Hobden indignantly.

'My liddle eye didn't see un, then. It looked as if you meant it for—for Any One that might need it. But settin' that aside, d'ye believe or—*do* ye?'

'I ain't sayin' nothin', because I've heard naught, an' I've seen naught. But if you was to say there was more things after dark in the shaws than men, or fur, or feather, or fin, I dunno as I'd go far about to call you a liar. Now turnagain, Tom. What's your say?'

'I'm like you. I say nothin'. But I'll tell you a tale, an' you can fit it *as* how you please.'

'Passel o' no-sense stuff,' growled Hobden, but he filled his pipe.

'The Marsh men they call it Dymchurch Flit,' Tom went on slowly. 'Hap you have heard it?'

'My woman she've told it me scores o' times. Dunno as I didn't end by belieftin' it—sometimes.'

Hobden crossed over as he spoke, and sucked with his pipe at the yellow lanthorn flame. Tom rested one great elbow on one great knee, where he sat among the coal.

'Have you ever bin in the Marsh?' he said to Dan.

'Only as far as Rye, once,' Dan answered.

'Ah, that's but the edge. Back behind of her there's steeples settin' beside churches, an' wise women settin' beside their doors, an' the sea settin' above the land, an' ducks herdin' wild in the diks' (he meant ditches). 'The Marsh is justabout riddled with diks an' sluices, an' tide-gates an' water-lets. You can hear 'em bubblin' an' grummelin' when the tide works in 'em, an' then you hear the sea rangin' left an' right-handed all up along the Wall. You've seen how flat she is—the Marsh? You'd think nothin' easier than to walk eend-on acrost her? Ah, but the diks an' the water-lets, they twists the roads about as ravelly as witch-yarn on the spindles. So ye get all turned round in broad daylight.'

'That's because they've dreened the waters into the diks,'

said Hobden. 'When I courted my woman the rushes was green—Eh me! the rushes was green—an' the Bailiff o' the Marshes he rode up and down as free as the fog.'

'Who was he?' said Dan.

'Why, the Marsh fever an' ague. He've clapped me on the shoulder once or twice till I shook proper. But now the dreenin' off of the waters have done away with the fevers; so they make a joke, like, that the Bailiff o' the Marshes broke his neck in a dik. A won'erful place for bees an' ducks 'tis too.'

'An' old,' Tom went on. 'Flesh an' Blood have been there since Time Everlastin' Beyond. Well, now, speakin' among themselves, the Marsh men say that from Time Everlastin' Beyond, the Pharisees favoured the Marsh above the rest of Old England. I lay the Marsh men ought to know. They've been out after dark, father an' son, smugglin' some one thing or t'other, since ever wool grew to sheep's backs. They say there was always a middlin' few Pharisees to be seen on the Marsh. Impident as rabbits, they was. They'd dance on the nakid roads in the nakid daytime; they'd flash their liddle green lights along the diks, comin' an' goin', like honest smugglers. Yes, an' times they'd lock the church doors against parson an' clerk of Sundays.'

'That 'ud be smugglers layin' in the lace or the brandy till they could run it out o' the Marsh. I've told my woman so,' said Hobden.

'I'll lay she didn't belief it, then—not if she was a Whitgift. A won'erful choice place for Pharisees, the Marsh, by all accounts, till Queen Bess's father he come in with his Reformatories.'

'Would that be a Act of Parliament like?' Hobden asked.

'Sure-ly. Can't do nothing in Old England without Act,

Warrant, an' Summons. He got his Act allowed him, an', they say, Queen Bess's father he used the parish churches something shameful. Justabout tore the gizzards out of I dunnamany. Some folk in England they held with 'em; but some they saw it different, an' it eended in 'em takin' sides an' burnin' each other no bounds, accordin' which side was top, time bein'. That tarrified the Pharisees: for Good-will among Flesh an' Blood is meat an' drink to 'em, an' ill-will is poison.'

'Same as bees,' said the Bee Boy. 'Bees won't stay by a house where there's hating.'

'True,' said Tom. 'This Reformatories tarrified the Pharisees same as the reaper goin' round a last stand o' wheat tarrifies rabbits. They packed into the Marsh from all parts, and they says, "Fair or foul, we must flit out o' this, for Merry England's done with, an' we're reckoned among the Images." '

'Did they *all* see it that way?' said Hobden.

'All but one that was called Robin—if you've heard of him. What are you laughin' at?' Tom turned to Dan. 'The Pharisees's trouble didn't tech Robin, because he'd cleaved middlin' close to people, like. No more he never meant to go out of Old England—not he; so he was sent messagin' for help among Flesh an' Blood. But Flesh an' Blood must always think of their own concerns, an' Robin couldn't get *through* at 'em, ye see. They thought it was tide-echoes off the Marsh.'

'What did you—what did the fai—Pharisees want?' Una asked.

'A boat, to be sure. Their liddle wings could no more cross Channel than so many tired butterflies. A boat an' a crew they desired to sail 'em over to France, where yet awhile folks hadn't tore down the Images. They couldn't abide cruel Canterbury Bells ringin' to Bulverhithe for more pore men an' women to be burnded, nor the King's proud messenger ridin' through the land givin' orders to tear down the Images. They couldn't abide it no shape. Nor yet they couldn't get their boat an' crew to flit by without Leave an' Good-will from Flesh an' Blood; an' Flesh an' Blood came an' went about its own business the while the Marsh was swarvin' up, an' swarvin' up with Pharisees from all England over, strivin' all means to get *through* at Flesh an' Blood to tell 'em their sore need. . . . I don't know as you've ever heard say Pharisees are like chickens?'

'My woman used to say that too,' said Hobden, folding his brown arms.

'They be. You run too many chickens together, an' the ground sickens, like, an' you get a squat, an' your chickens die. Same way, you crowd Pharisees all in one place—*they* don't die, but Flesh an' Blood walkin' among 'em is apt to sick up an' pine off. *They* don't mean it, an' Flesh an' Blood don't know it, but that's the truth—as I've heard. The Pharisees through bein' all stenched up an' frighted, an' tryin' to come *through* with their supplications, they nature-ally changed the thin airs an' humours in Flesh an' Blood. It lay on the Marsh like thunder. Men saw their churches ablaze with the wildfire in the windows after dark; they saw their cattle scatterin' an' no man scarin'; their sheep flockin' an' no man drivin'; their horses latherin' an' no man leadin'; they saw the liddle low green lights more than ever in the dik-sides; they heard the liddle feet patterin' more than ever round the houses; an' night an' day, day an' night, 'twas all as though they were bein' creeped up on, an' hinted at by Some One or other that couldn't rightly shape their trouble. Oh, I lay they sweated! Man an' maid, woman an' child, their nature done 'em no service all the weeks while the Marsh was swarvin' up with Pharisees. But they was Flesh an' Blood, an' Marsh men before all. They reckoned the signs sinnified trouble for the Marsh. Or that the sea 'ud rear up against Dymchurch Wall an' they'd be drowned like Old Winchelsea; or that the Plague was comin'. So they looked for the meanin' in the sea or in the clouds—far an' high up. They never thought to look near an' knee-high, where they could see naught.

'Now there was a poor widow at Dymchurch under the Wall, which, lacking man or property, she had the more time for feeling; and she come to feel there was a Trouble outside her doorstep bigger an' heavier than aught she'd ever carried over it. She had two sons—one born blind, an' t'other struck dumb through fallin' off the Wall when he was liddle. They was men grown, but not wage-earnin', an' she worked for 'em, keepin' bees and answerin' Questions.'

'What sort of questions?' said Dan.

'Like where lost things might be found, an' what to put about a crooked baby's neck, an' how to join parted sweethearts. She felt the Trouble on the Marsh same as eels feel thunder. She was a wise woman.'

'My woman was won'erful weather-tender, too,' said Hobden. 'I've seen her brish sparks like off an anvil out of her hair in thunderstorms. But she never laid out to answer Questions.'

'This woman was a Seeker, like, an' Seekers they sometimes find. One night, while she lay abed, hot an' achin', there come a Dream an' tapped at her window, an' "Widow Whitgift," it said, "Widow Whitgift!"

'First, by the wings an' the whistlin', she thought it was peewits, but last she arose an' dressed herself, an' opened her door to the Marsh, an' she felt the Trouble an' the Groanin' all about her, strong as fever an' ague, an' she calls: "What is it? Oh, what is it?"

'Then 'twas all like the frogs in the diks peepin': then 'twas all like the reeds in the diks clip-clappin'; an' then the great Tide-wave rummelled along the Wall, an' she couldn't hear proper.

'Three times she called, an' three times the Tide-wave did her down. But she catched the quiet between, an' she cries out: "What is the Trouble on the Marsh that's been lying down with my heart an' arising with my body this month gone?" She felt a liddle hand lay hold on her gown-hem, an' she stooped to the pull o' that liddle hand.'

Tom Shoesmith spread his huge fist before the fire and smiled at it as he went on.

' "Will the sea drown the Marsh?" she says. She was a Marsh woman first an' foremost.

' "No," says the liddle voice. "Sleep sound for all o' that."

' "Is the Plague comin' to the Marsh?" she says. Them was all the ills she knowed.

' "No. Sleep sound for all o' that," says Robin.

'She turned about, half mindful to go in, but the liddle voices grieved that shrill an' sorrowful she turns back, an' she cries: "If it is not a Trouble of Flesh an' Blood, what can I do?"

'The Pharisees cried out upon her from all round to fetch them a boat to sail to France, an' come back no more.

' "There's a boat on the Wall," she says, "but I can't push it down to the sea, nor sail it when 'tis there."

' "Lend us your sons," says all the Pharisees. "Give 'em Leave an' Good-will to sail it for us, Mother—O Mother!"

' "One's dumb, an' t'other's blind," she says. "But all the dearer me for that; and you'll lose them in the big sea." The voices justabout pierced through her; an' there was childern's voices too. She stood out all she could, but she couldn't rightly stand against *that*. So she says: "If you can draw my sons for your job, I'll not hinder 'em. You can't ask no more of a Mother."

'She saw them liddle green lights dance an' cross till she was dizzy; she heard them liddle feet patterin' by the thousand; she heard cruel Canterbury Bells ringing to Bulverhithe, an' she heard the great Tide-wave ranging along the Wall. That was while the Pharisees was workin' a Dream to wake her two sons asleep: an' while she bit on her fingers she saw them two she'd bore come out an' pass her with never a word. She followed 'em, cryin' pitiful, to the old boat on the Wall, an' that they took an' runned down to the sea.

'When they'd stepped mast an' sail the blind son speaks: "Mother, we're waitin' your Leave an' Good-will to take Them over." '

Tom Shoesmith threw back his head and half shut his eyes.

'Eh, me!' he said. 'She was a fine, valiant woman, the Widow Whitgift. She stood twistin' the eends of her long hair over her fingers, an' she shook like a poplar, makin' up her mind. The Pharisees all about they hushed their childern from cryin' an' they waited dumb-still. She was all their dependence. 'Thout her Leave an' Good-will they could not pass; for she was the Mother. So she shook like a aps-tree makin' up her mind. 'Last she drives the word past her teeth, an' "Go!" she says. "Go with my Leave an' Good-will."

'Then I saw—then, they say, she had to brace back same as if she was wadin' in tide-water; for the Pharisees just about flowed past her—down the beach to the boat, *I* dunnamany of 'em—with their wives an' childern an' valooables, all escapin' out of cruel Old England. Silver you could hear clinkin', an' liddle bundles hove down dunt on the bottom-boards, an' passels o' liddle swords an' shields raklin', an' liddle fingers an' toes scratchin' on the boatside to board her when the two sons

pushed her off. That boat she sunk lower an' lower, but all the
Widow could see in it was her boys movin' hampered-like to
get at the tackle. Up sail they did, an' away they went, deep as
a Rye barge; away into the off-shore mistës, an' the Widow
Whitgift she sat down an' eased her grief till mornin' light.'

'I never heard she was *all* alone,' said Hobden.

'I remember now. The one called Robin he stayed with her,
they tell. She was all too grievious to listen to his promises.'

'Ah! She should ha' made her bargain beforehand. I allus
told my woman so!' Hobden cried.

'No. She loaned her sons for a pure love-loan, bein' as she
sensed the Trouble on the Marshes, an' was simple good-willin'
to ease it.' Tom laughed softly. 'She done that. Yes, she done
that! From Hithe to Bulverhithe, fretty man an' maid, ailin'
woman an' wailin' child, they took the advantage of the
change in the thin airs just about *as* soon as the Pharisees
flitted. Folks come out fresh an' shinin' all over the Marsh like
snails after wet. An' that while the Widow Whitgift sat grievin'
on the Wall. She might have belieft us—she might have trusted
her sons would be sent back! She fussed, no bounds, when their
boat come in after three days.'

'And, of course, the sons were both quite cured?' said Una.

'No-o. That would have been out o' nature. She got 'em
back *as* she sent 'em. The blind man he hadn't seen naught of
anythin', an' the dumb man nature-ally he couldn't say aught
of what he'd seen. I reckon that was why the Pharisees pitched
on 'em for the ferryin' job.'

'But what did you—what did Robin promise the Widow?'
said Dan.

'What *did* he promise, now?' Tom pretended to think.
'Wasn't your woman a Whitgift, Ralph? Didn't she ever say?'

'She told me a passel o' no-sense stuff when he was born.'

Hobden pointed at his son. 'There was always to be one of 'em that could see further into a millstone than most.'

'Me! That's me!' said the Bee Boy so suddenly that they all laughed.

'I've got it now!' cried Tom, slapping his knee. 'So long as Whitgift blood lasted, Robin promised there would allers be one o' her stock that—that no Trouble 'ud lie on, no Maid 'ud sigh on, no Night could frighten, no Fright could harm, no Harm could make sin, an' no Woman could make a fool of.'

'Well, ain't that just me?' said the Bee Boy, where he sat in the silver square of the great September moon that was staring into the oast-house door.

'They was the exact words she told me when we first found he wasn't like others. But it beats me how you known 'em,' said Hobden.

'Aha! There's more under my hat besides hair!' Tom laughed and stretched himself. 'When I've seen these two young folk home, we'll make a night of old days, Ralph, with passin' old tales—eh? An' where might you live?' he said, gravely, to Dan. 'An' do you think your Pa 'ud give me a drink for takin' you there, Missy?'

They giggled so at this that they had to run out. Tom picked them both up, set one on each broad shoulder, and tramped across the ferny pasture where the cows puffed milky puffs at them in the moonlight.

'Oh, Puck! Puck! I guessed you right from when you talked about the salt. How could you ever do it?' Una cried, swinging along delighted.

'Do what?' he said, and climbed the stile by the pollard oak.

'Pretend to be Tom Shoesmith,' said Dan, and they ducked to avoid the two little ashes that grow by the bridge over the brook. Tom was almost running.

'Yes. That's my name, Mus' Dan,' he said, hurrying over the silent shining lawn, where a rabbit sat by the big white-thorn near the croquet ground. 'Here you be.' He strode into the old kitchen yard, and slid them down as Ellen came to ask questions.

'I'm helping in Mus' Spray's oast-house,' he said to her. 'No, I'm no foreigner. I knowed this country 'fore your mother was born; an'—yes, it's dry work oastin', Miss. Thank you.'

Ellen went to get a jug, and the children went in—magicked once more by Oak, Ash, and Thorn!

A THREE-PART SONG

I'm just in love with all these three,
The Weald an' the Marsh an' the Down countrie;
Nor I don't know which I love the most,
The Weald or the Marsh or the white chalk coast!

I've buried my heart in a ferny hill,
Twix' a liddle low shaw an' a great high gill.
Oh, hop-bine yaller an' wood-smoke blue,
I reckon you'll keep her middling true!

I've loosed my mind for to out an' run
On a Marsh that was old when Kings begun:
Oh, Romney level an' Brenzett reeds,
I reckon you know what my mind needs!

I've given my soul to the Southdown grass,
An' sheep-bells tinkled where you pass.
Oh, Firle an' Ditchling an' sails at sea,
I reckon you keep my soul for me!

THE TREASURE AND THE LAW

SONG OF THE FIFTH RIVER

When first by Eden Tree
The Four Great Rivers ran,
To each was appointed a Man
Her Prince and Ruler to be.

But after this was ordained,
(The ancient legends tell),
There came dark Israel,
For whom no River remained.

Then He That is Wholly Just
Said to him: 'Fling on the ground
A handful of yellow dust,
And a Fifth Great River shall run,
Mightier than these Four,
In secret the Earth around;
And Her secret evermore
Shall be shown to thee and thy Race.'

So it was said and done.
And, deep in the veins of Earth,
And, fed by a thousand springs
That comfort the market-place,
Or sap the power of Kings,
The Fifth Great River had birth,
Even as it was foretold—
The Secret River of Gold!

And Israel laid down
His sceptre and his crown,
To brood on that River bank,
Where the waters flashed and sank,
And burrowed in earth and fell,
And bided a season below;
For reason that none might know,
Save only Israel.

He is Lord of the Last—
The Fifth, most wonderful, Flood.
He hears Her thunder past
And Her song is in his blood.
He can foresay: 'She will fall,'
For he knows which fountain dries
Behind which desert-belt
A thousand leagues to the South.
He can foresay: 'She will rise.'
He knows what far snows melt
Along what mountain-wall
A thousand leagues to the North.
He snuffs the coming drouth
As he snuffs the coming rain,
He knows what each will bring forth,
And turns it to his gain.

A Prince without a Sword,
A Ruler without a Throne;
Israel follows his quest.
In every land a guest,
Of many lands a lord,
In no land King is he.

SONG OF THE FIFTH RIVER

But the Fifth Great River keeps
The secret of Her deeps
For Israel alone,
As it was ordered to be.

THE TREASURE AND THE LAW

NOW IT WAS THE THIRD WEEK in November, and the woods rang with the noise of pheasant-shooting. No one hunted that steep, cramped country except the village beagles, who, as often as not, escaped from their kennels and made a day of their own. Dan and Una found a couple of them towling round the kitchen-garden after the laundry cat. The little brutes were only too pleased to go rabbiting, so the children ran them all along the brook pastures and into Little Lindens farm-yard, where the old sow vanquished them—and up to the quarry-hole, where they started a fox. He headed for Far Wood, and there they frightened out all the pheasants, who were sheltering from a big beat across the valley. Then the cruel guns began again, and they grabbed the beagles lest they should stray and get hurt.

'I wouldn't be a pheasant—in November—for a lot,' Dan panted, as he caught Folly by the neck. 'Why did you laugh that horrid way?'

'I didn't,' said Una, sitting on Flora, the fat lady-dog. 'Oh, look! The silly birds are going back to their own woods instead of ours, where they would be safe.'

'Safe till it pleased you to kill them.' An old man, so tall he was almost a giant, stepped from behind the clump of hollies by Volaterrae. The children jumped, and the dogs dropped like setters. He wore a sweeping gown of dark thick stuff, lined and edged with yellowish fur, and he bowed a bent-down bow that made them feel both proud and ashamed.

Then he looked at them steadily, and they stared back without doubt or fear.

'You are not afraid?' he said, running his hands through his splendid grey beard. 'Not afraid that those men yonder'—he jerked his head towards the incessant pop-pop of the guns from the lower woods—'will do you hurt?'

'We-ell'—Dan liked to be accurate, especially when he was shy—'old Hobd—a friend of mine told me that one of the beaters got peppered last week—hit in the leg, I mean. You see, Mr. Meyer *will* fire at rabbits. But he gave Waxy Garnett a quid—sovereign, I mean—and Waxy told Hobden he'd have stood both barrels for half the money.'

'He doesn't understand,' Una cried, watching the pale, troubled face. 'Oh, I wish——'

She had scarcely said it when Puck rustled out of the hollies and spoke to the man quickly in foreign words. Puck wore a long cloak too—the afternoon was just frosting down—and it changed his appearance altogether.

'Nay, nay!' he said at last. 'You did not understand the boy. A freeman was a little hurt, by pure mischance, at the hunting.'

'I know that mischance! What did his lord do? Laugh and ride over him?' the old man sneered.

'It was one of your own people did the hurt, Kadmiel.' Puck's eyes twinkled maliciously. 'So he gave the freeman a piece of gold, and no more was said.'

'A Jew drew blood from a Christian and no more was said?' Kadmiel cried. 'Never! When did they torture him?'

'No man may be bound, or fined, or slain till he has been judged by his peers,' Puck insisted. 'There is but one Law in Old England for Jew or Christian—the Law that was signed at Runnymede.'

'Why, that's Magna Charta!' Dan whispered. It was one of

the few history dates that he could remember. Kadmiel turned
on him with a sweep and a whirr of his spicy-scented gown.

'Dost *thou* know of that, babe?' he cried, and lifted his
hands in wonder.

'Yes,' said Dan firmly.

> *'Magna Charta was signed by John,*
> *That Henry the Third put his heel upon.*

And old Hobden says that if it hadn't been for *her* (he calls
everything "her," you know), the keepers would have him
clapped in Lewes Jail all the year round.'

Again Puck translated to Kadmiel in the strange, solemn-
sounding language, and at last Kadmiel laughed.

'Out of the mouths of babes do we learn,' said he. 'But tell
me now, and I will not call you a babe but a Rabbi, *why* did
the King sign the roll of the New Law at Runnymede? For he
was a King.'

Dan looked sideways at his sister. It was her turn.

'Because he jolly well had to,' said Una softly. 'The Barons
made him.'

'Nay,' Kadmiel answered, shaking his head. 'You Christians
always forget that gold does more than the sword. Our good
King signed because he could not borrow more money from
us bad Jews.' He curved his shoulders as he spoke. 'A King
without gold is a snake with a broken back, and'—his nose
sneered up and his eyebrows frowned down—'it is a good deed
to break a snake's back. That was my work,' he cried, triumphantly, to Puck. 'Spirit of Earth, bear witness that that was *my*
work!' He shot up to his full towering height, and his words
rang like a trumpet. He had a voice that changed its tone
almost as an opal changes colour—sometimes deep and thun-

dery, sometimes thin and waily, but always it made you listen.

'Many people can bear witness to that,' Puck answered. 'Tell these babes how it was done. Remember, Master, they do not know Doubt or Fear.'

'So I saw in their faces when we met,' said Kadmiel. 'Yet surely, surely they are taught to spit upon Jews?'

'Are they?' said Dan, much interested. 'Where at?'

Puck fell back a pace, laughing. 'Kadmiel is thinking of King John's reign,' he explained. 'His people were badly treated then.'

'Oh, we know *that*,' they answered, and (it was very rude of them, but they could not help it) they stared straight at Kadmiel's mouth to see if his teeth were all there. It stuck in their lesson-memory that King John used to pull out Jews' teeth to make them lend him money.

Kadmiel understood the look and smiled bitterly.

'No. Your King never drew my teeth: I think, perhaps, I drew his. Listen! I was not born among Christians, but among Moors—in Spain—in a little white town under the mountains. Yes, the Moors are cruel, but at least their learned men dare to think. It was prophesied of me at my birth that I should be a Lawgiver to a People of a strange speech and a hard language. We Jews are always looking for the Prince and the Lawgiver to come. Why not? My people in the town (we were very few) set me apart as a child of the prophecy— the Chosen of the Chosen. We Jews dream so many dreams. You would never guess it to see us slink about the rubbish-heaps in our quarter; but at the day's end—doors shut, candles lit—aha! *then* we become the Chosen again.'

He paced back and forth through the wood as he talked. The rattle of the shot-guns never ceased, and the dogs whimpered a little and lay flat on the leaves.

'I was a Prince. Yes! Think of a little Prince who had never

known rough words in his own house handed over to shouting, bearded Rabbis, who pulled his ears and filliped his nose,
all that he might learn—learn—learn to be King when his
time came. Hé! Such a little Prince it was! One eye he kept on
the stone-throwing Moorish boys, and the other it roved about
the streets looking for his Kingdom. Yes, and he learned to
cry softly when he was hunted up and down those streets. He
learned to do all things without noise. He played beneath his
father's table when the Great Candle was lit, and he listened
as children listen to the talk of his father's friends above the
table. They came across the mountains, from out of all the
world, for my Prince's father was their counsellor. They came
from behind the armies of Sala-ud-Din: from Rome: from
Venice: from England. They stole down our alley, they tapped
secretly at our door, they took off their rags, they arrayed
themselves, and they talked to my father at the wine. All over
the world the heathen fought each other. They brought news
of these wars, and while he played beneath the table, my
Prince heard these meanly-dressed ones decide between themselves how, and when, and for how long King should draw
sword against King, and People rise up against People. Why
not? There can be no war without gold, and we Jews know
how the earth's gold moves with the seasons, and the crops,
and the winds; circling and looping and rising and sinking
away like a river—a wonderful underground river. How
should the foolish Kings know *that* while they fight and steal
and kill?'

The children's faces showed that they knew nothing at all
as, with open eyes, they trotted and turned beside the long-
striding old man. He twitched his gown over his shoulders,
and a square plate of gold, studded with jewels, gleamed for
an instant through the fur, like a star through flying snow.

'No matter,' he said. 'But, credit me, my Prince saw peace

or war decided not once, but many times, by the fall of a
coin spun between a Jew from Bury and a Jewess from Alex-
andria, in his father's house, when the Great Candle was lit.
Such power had we Jews among the Gentiles. Ah, my little
Prince! Do you wonder that he learned quickly? Why not?'
He muttered to himself and went on:—

'My trade was that of a physician. When I had learned it
in Spain I went to the East to find my Kingdom. Why not?
A Jew is as free as a sparrow—or a dog. He goes where he is
hunted. In the East I found libraries where men dared to
think—schools of medicine where they dared to learn. I was
diligent in my business. Therefore I stood before Kings. I
have been a brother to Princes and a companion to beggars,
and I have walked between the living and the dead. There
was no profit in it. I did not find my Kingdom. So, in the tenth
year of my travels, when I had reached the Uttermost Eastern
Sea, I returned to my father's house. God had wonderfully
preserved my people. None had been slain, none even
wounded, and only a few scourged. I became once more a
son of my father's house. Again the Great Candle was lit;
again the meanly-apparelled ones tapped on our door after
dusk; and again I heard them weigh out peace and war, as
they weighed out the gold on the table. But I was not rich—
not very rich. Therefore, when those that had power and
knowledge and wealth talked together, I sat in the shadow.
Why not?

'Yet all my wanderings had shown me one sure thing, which
is, that a King without money is like a spear without a head.
He cannot do much harm. I said, therefore, to Elias of Bury,
a great one among our people: "Why do our people lend any
more to the Kings that oppress us?" "Because," said Elias, "if
we refuse they stir up their people against us, and the People

are tenfold more cruel than Kings. If thou doubtest, come with me to Bury in England and live as I live."

'I saw my mother's face across the candle-flame, and I said, "I will come with thee to Bury. Maybe my Kingdom shall be there."

'So I sailed with Elias to the darkness and the cruelty of Bury in England, where there are no learned men. How can a man be wise if he hate? At Bury I kept his accounts for Elias, and I saw men kill Jews there by the tower. No—none laid hands on Elias. He lent money to the King, and the King's favour was about him. A King will not take the life so long as there is any gold. This King—yes, John—oppressed his people bitterly because they would not give him money. Yet his land was a good land. If he had only given it rest he might have cropped it as a Christian crops his beard. But even *that* little he did not know, for God had deprived him of all understanding, and had multiplied pestilence, and famine, and despair upon the people. Therefore his people turned against us Jews, who are all people's dogs. Why not? Lastly the Barons and the people rose together against the King because of his cruelties. Nay—nay—the Barons did not love the people, but they saw that if the King cut up and destroyed the common people, he would presently destroy the Barons. They joined then, as cats and pigs will join to slay a snake. I kept the accounts, and I watched all these things, for I remembered the Prophecy.

'A great gathering of Barons (to most of whom we had lent money) came to Bury, and there, after much talk and a thousand runnings-about, they made a roll of the New Laws that they would force on the King. If he swore to keep those Laws, they would allow him a little money. That was the King's God—Money—to waste. They showed us the roll of the New

Laws. Why not? We had lent them money. We knew all their counsels—we Jews shivering behind our doors in Bury.' He threw out his hands suddenly. 'We did not seek to be paid *all* in money. We sought Power—Power—Power! That is *our* God in our captivity. Power to use!

'I said to Elias: "These New Laws are good. Lend no more money to the King: so long as he has money he will lie and slay the people."

' "Nay," said Elias. "I know this people. They are madly cruel. Better one King than a thousand butchers. I have lent a little money to the Barons, or they would torture us, but my most I will lend to the King. He hath promised me a place near him at Court, where my wife and I shall be safe."

' "But if the King be made to keep these New Laws," I said, "the land will have peace, and our trade will grow. If we lend he will fight again."

' "Who made thee a Lawgiver in England?" said Elias. "*I* know this people. Let the dogs tear one another! I will lend the King ten thousand pieces of gold, and he can fight the Barons at his pleasure."

' "There are not two thousand pieces of gold in all England this summer," I said, for I kept the accounts, and I knew how the earth's gold moved—that wonderful underground river. Elias barred home the windows, and, his hands about his mouth, he told me how, when he was trading with small wares in a French ship, he had come to the Castle of Pevensey.'

'Oh!' said Dan. 'Pevensey again!' and looked at Una, who nodded and skipped.

'There, after they had scattered his pack up and down the Great Hall, some young knights carried him to an upper room, and dropped him into a well in a wall, that rose and fell with the tide. They called him Joseph, and threw torches at his wet head. Why not?'

'Why, of course!' cried Dan. 'Didn't you know it was——'
Puck held up his hand to stop him, and Kadmiel, who never
noticed, went on.

'When the tide dropped he thought he stood on old armour,
but feeling with his toes, he raked up bar on bar of soft gold.
Some wicked treasure of the old days put away, and the secret
cut off by the sword. I have heard the like before.'

'So have we,' Una whispered. 'But it wasn't wicked a bit.'

'Elias took a little of the stuff with him, and thrice yearly
he would return to Pevensey as a chapman, selling at no price
or profit, till they suffered him to sleep in the empty room,
where he would plumb and grope, and steal away a few bars.
The great store of it still remained, and by long brooding he
had come to look on it as his own. Yet when we thought how
we should lift and convey it, we saw no way. This was before
the Word of the Lord had come to me. A walled fortress possessed by Normans; in the midst a forty-foot tide-well out of
which to remove secretly many horse-loads of gold! Hopeless!
So Elias wept. Adah, his wife, wept too. She had hoped to
stand beside the Queen's Christian tiring-maids at Court, when
the King should give them that place at Court which he had
promised. Why not? She was born in England—an odious
woman.

'The present evil to us was that Elias, out of his strong
folly, had, as it were, promised the King that he would arm
him with more gold. Wherefore the King in his camp stopped
his ears against the Barons and the people. Wherefore men
died daily. Adah so desired her place at Court, she besought
Elias to tell the King where the treasure lay, that the King
might take it by force, and—they would trust to his gratitude.
Why not? This Elias refused to do, for he looked on the gold
as his own. They quarrelled, and they wept at the evening
meal, and late in the night came one Langton—a priest, al-

most learned—to borrow more money for the Barons. Elias
and Adah went to their chamber.'

Kadmiel laughed scornfully in his beard. The shots across
the valley stopped as the shooting party changed their ground
for the last beat.

'So it was I, not Elias,' he went on quietly, 'that made terms
with Langton touching the fortieth of the New Laws.'

'What terms?' said Puck quickly. 'The Fortieth of the Great
Charter says: "To none will we sell, refuse, or delay right or
justice." '

'True, but the Barons had written first: *To no free man*. It
cost me two hundred broad pieces of gold to change those
narrow words. Langton, the priest, understood. "Jew though
thou art," said he, "the change is just, and if ever Christian
and Jew come to be equal in England thy people may thank
thee." Then he went out stealthily, as men do who deal with
Israel by night. I think he spent my gift upon his altar. Why
not? I have spoken with Langton. He was such a man as I
might have been if—if we Jews had been a people. But yet,
in many things, a child.

'I heard Elias and Adah abovestairs quarrel, and, knowing
the woman was the stronger, I saw that Elias would tell the
King of the gold and that the King would continue in his
stubbornness. Therefore I saw that the gold must be put away
from the reach of any man. Of a sudden, the Word of the
Lord came to me saying: "The Morning is come, O thou that
dwellest in the land." '

Kadmiel halted, all black against the pale green sky beyond
the wood—a huge robed figure, like the Moses in the picture-
Bible.

'I rose. I went out, and as I shut the door on that House
of Foolishness, the woman looked from the window and whis-

pered: "I have prevailed on my husband to tell the King!"
I answered: "There is no need. The Lord is with me."

'In that hour the Lord gave me full understanding of all
that I must do; and His Hand covered me in my ways. First
I went to London, to a physician of our people, who sold me
certain drugs that I needed. You shall see why. Thence I went
swiftly to Pevensey. Men fought all around me, for there were
neither rulers nor judges in the abominable land. Yet when
I walked by them they cried out that I was one Ahasuerus,
a Jew, condemned, as they believe, to live for ever, and they
fled from me everyways. Thus the Lord saved me for my work,
and at Pevensey I bought me a little boat and moored it on
the mud beneath the Marsh-gate of the Castle. That also God
showed me.'

He was as calm as though he were speaking of some stranger,
and his voice filled the little bare wood with rolling music.

'I cast'—his hand went to his breast, and again the strange
jewel gleamed—'I cast the drugs which I had prepared into
the common well of the Castle. Nay, I did no harm. The more
we physicians know, the less do we do. Only the fool says:
"I dare." I caused a blotched and itching rash to break out
upon their skins, but I knew it would fade in fifteen days. I
did not stretch out my hand against their life. They in the
Castle thought it was the Plague, and they ran out, taking
with them their very dogs.

'A Christian physician, seeing that I was a Jew and a
stranger, vowed that I had brought the sickness from London.
This is the one time I have ever heard a Christian leech speak
truth of any disease. Thereupon the people beat me, but a
merciful woman said: "Do not kill him now. Push him into
our Castle with his Plague, and if, as he says, it will abate on
the fifteenth day, we can kill him then." Why not? They

drove me across the drawbridge of the Castle, and fled back to
their booths. Thus I came to be alone with the treasure.'

'But did you know this was all going to happen just right?'
said Una.

'My Prophecy was that I should be a Lawgiver to a People
of a strange land and a hard speech. I knew I should not die.
I washed my cuts. I found the tide-well in the wall, and from
Sabbath to Sabbath I dove and dug there in that empty, Chris-
tian-smelling fortress. Hé! I spoiled the Egyptians! Hé! If they
had only known! I drew up many good loads of gold, which
I loaded by night into my boat. There had been gold-dust too,
but that had been washed out by the tides.'

'Didn't you ever wonder who had put it there?' said Dan,
stealing a glance at Puck's calm, dark face under the hood of
his gown. Puck shook his head and pursed his lips.

'Often; for the gold was new to me,' Kadmiel replied. 'I
know the Golds. I can judge them in the dark; but this was
heavier and redder than any we deal in. Perhaps it was the
very gold of Parvaim. Eh, why not? It went to my heart to
heave it on to the mud, but I saw well that if the evil thing
remained, or if even the hope of finding it remained, the King
would not sign the New Laws, and the land would perish.'

'Oh, Marvel!' said Puck, beneath his breath, rustling in
the dead leaves.

'When the boat was loaded I washed my hands seven times,
and pared beneath my nails, for I would not keep one grain.
I went out by the little gate where the Castle's refuse is thrown.
I dared not hoist sail lest men should see me; but the Lord
commanded the tide to bear me carefully, and I was far from
land before the morning.'

'Weren't you afraid?' said Una.

'Why? There were no Christians in the boat. At sunrise I

made my prayer, and cast the gold—all—all that gold into the deep sea! A King's ransom—no, the ransom of a People! When I had loosed hold of the last bar, the Lord commanded the tide to return me to a haven at the mouth of a river, and thence I walked across a wilderness to Lewes, where I have brethren. They opened the door to me, and they say—I had not eaten for two days—they say that I fell across the threshold, crying: "I have sunk an army with horsemen in the sea!" '

'But you hadn't,' said Una. 'Oh, yes! I see! You meant that King John might have spent it on that?'

'Even so,' said Kadmiel.

The firing broke out again close behind them. The pheasants poured over the top of a belt of tall firs. They could see young Mr. Meyer, in his new yellow gaiters, very busy and excited at the end of the line, and they could hear the thud of the falling birds.

'But what did Elias of Bury do?' Puck demanded. 'He had promised money to the King.'

Kadmiel smiled grimly. 'I sent him word from London that the Lord was on my side. When he heard that the Plague had broken out in Pevensey, and that a Jew had been thrust into the Castle to cure it, he understood my word was true. He and Adah hurried to Lewes and asked me for an accounting. He still looked on the gold as his own. I told them where I had laid it, and I gave them full leave to pick it up. . . . Eh, well! The curses of a fool and the dust of a journey are two things no wise man can escape. . . . But I pitied Elias! The King was wroth with him because he could not lend; the Barons were wroth too because they heard that he would have lent to the King; and Adah was wroth with him because she was an odious woman. They took ship from Lewes to Spain. That was wise!'

'And you? Did you see the signing of the Law at Runny-mede?' said Puck, as Kadmiel laughed noiselessly.

'Nay. Who am I to meddle with things too high for me? I returned to Bury, and lent money on the autumn crops. Why not?'

There was a crackle overhead. A cock-pheasant that had sheered aside after being hit spattered down almost on top of them, driving up the dry leaves like a shell. Flora and Folly threw themselves at it; the children rushed forward, and when they had beaten them off and smoothed down the plumage Kadmiel had disappeared.

'Well,' said Puck calmly, 'what did you think of it? Weland gave the Sword! The Sword gave the Treasure, and the Treasure gave the Law. It's as natural as an oak growing.'

'I don't understand. Didn't he know it was Sir Richard's old treasure?' said Dan. 'And why did Sir Richard and Brother Hugh leave it lying about? And—and——'

'Never mind,' said Una politely. 'He'll let us come and go and look and know another time. Won't you, Puck?'

'Another time maybe,' Puck answered. 'Brr! It's cold—and late. I'll race you towards home!'

They hurried down into the sheltered valley. The sun had almost sunk behind Cherry Clack, the trodden ground by the cattle-gates was freezing at the edges, and the new-waked north wind blew the night on them from over the hills. They picked up their feet and flew across the browned pastures, and when they halted, panting in the steam of their own breath, the dead leaves whirled up behind them. There was Oak and Ash and Thorn enough in that year-end shower to magic away a thousand memories.

So they trotted to the brook at the bottom of the lawn, wondering why Flora and Folly had missed the quarry-hole fox.

Old Hobden was just finishing some hedge-work. They saw his white smock glimmer in the twilight where he faggoted the rubbish.

'Winter, he's come, I reckon, Mus' Dan,' he called. 'Hard times now till Heffle Cuckoo Fair. Yes, we'll all be glad to see the Old Woman let the Cuckoo out o' the basket for to start lawful Spring in England.'

They heard a crash, and a stamp and a splash of water as though a heavy old cow were crossing almost under their noses.

Hobden ran forward angrily to the ford.

'Gleason's bull again, playin' Robin all over the Farm! Oh, look, Mus' Dan—his great footmark as big as a trencher. No bounds to his impidence! He might count himself to be a man or—or Somebody——'

A voice the other side of the brook boomed:—

> *'I wonder who his cloak would turn*
> *When Puck had led him round,*
> *Or where those walking fires would burn——'*

Then the children went in singing 'Farewell, Rewards and Fairies' at the tops of their voices. They had forgotten that they had not even said good-night to Puck.

THE CHILDREN'S SONG

Land of our Birth, we pledge to thee
Our love and toil in the years to be;
When we are grown and take our place
As men and women with our race.

Father in Heaven Who lovest all,
Oh, help Thy children when they call;
That they may build from age to age
An undefilèd heritage.

Teach us to bear the yoke in youth,
With steadfastness and careful truth;
That, in our time, Thy Grace may give
The Truth whereby the Nations live.

Teach us to rule ourselves alway,
Controlled and cleanly night and day;
That we may bring, if need arise,
No maimed or worthless sacrifice.

Teach us to look in all our ends,
On Thee for judge, and not our friends;
That we, with Thee, may walk uncowed
By fear or favour of the crowd.

Teach us the Strength that cannot seek,
By deed or thought, to hurt the weak;
That, under Thee, we may possess
Man's strength to comfort man's distress.

PUCK OF POOK'S HILL

Teach us Delight in simple things,
And Mirth that has no bitter springs;
Forgiveness free of evil done,
And Love to all men 'neath the sun!

Land of our Birth, our faith, our pride,
For whose dear sake our fathers died;
O Motherland, we pledge to thee
Head, heart, and hand through the years to be!

REWARDS AND FAIRIES

CONTENTS

REWARDS AND FAIRIES

Rewards and Fairies was first published in 1910

A CHARM

Take of English earth as much
As either hand may rightly clutch.
In the taking of it breathe
Prayer for all who lie beneath—
Not the great nor well-bespoke,
But the mere uncounted folk
Of whose life and death is none
Report or lamentation.
    Lay that earth upon thy heart,
    And thy sickness shall depart!

It shall sweeten and make whole
Fevered breath and festered soul;
It shall mightily restrain
Over-busy hand and brain;
It shall ease thy mortal strife
'Gainst the immortal woe of life,
Till thyself restored shall prove
By what grace the Heavens do move.

Take of English flowers these—
Spring's full-facèd primroses,
Summer's wild wide-hearted rose,
Autumn's wall-flower of the close,
And, thy darkness to illume,
Winter's bee-thronged ivy-bloom.
Seek and serve them where they bide
From Candlemas to Christmas-tide,
    For these simples used aright
    Shall restore a failing sight.

REWARDS AND FAIRIES

These shall cleanse and purify
Webbed and inward-turning eye;
These shall show thee treasure hid,
Thy familiar fields amid,
At thy threshold, on thy hearth,
Or about thy daily path;
And reveal (which is thy need)
Every man a King indeed!

INTRODUCTION

ONCE UPON A TIME, Dan and Una, brother and sister, living in the English country, had the good fortune to meet with Puck, *alias* Robin Goodfellow, *alias* Nick o' Lincoln, *alias* Lob-lie-by-the-Fire, the last survivor in England of those whom mortals call Fairies. Their proper name, of course, is 'The People of the Hills.' This Puck, by means of the magic of Oak, Ash, and Thorn, gave the children power—

To see what they should see and hear what they should hear,
Though it should have happened three thousand year.

The result was that from time to time, and in different places on the farm and in the fields and the country about, they saw and talked to some rather interesting people. One of these, for instance, was a Knight of the Norman Conquest, another a young Centurion of a Roman Legion stationed in England, another a builder and decorator of King Henry VII.'s time; and so on and so forth; as I have tried to explain in a book called *Puck of Pook's Hill.*

A year or so later, the children met Puck once more, and though they were then older and wiser, and wore boots regularly instead of going barefooted when they got the chance, Puck was as kind to them as ever, and introduced them to more people of the old days.

He was careful, of course, to take away their memory of their walks and conversations afterwards, but otherwise he did not interfere; and Dan and Una would find the strangest sort of persons in their gardens or woods.

In the stories that follow I am trying to tell something about those people.

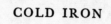

COLD IRON

COLD IRON

WHEN DAN AND UNA had arranged to go out before breakfast, they did not remember that it was Midsummer Morning. They only wanted to see the otter which, old Hobden said, had been fishing their brook for weeks; and early morning was the time to surprise him. As they tiptoed out of the house into the wonderful stillness, the Church clock struck five. Dan took a few steps across the dew-blobbed lawn, and looked at his black footprints.

'I think we ought to be kind to our poor boots,' he said. 'They'll get horrid wet.'

It was their first summer in boots, and they hated them, so they took them off, and slung them round their necks, and paddled joyfully over the dripping turf where the shadows lay the wrong way, like evening in the East.

The sun was well up and warm, but by the brook the last of the night mist still fumed off the water. They picked up the chain of otter's footprints on the mud, and followed it from the bank, between the weeds and the drenched mowing, while the birds shouted with surprise. Then the track left the brook and became a smear, as though a log had been dragged along.

They traced it into Three Cows meadow, over the mill-sluice to the Forge, round Hobden's garden, and then up the slope till it ran out on the short turf and fern of Pook's Hill, and they heard the cock-pheasants crowing in the woods behind them.

'No use!' said Dan, questing like a puzzled hound. 'The

dew's drying off, and old Hobden says otters'll travel for miles.'

'I'm sure we've travelled miles.' Una fanned herself with her hat. 'How still it is! It's going to be a regular roaster.' She looked down the valley, where no chimney yet smoked.

'Hobden's up!' Dan pointed to the open door of the Forge cottage. 'What d'you suppose he has for breakfast?'

'One of *them*. He says they eat good all times of the year.' Una jerked her head at some stately pheasants going down to the brook for a drink.

A few steps farther on a fox broke almost under their bare feet, yapped, and trotted off.

'Ah, Mus' Reynolds—Mus' Reynolds'—Dan was quoting from old Hobden,—'if I knowed all you knowed, I'd know something.'[1]

'I say,'—Una lowered her voice—'you know that funny feeling of things having happened before. I felt it when you said "Mus' Reynolds." '

'So did I,' Dan began. 'What is it?'

They faced each other, stammering with excitement.

'Wait a shake! I'll remember in a minute. Wasn't it something about a fox—last year? Oh, I nearly had it then!' Dan cried.

'Be quiet!' said Una, prancing excitedly. 'There was something happened before we met the fox last year. Hills! Broken Hills—the play at the theatre—see what you see——'

'I remember now,' Dan shouted. 'It's as plain as the nose on your face—Pook's Hill—Puck's Hill—Puck!'

'I remember, too,' said Una. 'And it's Midsummer Day again!'

The young fern on a knoll rustled, and Puck walked out, chewing a green-topped rush.

[1] See 'The Winged Hats' in *Puck of Pook's Hill*.

COLD IRON

'Good Midsummer Morning to you! Here's a happy meeting,' said he. They shook hands all round, and asked questions.

'You've wintered well,' he said after a while, and looked them up and down. 'Nothing much wrong with you, seemingly.'

'They've put us into boots,' said Una. 'Look at my feet—they're all pale white, and my toes are squdged together awfully.'

'Yes—boots make a difference.' Puck wriggled his brown, square, hairy foot, and cropped a dandelion flower between the big toe and the next.

'I could do that—last year,' Dan said dismally, as he tried and failed. 'And boots simply ruin one's climbing.'

'There must be some advantage to them, I suppose,' said Puck, 'or folk wouldn't wear them. Shall we come this way?'

They sauntered along side by side till they reached the gate at the far end of the hillside. Here they halted just like cattle, and let the sun warm their backs while they listened to the flies in the wood.

'Little Lindens is awake,' said Una, as she hung with her chin on the top rail. 'See the chimney smoke?'

'To-day's Thursday, isn't it?' Puck turned to look at the old pink farmhouse across the little valley. 'Mrs. Vincey's baking day. Bread should rise well this weather.' He yawned, and that set them both yawning.

The bracken about rustled and ticked and shook in every direction. They felt that little crowds were stealing past.

'Doesn't that sound like—er—the People of the Hills?' said Una.

'It's the birds and wild things drawing up to the woods before people get about,' said Puck, as though he were Ridley the keeper.

'Oh, we know that. I only said it sounded like.'

'As I remember 'em, the People of the Hills used to make more noise. They'd settle down for the day rather like small birds settling down for the night. But that was in the days when they carried the high hand. Oh, me! The deeds that I've had act and part in, you'd scarcely believe!'

'I like that!' said Dan. 'After all you told us last year, too!'

'Only, the minute you went away, you made us forget everything,' said Una.

Puck laughed and shook his head. 'I shall this year, too. I've given you seizin of Old England, and I've taken away your Doubt and Fear, but your memory and remembrance between whiles I'll keep where old Billy Trott kept his night-lines—and that's where he could draw 'em up and hide 'em at need. Does that suit?' He twinkled mischievously.

'It's got to suit,' said Una, and laughed. 'We can't magic back at you.' She folded her arms and leaned against the gate. 'Suppose, now, you wanted to magic me into something—an otter? Could you?'

'Not with those boots round your neck.'

'I'll take them off.' She threw them on the turf. Dan's followed immediately. 'Now!' she said.

'Less than ever now you've trusted me. Where there's true faith, there's no call for magic.' Puck's slow smile broadened all over his face.

'But what have boots to do with it?' said Una, perching on the gate.

'There's Cold Iron in them,' said Puck, and settled beside her. 'Nails in the soles, I mean. It makes a difference.'

'How?'

'Can't you feel it does? You wouldn't like to go back to bare feet again, same as last year, would you? Not really?'

'No—o. I suppose I shouldn't—not for always. I'm growing up, you know,' said Una.

COLD IRON

'But you told us last year, in the Long Slip—at the theatre —that you didn't mind Cold Iron,' said Dan.

'*I* don't; but folk in housen, as the People of the Hills call them, must be ruled by Cold Iron. Folk in housen are born on the near side of Cold Iron—there's iron in every man's house, isn't there? They handle Cold Iron every day of their lives, and their fortune's made or spoilt by Cold Iron in some shape or other. That's how it goes with Flesh and Blood, and one can't prevent it.'

'I don't quite see. How do you mean?' said Dan.

'It would take me some time to tell you.'

'Oh, it's ever so long to breakfast,' said Dan. 'We looked in the larder before we came out.' He unpocketed one big hunk of bread and Una another, which they shared with Puck.

'That's Little Lindens' baking,' he said, as his white teeth sunk in it. 'I know Mrs. Vincey's hand.' He ate with a slow sideways thrust and grind, just like old Hobden, and, like Hobden, hardly dropped a crumb. The sun flashed on Little Lindens' windows, and the cloudless sky grew stiller and hotter in the valley.

'Ah—Cold Iron,' he said at last to the impatient children. 'Folk in housen, as the People of the Hills say, grow careless about Cold Iron. They'll nail the Horseshoe over the front door, and forget to put it over the back. Then, some time or other, the People of the Hills slip in, find the cradle-babe in the corner, and——'

'Oh, I know. Steal it and leave a changeling,' Una cried.

'No,' said Puck firmly. 'All that talk of changelings is people's excuse for their own neglect. Never believe 'em. I'd whip 'em at the cart-tail through three parishes if I had my way.'

'But they don't do it now,' said Una.

'Whip, or neglect children? Umm! Some folks and some fields never alter. But the People of the Hills didn't work any changeling tricks. They'd tiptoe in and whisper and weave round the cradle-babe in the chimney-corner—a fag-end of a charm here, or half a spell there—like kettles singing; but when the babe's mind came to bud out afterwards, it would act differently from other people in its station. That's no advantage to man or maid. So I wouldn't allow it with my folks' babies here. I told Sir Huon so once.'

'Who was Sir Huon?' Dan asked, and Puck turned on him in quiet astonishment.

'Sir Huon of Bordeaux—he succeeded King Oberon. He had been a bold knight once, but he was lost on the road to Babylon, a long while back. Have you ever heard "How many miles to Babylon?"?'

'Of course,' said Dan, flushing.

'Well, Sir Huon was young when that song was new. But about tricks on mortal babies. I said to Sir Huon in the fern here, on just such a morning as this: "If you crave to act and influence on folk in housen, which I know is your desire, why don't you take some human cradle-babe by fair dealing, and bring him up among yourselves on the far side of Cold Iron— as Oberon did in time past? Then you could make him a splendid fortune, and send him out into the world." "Time past is past time," says Sir Huon. "I doubt if we could do it. For one thing, the babe would have to be taken without wronging man, woman, or child. For another, he'd have to be born on the far side of Cold Iron—in some house where no Cold Iron ever stood; and for yet the third, he'd have to be kept from Cold Iron all his days till we let him find his fortune. No, it's not easy," he said, and he rode off, thinking. You see, Sir Huon had been a man once.

'I happened to attend Lewes Market next Woden's Day even, and watched the slaves being sold there—same as pigs are sold at Robertsbridge Market nowadays. Only, the pigs have rings on their noses, and the slaves had rings round their necks.'

'What sort of rings?' said Dan.

'A ring of Cold Iron, four fingers wide, and a thumb thick, just like a quoit, but with a snap to it for to snap round the slave's neck. They used to do a big trade in slave-rings at the Forge here, and ship them to all parts of Old England, packed in oak sawdust. But, as I was saying, there was a farmer out of the Weald who had bought a woman with a babe in her arms, and he didn't want any encumbrances to her driving his beasts home for him.'

'Beast himself!' said Una, and kicked her bare heel on the gate.

'So he blamed the auctioneer. "It's none o' my baby," the wench puts in. "I took it off a woman in our gang who died on Terrible Down yesterday." "I'll take it off to the Church then," says the farmer. "Mother Church 'll make a monk of it, and we'll step along home."

'It was dusk then. He slipped down to St. Pancras' Church, and laid the babe at the cold chapel door. I breathed on the back of his stooping neck—and—I've *heard* he never could be warm at any fire afterwards. I should have been surprised if he could! Then I whipped up the babe, and came flying home here like a bat to his belfry.

'On the dewy break of morning of Thor's own day—just such a day as this—I laid the babe outside the Hill here, and the People flocked up and wondered at the sight.

' "You've brought him, then?" Sir Huon said, staring like any mortal man.

' "Yes, and he's brought his mouth with him too," I said. The babe was crying loud for his breakfast.

' "What is he?" says Sir Huon, when the women-folk had drawn him under to feed him.

' "Full Moon and Morning Star may know," I says. "*I* don't. By what I could make out of him in the moonlight, he's without brand or blemish. I'll answer for it that he's born on the far side of Cold Iron, for he was born under a shaw on Terrible Down, and I've wronged neither man, woman, nor child in taking him, for he is the son of a dead slave-woman."

' "All to the good, Robin," Sir Huon said. "He'll be the less anxious to leave us. Oh, we'll give him a splendid fortune, and he shall act and influence on folk in housen as we have always craved." His Lady came up then, and drew him under to watch the babe's wonderful doings.'

'Who was his Lady?' said Dan.

'The Lady Esclairmonde. She had been a woman once, till she followed Sir Huon across the fern, as we say. Babies are no special treat to me—I've watched too many of them—so I stayed on the Hill. Presently I heard hammering down at the Forge there.' Puck pointed towards Hobden's cottage. 'It was too early for any workmen, but it passed through my mind that the breaking day was Thor's own day. A slow North-East wind blew up and set the oaks sawing and fretting in a way I remembered; so I slipped over to see what I could see.'

'And what did you see?'

'A smith forging something or other out of Cold Iron. When it was finished, he weighed it in his hand (his back was towards me), and tossed it from him a longish quoit-throw down the valley. I saw Cold Iron flash in the sun, but I couldn't quite make out where it fell. *That* didn't trouble me. I knew it would be found sooner or later by some one.'

'How did you know?' Dan went on.

'Because I knew the Smith that made it,' said Puck quietly.

'Wayland Smith?'[1] Una suggested.

'No. I should have passed the time o' day with Wayland Smith, of course. This other was different. So'—Puck made a queer crescent in the air with his finger—'I counted the blades of grass under my nose till the wind dropped and he had gone —he and his Hammer.'

'Was it Thor then?' Una murmured under her breath.

'Who else? It was Thor's own day.' Puck repeated the sign. 'I didn't tell Sir Huon or his Lady what I'd seen. Borrow trouble for yourself if that's your nature, but don't lend it to your neighbours. Moreover, I might have been mistaken about the Smith's work. He might have been making things for mere amusement, though it wasn't like him, or he might have thrown away an old piece of made iron. One can never be sure. So I held my tongue and enjoyed the babe. He was a wonderful child—and the People of the Hills were so set on him, they wouldn't have believed me. He took to me wonderfully. As soon as he could walk he'd putter forth with me all about my Hill here. Fern makes soft falling! He knew when day broke on earth above, for he'd thump, thump, thump, like an old buck-rabbit in a bury, and I'd hear him say "Opy!" till some one who knew the Charm let him out, and then it would be "Robin! Robin!" all round Robin Hood's barn, as we say, till he'd found me.'

'The dear!' said Una. 'I'd like to have seen him!'

'Yes, he was a boy. And when it came to learning his words —spells and such-like—he'd sit on the Hill in the long shadows, worrying out bits of charms to try on passers-by. And when the bird flew to him, or the tree bowed to him for pure love's sake (like everything else on my Hill), he'd shout, "Robin! Look—see! Look, see, Robin!" and sputter out some

[1] See 'Weland's Sword' in *Puck of Pook's Hill*.

spell or other that they had taught him, *all* wrong end first, till I hadn't the heart to tell him it was his own dear self and not the words that worked the wonder. When he got more abreast of his words, and could cast spells for sure, as we say, he took more and more notice of things and people in the world. People, of course, always drew him, for he was mortal all through.

'Seeing that he was free to move among folk in housen, under or over Cold Iron, I used to take him along with me night-walking, where he could watch folk, and I could keep him from touching Cold Iron. That wasn't so difficult as it sounds, because there are plenty of things besides Cold Iron in housen to catch a boy's fancy. He *was* a handful, though! I shan't forget when I took him to Little Lindens—his first night under a roof. The smell of the rushlights and the bacon on the beams—they were stuffing a feather-bed too, and it was a drizzling warm night—got into his head. Before I could stop him—we were hiding in the bakehouse—he'd whipped up a storm of wildfire, with flashlights and voices, which sent the folk shrieking into the garden, and a girl overset a hive there, and—of course *he* didn't know till then such things could touch him—he got badly stung, and came home with his face looking like kidney potatoes!

'You can imagine how angry Sir Huon and Lady Esclair-monde were with poor Robin! They said the Boy was never to be trusted with me night-walking any more—and he took about as much notice of their order as he did of the bee-stings. Night after night, as soon as it was dark, I'd pick up his whistle in the wet fern, and off we'd flit together among folk in housen till break of day—he asking questions, and I answering according to my knowledge. Then we fell into mischief again!' Puck shook till the gate rattled.

COLD IRON

'We came across a man up at Brightling who was beating his wife with a bat in the garden. I was just going to toss the man over his own woodlump when the Boy jumped the hedge and ran at him. Of course the woman took her husband's part, and while the man beat him, the woman scratted his face. It wasn't till I danced among the cabbages like Brightling Beacon all ablaze that they gave up and ran indoors. The Boy's fine green-and-gold clothes were torn all *to* pieces, and he had been welted in twenty places with the man's bat, and scratted by the woman's nails to pieces. He looked like a Robertsbridge hopper on a Monday morning.

' "Robin," said he, while I was trying to clean him down with a bunch of hay, "I don't quite understand folk in housen. I went to help that old woman, and she hit me, Robin!"

' "What else did you expect?" I said. "That was the one time when you might have worked one of your charms, instead of running into three times your weight."

' "I didn't think," he says. "But I caught the man one on the head that was as good as any charm. Did you see it work, Robin?"

' "Mind your nose," I said. "Bleed it on a dockleaf—not your sleeve, for pity's sake." I knew what the Lady Esclairmonde would say.

'*He* didn't care. He was as happy as a gipsy with a stolen pony, and the front part of his gold coat, all blood and grass stains, looked like ancient sacrifices.

'Of course the People of the Hills laid the blame on me. The Boy could do nothing wrong, in their eyes.

' "You are bringing him up to act and influence on folk in housen, when you're ready to let him go," I said. "Now he's begun to do it, why do you cry shame on me? That's no shame. It's his nature drawing him to his kind."

' "But we don't want him to begin *that* way," the Lady Esclairmonde said. "We intend a splendid fortune for him—not
your flitter-by-night, hedge-jumping, gipsy-work."

' "I don't blame you, Robin," says Sir Huon, "but I *do*
think you might look after the Boy more closely."

' "I've kept him away from Cold Iron these sixteen years,"
I said. "You know as well as I do, the first time he touches
Cold Iron he'll find his own fortune, in spite of everything
you intend for him. You owe me something for that."

'Sir Huon, having been a man, was going to allow me the
right of it, but the Lady Esclairmonde, being the Mother of
all Mothers, overpersuaded him.

' "We're very grateful," Sir Huon said, "but we think that
just for the present you are about too much with him on the
Hill."

' "Though you have said it," I said, "I will give you a second
chance." I did not like being called to account for my doings
on my own Hill. I wouldn't have stood it even that far except
I loved the Boy.

' "No! No!" says the Lady Esclairmonde. "He's never any
trouble when he's left to me and himself. It's your fault."

' "You have said it," I answered. "Hear me! From now on
till the Boy has found his fortune, whatever that may be, I
vow to you all on my Hill, by Oak, and Ash, and Thorn, *and*
by the Hammer of Asa Thor" '—again Puck made that curious
double-cut in the air—' "that you may leave me out of all
your counts and reckonings." Then I went out'—he snapped
his fingers—'like the puff of a candle, and though they called
and cried, they made nothing by it. I didn't promise not to
keep an eye on the Boy, though. I watched him close—close—
close!

'When he found what his people had forced me to do, he

gave them a piece of his mind, but they all kissed and cried round him, and being only a boy, he came over to their way of thinking (I don't blame him), and called himself unkind and ungrateful; and it all ended in fresh shows and plays, and magics to distract him from folk in housen. Dear heart alive! How he used to call and call on me, and I couldn't answer, or even let him know that I was near!'

'Not even once?' said Una. 'If he was very lonely?'

'No, he couldn't,' said Dan, who had been thinking. 'Didn't you swear by the Hammer of Thor that you wouldn't, Puck?'

'By that Hammer!' was the deep rumbled reply. Then he came back to his soft speaking voice. 'And the Boy *was* lonely, when he couldn't see me any more. He began to try to learn all learning (he had good teachers), but I saw him lift his eyes from the big black books towards folk in housen all the time. He studied song-making (good teachers he had too!), but he sang those songs with his back toward the Hill, and his face toward folk. *I* know! I have sat and grieved over him grieving within a rabbit's jump of him. Then he studied the High, Low, and Middle Magic. He had promised the Lady Esclairmonde he would never go near folk in housen; so he had to make shows and shadows for his mind to chew on.'

'What sort of shows?' said Dan.

'Just boy's Magic as we say. I'll show you some, some time. It pleased him for the while, and it didn't hurt any one in particular except a few men coming home late from the taverns. But I knew what it was a sign of, and I followed him like a weasel follows a rabbit. As good a boy as ever lived! I've seen him with Sir Huon and the Lady Esclairmonde stepping just as they stepped to avoid the track of Cold Iron in a furrow, or walking wide of some old ash-tot because a man had left his swop-hook or spade there; and all his heart aching to go straightforward among folk in housen all the time. Oh, a good boy! They always intended a fine fortune for him—but they could never find it in their heart to let him begin. I've heard that many warned them, but they wouldn't be warned. So it happened *as* it happened.

'One hot night I saw the Boy roving about here wrapped in his flaming discontents. There was flash on flash against the clouds, and rush on rush of shadows down the valley till the shaws were full of his hounds giving tongue, and the wood-ways were packed with his knights in armour riding down into the water-mists—all his own Magic, of course. Behind them you could see great castles lifting slow and splendid on arches of moonshine, with maidens waving their hands at the windows, which all turned into roaring rivers; and then would come the darkness of his own young heart wiping out the whole slateful. But boy's Magic doesn't trouble me—or Merlin's either for that matter. I followed the Boy by the flashes and the whirling wildfire of his discontent, and oh, but I grieved for him! Oh, but I grieved for him! He pounded back and forth like a bullock in a strange pasture—sometimes alone —sometimes waist-deep among his shadow-hounds—sometimes leading his shadow-knights on a hawk-winged horse to rescue his shadow-girls. I never guessed he had such Magic at his command; but it's often that way with boys.

'Just when the owl comes home for the second time, I saw Sir Huon and the Lady ride down my Hill, where there's not much Magic allowed except mine. They were very pleased at the Boy's Magic—the valley flared with it—and I heard them settling his splendid fortune when they should find it in their hearts to let him go to act and influence among folk in housen. Sir Huon was for making him a great King somewhere or other, and the Lady was for making him a marvellous wise man whom all should praise for his skill and kindness. She was very kind-hearted.

'Of a sudden we saw the flashes of his discontents turned back on the clouds, and his shadow-hounds stopped baying.

' "There's Magic fighting Magic over yonder," the Lady Esclairmonde cried, reining up. "Who is against him?"

'I could have told her, but I did not count it any of my business to speak of Asa Thor's comings and goings.'

'How did you know?' said Una.

'A slow North-East wind blew up, sawing and fretting through the oaks in a way I remembered. The wildfire roared up, one last time in one sheet, and snuffed out like a rush-light, and a bucketful of stinging hail fell. We heard the Boy walking in the Long Slip—where I first met you.

' "Here, oh, come here!" said the Lady Esclairmonde, and stretched out her arms in the dark.

'He was coming slowly, but he stumbled in the footpath, being, of course, mortal man.

' "Why, what's this?" he said to himself. We three heard him.

' "Hold, lad, hold! 'Ware Cold Iron!" said Sir Huon, and they two swept 'down like night-jars, crying as they rode.

'I ran at their stirrups, but it was too late. We felt that the Boy had touched Cold Iron somewhere in the dark, for the Horses of the Hill shied off, and whipped round, snorting.

'Then I judged it was time for me to show myself in my own shape; so I did.

' "Whatever it is," I said, "he has taken hold of it. Now we must find out whatever it *is* that he has taken hold of; for that will be his fortune."

' "Come here, Robin," the Boy shouted, as soon as he heard my voice. "I don't know what I've hold of."

' "It is in your hands," I called back. "Tell us if it is hard and cold, with jewels atop. For that will be a King's Sceptre."

' "Not by a furrow-long," he said, and stooped and tugged in the dark. We heard him.

' "Has it a handle and two cutting edges?" I called. "For that'll be a Knight's Sword."

' "No, it hasn't," he says. "It's neither ploughshare, whittle, hook, nor crook, nor aught I've yet seen men handle." By this time he was scratting in the dirt to prise it up.

' "Whatever it is, you know who put it there, Robin," said Sir Huon to me, "or you would not ask those questions. You should have told me as soon as you knew."

' "What could you or I have done against the Smith that made it and laid it for him to find?" I said, and I whispered Sir Huon what I had seen at the Forge on Thor's Day, when the babe was first brought to the Hill.

' "Oh, good-bye, our dreams!" said Sir Huon. "It's neither sceptre, sword, nor plough! Maybe yet it's a bookful of learning, bound with iron clasps. There's a chance for a splendid fortune in that sometimes."

'But we knew we were only speaking to comfort ourselves, and the Lady Esclairmonde, having been a woman, said so.

' "Thur aie! Thor help us!" the Boy called. "It is round, without end, Cold Iron, four fingers wide and a thumb thick, and there is writing on the breadth of it."

' "Read the writing if you have the learning," I called. The darkness had lifted by then, and the owl was out over the fern again.

'He called back, reading the runes on the iron:—

"Few can see
Further forth

COLD IRON

Than when the child
Meets the Cold Iron."

And there he stood, in clear starlight, with a new, heavy, shining slave-ring round his proud neck.

' "Is this how it goes?" he asked, while the Lady Esclairmonde cried.

' "That is how it goes," I said. He hadn't snapped the catch home yet, though.

' "What fortune does it mean for him?" said Sir Huon, while the Boy fingered the ring. "You who walk under Cold Iron, you must tell us and teach us."

' "Tell I can, but teach I cannot," I said. "The virtue of the Ring is only that he must go among folk in housen henceforward, doing what they want done, or what he knows they need, all Old England over. Never will he be his own master, nor yet ever any man's. He will get half he gives, and give twice what he gets, till his life's last breath; and if he lays aside his load before he draws that last breath, all his work will go for naught."

' "Oh, cruel, wicked Thor!" cried the Lady Esclairmonde. "Ah, look, see, all of you! The catch is still open! He hasn't locked it. He can still take it off. He can still come back. Come back!" She went as near as she dared, but she could not lay hands on Cold Iron. The Boy could have taken it off, yes. We waited to see if he would, but he put up his hand, and the snap locked home.

' "What else could I have done?" said he.

' "Surely, then, you will do," I said. "Morning's coming, and if you three have any farewells to make, make them now, for, after sunrise, Cold Iron must be your master."

'So the three sat down, cheek by wet cheek, telling over their farewells till morning light. As good a boy as ever lived, he was.'

'And what happened to him?' asked Dan.

'When morning came, Cold Iron was master of him and his fortune, and he went to work among folk in housen. Presently he came across a maid like-minded with himself, and they were wedded, and had bushels of children, as the saying is. Perhaps you'll meet some of his breed, this year.'

'Thank you,' said Una. 'But what did the poor Lady Esclairmonde do?'

'What *can* you do when Asa Thor lays the Cold Iron in a lad's path? She and Sir Huon were comforted to think they had given the Boy good store of learning to act and influence on folk in housen. For he *was* a good boy! Isn't it getting on for breakfast-time? I'll walk with you a piece.'

When they were well in the centre of the bone-dry fern, Dan nudged Una, who stopped and put on a boot as quickly as she could.

'Now,' she said, 'you can't get any Oak, Ash, and Thorn leaves from here, and'—she balanced wildly on one leg—'I'm standing on Cold Iron. What'll you do if we don't go away?'

'E-eh? Of all mortal impudence!' said Puck, as Dan, also in one boot, grabbed his sister's hand to steady himself. He walked round them, shaking with delight. 'You think I can only work with a handful of dead leaves? This comes of taking away your Doubt and Fear! I'll show you!'

A minute later they charged into old Hobden at his simple breakfast of cold roast pheasant, shouting that there was a wasps' nest in the fern which they had nearly stepped on, and asking him to come and smoke it out.

'It's too early for wops-nestës, an' I don't go diggin' in the

Hill, not for shillin's,' said the old man placidly. 'You've a thorn in your foot, Miss Una. Sit down, and put on your t'other boot. You're too old to be caperin' barefoot on an empty stomach. Stay it with this chicken o' mine.'

COLD IRON

'Gold is for the mistress—silver for the maid!
Copper for the craftsman cunning at his trade.'
'Good!' said the Baron, sitting in his hall,
'But Iron—Cold Iron—is master of them all!'

So he made rebellion 'gainst the King his liege,
Camped before his citadel and summoned it to siege—
'Nay!' said the cannoneer on the castle wall,
'But Iron—Cold Iron—shall be master of you all!'

Woe for the Baron and his knights so strong,
When the cruel cannon-balls laid 'em all along!
He was taken prisoner, he was cast in thrall,
And Iron—Cold Iron—was master of it all!

Yet his King spake kindly (Oh, how kind a Lord!)
'What if I release thee now and give thee back thy sword?'
'Nay!' said the Baron, 'mock not at my fall,
For Iron—Cold Iron—is master of men all.'

'Tears are for the craven, prayers are for the clown—
Halters for the silly neck that cannot keep a crown.'
'As my loss is grievous, so my hope is small,
For Iron—Cold Iron—must be master of men all!'

Yet his King made answer (few such Kings there be!)
'Here is Bread and here is Wine—sit and sup with me.
Eat and drink in Mary's Name, the whiles I do recall
How Iron—Cold Iron—can be master of men all!'

*He took the Wine and blessed It; He blessed and brake the
    Bread.*
*With His own Hands He served Them, and presently He
    said:*
*'Look! These Hands they pierced with nails outside my city
    wall*
Show Iron—Cold Iron—to be master of men all!

'Wounds are for the desperate, blows are for the strong,
Balm and oil for weary hearts all cut and bruised with wrong.
I forgive thy treason—I redeem thy fall—
For Iron—Cold Iron—must be master of men all!'

'Crowns are for the valiant—sceptres for the bold!
Thrones and powers for mighty men who dare to take and
    hold.'
'Nay!' said the Baron, kneeling in his hall,
'But Iron—Cold Iron—is master of men all!
    Iron, out of Calvary, is master of men all!'

GLORIANA

THE TWO COUSINS

Valour and Innocence
Have latterly gone hence
To certain death by certain shame attended.
Envy—ah! even to tears!—
The fortune of their years
Which, though so few, yet so divinely ended.

Scarce had they lifted up
Life's full and fiery cup,
Than they had set it down untouched before them.
Before their day arose
They beckoned it to close—
Close in destruction and confusion o'er them.

They did not stay to ask
What prize should crown their task,
Well sure that prize was such as no man strives for;
But passed into eclipse,
Her kiss upon their lips—
Even Belphoebe's, whom they gave their lives for!

GLORIANA

Willow Shaw, the little fenced wood where the hop-poles are stacked like Indian wigwams, had been given to Dan and Una for their very own kingdom when they were quite small. As they grew older, they contrived to keep it most particularly private. Even Phillips, the gardener, told them every time that he came in to take a hop-pole for his beans, and old Hobden would no more have thought of setting his rabbit-wires there without leave, given fresh each spring, than he would have torn down the calico and marking-ink notice on the big willow which said: 'Grown-ups not allowed in the Kingdom unless brought.'

Now you can understand their indignation when, one blowy July afternoon, as they were going up for a potato-roast, they saw somebody moving among the trees. They hurled themselves over the gate, dropping half the potatoes, and while they were picking them up Puck came out of a wigwam.

'Oh, it's you, is it?' said Una. 'We thought it was people.'

'I saw you were angry—from your legs,' he answered with a grin.

'Well, it's our own Kingdom—not counting you, of course.'

'That's rather why I came. A lady here wants to see you.'

'What about?' said Dan cautiously.

'Oh, just Kingdoms and things. She knows about Kingdoms.'

There was a lady near the fence dressed in a long dark

cloak that hid everything except her high red-heeled shoes. Her face was half covered by a black silk fringed mask, without goggles. And yet she did not look in the least as if she motored.

Puck led them up to her and bowed solemnly. Una made the best dancing-lesson curtsy she could remember. The lady answered with a long, deep, slow, billowy one.

'Since it seems that you are a Queen of this Kingdom,' she said, 'I can do no less than acknowledge your sovereignty.' She turned sharply on staring Dan. 'What's in your head, lad? Manners?'

'I was thinking how wonderfully you did that curtsy,' he answered.

She laughed a rather shrill laugh. 'You're a courtier already. Do you know anything of dances, wench—or Queen, must I say?'

'I've had some lessons, but I can't really dance a bit,' said Una.

'You should learn, then.' The lady moved forward as though she would teach her at once. 'It gives a woman alone among men or her enemies time to think how she shall win or—lose. A woman can only work in man's playtime. Heigho!' She sat down on the bank.

Old Middenboro, the lawn-mower pony, stumped across the paddock and hung his sorrowful head over the fence.

'A pleasant Kingdom,' said the lady, looking round. 'Well enclosed. And how does your Majesty govern it? Who is your Minister?'

Una did not quite understand. 'We don't play that,' she said.

'Play?' The lady threw up her hands and laughed.

'We have it for our own, together,' Dan explained.

'And d'you never quarrel, young Burleigh?'

'Sometimes, but then we don't tell.'

The lady nodded. 'I've no brats of my own, but I understand keeping a secret between Queens and their Ministers. *Ay de mi!* But with no disrespect to present majesty, methinks your realm is small, and therefore likely to be coveted by man and beast. For example'—she pointed to Middenboro— 'yonder old horse, with the face of a Spanish friar—does he never break in?'

'He can't. Old Hobden stops all our gaps for us,' said Una, 'and we let Hobden catch rabbits in the Shaw.'

The lady laughed like a man. 'I see! Hobden catches conies —rabbits—for himself, and guards your defences for you. Does he make a profit out of his coney-catching?'

'We never ask,' said Una. 'Hobden's a particular friend of ours.'

'Hoity-toity!' the lady began angrily. Then she laughed. 'But I forget. It is your Kingdom. I knew a maid once that had a larger one than this to defend, and so long as her men kept the fences stopped, she asked 'em no questions either.'

'Was she trying to grow flowers?' said Una.

'No, trees—perdurable trees. Her flowers all withered.' The lady leaned her head on her hand.

'They do if you don't look after them. We've got a few. Would you like to see? I'll fetch you some.' Una ran off to the rank grass in the shade behind the wigwam, and came back with a handful of red flowers. 'Aren't they pretty?' she said. 'They're Virginia stock.'

'Virginia?' said the lady, and lifted them to the fringe of her mask.

'Yes. They come from Virginia. Did your maid ever plant any?'

'Not herself—but her men adventured all over the earth to pluck or to plant flowers for her crown. They judged her worthy of them.'

'And was she?' said Dan cheerfully.

'*Quien sabe?* [who knows?] But at least, while her men toiled abroad she toiled in England, that they might find a safe home to come back to.'

'And what was she called?'

'Gloriana—Belphoebe—Elizabeth of England.' Her voice changed at each word.

'You mean Queen Bess?'

The lady bowed her head a little towards Dan. 'You name her lightly enough, young Burleigh. What might you know of her?' said she.

'Well, I—I've seen the little green shoes she left at Brickwall House—down the road, you know. They're in a glass case—awfully tiny things.'

'Oh, Burleigh, Burleigh!' she laughed. 'You are a courtier too soon.'

'But they are,' Dan insisted. 'As little as dolls' shoes. Did you really know her well?'

'Well. She was a—woman. I've been at her Court all my life. Yes, I remember when she danced after the banquet at Brickwall. They say she danced Philip of Spain out of a brand-new kingdom that day. Worth the price of a pair of old shoes—hey?'

She thrust out one foot, and stooped forward to look at its broad flashing buckle.

'You've heard of Philip of Spain—long-suffering Philip,' she said, her eyes still on the shining stones. 'Faith, what some men will endure at some women's hands passes belief! If *I* had been a man, and a woman had played with me as Elizabeth played with Philip, I would have——' She nipped off one of the Virginia stocks and held it up between finger and thumb. 'But for all that'—she began to strip the leaves one by one—'they say—and I am persuaded—that Philip loved her.' She tossed her head sideways.

'I don't quite understand,' said Una.

'The high heavens forbid that you should, wench!' She swept the flowers from her lap and stood up in the rush of shadows that the wind chased through the wood.

'I should like to know about the shoes,' said Dan.

'So ye shall, Burleigh. So ye shall, if ye watch me. 'Twill be as good as a play.'

'We've never been to a play,' said Una.

The lady looked at her and laughed. 'I'll make one for you. Watch! You are to imagine that she—Gloriana, Belphoebe, Elizabeth—has gone on a progress to Rye to comfort her sad heart (maids are often melancholic), and while she halts at Brickwall House, the village—what was its name?' She pushed Puck with her foot.

'Norgem,' he croaked, and squatted by the wigwam.

'Norgem village loyally entertains her with a masque or play, and a Latin oration spoken by the parson, for whose false quantities, if *I'd* made 'em in my girlhood, I should have been whipped.'

'You whipped?' said Dan.

'Soundly, sirrah, soundly! She stomachs the affront to her scholarship, makes her grateful, gracious thanks from the teeth outwards, thus'—(the lady yawned)—'Oh, a Queen may love her subjects in her heart, and yet be dog-wearied of 'em in body and mind—and so sits down'—her skirts foamed about her as she sat—'to a banquet beneath Brickwall Oak. Here for her sins she is waited upon by—— What were the young cockerels' names that served Gloriana at table?'

'Frewens, Courthopes, Fullers, Husseys,' Puck began.

She held up her long jewelled hand. 'Spare the rest! They were the best blood of Sussex, and by so much the more clumsy in handling the dishes and plates. Wherefore'—she looked funnily over her shoulder—'you are to think of Gloriana in a green and gold-laced habit, dreadfully expecting that the jostling youths behind her would, of pure jealousy or devotion, spatter it with sauces and wines. The gown was Philip's gift, too! At this happy juncture a Queen's messenger, mounted and mired, spurs up the Rye road and delivers her a letter'—she giggled—'a letter from a good, simple, frantic Spanish gentleman called—Don Philip.'

'That wasn't Philip, King of Spain?' Dan asked.

'Truly, it was. 'Twixt you and me and the bedpost, young Burleigh, these kings and queens are very like men and women, and I've heard they write each other fond, foolish letters that none of their ministers should open.'

'Did her ministers ever open Queen Elizabeth's letters?' said Una.

'Faith, yes! But she'd have done as much for theirs, any day. You are to think of Gloriana, then (they say she had a pretty hand), excusing herself thus to the company—for the Queen's time is never her own—and, while the music strikes up, reading Philip's letter, as I do.' She drew a real letter from her pocket, and held it out almost at arm's length, like the old post-mistress in the village when she reads telegrams.

'Hm! Hm! Hm! Philip writes as ever most lovingly. He says his Gloriana is cold, for which reason he burns for her through a fair written page.' She turned it with a snap. 'What's here? Philip complains that certain of her gentlemen have fought against his generals in the Low Countries. He prays her to hang 'em when they re-enter her realms. (Hm, that's as may be.) Here's a list of burnt shipping slipped between two vows of burning adoration. Oh, poor Philip! His admirals at sea—no less than three of 'em—have been boarded, sacked, and scuttled on their lawful voyages by certain English mariners (gentlemen, he will not call them), who are now at large and working more piracies in *his* American ocean, which the Pope gave him. (He and the Pope should guard it, then!) Philip hears, but his devout ears will not credit it, that Gloriana in some fashion countenances these villains' misdeeds, shares in their booty, and—oh, shame!—has even lent them ships royal for their sinful thefts. Therefore he requires (which is a word Gloriana loves not), *requires* that she shall hang 'em when they return to England, and afterwards shall account to him for all the goods and gold they have plundered. A most loving request! If Gloriana will not be Philip's bride, she shall be his broker and his butcher! Should she still be stiff-necked, he writes—see where the pen digged the innocent paper!—that he hath both the means and the intention to be revenged on her. Aha! Now we come to the Spaniard in his shirt!' (She waved the letter merrily.) 'Listen here! Philip will prepare for Gloriana a destruction from the West —a destruction from the West—far exceeding that which Pedro de Avila wrought upon the Huguenots. And he rests and remains, kissing her feet and her hands, her slave, her enemy, or her conqueror, as he shall find that she uses him.'

She thrust back the letter under her cloak, and went on acting, but in a softer voice. 'All this while—hark to it—the wind blows through Brickwall Oak, the music plays, and, with the company's eyes upon her, the Queen of England must think what this means. She cannot remember the name of Pedro de Avila, nor what he did to the Huguenots, nor when, nor where. She can only see darkly some dark motion moving in Philip's dark mind, for he hath never written before in this fashion. She must smile above the letter as though it were good news from her ministers—the smile that tires the mouth and the poor heart. What shall she do?' Again her voice changed.

'You are to fancy that the music of a sudden wavers away. Chris Hatton, Captain of her bodyguard, quits the table all red and ruffled, and Gloriana's virgin ear catches the clash of swords at work behind a wall. The mothers of Sussex look round to count their chicks—I mean those young game-cocks that waited on her. Two dainty youths have stepped aside into Brickwall garden with rapier and dagger on a private point of honour. They are haled out through the gate, disarmed and glaring—the lively image of a brace of young Cupids transformed into pale, panting Cains. Ahem! Gloriana beckons awfully—thus! They come up for judgment. Their lives and estates lie at her mercy whom they have doubly offended, both as Queen and woman. But la! what will not foolish young men do for a beautiful maid?'

'Why? What did she do? What had they done?' said Una.

'Hsh! You mar the play! Gloriana had guessed the cause of the trouble. They were handsome lads. So she frowns a while and tells 'em not to be bigger fools than their mothers had made 'em, and warns 'em, if they do not kiss and be friends on the instant, she'll have Chris Hatton horse and birch 'em in the style of the new school at Harrow. (Chris looks sour at that.) Lastly, because she needed time to think on Philip's letter burning in her pocket, she signifies her pleasure to dance with 'em and teach 'em better manners. Whereat the revived company call down Heaven's blessing on her gracious head; Chris and the others prepare Brickwall House for a dance; and she walks in the clipped garden between those two lovely young sinners who are both ready to sink for shame. They confess their fault. It appears that midway in the banquet the elder—they were cousins—conceived that the Queen looked upon him with special favour. The younger, taking the look to himself, after some words gives the elder the lie. Hence, as she guessed, the duel.'

'And which had she really looked at?' Dan asked.

'Neither—except to wish them farther off. She was afraid all the while they'd spill dishes on her gown. She tells 'em this, poor chicks—and it completes their abasement. When they had grilled long enough, she says: "And so you would have fleshed your maiden swords for me—for me?" Faith, they would have been at it again if she'd egged 'em on! but their swords—oh, prettily they said it!—had been drawn for her once or twice already.

' "And where?" says she. "On your hobby-horses before you were breeched?"

' "On my ownship," says the elder. "My cousin was vice-admiral of our venture in his pinnace. We would not have you think of us as brawling children."

' "No, no," says the younger, and flames like a very Tudor rose. "At least the Spaniards know us better."

' "Admiral Boy—Vice-Admiral Babe," says Gloriana, "I cry your pardon. The heat of these present times ripens childhood to age more quickly than I can follow. But we are at peace with Spain. Where did you break your Queen's peace?"

' "On the sea called the Spanish Main, though 'tis no more Spanish than my doublet," says the elder. Guess how that warmed Gloriana's already melting heart! She would never suffer any sea to be called Spanish in her private hearing.

' "And why was I not told? What booty got you, and where have you hid it? Disclose," says she. "You stand in some danger of the gallows for pirates."

' "The axe, most gracious lady," says the elder, "for we are gentle born." He spoke truth, but no woman can brook contradiction. "Hoity-toity!" says she, and, but that she remembered that she was Queen, she'd have cuffed the pair of 'em. "It shall be gallows, hurdle, and dung-cart if I choose."

' "Had our Queen known of our going beforehand, Philip might have held her to blame for some small things we did on the seas," the younger lisps.

' "As for treasure," says the elder, "we brought back but our bare lives. We were wrecked on the Gascons' Graveyard, where our sole company for three months was the bleached bones of De Avila's men."

'Gloriana's mind jumped back to Philip's last letter.

' "De Avila that destroyed the Huguenots? What d'you know of him?" she says. The music called from the house here, and they three turned back between the yews.

' "Simply that De Avila broke in upon a plantation of Frenchmen on that coast, and very Spaniardly hung them all for heretics—eight hundred or so. The next year Dominique de Gorgues, a Gascon, broke in upon De Avila's men, and very justly hung 'em all for murderers—five hundred or so. No Christians inhabit there now," says the elder lad, "though 'tis a goodly land north of Florida."

' "How far is it from England?" asks prudent Gloriana.

' "With a fair wind, six weeks. They say that Philip will plant it again soon." This was the younger, and he looked at her out of the corner of his innocent eye.

'Chris Hatton, fuming, meets and leads her into Brickwall Hall, where she dances—thus. A woman can think while she dances—can think. I'll show you. Watch!'

She took off her cloak slowly, and stood forth in dove-coloured satin, worked over with pearls that trembled like running water in the running shadows of the trees. Still talking—more to herself than to the children—she swam into a

majestical dance of the stateliest balancings, the haughtiest
wheelings and turnings aside, the most dignified sinkings, the
gravest risings, all joined together by the elaboratest inter-
lacing steps and circles.

They leaned forward breathlessly to watch the splendid
acting.

'Would a Spaniard,' she began, looking on the ground,
'speak of his revenge till his revenge were ripe? No. Yet a man
who loved a woman might threaten her in the hope that his
threats would make her love him. Such things have been.'
She moved slowly across a bar of sunlight. 'A destruction
from the West may signify that Philip means to descend on
Ireland. But then my Irish spies would have had some warning. The Irish keep no secrets. No—it is not Ireland. Now
why—why—why'—the red shoes clicked and paused—'does
Philip name Pedro Melendez de Avila, a general in his Americas, unless'—she turned more quickly—'unless he intends to
work his destruction from the Americas? Did he say De Avila
only to put her off her guard, or for this once has his black
pen betrayed his black heart? We'—she raised herself to her
full height—'England must forestall Master Philip. But not
openly,'—she sank again—'we cannot fight Spain openly—not
yet—not yet.' She stepped three paces as though she were pegging down some snare with her twinkling shoe-buckles. 'The
Queen's mad gentlemen may fight Philip's poor admirals
where they find 'em, but England, Gloriana, Harry's daughter,
must keep the peace. Perhaps, after all, Philip loves her—as
many men and boys do. That may help England. Oh, *what*
shall help England?'

She raised her head—the masked head that seemed to have
nothing to do with the busy feet—and stared straight at the
children.

'I think this is rather creepy,' said Una with a shiver. 'I wish she'd stop.'

The lady held out her jewelled hand as though she were taking some one else's hand in the Grand Chain.

'Can a ship go down into the Gascons' Graveyard and wait there?' she asked into the air, and passed on rustling.

'She's pretending to ask one of the cousins, isn't she?' said Dan, and Puck nodded.

Back she came in the silent, swaying, ghostly dance. They saw she was smiling beneath the mask, and they could hear her breathing hard.

'I cannot lend you any my ships for the venture; Philip would hear of it,' she whispered over her shoulder; 'but as much guns and powder as you ask, if you do not ask too——' Her voice shot up and she stamped her foot thrice. 'Louder! Louder, the music in the gallery! Oh, me, but I have burst out of my shoe!'

She gathered her skirts in each hand, and began a curtsy. 'You will go at your own charges,' she whispered straight before her. 'Oh, enviable and adorable age of youth!' Her eyes shone through the mask-holes. 'But I warn you you'll repent it. Put not your trust in princes—or Queens. Philip's ships 'll blow you out of water. You'll not be frightened? Well, we'll talk on it again, when I return from Rye, dear lads.'

The wonderful curtsy ended. She stood up. Nothing stirred on her except the rush of the shadows.

'And so it was finished,' she said to the children. 'Why d'you not applaud?'

'What was finished?' said Una.

'The dance,' the lady replied offendedly. 'And a pair of green shoes.'

'I don't understand a bit,' said Una.

'Eh? What did *you* make of it, young Burleigh?'

'I'm not quite sure,' Dan began, 'but——'

'You never can be—with a woman. But——'

'But I thought Gloriana meant the cousins to go back to the Gascons' Graveyard, wherever that was.'

' 'Twas Virginia afterwards. Her plantation of Virginia.'

'Virginia afterwards, and stop Philip from taking it. Didn't she say she'd lend 'em guns?'

'Right so. But not ships—*then*.'

'And I thought you meant they must have told her they'd do it off their own bat, without getting her into a row with Philip. Was I right?'

'Near enough for a Minister of the Queen. But remember she gave the lads full time to change their minds. She was three long days at Rye Royal—knighting of fat Mayors. When she came back to Brickwall, they met her a mile down the road, and she could feel their eyes burn through her riding-mask. Chris Hatton, poor fool, was vexed at it.

' "You would not birch them when I gave you the chance," says she to Chris. "Now you must get me half an hour's private speech with 'em in Brickwall garden. Eve tempted Adam in a garden. Quick, man, or I may repent!" '

'She was a Queen. Why did she not send for them herself?' said Una.

The lady shook her head. 'That was never her way. I've seen her walk to her own mirror by bye-ends, and the woman that cannot walk straight *there* is past praying for. Yet I would have you pray for her! What else—what else in England's name could she have done?' She lifted her hand to her throat for a moment. 'Faith,' she cried, 'I'd forgotten the little green shoes! She left 'em at Brickwall—so she did. And I remember she gave the Norgem parson—John Withers, was he?

—a text for his sermon—"Over Edom have I cast out my shoe." Neat, if he'd understood!'

'I don't understand,' said Una. 'What about the two cousins?'

'You are as cruel as a woman,' the lady answered. '*I* was not to blame. I told you I gave 'em time to change their minds. On my honour (*ay de mi!*), she asked no more of 'em at first than to wait a while off that coast—the Gascons' Graveyard—to hover a little if their ships chanced to pass that way—they had only one tall ship and a pinnace—only to watch and bring me word of Philip's doings. One must watch Philip always. What a murrain right had he to make any plantation there, a hundred leagues north of his Spanish Main, and only six weeks from England? By my dread father's soul, I tell you he had none—none!' She stamped her red foot again, and the two children shrunk back for a second.

'Nay, nay. You must not turn from me too! She laid it all fairly before the lads in Brickwall garden between the yews. I told 'em that if Philip sent a fleet (and to make a plantation he could not well send less), their poor little cockboats could not sink it. They answered that, with submission, the fight would be their own concern. She showed 'em again that there could be only one end to it—quick death on the sea, or slow death in Philip's prisons. They asked no more than to embrace death for my sake. Many men have prayed to me for life. I've refused 'em, and slept none the worse after; but when my men, my tall, fantastical young men, beseech me on their knees for leave to die for me, it shakes me—ah, it shakes me to the marrow of my old bones.'

Her chest sounded like a board as she hit it.

'She showed 'em all. I told 'em that this was no time for open war with Spain. If by miracle inconceivable they pre-

vailed against Philip's fleet, Philip would hold me account-
able. For England's sake, to save war, I should e'en be forced
(I told 'em so) to give him up their young lives. If they failed,
and again by some miracle escaped Philip's hand, and crept
back to England with their bare lives, they must lie—oh, I
told 'em all—under my sovereign displeasure. She could not
know them, see them, nor hear their names, nor stretch
out a finger to save them from the gallows, if Philip chose
to ask it.

' "Be it the gallows, then," says the elder. (I could have
wept, but that my face was made for the day.)

' "Either way—any way—this venture is death, which I
know you fear not. But it is death with assured dishonour,"
I cried.

' "Yet our Queen will know in her heart what we have
done," says the younger.

' "Sweetheart," I said. "A queen has no heart."

' "But she is a woman, and a woman would not forget,"
says the elder. "We will go!" They knelt at my feet.

' "Nay, dear lads—but here!" I said, and I opened my arms
to them and I kissed them.

' "Be ruled by me," I said. "We'll hire some ill-featured old
tarry-breeks of an admiral to watch the Graveyard, and you
shall come to Court."

' "Hire whom you please," says the elder; "we are ruled by
you, body and soul"; and the younger, who shook most when
I kissed 'em, says between his white lips, "I think you have
power to make a god of a man."

' "Come to Court and be sure of it," I said.

'They shook their heads and I knew—I knew, that go they
would. If I had not kissed them—perhaps I might have prevailed.'

'Then why did you do it?' said Una. 'I don't think you knew really what you wanted done.'

'May it please your Majesty'—the lady bowed her head low—'this Gloriana whom I have represented for your pleasure was a woman and a Queen. Remember her when you come to your Kingdom.'

'But did the cousins go to the Gascons' Graveyard?' said Dan, as Una frowned.

'They went,' said the lady.

'Did they ever come back?' Una began; but—'Did they stop King Philip's fleet?' Dan interrupted.

The lady turned to him eagerly.

'D'you think they did right to go?' she asked.

'I don't see what else they could have done,' Dan replied, after thinking it over.

'D'you think she did right to send 'em?' The lady's voice rose a little.

'Well,' said Dan, 'I don't see what else she could have done, either—do you? How did they stop King Philip from getting Virginia?'

'There's the sad part of it. They sailed out that autumn from Rye Royal, and there never came back so much as a single rope-yarn to show what had befallen them. The winds blew, and they were not. Does that make you alter your mind, young Burleigh?'

'I expect they were drowned, then. Anyhow, Philip didn't score, did he?'

'Gloriana wiped out her score with Philip later. But if Philip had won, would you have blamed Gloriana for wasting those lads' lives?'

'Of course not. She was bound to try to stop him.'

The lady coughed. 'You have the root of the matter in you. Were I Queen, I'd make you Minister.'

'We don't play that game,' said Una, who felt that she disliked the lady as much as she disliked the noise the high wind made tearing through Willow Shaw.

'Play!' said the lady with a laugh, and threw up her hands affectedly. The sunshine caught the jewels on her many rings and made them flash till Una's eyes dazzled, and she had to rub them. Then she saw Dan on his knees picking up the potatoes they had spilled at the gate.

'There wasn't anybody in the Shaw, after all,' he said. 'Didn't you think you saw some one?'

'I'm most awfully glad there isn't,' said Una. Then they went on with the potato-roast.

THE LOOKING-GLASS

Queen Bess was Harry's daughter!

The Queen was in her chamber, and she was middling old.
Her petticoat was satin and her stomacher was gold.
Backwards and forwards and sideways did she pass,
Making up her mind to face the cruel looking-glass.
  The cruel looking-glass that will never show a lass
  As comely or as kindly or as young as once she was!

The Queen was in her chamber, a-combing of her hair,
There came Queen Mary's spirit and it stood behind her chair,
Singing, 'Backwards and forwards and sideways may you pass,
But I will stand behind you till you face the looking-glass.
  The cruel looking-glass that will never show a lass
  As lovely or unlucky or as lonely as I was!'

The Queen was in her chamber, a-weeping very sore,
There came Lord Leicester's spirit and it scratched upon the
    door,
Singing, 'Backwards and forwards and sideways may you pass,
But I will walk beside you till you face the looking-glass.
  The cruel looking-glass that will never show a lass
  As hard and unforgiving or as wicked as you was!'

The Queen was in her chamber; her sins were on her head;
She looked the spirits up and down and statelily she said:
'Backwards and forwards and sideways though I've been,
Yet I am Harry's daughter and I am England's Queen!'

REWARDS AND FAIRIES

And she faced the looking-glass (and whatever else there was),
And she saw her day was over and she saw her beauty pass
In the cruel looking-glass that can always hurt a lass
More hard than any ghost there is or any man there was!

THE WRONG THING

A TRUTHFUL SONG

I

THE BRICKLAYER:—

I tell this tale, which is strictly true,
　　Just by way of convincing you
How very little since things were made
　　Things have altered in the building trade.

A year ago, come the middle o' March,
We was building flats near the Marble Arch,
When a thin young man with coal-black hair
Came up to watch us working there.

Now there wasn't a trick in brick or stone
That this young man hadn't seen or known;
Nor there wasn't a tool from trowel to maul
But this young man could use 'em all!

Then up and spoke the plumbyers bold,
Which was laying the pipes for the hot and cold:
'Since you with us have made so free,
Will you kindly say what your name might be?'

The young man kindly answered them:
'It might be Lot or Methusalem,
Or it might be Moses (a man I hate),
Whereas it is Pharaoh surnamed the Great.

REWARDS AND FAIRIES

'Your glazing is new and your plumbing's strange,
But otherwise I perceive no change,
And in less than a month, if you do as I bid,
I'd learn you to build me a Pyramid.'

II

THE SAILOR:—

I tell this tale, which is stricter true,
   Just by way of convincing you
How very little since things was made
   Things have altered in the shipwright's trade.

In Blackwall Basin yesterday
A China barque re-fitting lay,
When a fat old man with snow-white hair
Came up to watch us working there.

Now there wasn't a knot which the riggers knew
But the old man made it—and better too;
Nor there wasn't a sheet, or a lift, or a brace,
But the old man knew its lead and place.

Then up and spake the caulkyers bold,
Which was packing the pump in the after-hold:
'Since you with us have made so free,
Will you kindly tell what your name might be?'

The old man kindly answered them:
'It might be Japhet, it might be Shem,
Or it might be Ham (though his skin was dark),
Whereas it is Noah, commanding the Ark.

A TRUTHFUL SONG

'Your wheel is new and your pumps are strange,
But otherwise I perceive no change,
And in less than a week, if she did not ground,
I'd sail this hooker the wide world round!'

BOTH: We tell these tales, which are strictest true, etc.

THE WRONG THING

DAN HAD GONE IN FOR building model boats; but after he had filled the schoolroom with chips, which he expected Una to clear away, they turned him out of doors and he took all his tools up the hill to Mr. Springett's yard, where he knew he could make as much mess as he chose. Old Mr. Springett was a builder, contractor, and sanitary engineer, and his yard, which opened off the village street, was always full of interesting things. At one end of it was a long loft, reached by a ladder, where he kept his iron-bound scaffold-planks, tins of paints, pulleys, and odds and ends he had found in old houses. He would sit here by the hour watching his carts as they loaded or unloaded in the yard below, while Dan gouged and grunted at the carpenter's bench near the loft window. Mr. Springett and Dan had always been particular friends, for Mr. Springett was so old he could remember when railways were being made in the southern counties of England, and people were allowed to drive dogs in carts.

One hot, still afternoon—the tar-paper on the roof smelt like ships—Dan, in his shirt-sleeves, was smoothing down a new schooner's bow, and Mr. Springett was talking of barns and houses he had built. He said he never forgot any stick or stone he had ever handled, or any man, woman, or child he had ever met. Just then he was very proud of the Village Hall at the entrance to the village, which he had finished a few weeks before.

'An' I don't mind tellin' you, Mus' Dan,' he said, 'that the Hall will be my last job top of this mortal earth. I didn't make ten pounds—no, nor yet five—out o' the whole contrac', but my name's lettered on the foundation stone—*Ralph Springett, Builder*—and the stone she's bedded on four foot good concrete. If she shifts any time these five hundred years, I'll sure-ly turn in my grave. I told the Lunnon architec' so when he come down to oversee my work.'

'What did he say?' Dan was sandpapering the schooner's port bow.

'Nothing. The Hall ain't more than one of his small jobs for *him*, but 'tain't small to me, an' my name is cut and lettered, frontin' the village street, I do hope an' pray, for time everlastin'. You'll want the little round file for that holler in her bow. Who's there?' Mr. Springett turned stiffly in his chair.

A long pile of scaffold-planks ran down the centre of the loft. Dan looked, and saw Hal o' the Draft's touzled head beyond them.[1]

'Be you the builder of the Village Hall?' he asked of Mr. Springett.

'I be,' was the answer. 'But if you want a job——'

Hal laughed. 'No, faith!' he said. 'Only the Hall is as good and honest a piece of work as I've ever run a rule over. So, being born hereabouts, and being reckoned a master among masons, and accepted as a master mason, I made bold to pay my brotherly respects to the builder.'

'Aa—um!' Mr. Springett looked important. 'I be a bit rusty, but I'll try ye!'

He asked Hal several curious questions, and the answers must have pleased him, for he invited Hal to sit down. Hal moved up, always keeping behind the pile of planks so that only his head showed, and sat down on a trestle in the dark

[1] See 'Hal o' the Draft' in *Puck of Pook's Hill*.

corner at the back of Mr. Springett's desk. He took no notice
of Dan, but talked at once to Mr. Springett about bricks, and
cement, and lead and glass, and after a while Dan went on
with his work. He knew Mr. Springett was pleased, because
he tugged his white sandy beard, and smoked his pipe in
short puffs. The two men seemed to agree about everything,
but when grown-ups agree they interrupt each other almost
as much as if they were quarrelling. Hal said something about
workmen.

'Why, that's what *I* always say,' Mr. Springett cried. 'A
man who can only do one thing, he's but next-above-fool to
the man that can't do nothin'. That's where the Unions make
their mistake.'

'My thought to the very dot.' Dan heard Hal slap his tight-
hosed leg. 'I've suffered in my time from these same Guilds—
Unions, d'you call 'em? All their precious talk of the mysteries
of their trades—why, what does it come to?'

'Nothin'! You've justabout hit it,' said Mr. Springett, and
rammed his hot tobacco with his thumb.

'Take the art of wood-carving,' Hal went on. He reached
across the planks, grabbed a wooden mallet, and moved his
other hand as though he wanted something. Mr. Springett
without a word passed him one of Dan's broad chisels. 'Ah!
Wood-carving, for example. If you can cut wood and have a
fair draft of what ye mean to do, a' Heaven's name take
chisel and maul and let drive at it, say I! You'll soon find all
the mystery, forsooth, of wood-carving under your proper
hand!' Whack, came the mallet on the chisel, and a sliver of
wood curled up in front of it. Mr. Springett watched like an
old raven.

'All art is one, man—one!' said Hal between whacks; 'and
to wait on another man to finish out——'

'To finish out your work ain't no sense,' Mr. Springett cut in. 'That's what I'm always sayin' to the boy here.' He nodded towards Dan. 'That's what I said when I put the new wheel into Brewster's Mill in Eighteen hundred Seventy-two. I reckoned I was millwright enough for the job 'thout bringin' a man from Lunnon. An' besides, dividin' work eats up profits, no bounds.'

Hal laughed his beautiful deep laugh, and Mr. Springett joined in till Dan laughed too.

'You handle your tools, I can see,' said Mr. Springett. 'I reckon, if you're any way like me, you've found yourself hindered by those—Guilds, did you call 'em?—Unions, we say.'

'You may say so!' Hal pointed to a white scar on his cheek-bone. 'This is a rememberance from the Master watching-Foreman of Masons on Magdalen Tower, because, please you, I dared to carve stone without their leave. They said a stone had slipped from the cornice by accident.'

'I know them accidents. There's no way to disprove 'em. An' stones ain't the only things that slip,' Mr. Springett grunted. Hal went on:

'I've seen a scaffold-plank keckle and shoot a too-clever workman thirty foot on to the cold chancel floor below. And a rope can break——'

'Yes, natural as nature; an' lime 'll fly up in a man's eyes without any breath o' wind sometimes,' said Mr. Springett. 'But who's to show 'twasn't a accident?'

'Who do these things?' Dan asked, and straightened his back at the bench as he turned the schooner end-for-end in the vice to get at her counter.

'Them which don't wish other men to work no better nor quicker than they do,' growled Mr. Springett. 'Don't pinch her so hard in the vice, Mus' Dan. Put a piece o' rag in the jaws, or you'll bruise her. More than that'—he turned towards Hal—'if a man has his private spite laid up against you, the Unions give him his excuse for workin' it off.'

'Well I know it,' said Hal.

'They never let you go, them spiteful ones. I knowed a plasterer in Eighteen hundred Sixty-one—down to the Wells. He was a Frenchy—a bad enemy he was.'

'I had mine too. He was an Italian, called Benedetto. I met him first at Oxford on Magdalen Tower when I was learning my trade—or trades, I should say. A bad enemy he was, as you say, but he came to be my singular good friend,' said Hal as he put down the mallet and settled himself comfortably.

'What might his trade have been—plasterin'?' Mr. Springett asked.

'Plastering of a sort. He worked in stucco—fresco we call it. Made pictures on plaster. Not but what he had a fine sweep of the hand in drawing. He'd take the long sides of a cloister, trowel on his stuff, and roll out his great all-abroad pictures of saints and croppy-topped trees quick as a webster unrolling cloth almost. Oh, Benedetto could draw, but 'a was a little-minded man, professing to be full of secrets of colour or plaster—common tricks, all of 'em—and his one single talk was how Tom, Dick or Harry had stole this or t'other secret art from him.'

'I know that sort,' said Mr. Springett. 'There's no keeping peace or making peace with such. An' they're mostly born an' bone idle.'

'True. Even his fellow-countrymen laughed at his jealousy. We two came to loggerheads early on Magdalen Tower. I was a youngster then. Maybe I spoke my mind about his work.'

'You shouldn't never do that.' Mr. Springett shook his head. 'That sort lay it up against you.'

'True enough. This Benedetto did most specially. Body o' me, the man lived to hate me! But I always kept my eyes open on a plank or a scaffold. I was mighty glad to be shut of him when he quarrelled with his Guild foreman, and went off, nose in air, and paints under his arm. But'—Hal leaned forward—'if you hate a man or a man hates you——'

'*I* know. You're everlastin' running acrost him,' Mr. Springett interrupted. 'Excuse me, sir.' He leaned out of the window, and shouted to a carter who was loading a cart with bricks.

'Ain't you no more sense than to heap 'em up that way?' he said. 'Take an' throw a hundred of 'em off. It's more than the team can compass. Throw 'em off, I tell you, and make another trip for what's left over. Excuse me, sir. You was sayin'——'

'I was saying that before the end of the year I went to Bury to strengthen the lead-work in the great Abbey east window there.'

'Now that's just one of the things I've never done. But I mind there was a cheap excursion to Chichester in Eighteen hundred Seventy-nine, an' I went an' watched 'em leadin' a won'erful fine window in Chichester Cathedral. I stayed watchin' till 'twas time for us to go back. Dunno as I had two drinks p'raps, all that day.'

Hal smiled. 'At Bury, then, sure enough, I met my enemy Benedetto. He had painted a picture in plaster on the south wall of the Refectory—a noble place for a noble thing—a picture of Jonah.'

'Ah! Jonah an' his whale. I've never been as fur as Bury. You've worked about a lot,' said Mr. Springett, with his eyes on the carter below.

'No. Not the whale. This was a picture of Jonah and the pompion that withered. But all that Benedetto had shown was a peevish greybeard huggled up in angle-edged drapery beneath a pompion on a wooden trellis. This last, being a dead thing, he'd drawn it as 'twere to the life. But fierce old Jonah, bared in the sun, angry even to death that his cold prophecy was disproven—Jonah, ashamed, and already hearing the children of Nineveh running to mock him—ah, that was what Benedetto had *not* drawn!'

'He better ha' stuck to his whale, then,' said Mr. Springett.

'He'd ha' done no better with that. He draws the damp cloth off the picture, an' shows it to me. I was a craftsman too, d'ye see?

' " 'Tis good," I said, "but it goes no deeper than the plaster."

' "What?" he said in a whisper.

' "Be thy own judge, Benedetto," I answered. "Does it go deeper than the plaster?"

'He reeled against a piece of dry wall. "No," he says, "and I know it. I could not hate thee more than I have done these five years, but if I live, I will try, Hal. I will try." Then he goes away. I pitied him, but I had spoken truth. His picture went no deeper than the plaster.'

'Ah!' said Mr. Springett, who had turned quite red. 'You was talkin' so fast I didn't understand what you was drivin' at. I've seen men—good workmen they was—try to do more than they could do, and—and they couldn't compass it. They knowed it, and it nigh broke their hearts like. You was in your right, o' course, sir, to say what you thought o' his work; but if you'll excuse me, was you in your duty?'

'I was wrong to say it,' Hal replied. 'God forgive me—I was young! He was workman enough himself to know where he failed. But it all came evens in the long run. By the same token, did ye ever hear o' one Torrigiano—Torrisany we called him?'

'I can't say I ever did. Was he a Frenchy like?'

'No, a hectoring, hard-mouthed, long-sworded Italian builder, as vain as a peacock and as strong as a bull, but, mark you, a master workman. More than that—he could get his best work out of the worst men.'

'Which it's a gift. I had a foreman-bricklayer like him once,' said Mr. Springett. 'He used to prod 'em in the back like with a pointing-trowel, and they did wonders.'

'I've seen our Torrisany lay a 'prentice down with one buffet and raise him with another—to make a mason of him. I worked under him at building a chapel in London—a chapel and a tomb for the King.'

'I never knew kings went to chapel much,' said Mr. Springett. 'But I always hold with a man—don't care who he be—seein' about his own grave before he dies. 'Tisn't the sort of thing to leave to your family after the will's read. I reckon 'twas a fine vault?'

'None finer in England. This Torrigiano had the contract for it, as you'd say. He picked master craftsmen from all parts—England, France, Italy, the Low Countries—no odds to him so long as they knew their work, and he drove them like—like pigs at Brightling Fair. He called us English all pigs. We suffered it because he was a master in his craft. If he misliked any work that a man had done, with his own great hands he'd rive it out, and tear it down before us all. "Ah, you pig—you English pig!" he'd scream in the dumb wretch's face. "You answer me? You look at me? You think at me? Come out with me into the cloisters. I will teach you carving myself. I will gild you all over!" But when his passion had blown out, he'd slip his arm round the man's neck, and impart knowledge worth gold. 'Twould have done your heart good, Mus' Springett, to see the two hundred of us—masons, jewellers, carvers, gilders, iron-workers and the rest—all toiling like cock-angels, and this mad Italian hornet fleeing from one to next up and down the chapel. Done your heart good, it would!'

'I believe you,' said Mr. Springett. 'In Eighteen hundred Fifty-four, I mind, the railway was bein' made into Hastin's. There was two thousand navvies on it—all young—all strong —an' I was one of 'em. Oh, dearie me! Excuse me, sir, but was your enemy workin' with you?'

'Benedetto? Be sure he was. He followed me like a lover. He painted pictures on the chapel ceiling—slung from a chair. Torrigiano made us promise not to fight till the work should be finished. We were both master craftsmen, do ye see, and he needed us. None the less, I never went aloft to carve 'thout testing all my ropes and knots each morning. We were never far from each other. Benedetto 'ud sharpen his knife on his sole while he waited for his plaster to dry—*wheet, wheet, wheet*. I'd hear it where I hung chipping round a pillar-head, and we'd nod to each other friendly-like. Oh, he was a craftsman, was Benedetto, but his hate spoiled his eye and his hand. I mind the night I had finished the models for the bronze saints round the tomb; Torrigiano embraced me before all the chapel, and bade me to supper. I met Benedetto when I came out. He was slavering in the porch like a mad dog.'

'Workin' himself up to it?' said Mr. Springett. 'Did he have it in at ye that night?'

'No, no. That time he kept his oath 'to Torrigiano. But I pitied him. Eh, well! Now I come to my own follies. I had never thought too little of myself; but after Torrisany had put his arm round my neck, I—I'—Hal broke into a laugh—'I lay there was not much odds 'twixt me and a cock-sparrow in his pride.'

'I was pretty middlin' young once on a time,' said Mr. Springett.

'Then ye know that a man can't drink and dice and dress fine, and keep company above his station, but his work suffers for it, Mus' Springett.'

'I never held much with dressin' up, but—you're right! The worst mistakes I ever made they was made of a Monday morning,' Mr. Springett answered. 'We've all been one sort of fool or t'other. Mus' Dan, Mus' Dan, take the smallest gouge, or you'll be spluttin' her stern works clean out. Can't ye see the grain of the wood don't favour a chisel?'

'I'll spare you some of my follies. But there was a man called Brygandyne—Bob Brygandyne—Clerk of the King's Ships, a little, smooth, bustling atomy, as clever as a woman to get work done for nothin'—a won'erful smooth-tongued pleader. He made much o' me, and asked me to draft him out a drawing, a piece of carved and gilt scroll-work for the bows of one ·of the King's Ships—the *Sovereign* was her name.'

'Was she a man-of-war?' asked Dan.

'She was a warship, and a woman called Catherine of Castile desired the King to give her the ship for a pleasure-ship of her own. *I* did not know at the time, but she'd been at Bob to get this scroll-work done and fitted that the King might see it. I made him the picture, in an hour, all of a heat after supper—one great heaving play of dolphins and a Neptune or so reining in webby-footed sea-horses, and Arion with his harp high atop of them. It was twenty-three foot long, and maybe nine foot deep—painted and gilt.'

'It must ha' justabout looked fine,' said Mr. Springett.

'That's the curiosity of it. 'Twas bad—rank bad. In my conceit I must needs show it to Torrigiano, in the chapel. He straddles his legs, hunches his knife behind him, and whistles like a storm-cock through a sleet-shower. Benedetto was behind him. We were never far apart, I've told you.

' "That is pig's work," says our Master. "Swine's work. You make any more such things, even after your fine Court suppers, and you shall be sent away."

'Benedetto licks his lips like a cat. "Is it so bad then, Master?" he says. "What a pity!"

' "Yes," says Torrigiano. "Scarcely *you* could do things so bad. I will condescend to show."

'He talks to me then and there. No shouting, no swearing (it was too bad for that); but good, memorable counsel, bitten in slowly. Then he sets me to draft out a pair of iron gates, to take, as he said, the taste of my naughty dolphins out of my mouth. Iron's sweet stuff if you don't torture her, and hammered work is all pure, truthful line, with a reason and a support for every curve and bar of it. A week at that settled my stomach handsomely, and the Master let me put the work through the smithy, where I sweated out more of my foolish pride.'

'Good stuff is good iron,' said Mr. Springett. 'I done a pair of lodge gates once in Eighteen hundred Sixty-three.'

'Oh, I forgot to say that Bob Brygandyne whipped away my draft of the ship's scroll-work, and would not give it back to me to re-draw. He said 'twould do well enough. Howsoever, my lawful work kept me too busied to remember him. Body o' me, but I worked that winter upon the gates and the bronzes for the tomb as I'd never worked before! I was leaner than a lath, but I lived—I lived then!' Hal looked at Mr.

Springett with his wise, crinkled-up eyes, and the old man smiled back.

'Ouch!' Dan cried. He had been hollowing out the schooner's after-deck, the little gouge had slipped and gashed the ball of his left thumb,—an ugly, triangular tear.

'That came of not steadying your wrist,' said Hal calmly. 'Don't bleed over the wood. *Do* your work with your heart's blood, but no need to let it show.' He rose and peered into a corner of the loft.

Mr. Springett had risen too, and swept down a ball of cobwebs from a rafter.

'Clap that on,' was all he said, 'and put your handkerchief atop. 'Twill cake over in a minute. It don't hurt now, do it?'

'No,' said Dan indignantly. 'You know it has happened lots of times. I'll tie it up myself. Go on, sir.'

'And it'll happen hundreds of times more,' said Hal with a friendly nod as he sat down again. But he did not go on till Dan's hand was tied up properly. Then he said:

'One dark December day—too dark to judge colour—we was all sitting and talking round the fires in the chapel (you heard good talk there), when Bob Brygandyne bustles in and —"Hal, you're sent for," he squeals. I was at Torrigiano's feet on a pile of putlocks, as I might be here, toasting a herring on my knife's point. 'Twas the one English thing our Master liked—salt herring.

' "I'm busy, about my art," I calls.

' "Art?" says Bob. "What's Art compared to your scroll-work for the *Sovereign*? Come."

' "Be sure your sins will find you out," says Torrigiano. "Go with him and see." As I followed Bob out I was aware of Benedetto, like a black spot when the eyes are tired, sliddering up behind me.

'Bob hurries through the streets in the raw fog, slips into
a doorway, up stairs, along passages, and at last thrusts
me into a little cold room vilely hung with Flemish tapestries, and no furnishing except a table and my draft of the
Sovereign's scroll-work. Here he leaves me. Presently comes
in a dark, long-nosed man in a fur cap.

' "Master Harry Dawe?" said he.

' "The same," I says. "Where a plague has Bob Brygandyne
gone?"

'His thin eyebrows surged up a piece and come down again
in a stiff bar. "He went to the King," he says.

' "All one. What's your pleasure with me?" I says, shivering,
for it was mortal cold.

'He lays his hand flat on my draft. "Master Dawe," he says,
"do you know the present price of gold leaf for all this wicked
gilding of yours?"

'By that I guessed he was some cheese-paring clerk or other
of the King's Ships, so I gave him the price. I forget it now,
but it worked out to thirty pounds—carved, gilt, and fitted
in place.

' "Thirty pounds!" he said, as though I had pulled a tooth
of him. "You talk as though thirty pounds was to be had
for the asking. None the less," he says, "your draft's a fine
piece of work."

'I'd been looking at it ever since I came in, and 'twas viler
even than I judged it at first. My eye and hand had been
purified the past months, d'ye see, by my iron work.

' "I could do it better now," I said. The more I studied my
squabby Neptunes the less I liked 'em; and Arion was a
pure flaming shame atop of the unbalanced dolphins.

' "I doubt it will be fresh expense to draft it again," he
says.

' "Bob never paid me for the first draft. I lay he'll never pay me for the second. 'Twill cost the King nothing if I re-draw it," I says.

' "There's a woman wishes it to be done quickly," he says. "We'll stick to your first drawing, Master Dawe. But thirty pounds is thirty pounds. You must make it less."

'And all the while the faults in my draft fair leaped out and hit me between the eyes. At any cost, I thinks to myself, I must get it back and re-draft it. He grunts at me impatiently, and a splendid thought comes to me, which shall save me. By the same token, 'twas quite honest.'

'They ain't always,' said Mr. Springett. 'How did you get out of it?'

'By the truth. I says to Master Fur Cap, as I might to you here, I says, "I'll tell you something, since you seem a knowledgeable man. Is the *Sovereign* to lie in Thames river all her days, or will she take the high seas?"

' "Oh," he says quickly, "the King keeps no cats that don't catch mice. She must sail the seas, Master Dawe. She'll be hired to merchants for the trade. She'll be out in all shapes o' weathers. Does that make any odds?"

' "Why, then," says I, "the first heavy sea she sticks her nose into'll claw off half that scroll-work, and the next will finish it. If she's meant for a pleasure-ship give me my draft again, and I'll porture you a pretty, light piece of scroll-work, good cheap. If she's meant for the open sea, pitch the draft into the fire. She can never carry that weight on her bows."

'He looks at me squintlings and plucks his under-lip.

' "Is this your honest, unswayed opinion?" he says.

' "Body o' me! Ask about!" I says. "Any seaman could tell you 'tis true. I'm advising you against my own profit, but why I do so is my own concern."

' "Not altogether," he says. "It's some of mine. You've saved me thirty pounds, Master Dawe, and you've given me good arguments to use against a wilful woman that wants my fine new ship for her own toy. We'll not have any scroll-work." His face shined with pure joy.

' "Then see that the thirty pounds you've saved on it are honestly paid the King," I says, "and keep clear o' women-folk." I gathered up my draft and crumpled it under my arm. "If that's all you need of me I'll be gone," I says. "I'm pressed."

'He turns him round and fumbles in a corner. "Too pressed to be made a knight, Sir Harry?" he says, and comes at me smiling, with three-quarters of a rusty sword.

'I pledge you my Mark I never guessed it was the King till that moment. I kneeled, and he tapped me on the shoulder.

' "Rise up, Sir Harry Dawe," he says, and, in the same breath, "I'm pressed, too," and slips through the tapestries, leaving me like a stuck calf.

'It come over me, in a bitter wave like, that here was I, a master craftsman, who had worked no bounds, soul or body, to make the King's tomb and chapel a triumph and a glory for all time; and here, d'ye see, I was made knight, not for any-thing I'd slaved over, or given my heart and guts to, but ex-pressedly because I'd saved him thirty pounds and a tongue-lashing from Catherine of Castile—she that had asked for the ship. That thought shrivelled me withinsides while I was fold-ing away my draft. On the heels of it—maybe you'll see why—I began to grin to myself. I thought of the earnest simplicity of the man—the King, I should say—because I'd saved him the money; his smile as though he'd won half France! I thought of my own silly pride and foolish expectations that

some day he'd honour me as a master craftsman. I thought of
the broken-tipped sword he'd found behind the hangings; the
dirt of the cold room, and his cold eye, wrapped up in his
own concerns, scarcely resting on me. Then I remembered
the solemn chapel roof and the bronzes about the stately tomb
he'd lie in, and—d'ye see?—the unreason of it all—the mad
high humour of it all—took hold on me till I sat me down on a
dark stair-head in a passage, and laughed till I could laugh
no more. What else could I have done?

'I never heard his feet behind me—he always walked like
a cat—but his arm slid round my neck, pulling me back
where I sat, till my head lay on his chest, and his left hand
held the knife plumb over my heart—Benedetto! Even so I
laughed—the fit was beyond my holding—laughed while he
ground his teeth in my ear. He was stark crazed for the time.

' "Laugh," he said. "Finish the laughter. I'll not cut ye
short. Tell me now"—he wrenched at my head—"why the
King chose to honour you,—you—you—you lickspittle Englishman? I am full of patience now. I have waited so long."
Then he was off at score about his Jonah in Bury Refectory,
and what I'd said of it, and his pictures in the chapel which
all men praised and none looked at twice (as if that was *my*
fault!), and a whole parcel of words and looks treasured up
against me through years.

' "Ease off your arm a little," I said. "I cannot die by choking, for I am just dubbed knight, Benedetto."

' "Tell me, and I'll confess ye, Sir Harry Dawe, Knight.
There's a long night before ye. Tell," says he.

'So I told him—his chin on my crown—told him all; told
it as well and with as many words as I have ever told a tale
at a supper with Torrigiano. I knew Benedetto would understand, for, mad or sad, he was a craftsman. I believed it to

be the last tale I'd ever tell top of mortal earth, and I would not put out bad work before I left the Lodge. All art's one art, as I said. I bore Benedetto no malice. My spirits, d'ye see, were catched up in a high, solemn exaltation, and I saw all earth's vanities foreshortened and little, laid out below me like a town from a cathedral scaffolding. I told him what befell, and what I thought of it. I gave him the King's very voice at "Master Dawe, you've saved me thirty pounds!"; his peevish grunt while he looked for the sword; and how the badger-eyed figures of Glory and Victory leered at me from the Flemish hangings. Body o' me, 'twas a fine, noble tale, and, as I thought, my last work on earth.

'"That is how I was honoured by the King," I said. "They'll hang ye for killing me, Benedetto. And, since you've killed in the King's Palace, they'll draw and quarter you; but you're too mad to care. Grant me, though, ye never heard a better tale."

'He said nothing, but I felt him shake. My head on his chest shook; his right arm fell away, his left dropped the knife, and he leaned with both hands on my shoulder— shaking—shaking! I turned me round. No need to put my foot on his knife. The man was speechless with laughter— honest craftsman's mirth. The first time I'd ever seen him laugh. You know the mirth that cuts off the very breath, while ye stamp and snatch at the short ribs? That was Benedetto's case.

'When he began to roar and bay and whoop in the passage, I haled him out into the street, and there we leaned against the wall and had it all over again—waving our hands and wagging our heads—till the watch came to know if we were drunk.

'Benedetto says to 'em, solemn as an owl: "You have saved

me thirty pound, Mus' Dawe," and off he pealed. In some sort we were mad-drunk—I because dear life had been given back to me, and he because, as he said afterwards, because the old crust of hatred round his heart was broke up and carried away by laughter. His very face had changed too.

' "Hal," he cries, "I forgive thee. Forgive me too, Hal. Oh, you English, you English! Did it gall thee, Hal, to see the rust on the dirty sword? Tell me again, Hal, how the King grunted with joy. Oh, let us tell the Master."

'So we reeled back to the chapel, arms round each other's necks, and when we could speak—he thought we'd been fighting—we told the Master. Yes, we told Torrigiano, and he laughed till he rolled on the new cold pavement. Then he knocked our heads together.

' "Ah, you English!" he cried. "You are more than pigs. You are English. Now you are well punished for your dirty fishes. Put the draft in the fire, and never do so any more. You are a fool, Hal, and you are a fool, Benedetto, but I need your works to please this beautiful English King——"

' "And I meant to kill Hal," says Benedetto. "Master, I meant to kill him because the English King had made him a knight."

' "Ah!" says the Master, shaking his finger. "Benedetto, if you had killed my Hal, I should have killed you—in the cloister. But you are a craftsman too, so I should have killed you like a craftsman, very, very slowly—in an hour, if I could spare the time!" That was Torrigiano—the Master!'

Mr. Springett sat quite still for some time after Hal had finished. Then he turned dark red; then he rocked to and fro; then he coughed and wheezed till the tears ran down his face. Dan knew by this that he was laughing, but it surprised Hal at first.

'Excuse me, sir,' said Mr. Springett, 'but I was thinkin' of some stables I built for a gentleman in Eighteen hundred Seventy-four. They was stables in blue brick—very particular work. Dunno as they weren't the best job which ever I'd done. But the gentleman's lady—she'd come from Lunnon, new married—she was all for buildin' what she called a haw-haw —what you an' me 'ud call a dik—right acrost his park. A middlin' big job which I'd have had the contract of, for she spoke to me in the library about it. But I told her there was a line o' springs just where she wanted to dig her ditch, an' she'd flood the park if she went on.'

'Were there any springs at all?' said Hal.

'Bound to be springs everywhere if you dig deep enough, ain't there? But what I said about the springs put her out o' conceit o' diggin' haw-haws, an' she took an' built a white tile dairy instead. But when I sent in my last bill for the stables, the gentleman he paid it 'thout even lookin' at it, and I hadn't forgotten nothin', I do assure you. More than that, he slips two five-pound notes into my hand in the library, an' "Ralph," he says—he allers called me by name— "Ralph," he says, "you've saved me a heap of expense an' trouble this autumn." I didn't say nothin', o' course. I knowed he didn't want any haw-haws digged acrost his park no more'n *I* did, but I never said nothin'. No more he didn't say nothin' about my blue-brick stables, which was really the best an' honestest piece o' work I'd done in quite a while. He give me ten pounds for savin' him a hem of a deal o' trouble at home. I reckon things are pretty much alike, all times, in all places.'

Hal and he laughed together. Dan couldn't quite understand what they thought so funny, and went on with his work for some time without speaking.

When he looked up, Mr. Springett, alone, was wiping his eyes with his green-and-yellow pocket-handkerchief.

'Bless me, Mus' Dan, I've been asleep,' he said. 'An' I've dreamed a dream which has made me laugh—laugh as I ain't laughed in a long day. I can't remember what 'twas all about, but they do say that when old men take to laughin' in their sleep, they're middlin' ripe for the next world. Have you been workin' honest, Mus' Dan?'

'Ra-ather,' said Dan, unclamping the schooner from the vice. 'And look how I've cut myself with the small gouge.'

'Ye-es. You want a lump o' cobwebs to that,' said Mr. Springett. 'Oh, I see you've put it on already. That's right, Mus' Dan.'

KING HENRY VII. AND THE SHIPWRIGHTS

Harry our King in England from London town is gone,
And comen to Hamull on the Hoke in the countie of Suthamp-
* ton.*
For there lay the Mary of the Tower, *his ship of war so strong,*
And he would discover, certaynely, if his shipwrights did him
* wrong.*

He told not none of his setting forth, nor yet where he would
*   go*
(But only my Lord of Arundel), and meanly did he show,
In an old jerkin and patched hose that no man might him
* mark;*
With his frieze hood and cloak about, he looked like any clerk.

He was at Hamull on the Hoke about the hour of the tide,
And saw the Mary *haled into dock, the winter to abide,*
With all her tackle and habiliments which are the King his
* own;*
But then ran on his false shipwrights and stripped her to the
* bone.*

They heaved the main-mast overboard, that was of a trusty
* tree,*
And they wrote down it was spent and lost by force of
* weather at sea.*
But they sawen it into planks and strakes as far as it might go,
To maken beds for their own wives and little children also.

There was a knave called Slingawai, he crope beneath the
deck,
Crying: 'Good felawes, come and see! The ship is nigh a
wreck!
For the storm that took our tall main-mast, it blew so fierce
and fell,
Alack! it hath taken the kettles and pans, and this brass pott
as well!'

With that he set the pott on his head and hied him up the
hatch,
While all the shipwrights ran below to find what they might
snatch;
All except Bob Brygandyne and he was a yeoman good,
He caught Slingawai round the waist and threw him on to the
mud.

'I have taken plank and rope and nail, without the King his
leave,
After the custom of Portesmouth, but I will not suffer a thief.
Nay, never lift up thy hand at me! There's no clean hands
in the trade.
Steal in measure,' quo' Brygandyne. 'There's measure in all
things made!'

'Gramercy, yeoman!' said our King. 'Thy counsel liketh me.'
And he pulled a whistle out of his neck and whistled whistles
three.
Then came my Lord of Arundel pricking across the down,
And behind him the Mayor and Burgesses of merry Suthamp-
ton town.

KING HENRY VII. AND THE SHIPWRIGHTS

They drew the naughty shipwrights up, with the kettles in their hands,
And bound them round the forecastle to wait the King's commands.
But 'Since ye have made your beds,' said the King, 'ye needs must lie thereon.
For the sake of your wives and little ones—felawes, get you gone!'

When they had beaten Slingawai, out of his own lips,
Our King appointed Brygandyne to be Clerk of all his ships.
'Nay, never lift up thy hands to me—there's no clean hands in the trade.
But steal in measure,' said Harry our King. 'There's measure in all things made!'

God speed the *Mary of the Tower,* the *Sovereign* and *Grace Dieu,*
The *Sweepstakes* and the *Mary Fortune,* and the *Henry of Bristol* too!
All tall ships that sail on the sea, or in our harbours stand,
That they may keep measure with Harry our King and peace in Engeland!

MARKLAKE WITCHES

THE WAY THROUGH THE WOODS

They shut the road through the woods
    Seventy years ago.
Weather and rain have undone it again,
    And now you would never know
There was once a road through the woods
    Before they planted the trees.
It is underneath the coppice and heath,
    And the thin anemones.
        Only the keeper sees
That, where the ring-dove broods,
    And the badgers roll at ease,
There was once a road through the woods.

Yet, if you enter the woods
    Of a summer evening late,
When the night-air cools on the trout-ringed pools
    Where the otter whistles his mate
(They fear not men in the woods
    Because they see so few),
You will hear the beat of a horse's feet
    And the swish of a skirt in the dew,
        Steadily cantering through
The misty solitudes,
    As though they perfectly knew
The old lost road through the woods . . .
But there is no road through the woods!

MARKLAKE WITCHES

WHEN DAN TOOK UP BOAT-BUILDING, Una coaxed Mrs. Vincey, the farmer's wife at Little Lindens, to teach her to milk. Mrs. Vincey milks in the pasture in summer, which is different from milking in the shed, because the cows are not tied up, and until they know you they will not stand still. After three weeks Una could milk Red Cow or Kitty Shorthorn quite dry, without her wrists aching, and then she allowed Dan to look. But milking did not amuse him, and it was pleasanter for Una to be alone in the quiet pastures with quiet-spoken Mrs. Vincey. So, evening after evening, she slipped across to Little Lindens, took her stool from the fern-clump beside the fallen oak, and went to work, her pail between her knees, and her head pressed hard into the cow's flank. As often as not, Mrs. Vincey would be milking cross Pansy at the other end of the pasture, and would not come near till it was time to strain and pour off.

Once, in the middle of a milking, Kitty Shorthorn boxed Una's ear with her tail.

'You old pig!' said Una, nearly crying, for a cow's tail can hurt.

'Why didn't you tie it down, child?' said a voice behind her.

'I meant to, but the flies are so bad I let her off—and this is what she's done!' Una looked round, expecting Puck, and saw a curly-haired girl, not much taller than herself, but older, dressed in a curious high-waisted, lavender-coloured riding-habit, with a high hunched collar and a deep cape and a belt fastened with a steel clasp. She wore a yellow velvet cap and tan gauntlets, and carried a real hunting-crop. Her cheeks were pale except for two pretty pink patches in the middle, and she talked with little gasps at the end of her sentences, as though she had been running.

'You don't milk so badly, child,' she said, and when she smiled her teeth showed small and even and pearly.

'Can you milk?' Una asked, and then flushed, for she heard Puck's chuckle.

He stepped out of the fern and sat down, holding Kitty Shorthorn's tail. 'There isn't much,' he said, 'that Miss Philadelphia doesn't know about milk—or, for that matter, butter and eggs. She's a great housewife.'

'Oh,' said Una. 'I'm sorry I can't shake hands. Mine are all milky; but Mrs. Vincey is going to teach me butter-making this summer.'

'Ah! *I'm* going to London this summer,' the girl said, 'to my aunt in Bloomsbury.' She coughed as she began to hum, ' "Oh, what a town! What a wonderful metropolis!" '

'You've got a cold,' said Una.

'No. Only my stupid cough. But it's vastly better than it was last winter. It will disappear in London air. Every one says so. D'you like doctors, child?'

'I don't know any,' Una replied. 'But I'm sure I shouldn't.'

'Think yourself lucky, child. I beg your pardon,' the girl laughed, for Una frowned.

'I'm not a child, and my name's Una,' she said.

'Mine's Philadelphia. But everybody except René calls me Phil. I'm Squire Bucksteed's daughter—over at Marklake yonder.' She jerked her little round chin towards the south behind Dallington. 'Sure-ly you know Marklake?'

'We went a picnic to Marklake Green once,' said Una. 'It's awfully pretty. I like all those funny little roads that don't lead anywhere.'

'They lead over our land,' said Philadelphia stiffly, 'and the coach road is only four miles away. One can go anywhere from the Green. I went to the Assize Ball at Lewes last year.' She spun round and took a few dancing steps, but stopped with her hand to her side.

'It gives me a stitch,' she explained. 'No odds. 'Twill go away in London air. That's the latest French step, child. René taught it me. D'you hate the French, chi—Una?'

'Well, I hate French, of course, but I don't mind Ma'm'selle. She's rather decent. Is René your French governess?'

Philadelphia laughed till she caught her breath again.

'Oh, no! René's a French prisoner—on parole. That means he's promised not to escape till he has been properly exchanged for an Englishman. He's only a doctor, so I hope they won't think him worth exchanging. My uncle captured him last year in the *Ferdinand* privateer, off Belle Isle, and he cured my uncle of a r-r-raging toothache. Of course, after *that* we couldn't let him lie among the common French prisoners at Rye, and so he stays with us. He's of very old family —a Breton, which is nearly next door to being a true Briton, my father says—and he wears his hair clubbed—not powdered. *Much* more becoming, don't you think?'

'I don't know what you're——' Una began, but Puck, the other side of the pail, winked, and she went on with her milking.

'He's going to be a great French physician when the war is over. He makes me bobbins for my lace-pillow now—he's very clever with his hands; but he'd doctor our people on the Green if they would let him. Only our Doctor—Doctor Break

—says he's an emp—— or imp something—worse than im-postor. But my Nurse says——'

'Nurse! You're ever so old. What have you got a nurse for?' Una finished milking, and turned round on her stool as Kitty Shorthorn grazed off.

'Because I can't get rid of her. Old Cissie nursed my mother, and she says she'll nurse me till she dies. The idea! She never lets me alone. She thinks I'm delicate. She has grown infirm in her understanding, you know. Mad—quite mad, poor Cissie!'

'Really mad?' said Una. 'Or just silly?'

'Crazy, I should say—from the things she does. Her devo-tion to me is terribly embarrassing. You know I have all the keys of the Hall except the brewery and the tenants' kitchen. I give out all stores and the linen and plate.'

'How jolly! I love store-rooms and giving out things.'

'Ah, it's a great responsibility, you'll find, when you come to my age. Last year Dad said I was fatiguing myself with my duties, and he actually wanted me to give up the keys to old Amoore, our housekeeper. I wouldn't. I hate her. I said, "No, sir. I am Mistress of Marklake Hall just as long as I live, because I'm never going to be married, and I shall give out stores and linen till I die!"'

'And what did your father say?'

'Oh. I threatened to pin a dishclout to his coat-tail. He ran away. Every one's afraid of Dad, except me.' Philadelphia stamped her foot. 'The idea! If I can't make my own father happy in his own house, I'd like to meet the woman that can, and—and—I'd have the living hide off her!'

She cut with her long-thonged whip. It cracked like a pistol-shot across the still pasture. Kitty Shorthorn threw up her head and trotted away.

'I beg your pardon,' Philadelphia said; 'but it makes me furious. Don't you hate those ridiculous old quizzes with their feathers and fronts, who come to dinner and call you "child" in your own chair at your own table?'

'I don't always come to dinner,' said Una, 'but I hate being called "child." Please tell me about store-rooms and giving out things.'

'Ah, it's a great responsibility—particularly with that old cat Amoore looking at the lists over your shoulder. And such a shocking thing happened last summer! Poor crazy Cissie, my Nurse that I was telling you of, she took three solid silver tablespoons.'

'Took! But isn't that stealing?' Una cried.

'Hsh!' said Philadelphia, looking round at Puck. 'All I say is she took them without my leave. I made it right afterwards. So, as Dad says—and he's a magistrate—, it wasn't a legal offence; it was only compounding a felony.'

'It sounds awful,' said Una.

'It was. My dear, I was furious! I had had the keys for ten months, and I'd never lost anything before. I said nothing at first, because a big house offers so many chances of things being mislaid, and coming to hand later. "Fetching up in the lee-scuppers," my uncle calls it. But next week I spoke to old Cissie about it when she was doing my hair at night, and she said I wasn't to worry my heart for trifles!'

'Isn't it like 'em?' Una burst out. 'They see you're worried over something that really matters, and they say, "Don't worry"; as if *that* did any good!'

'I quite agree with you, my dear; quite agree with you! I told Ciss the spoons were solid silver, and worth forty shillings, so if the thief were found, he'd be tried for his life.'

'Hanged, do you mean?' Una said.

'They ought to be; but Dad says no jury will hang a man nowadays for a forty-shilling theft. They transport 'em into penal servitude at the uttermost ends of the earth beyond the seas, for the term of their natural life. I told Cissie that, and I saw her tremble in my mirror. Then she cried, and caught hold of my knees, and I couldn't for my life understand what it was all about,—she cried so. *Can* you guess, my dear, what that poor crazy thing had done? It was midnight before I pieced it together. She had given the spoons to Jerry Gamm, the Witchmaster on the Green, so that he might put a charm on me! Me!'

'Put a charm on you? Why?'

'That's what *I* asked; and then I saw how mad poor Cissie was! You know this stupid little cough of mine? It will disappear as soon as I go to London. She was troubled about *that,* and about my being so thin, and she told me Jerry had promised her, if she would bring him three silver spoons, that he'd charm my cough away and make me plump—"flesh-up," she said. I couldn't help laughing; but it was a terrible night! I had to put Cissie into my own bed, and stroke her hand till she cried herself to sleep. What else could I have done? When she woke, and I coughed—I suppose I *can* cough in my own room if I please—she said that she'd killed me, and asked me to have her hanged at Lewes sooner than send her to the uttermost ends of the earth away from me.'

'How awful! What did you do, Phil?'

'Do? I rode off at five in the morning to talk to Master Jerry, with a new lash on my whip. Oh, I was *furious!* Witchmaster or no Witchmaster, I meant to——'

'Ah! what's a Witchmaster?'

'A master of witches, of course. *I* don't believe there are witches; but people say every village has a few, and Jerry was the master of all ours at Marklake. He has been a smuggler, and a man-of-war's man, and now he pretends to be a carpenter and joiner—he can make almost anything—but he really is a white wizard. He cures people by herbs and charms. He can cure them after Doctor Break has given them up, and that's why Doctor Break hates him so. He used to make me toy carts, and charm off my warts when I was a child.' Philadelphia spread out her hands with the delicate shiny little nails. 'It isn't counted lucky to cross him. He has his ways of getting even with you, they say. But *I* wasn't afraid of Jerry! I saw him working in his garden, and I leaned out of my saddle and double-thonged him between the shoulders, over the hedge. Well, my dear, for the first time since Dad gave him to me, my Troubadour (I wish you could see the sweet creature!) shied across the road, and I spilled out into the hedge-top. *Most* undignified! Jerry pulled me through to his side and brushed the leaves off me. I was horribly pricked, but I didn't care. "Now, Jerry," I said, "I'm going to take the hide off you first, and send you to Lewes afterwards. You well know why." "Oh!" he said, and he sat down among his bee-hives. "Then I reckon you've come about old Cissie's business, my dear." "I reckon I justabout have," I said. "Stand away from these hives. I can't get at you there." "That's why I be where I be," he said. "If you'll excuse me, Miss Phil, I don't hold with bein' flogged before breakfast, at my time o' life." He's a huge big man, but he looked so comical squatting among the hives that—I know I oughtn't to—I laughed, and he laughed. I always laugh at the wrong time. But I soon recovered my dignity, and I said. "Then give me back what you made poor Cissie steal!"

' "Your pore Cissie," he said. "She's a hatful o' trouble. But you shall have 'em, Miss Phil. They're all ready put by for you." And, would you believe it, the old sinner pulled my three silver spoons out of his dirty pocket, and polished them on his cuff! "Here they be," he says, and he gave them to me, just as cool as though I'd come to have my warts charmed. That's the worst of people having known you when you were young. But I preserved my composure. "Jerry," I said, "what in the world are we to do? If you'd been caught with these things on you, you'd have been hanged."

' "I know it," he said. "But they're yours now."

' "But you made my Cissie steal them," I said.

' "That I didn't," he said. "Your Cissie, she was pickin' at me an' tarrifyin' me all the long day an' every day for weeks, to put a charm on you, Miss Phil, an' take away your little spitty cough."

' "Yes, I knew that, Jerry, and to make me flesh-up!" I said. "I'm much obliged to you, but I'm not one of your pigs!"

' "Ah! I reckon she've been talking to you, then," he said. "Yes, she give me no peace, and bein' tarrified—for I don't hold with old women—I laid a task on her which I thought 'ud silence her. *I* never reckoned the old scrattle 'ud risk her neckbone at Lewes Assizes for your sake, Miss Phil. But she did. She up an' stole, I tell ye, as cheerful as a tinker. You might ha' knocked me down with any one of them liddle spoons when she brung 'em in her apron."

' "Do you mean to say, then, that you did it to try my poor Cissie?" I screamed at him.

' "What else for, dearie?" he said. "*I* don't stand in need of hedge-stealings. I'm a freeholder, with money in the bank; and now I won't trust women no more! Silly old besom! I do beleft she'd ha' stole the Squire's big fob-watch, if I'd required her."

' "Then you're a wicked, wicked old man," I said, and I

was so angry that I couldn't help crying, and of course that made me cough.

'Jerry was in a fearful taking. He picked me up and carried me into his cottage—it's full of foreign curiosities—and he got me something to eat and drink, and he said he'd be hanged by the neck any day if it pleased me. He said he'd even tell old Cissie he was sorry. That's a great come-down for a Witchmaster, you know.

'I was ashamed of myself for being so silly, and I dabbed my eyes and said, "The least you can do now is to give poor Ciss some sort of a charm for me."

' "Yes, that's only fair dealings," he said. "You know the names of the Twelve Apostles, dearie? You say them names, one by one, before your open window, rain or storm, wet or shine, five times a day fasting. But mind you, 'twixt every name you draw in your breath through your nose, right down to your pretty liddle toes, as long and as deep as you can, and let it out slow through your pretty liddle mouth. There's virtue for your cough in those names spoke that way. And I'll give you something you can see, moreover. Here's a stick of maple, which is the warmest tree in the wood." '

'That's true,' Una interrupted. 'You can feel it almost as warm as yourself when you touch it.'

' "It's cut one inch long for your every year," Jerry said. "That's sixteen inches. You set it in your window so that it holds up the sash, and thus you keep it, rain or shine, or wet or fine, day and night. I've said words over it which will have virtue on your complaints."

' "I haven't any complaints, Jerry," I said. "It's only to please Cissie."

' "I know that as well as you do, dearie," he said. And—and that was all that came of my going to give him a flogging.

337

I wonder whether he made poor Troubadour shy when I lashed at him? Jerry has his ways of getting even with people.'

'I wonder,' said Una. 'Well, did you try the charm? Did it work?'

'What nonsense! I told René about it, of course, because he's a doctor. He's going to be a most famous doctor. That's why our doctor hates him. René said, "Oho! Your Master Gamm, he is worth knowing," and he put up his eyebrows—like this. He made joke of it all. He can see my window from the carpenter's shed, where he works, and if ever the maple stick fell down, he pretended to be in a fearful taking till I propped the window up again. He used to ask me whether I had said my Apostles properly, and how I took my deep breaths. Oh yes, and the next day, though he had been there ever so many times before, he put on his new hat and paid Jerry Gamm a visit of state—as a fellow-physician. Jerry never guessed René was making fun of him, and so he told René about the sick people in the village, and how he cured them with herbs after Doctor Break had given them up. Jerry could talk smugglers' French, of course, and I had taught René plenty of English, if only he wasn't so shy. They called each other Monsieur Gamm and Mosheur Lanark, just like gentlemen. I suppose it amused poor René. He hasn't much to do, except to fiddle about in the carpenter's shop. He's like all the French prisoners—always making knick-knacks; and Jerry had a little lathe at his cottage, and so—and so—René took to being with Jerry much more than I approved of. The Hall is so big and empty when Dad's away, and I will *not* sit with old Amoore—she talks so horridly about every one —specially about René.

'I was rude to René, I'm afraid; but I was properly served

out for it. One always is. You see, Dad went down to Hastings
to pay his respects to the General who commanded the
brigade there, and to bring him to the Hall afterwards. Dad
told me he was a very brave soldier from India—he was
Colonel of Dad's Regiment, the Thirty-third Foot, after Dad
left the Army, and then he changed his name from Wesley
to Wellesley, or else the other way about; and Dad said I was
to get out all the silver for him, and I knew that meant a big
dinner. So I sent down to the sea for early mackerel, and had
such a morning in the kitchen and the store-rooms. Old
Amoore nearly cried.

'However, my dear, I made all my preparations in ample
time, but the fish didn't arrive—it never does—and I wanted
René to ride to Pevensey and bring it himself. He had gone
over to Jerry, of course, as he always used, unless I requested
his presence beforehand. *I* can't send for René every time I
want him. He should be there. Now, don't you ever do what
I did, child, because it's in the highest degree unladylike; but
—but one of our woods runs up to Jerry's garden, and if you
climb—it's ungenteel, but I can climb like a kitten—there's
an old hollow oak just above the pigsty where you can hear
and see everything below. Truthfully, I only went to tell René
about the mackerel, but I saw him and Jerry sitting on the
seat playing with wooden toy trumpets. So I slipped into the
hollow, and choked down my cough, and listened. René had
never shown me any of these trumpets.'

'Trumpets? Aren't you too old for trumpets?' said Una.

'They weren't real trumpets, because Jerry opened his shirt-
collar, and René put one end of his trumpet against Jerry's
chest, and put his ear to the other. Then Jerry put his
trumpet against René's chest, and listened while René
breathed and coughed. I was afraid *I* would cough too.

' "This hollywood one is the best," said Jerry. " 'Tis won'erful like hearin' a man's soul whisperin' in his innards; but
unless I've a buzzin' in my ears, Mosheur Lanark, you make
much about the same kind o' noises as old Gaffer Macklin—
but not quite so loud as young Copper. It sounds like breakers
on a reef—a long way off. Comprenny?"

' "Perfectly," said René. "I drive on the breakers. But before I strike, I shall save hundreds, thousands, millions perhaps, by my little trumpets. Now tell me what sounds the old
Gaffer Macklin have made in his chest, and what the young
Copper also."

'Jerry talked for nearly a quarter of an hour about sick
people in the village, while René asked questions. Then he
sighed, and said, "You explain very well, Monsieur Gamm,
but if only I had your opportunities to listen for myself!
Do you think these poor people would let me listen to them
through my trumpet—for a little money? No?"—René's as
poor as a church mouse.

' "They'd kill you, Mosheur. It's all I can do to coax 'em
to abide it, and I'm Jerry Gamm," said Jerry. He's very proud
of his attainments.

' "Then these poor people are alarmed—No?" said René.

' "They've had it in at me for some time back because o'
my tryin' your trumpets on their sick; and I reckon by the talk
at the alehouse they won't stand much more. Tom Dunch an'
some of his kidney was drinkin' themselves riot-ripe when
I passed along after noon. Charms an' mutterin's an' bits o'
red wool an' black hens is in the way o' nature to these fools,
Mosheur; but anything likely to do 'em real service is devil's
work by their estimation. If I was you, I'd go home before they
come." Jerry spoke quite quietly, and René shrugged his
shoulders.

' "I am prisoner on parole, Monsieur Gamm," he said. "I
have no home."

'Now that was unkind of René. He's often told me that he
looked on England as his home. I suppose it's French politeness.

' "Then we'll talk o' something that matters," said Jerry.
"Not to name no names, Mosheur Lanark, what might be your
own opinion o' some one who ain't old Gaffer Macklin nor
young Copper? Is that person better or worse?"

' "Better—for time that is," said René. He meant for the
time being, but I never could teach him some phrases.

' "I thought so too," said Jerry. "But how about time to
come?"

'René shook his head, and then he blew his nose. You don't
know how odd a man looks blowing his nose when you are
sitting directly above him.

' "I've thought that too," said Jerry. He rumbled so deep
I could scarcely catch. "It don't make much odds to me, because I'm old. But you're young, Mosheur—you're young,"
and he put his hand on René's knee, and René covered it with
his hand. I didn't know they were such friends.

' "Thank you, *mon ami*," said René. "I am much oblige.
Let us return to our trumpet-making. But I forget"—he stood
up—"it appears that you receive this afternoon!"

'You can't see into Gamm's Lane from the oak, but the
gate opened, and fat little Doctor Break stumped in, mopping
his head, and half-a-dozen of our people followed him, very
drunk.

'You ought to have seen René bow; he does it beautifully.

' "A word with you, Laennec," said Doctor Break. "Jerry
has been practising some devilry or other on these poor
wretches, and they've asked me to be arbiter."

' "Whatever that means, I reckon it's safer than asking you
to be doctor," said Jerry, and Tom Dunch, one of our carters,
laughed.

' "That ain't right feeling of you, Tom," Jerry said, "seeing
how clever Doctor Break put away your thorn in the flesh
last winter." Tom's wife had died at Christmas, though
Doctor Break bled her twice a week. Doctor Break danced
with rage.

' "This is all beside the mark," he said. "These good people
are willing to testify that you've been impudently prying into
God's secrets by means of some papistical contrivance which
this person"—he pointed to poor René—"has furnished you
with. Why, here are the things themselves!" René was holding
a trumpet in his hand.

'Then all the men talked at once. They said old Gaffer
Macklin was dying from stitches in his side where Jerry had
put the trumpet—they called it the devil's ear-piece; and they
said it left round red witch-marks on people's skins, and dried
up their lights, and made 'em spit blood, and threw 'em into
sweats. Terrible things they said. You never heard such a
noise. I took advantage of it to cough.

'René and Jerry were standing with their backs to the pigsty.
Jerry fumbled in his big flap pockets and fished up a pair of
pistols. You ought to have seen the men give back when he
cocked his. He passed one to René.

' "Wait! Wait!" said René. "I will explain to the doctor if he
permits." He waved a trumpet at him, and the men at the
gate shouted, "Don't touch it, Doctor! Don't lay a hand to
the thing."

' "Come, come!" said René. "You are not so big fool as you
pretend. No?"

'Doctor Break backed toward the gate, watching Jerry's

pistol, and René followed him with his trumpet, like a nurse trying to amuse a child, and put the ridiculous thing to his ear to show how it was used, and talked of *la Gloire*, and *l'Humanité*, and *la Science*, while Doctor Break watched Jerry's pistol and swore. I nearly laughed aloud.

' "Now listen! Now listen!" said René. "This will be moneys in your pockets, my dear *confrère*. You will become rich."

'Then Doctor Break said something about adventurers who could not earn an honest living in their own country creeping into decent houses and taking advantage of gentlemen's confidence to enrich themselves by base intrigues.

'René dropped his absurd trumpet and made one of his best bows. I knew he was angry from the way he rolled his "r's."

' "Ver-r-ry good," said he. "For that I shall have much pleasure to kill you now and here. Monsieur Gamm,"—another bow to Jerry—"you will please lend him your pistol, or he shall have mine. I give you my word I know not which is best; and if he will choose a second from his friends over there"—another bow to our drunken yokels at the gate—"we will commence."

' "That's fair enough," said Jerry. "Tom Dunch, you owe it to the Doctor to be his second. Place your man."

' "No," said Tom. "No mixin' in gentry's quarrels for me." And he shook his head and went out, and the others followed him.

' "Hold on," said Jerry. "You've forgot what you set out to do up at the alehouse just now. You was goin' to search me for witch-marks; you was goin' to duck me in the pond; you was goin' to drag all my bits o' sticks out o' my little cottage here. What's the matter with you? Wouldn't you like to be with your old woman to-night, Tom?"

'But they didn't even look back, much less come. They ran to the village alehouse like hares.

' "No matter for these *canaille*," said René, buttoning up his coat so as not to show any linen. All gentlemen do that before a duel, Dad says—and he's been out five times. "You shall be his second, Monsieur Gamm. Give him the pistol."

'Doctor Break took it as if it was red-hot, but he said that if René resigned his pretensions in certain quarters he would pass over the matter. René bowed deeper than ever.

' "As for that," he said, "if you were not the ignorant which you are, you would have known long ago that the subject of your remarks is not for any living man."

'I don't know what the subject of his remarks might have been, but he spoke in a simply dreadful voice, my dear, and Doctor Break turned quite white, and said René was a liar; and then René caught him by the throat, and choked him black.

'Well, my dear, as if this wasn't deliciously exciting enough, just exactly at that minute I heard a strange voice on the other side of the hedge say, "What's this? What's this, Bucksteed?" and there was my father and Sir Arthur Wesley on horseback in the lane; and there was René kneeling on Doctor Break, and there was I up in the oak, listening with all my ears.

'I must have leaned forward too much, and the voice gave me such a start that I slipped. I had only time to make one jump on to the pigsty roof—another, before the tiles broke, on to the pigsty wall—and then I bounced down into the garden, just behind Jerry, with my hair full of bark. Imagine the situation!'

'Oh, I can!' Una laughed till she nearly fell off the stool.

'Dad said, "Phil—a—del—phia!" and Sir Arthur Wesley said, "Good Ged!" and Jerry put his foot on the pistol René had dropped. But René was splendid. He never even looked at me. He began to untwist Doctor Break's neckcloth as fast as he'd twisted it, and asked him if he felt better.

' "What's happened? What's happened?" said Dad.

' "A fit!" said René. "I fear my *confrère* has had a fit. Do not be alarmed. He recovers himself. Shall I bleed you a little, my dear Doctor?" Doctor Break was very good too. He said, "I am vastly obliged, Monsieur Laennec, but I am restored now." And as he went out of the gate he told Dad it was a syncope—a think. Then Sir Arthur said, "Quite right, Bucksteed. Not another word! They are both gentlemen." And he took off his cocked hat to Doctor Break and René.

'But poor Dad wouldn't let well alone. He kept saying, "Philadelphia, what does all this mean?"

' "Well, sir," I said, "I've only just come down. As far as I could see, it looked as though Doctor Break had had a sudden seizure." That was quite true—if you'd seen René seize him. Sir Arthur laughed. "Not much change there, Bucksteed," he said. "She's a lady—a thorough lady."

' "Heaven knows she doesn't look like one," said poor Dad. "Go home, Philadelphia."

'So I went home, my dear—don't laugh so!—right under Sir Arthur's nose—a most enormous nose—feeling as though I were twelve years old, going to be whipped. Oh, I *beg* your pardon, child!'

'It's all right,' said Una. 'I'm getting on for thirteen. I've never been whipped, but I know how you felt. All the same, it must have been funny!'

'Funny! If you'd heard Sir Arthur jerking out, "Good Ged, Bucksteed!" every minute as they rode behind me; and poor Dad saying, " 'Pon my honour, Arthur, I can't account for it!" Oh, how my cheeks tingled when I reached my room! But Cissie had laid out my very best evening dress, the white satin one, vandyked at the bottom with spots of morone foil, and the pearl knots, you know, catching up the drapery from the left shoulder. I had poor mother's lace tucker and her coronet comb.'

'Oh, you lucky!' Una murmured. '*And* gloves?'

'French kid, my dear'—Philadelphia patted her shoulder—'and morone satin shoes and a morone and gold crape fan. That restored my calm. Nice things always do. I wore my hair banded on my forehead with a little curl over the left ear. And when I descended the stairs, *en grande tenue*, old Amoore curtsied to me without my having to stop and look at her, which, alas! is too often the case. Sir Arthur highly approved of the dinner, my dear: the mackerel *did* come in time. We had all the Marklake silver out, and he toasted my health, and he asked me where my little bird's-nesting sister was. I *know* he did it to quiz me, so I looked him straight in the face, my dear, and I said, "I always send her to the nursery, Sir Arthur, when I receive guests at Marklake Hall." '

'Oh, how chee—clever of you. What did he say?' Una cried.

'He said, "Not much change there, Bucksteed. Ged, I deserved it," and he toasted me again. They talked about the French and what a shame it was that Sir Arthur only commanded a brigade at Hastings, and he told Dad of a battle in India at a place called Assaye. Dad said it was a terrible fight, but Sir Arthur described it as though it had been a whist-party—I suppose because a lady was present.'

'Of course you were the lady. I wish I'd seen you,' said Una.

'I wish you had, child. I had *such* a triumph after dinner. René and Doctor Break came in. They had quite made up their quarrel, and they told me they had the highest esteem for each other, and I laughed and said, "I heard every word of it up in the tree." You never saw two men so frightened in your life, and when I said, "What *was* 'the subject of your remarks,' René?" neither of them knew where to look. Oh, I quizzed them unmercifully. They'd seen me jump off the pigsty roof, remember.'

'But what *was* the subject of their remarks?' said Una.

'Oh, Doctor Break said it was a professional matter, so the laugh was turned on me. I was horribly afraid it might have been something unladylike and indelicate. But *that* wasn't my triumph. Dad asked me to play on the harp. Between just you and me, child, I had been practising a new song from London—I don't always live in trees—for weeks; and I gave it them for a surprise.'

'What was it?' said Una. 'Sing it.'

' "I have given my heart to a flower." Not very difficult fingering, but r-r-ravishing sentiment.'

Philadelphia coughed and cleared her throat.

'I've a deep voice for my age and size,' she explained. 'Contralto, you know, but it ought to be stronger,' and she began, her face all dark against the last of the soft pink sunset:—

> *'I have given my heart to a flower,*
> *Though I know it is fading away,*
> *Though I know it will live but an hour*
> *And leave me to mourn its decay!*

'Isn't that touchingly sweet? Then the last verse—I wish I had my harp, dear—goes as low as my register will reach.' She drew in her chin, and took a deep breath:—

> *'Ye desolate whirlwinds that rave,*
> *I charge you be good to my dear!*

She is all—she is all that I have,
And the time of our parting is near!'

'Beautiful!' said Una. 'And did they like it?'

'Like it? They were overwhelmed—*accablés*, as René says. My dear, if I hadn't seen it, I shouldn't have believed that I could have drawn tears, genuine tears, to the eyes of four grown men. But I did! René simply couldn't endure it! He's all French sensibility. He hid his face and said, *"Assez, Mademoiselle! C'est plus fort que moi! Assez!"* And Sir Arthur blew his nose and said, "Good Ged! This is worse than Assaye!" While Dad sat with the tears simply running down his cheeks.'

'And what did Doctor Break do?'

'He got up and pretended to look out of the window, but I saw his little fat shoulders jerk as if he had the hiccoughs. That *was* a triumph. I never suspected him of sensibility.'

'Oh, I wish I'd seen! I wish I'd been you,' said Una, clasping her hands. Puck rustled and rose from the fern, just as a big blundering cockchafer flew smack against Una's cheek.

When she had finished rubbing the place, Mrs. Vincey called to her that Pansy had been fractious, or she would have come long before to help her strain and pour off.

'It didn't matter,' said Una; 'I just waited. Is that old Pansy barging about the lower pasture now?'

'No,' said Mrs. Vincey, listening. 'It sounds more like a horse being galloped middlin' quick through the woods; but there's no road there. I reckon it's one of Gleason's colts loose. Shall I see you up to the house, Miss Una?'

'Gracious, no! thank you. What's going to hurt me?' said Una, and she put her stool away behind the oak, and strolled home through the gaps that old Hobden kept open for her.

BROOKLAND ROAD

I was very well pleased with what I knowed,
  I reckoned myself no fool—
Till I met with a maid on the Brookland Road
  That turned me back to school.

  Low down—low down!
  Where the liddle green lanterns shine—
  Oh! maids, I've done with 'ee all but one,
  And she can never be mine!

'Twas right in the middest of a hot June night,
  With thunder duntin' round,
And I seed her face by the fairy light
  That beats from off the ground.

She only smiled and she never spoke,
  She smiled and went away;
But when she'd gone my heart was broke,
  And my wits was clean astray.

Oh! Stop your ringing and let me be—
  Let be, O Brookland bells!
You'll ring Old Goodman[1] out of the sea,
  Before I wed one else!

Old Goodman's farm is rank sea sand,
  And was this thousand year;
But it shall turn to rich plough land
  Before I change my dear!

[1] Earl Godwin of the Goodwin Sands (?).

REWARDS AND FAIRIES

Oh! Fairfield Church is water-bound
   From Autumn to the Spring;
But it shall turn to high hill ground
   Before my bells do ring!

Oh! leave me walk on the Brookland Road,
   In the thunder and warm rain—
Oh! leave me look where my love goed
   And p'raps I'll see her again!

   Low down—low down!
   Where the liddle green lanterns shine—
   Oh! maids, I've done with 'ee all but one,
   And she can never be mine!

THE KNIFE AND THE NAKED CHALK

THE RUN OF THE DOWNS

The Weald is good, the Downs are best—
I'll give you the run of 'em, East to West.
Beachy Head and Winddoor Hill,
They were once and they are still.
Firle, Mount Caburn and Mount Harry
Go back as far as sums 'll carry.
Ditchling Beacon and Chanctonbury Ring,
They have looked on many a thing;
And what those two have missed between 'em
I reckon Truleigh Hill has seen 'em.
Highden, Bignor and Duncton Down
Knew Old England before the Crown.
Linch Down, Treyford and Sunwood
Knew Old England before the Flood.
And when you end on the Hampshire side—
Butser's old as Time and Tide.
   The Downs are sheep, the Weald is corn,
   You be glad you are Sussex born!

THE KNIFE AND THE NAKED CHALK

THE CHILDREN WENT TO THE SEASIDE for a month, and lived in a flint village on the bare windy chalk Downs, quite thirty miles away from home. They made friends with an old shepherd, called Mr. Dudeney, who had known their Father when their Father was little. He did not talk like their own people in the Weald of Sussex, and he used different names for farm things, but he understood how they felt, and let them go with him. He had a tiny cottage about half a mile from the village, where his wife made mead from thyme honey, and nursed sick lambs in front of a coal fire, while Old Jim, who was Mr. Dudeney's sheep-dog's father, lay at the door. They brought up beef bones for Old Jim (you must never give a sheep-dog mutton bones), and if Mr. Dudeney happened to be far in the Downs, Mrs. Dudeney would tell the dog to take them to him, and he did.

One August afternoon when the village water-cart had made the street smell specially townified, they went to look for their shepherd as usual, and, as usual, Old Jim crawled over the door-step and took them in charge. The sun was hot, the dry grass was very slippery, and the distances were very distant.

'It's just like the sea,' said Una, when Old Jim halted in the shade of a lonely flint barn on a bare rise. 'You see where you're going, and—you go there, and there's nothing between.'

Dan slipped off his shoes. 'When we get home I shall sit in the woods all day,' he said.

'Whuff!' said Old Jim, to show he was ready, and struck

across a long rolling stretch of turf. Presently he asked for his beef bone.

'Not yet,' said Dan. 'Where's Mr. Dudeney? Where's Master?'

Old Jim looked as if he thought they were mad, and asked again.

'Don't you give it him,' Una cried. 'I'm not going to be left howling in a desert.'

'Show, boy! Show!' said Dan, for the Downs seemed as bare as the palm of your hand.

Old Jim sighed, and trotted forward. Soon they spied the blob of Mr. Dudeney's hat against the sky a long way off.

'Right! All right!' said Dan. Old Jim wheeled round, took his bone carefully between his blunted teeth, and returned to the shadow of the old barn, looking just like a wolf. The children went on. Two kestrels hung bivvering and squealing above them. A gull flapped lazily along the white edge of the cliffs. The curves of the Downs shook a little in the heat, and so did Mr. Dudeney's distant head.

They walked toward it very slowly and found themselves staring into a horseshoe-shaped hollow a hundred feet deep, whose steep sides were laced with tangled sheep-tracks. The flock grazed on the flat at the bottom, under charge of Young Jim. Mr. Dudeney sat comfortably knitting on the edge of the slope, his crook between his knees. They told him what Old Jim had done.

'Ah, he thought you could see my head as soon as he did. The closeter you be to the turf the more you see things. You look warm-like,' said Mr. Dudeney.

'We be,' said Una, flopping down. '*And* tired.'

'Set beside o' me here. The shadow'll begin to stretch out in a little while, and a heat-shake o' wind will come up with it that'll overlay your eyes like so much wool.'

'We don't want to sleep,' said Una indignantly; but she settled herself as she spoke, in the first strip of early afternoon shade.

'O' course not. You come to talk with me same as your father used. *He* didn't need no dog to guide him to Norton Pit.'

'Well, he belonged here,' said Dan, and laid himself down at length on the turf.

'He did. And what beats me is why he went off to live among them messy trees in the Weald, when he might ha' stayed here and looked all about him. There's no profit to trees. They draw the lightning, and sheep shelter under 'em, and *so*, like as not, you'll lose a half-score ewes struck dead in one storm. Tck! Your father knew that.'

'Trees aren't messy.' Una rose on her elbow. 'And what about firewood? I don't like coal.'

'Eh? You lie a piece more uphill and you'll lie more natural,' said Mr. Dudeney, with his provoking deaf smile. 'Now press your face down and smell to the turf. That's Southdown thyme which makes our Southdown mutton beyond compare, and, my mother told me, 'twill cure anything except broken necks, or hearts. I forget which.'

They sniffed, and somehow forgot to lift their cheeks from the soft thymy cushions.

'You don't get nothing like that in the Weald. Watercress, maybe?' said Mr. Dudeney.

'But we've water—brooks full of it—where you paddle in hot weather,' Una replied, watching a yellow-and-violet-banded snail-shell close to her eye.

'Brooks flood. Then you must shift your sheep—let alone foot-rot afterward. I put more dependence on a dew-pond any day.'

'How's a dew-pond made?' said Dan, and tilted his hat over his eyes. Mr. Dudeney explained.

The air trembled a little as though it could not make up its mind whether to slide into the Pit or move across the open. But it seemed easiest to go downhill, and the children felt one soft puff after another slip and sidle down the slope in fragrant breaths that baffed on their eyelids. The little whisper of the sea by the cliffs joined with the whisper of the wind over the grass, the hum of insects in the thyme, the ruffle and rustle of the flock below, and a thickish mutter deep in the very chalk beneath them. Mr. Dudeney stopped explaining, and went on with his knitting.

They were roused by voices. The shadow had crept half-way down the steep side of Norton Pit, and on the edge of it, his back to them, Puck sat beside a half-naked man who seemed busy at some work. The wind had dropped, and in that funnel of ground every least noise and movement reached them like whispers up a water-pipe.

'That is clever,' said Puck, leaning over. 'How truly you shape it!'

'Yes, but what does The Beast care for a brittle flint tip? Bah!' The man flicked something contemptuously over his shoulder. It fell between Dan and Una—a beautiful dark-blue flint arrow-head still hot from the maker's hand.

The man reached for another stone, and worked away like a thrush with a snail-shell.

'Flint work is fool's work,' he said at last. 'One does it because one always did it; but when it comes to dealing with The Beast—no good!' He shook his shaggy head.

'The Beast was dealt with long ago. He has gone,' said Puck.

'He'll be back at lambing-time. *I* know him.' He chipped very carefully, and the flints squeaked.

'Not he. Children can lie out on the Chalk now all day through and go home safe.'

'Can they? Well, call The Beast by his True Name, and I'll believe it,' the man replied.

'Surely!' Puck leaped to his feet, curved his hands round his mouth and shouted: 'Wolf! Wolf!'

Norton Pit threw back the echo from its dry sides—'Wuff! Wuff!' like Young Jim's bark.

'You see? You hear?' said Puck. 'Nobody answers. Grey Shepherd is gone. Feet-in-the-Night has run off. There are no more wolves.'

'Wonderful!' The man wiped his forehead as though he were hot. 'Who drove him away? You?'

'Many men through many years, each working in his own country. Were you one of them?' Puck answered.

The man slid his sheepskin cloak to his waist, and without a word pointed to his side, which was all seamed and blotched with scars. His arms, too, were dimpled from shoulder to elbow with horrible white dimples.

'I see,' said Puck. 'It is The Beast's mark. What did you use against him?'

'Hand, hammer, and spear, as our fathers did before us.'

'So? Then how'—Puck twitched aside the man's dark-brown cloak—'how did a Flint-worker come by *that*? Show, man, show!' He held out his little hand.

The man slipped a long dark iron knife, almost a short sword, from his belt, and after breathing on it, handed it hilt-first to Puck, who took it with his head on one side, as you should when you look at the works of a watch, squinted down the dark blade, and very delicately rubbed his forefinger from the point to the hilt.

'Good!' said he, in a surprised tone.

'It should be. The Children of the Night made it,' the man answered.

'So I see by the iron. What might it have cost you?'

'This!' The man raised his hand to his cheek. Puck whistled like a Weald starling.

'By the Great Rings of the Chalk!' he cried. 'Was *that* your price? Turn sunward that I may see better, and shut your eye.'

He slipped his hand beneath the man's chin and swung him till he faced the children up the slope. They saw that his right eye was gone, and the eyelid lay shrunk. Quickly Puck turned him round again, and the two sat down.

'It was for the sheep. The sheep are the people,' said the man, in an ashamed voice. 'What else could I have done? *You* know, Old One.'

Puck sighed a little fluttering sigh. 'Take the knife. I listen.'

The man bowed his head, drove the knife into the turf, and while it still quivered said: 'This is witness between us that I speak the thing that has been. Before my Knife and the Naked Chalk I speak. Touch!'

Puck laid a hand on the hilt. It stopped shaking. The children wriggled a little nearer.

'I am of the People of the Worked Flint. I am the one son of the Priestess who sells the Winds to the Men of the Sea. I am the Buyer of the Knife—the Keeper of the People,' the man began, in a sort of singing shout. 'These are my names in this country of the Naked Chalk, between the Trees and the Sea.'

'Yours was a great country. Your names are great too,' said Puck.

'One cannot feed some things on names and songs.' The man hit himself on the chest. 'It is better—always better—to count one's children safe round the fire, their Mother among them.'

'Ahai!' said Puck. 'I think this will be a very old tale.'

'I warm myself and eat at any fire that I choose, but there is no *one* to light me a fire or cook my meat. I sold all that when I bought the Magic Knife for my people. It was not right that The Beast should master man. What else could I have done?'

'I hear. I know. I listen,' said Puck.

'When I was old enough to take my place in the Sheep-guard, The Beast gnawed all our country like a bone between his teeth. He came in behind the flocks at watering-time, and watched them round the Dew-ponds; he leaped into the folds between our knees at the shearing; he walked out alongside the grazing flocks, and chose his meat on the hoof while our boys threw flints at him; he crept by night into the huts, and licked the babe from between the mother's hands; he called his companions and pulled down men in broad daylight on the Naked Chalk. No—not always did he do so! *This* was his cunning! He would go away for a while to let us forget him. A year—two years perhaps—we neither smelt, nor heard, nor saw him. When our flocks had increased; when our men did not always look behind them; when children strayed from the fenced places; when our women walked alone to draw water —back, back, back came the Curse of the Chalk, Grey Shep-herd, Feet-in-the-Night—The Beast, The Beast, The Beast!

'He laughed at our little brittle arrows and our poor blunt spears. He learned to run in under the stroke of the hammer. I think he knew when there was a flaw in the flint. Often it does not show till you bring it down on his snout. Then— *Pouf!*—the false flint falls all to flinders, and you are left with the hammer-handle in your fist, and his teeth in your flank! I have felt them. At evening, too, in the dew, or when it has misted and rained, your spear-head lashings slack off, though you have kept them beneath your cloak all day. You are alone —but so close to the home ponds that you stop to tighten the sinews with hands, teeth, and a piece of driftwood. You bend

over and pull—so! That is the minute for which he has followed you since the stars went out. "Aarh!" he says. "Wurr-
aarh!" he says.' (Norton Pit gave back the growl like a pack of
real wolves.) 'Then he is on your right shoulder feeling for the
vein in your neck, and—perhaps your sheep run on without
you. To fight The Beast is nothing, but to be despised by The
Beast when he fights you—that is like his teeth in the heart!
Old One, why is it that men desire so greatly, and can do so
little?'

'I do not know. Did you desire so much?' said Puck.

'I desired to master The Beast. It is not right that The Beast
should master man. But my people were afraid. Even my
Mother, the Priestess, was afraid when I told her what I desired. We were accustomed to be afraid of The Beast. When
I was made a man, and a maiden—she was a Priestess—waited
for me at the Dew-ponds, The Beast flitted from off the Chalk.
Perhaps it was a sickness; perhaps he had gone to his Gods to
learn how to do us new harm. But he went, and we breathed
more freely. The women sang again; the children were not so
much guarded; our flocks grazed far out. I took mine yonder'
—he pointed inland to the hazy line of the Weald—'where
the new grass was best. They grazed north. I followed till we
were close to the Trees'—he lowered his voice—'close *there*
where the Children of the Night live.' He pointed north again.

'Ah, now I remember a thing,' said Puck. 'Tell me, why did
your people fear the Trees so extremely?'

'Because the Gods hate the Trees and strike them with
lightning. We can see them burning for days all along the
Chalk's edge. Besides, all the Chalk knows that the Children
of the Night, though they worship our Gods, are magicians.
When a man goes into their country, they change his spirit;
they put words into his mouth; they make him like talking

water. But a voice in my heart told me to go toward the north. While I watched my sheep there I saw three Beasts chasing a man, who ran toward the Trees. By this I knew he was a Child of the Night. We Flint-workers fear the Trees more than we fear The Beast. He had no hammer. He carried a knife like this one. A Beast leaped at him. He stretched out his knife. The Beast fell dead. The other Beasts ran away howling, which they would never have done from a Flint-worker. The man went in among the Trees. I looked for the dead Beast. He had been killed in a new way—by a single deep, clean cut, without bruise or tear, which had split his bad heart. Wonderful! So I saw that the man's knife was magic, and I thought how to get it,—thought strongly how to get it.

'When I brought the flocks to the shearing, my Mother the Priestess asked me, "What is the new thing which you have seen and I see in your face?" I said, "It is a sorrow to me"; and she answered, "All new things are sorrow. Sit in my place, and eat sorrow." I sat down in her place by the fire, where she talks to the ghosts in winter, and two voices spoke in my heart. One voice said, "Ask the Children of the Night for the Magic Knife. It is not fit that The Beast should master man." I listened to that voice.

'One voice said, "If you go among the Trees, the Children of the Night will change your spirit. Eat and sleep here." The other voice said, "Ask for the Knife." I listened to that voice.

'I said to my Mother in the morning, "I go away to find a thing for the people, but I do not know whether I shall return in my own shape." She answered, "Whether you live or die, or are made different, I am your Mother." '

'True,' said Puck. 'The Old Ones themselves cannot change men's mothers even if they would.'

'Let us thank the Old Ones! I spoke to my Maiden, the Priestess who waited for me at the Dew-ponds. She promised fine things too.' The man laughed. 'I went away to that place where I had seen the magician with the knife. I lay out two days on the short grass before I ventured among the Trees. I felt my way before me with a stick. I was afraid of the terrible talking Trees. I was afraid of the ghosts in the branches; of the soft ground underfoot; of the red and black waters. I was afraid, above all, of the Change. It came!'

They saw him wipe his forehead once again, and his strong back-muscles quivered till he laid his hand on the knife-hilt.

'A fire without a flame burned in my head; an evil taste grew in my mouth; my eyelids shut hot over my eyes; my breath was hot between my teeth, and my hands were like the hands of a stranger. I was made to sing songs and to mock the Trees, though I was afraid of them. At the same time I saw myself laughing, and I was very sad for this fine young man, who was myself. Ah! The Children of the Night know magic.'

'I think that is done by the Spirits of the Mist. They change a man if he sleeps among them,' said Puck. 'Had you slept in any mists?'

'Yes—but *I* know it was the Children of the Night. After three days I saw a red light behind the Trees, and I heard a heavy noise. I saw the Children of the Night dig red stones from a hole, and lay them in fires. The stones melted like tallow, and the men beat the soft stuff with hammers. I wished to speak to these men, but the words were changed in my mouth, and all I could say was, "Do not make that noise. It hurts my head." By this I knew that I was bewitched, and I clung to the Trees, and prayed the Children of the Night to take off their spells. They were cruel. They asked me many questions which they would never allow me to answer. They changed my words between my teeth till I wept. Then they led me into a hut and covered the floor with hot stones and dashed water on the stones, and sang charms till the sweat poured off me like water. I slept. When I waked, my own spirit —not the strange, shouting thing—was back in my body, and I was like a cool bright stone on the shingle between the sea and the sunshine. The magicians came to hear me—women and men—each wearing a Magic Knife. Their Priestess was their Ears and their Mouth.

'I spoke. I spoke many words that went smoothly along like sheep in order when their shepherd, standing on a mound, can count those coming, and those far off getting ready to come. I asked for Magic Knives for my people. I said that my people would bring meat, and milk, and wool, and lay them in the short grass outside the Trees, if the Children of the Night would leave Magic Knives for our people to take away. They were pleased. Their Priestess said, "For whose sake have you come?" I answered, "The sheep are the people. If The Beast kills our sheep, our people die. So I come for a Magic Knife to kill The Beast."

'She said, "We do not know if our God will let us trade with the people of the Naked Chalk. Wait till we have asked."

'When they came back from the Question-place (their Gods are our Gods), their Priestess said, "The God needs a proof that your words are true." I said, "What is the proof?" She said, "The God says that if you have come for the sake of your people you will give him your right eye to be put out; but if you have come for any other reason you will not give it. This proof is between you and the God. We ourselves are sorry."

'I said, "This is a hard proof. Is there no other road?"

'She said, "Yes. You can go back to your people with your

two eyes in your head if you choose. But then you will not get any Magic Knives for your people."

'I said, "It would be easier if I knew that I were to be killed."

'She said, "Perhaps the God knew this too. See! I have made my knife hot."

'I said, "Be quick, then!" With her knife heated in the flame she put out my right eye. She herself did it. I am the son of a Priestess. She was a Priestess. It was not work for any common man.'

'True! Most true,' said Puck. 'No common man's work, that. And, afterwards?'

'Afterwards I did not see out of that eye any more. I found also that a one eye does not tell you truly where things are. Try it!'

At this Dan put his hand over one eye, and reached for the flint arrow-head on the grass. He missed it by inches. 'It's true,' he whispered to Una. 'You can't judge distances a bit with only one eye.'

Puck was evidently making the same experiment, for the man laughed at him.

'I know it is so,' said he. 'Even now I am not always sure of my blow. I stayed with the Children of the Night till my eye healed. They said I was the son of Tyr, the God who put his right hand in a Beast's mouth. They showed me how they melted their red stone and made the Magic Knives of it. They told me the charms they sang over the fires and at the beatings. I can sing many charms.' Then he began to laugh like a boy.

'I was thinking of my journey home,' he said, 'and of the surprised Beast. He had come back to the Chalk. I saw him— I smelt his lairs as soon as ever I left the Trees. He did not know I had the Magic Knife—I hid it under my cloak—the

Knife that the Priestess gave me. Ho! Ho! That happy day
was too short! See! A Beast would wind me. "Wow!" he
would say. "Here is my Flint-worker!" He would come leaping, tail in air; he would roll; he would lay his head between
his paws out of merriness of heart at his warm, waiting meal.
He would leap—and, oh, his eye in mid-leap when he saw—
when he saw the knife held ready for him! It pierced his hide
as a rush pierces curdled milk. Often he had no time to howl.
I did not trouble to flay any beasts I killed. Sometimes I
missed my blow. Then I took my little flint hammer and beat
out his brains as he cowered. He made no fight. He knew the
Knife! But The Beast is very cunning. Before evening all The
Beasts had smelt the blood on my knife, and were running
from me like hares. *They* knew! Then I walked as a man
should—the Master of The Beast!

'So came I back to my Mother's house. There was a lamb to
be killed. I cut it in two halves with my knife, and I told her
all my tale. She said, "This is the work of a God." I kissed her
and laughed. I went to my Maiden who waited for me at the
Dew-ponds. There was a lamb to be killed. I cut it in two
halves with my knife, and told her all my tale. She said, "It is
the work of a God." I laughed, but she pushed me away, and
being on my blind side, ran off before I could kiss her. I went
to the Men of the Sheepguard at watering-time. There was a
sheep to be killed for their meat. I cut it in two halves with
my knife, and told them all my tale. They said, "It is the work
of a God." I said, "We talk too much about Gods. Let us eat
and be happy, and to-morrow I will take you to the Children
of the Night, and each man will find a Magic Knife."

'I was glad to smell our sheep again; to see the broad sky
from edge to edge, and to hear the sea. I slept beneath the
stars in my cloak. The men talked among themselves.

'I led them, the next day, to the Trees, taking with me meat, wool, and curdled milk, as I had promised. We found the Magic Knives laid out on the grass, as the Children of the Night had promised. They watched us from among the Trees. Their Priestess called to me and said, "How is it with your people?" I said, "Their hearts are changed. I cannot see their hearts as I used to." She said, "That is because you have only one eye. Come to me and I will be both your eyes." But I said, "I must show my people how to use their knives against The Beast, as you showed me how to use my knife." I said this because the Magic Knife does not balance like the flint. She said, "What you have done, you have done for the sake of a woman, and not for the sake of your people." I asked of her, "Then why did the God accept my right eye, and why are you so angry?" She answered, "Because any man can lie to a God, but no man can lie to a woman. And I am not angry with you. I am only very sorrowful for you. Wait a little, and you will see out of your one eye why I am sorry." So she hid herself.

'I went back with my people, each one carrying his Knife, and making it sing in the air—*tssee-sssse*. The Flint never sings. It mutters—*ump-ump*. The Beast heard. The Beast saw. *He* knew! Everywhere he ran away from us. We all laughed. As we walked over the grass my Mother's brother—the Chief on the Men's Side—he took off his Chief's necklace of yellow sea-stones.'

'How? Eh? Oh, I remember! Amber,' said Puck.

'And would have put them on my neck. I said, "No, I am content. What does my one eye matter if my other eye sees fat sheep and fat children running about safely?" My Mother's brother said to them, "I told you he would never take such things." Then they began to sing a song in the Old Tongue—*The Song of Tyr*. I sang with them, but my Mother's brother said, "This is *your* song, O Buyer of the Knife. Let *us* sing it, Tyr."

'Even then I did not understand, till I saw that—that no man stepped on my shadow; and I knew that they thought me to be a God, like the God Tyr, who gave his right hand to conquer a Great Beast.'

'By the Fire in the Belly of the Flint was that so?' Puck rapped out.

'By my Knife and the Naked Chalk, so it was! They made way for my shadow as though it had been a Priestess walking to the Barrows of the Dead. I was afraid. I said to myself, "My Mother and my Maiden will know I am not Tyr." But *still* I was afraid, with the fear of a man who falls into a steep flint-pit while he runs, and feels that it will be hard to climb out.

'When we came to the Dew-ponds all our people were there. The men showed their knives and told their tale. The sheep-guards also had seen The Beast flying from us. The Beast went west across the river in packs—howling! He knew the Knife had come to the Naked Chalk at last—at last! *He* knew! So my work was done. I looked for my Maiden among the Priestesses. She looked at me, but she did not smile. She made the sign to me that our Priestesses must make when they sacrifice to the Old Dead in the Barrows. I would have spoken, but my Mother's brother made himself my Mouth, as though I had been one of the Old Dead in the Barrows for whom our Priests speak to the people on Midsummer Mornings.'

'I remember. Well I remember those Midsummer Mornings!' said Puck.

'Then I went away angrily to my Mother's house. She would have knelt before me. Then I was more angry, but she said, "Only a God would have spoken to me thus, a Priestess. A man would have feared the punishment of the Gods." I looked at her and I laughed. I could not stop my unhappy laughing. They called me from the door by the name of Tyr himself. A young man with whom I had watched my first flocks, and chipped my first arrow, and fought my first Beast, called me by that name in the Old Tongue. He asked my leave to take my Maiden. His eyes were lowered, his hands were on his forehead. He was full of the fear of a God, but of *me*, a man, he had no fear when he asked. I did not kill him. I said, "Call the maiden." She came also without fear—this very one that had waited for me, that had talked with me, by our Dew-ponds. Being a Priestess, she lifted her eyes to me. As I looked on a hill or a cloud, so she looked at me. She spoke in the Old Tongue which Priestesses use when they make prayers to the Old Dead in the Barrows. She asked leave that she might light the fire in my companion's house—and that I should bless their children. I did not kill her. I heard my own voice, little and cold, say, "Let it be as you desire," and they went away hand in hand. My heart grew little and cold; a wind shouted in my ears; my eye darkened. I said to my Mother, "Can a God die?" I heard her say, "What is it? What is it, my son?" and I fell into darkness full of hammer-noises. I was not.'

'Oh, poor—poor God!' said Puck. 'And your wise Mother?'

'*She* knew. As soon as I dropped she knew. When my spirit came back I heard her whisper in my ear, "Whether you live or die, or are made different, I am your Mother." That was good—better even than the water she gave me and the going away of the sickness. Though I was ashamed to have fallen down, yet I was very glad. She was glad too. Neither of us wished to lose the other. There is only the one Mother for the one son. I heaped the fire for her, and barred the doors, and sat at her feet as before I went away, and she combed my hair, and sang.

370

THE KNIFE AND THE NAKED CHALK

I said at last, "What is to be done to the people who say that I am Tyr?"

'She said, "He who has done a God-like thing must bear himself like a God. I see no way out of it. The people are now your sheep till you die. You cannot drive them off."

'I said, "This is a heavier sheep than I can lift." She said, "In time it will grow easy. In time perhaps you will not lay it down for any maiden anywhere. Be wise—be very wise, my son, for nothing is left you except the words, and the songs, and the worship of a God." '

'Oh, poor God!' said Puck. 'But those are not altogether bad things.'

'I know they are not; but I would sell them all—all—all for one small child of my own, smearing himself with the ashes of our own house-fire.'

He wrenched his knife from the turf, thrust it into his belt and stood up.

'And yet, what else could I have done?' he said. 'The sheep are the people.'

'It is a very old tale,' Puck answered. 'I have heard the like of it not only on the Naked Chalk, but also among the Trees —under Oak, and Ash, and Thorn.'

The afternoon shadows filled all the quiet emptiness of Norton Pit. The children heard the sheep-bells and Young Jim's busy bark above them, and they scrambled up the slope to the level.

'We let you have your sleep out,' said Mr. Dudeney, as the flock scattered before them. 'It's making for tea-time now.'

'Look what I've found,' said Dan, and held up a little blue flint arrow-head as fresh as though it had been chipped that very day.

'Oh,' said Mr. Dudeney, 'the closeter you be to the turf the more you're apt to see things. I've found 'em often. Some says the fairies made 'em, but I says they was made by folks like ourselves—only a goodish time back. They're lucky to keep. Now, you couldn't ever have slept—not to any profit—among your father's trees same as you've laid out on Naked Chalk—could you?'

'One doesn't want to sleep in the woods,' said Una.

'Then what's the good of 'em?' said Mr. Dudeney. 'Might as well set in the barn all day. Fetch 'em 'long, Jim boy!'

The Downs, that looked so bare and hot when they came, were full of delicious little shadow-dimples; the smell of the thyme and the salt mixed together on the south-west drift from the still sea; their eyes dazzled with the low sun, and the long grass under it looked golden. The sheep knew where their fold was, so Young Jim came back to his master, and they all four strolled home, the scabious-heads swishing about their ankles, and their shadows streaking behind them like the shadows of giants.

SONG OF THE MEN'S SIDE

Once we feared The Beast—when he followed us we ran,
  Ran very fast though we knew
It was not right that The Beast should master Man;
  But what could we Flint-workers do?
The Beast only grinned at our spears round his ears—
  Grinned at the hammers that we made;
But now we will hunt him for the life with the Knife—
  And this is the Buyer of the Blade!

  Room for his shadow on the grass—let it pass!
    To left and right—stand clear!
  This is the Buyer of the Blade—be afraid!
    This is the great God Tyr!

Tyr thought hard till he hammered out a plan,
  For he knew it was not right
(And it is not right) that The Beast should master Man;
  So he went to the Children of the Night.
He begged a Magic Knife of their make for our sake.
  When he begged for the Knife they said:
'The price of the Knife you would buy is an eye!'
  And that was the price he paid.

  Tell it to the Barrows of the Dead—run ahead!
    Shout it so the Women's Side can hear!
  This is the Buyer of the Blade—be afraid!
    This is the great God Tyr!

REWARDS AND FAIRIES

Our women and our little ones may walk on the Chalk,
*   As far as we can see them and beyond.*
We shall not be anxious for our sheep when we keep
*   Tally at the shearing-pond.*
We can eat with both our elbows on our knees, if we please,
*   We can sleep after meals in the sun;*
For Shepherd-of-the-Twilight is dismayed at the Blade,
*   Feet-in-the-Night have run!*
Dog-without-a-Master goes away (Hai, Tyr aie!),
*   Devil-in-the-Dusk has run!*

Then:

        Room for his shadow on the grass—let it pass!
            To left and right—stand clear!
        This is the Buyer of the Blade—be afraid!
            This is the great God Tyr!

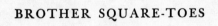

BROTHER SQUARE-TOES

PHILADELPHIA

If you're off to Philadelphia in the morning,
  You mustn't take my stories for a guide.
There's little left indeed of the city you will read of,
  And all the folk I write about have died.
Now few will understand if you mention Talleyrand,
  Or remember what his cunning and his skill did.
And the cabmen at the wharf do not know Count Zinnendorf,
  Nor the Church in Philadelphia he builded.

  It is gone, gone, gone with lost Atlantis
  (Never say I didn't give you warning).
  In Seventeen Ninety-three 'twas there for all to see,
  But it's not in Philadelphia this morning.

If you're off to Philadelphia in the morning,
  You mustn't go by everything I've said.
Bob Bicknell's Southern Stages have been laid aside for ages,
  But the Limited will take you there instead.
Toby Hirte can't be seen at One Hundred and Eighteen,
  North Second Street—no matter when you call;
And I fear you'll search in vain for the wash-house down the
    lane
  Where Pharaoh played the fiddle at the ball.

  It is gone, gone, gone with Thebes the Golden
  (Never say I didn't give you warning).
  In Seventeen Ninety-four 'twas a famous dancing-
    floor—
  But it's not in Philadelphia this morning.

REWARDS AND FAIRIES

If you're off to Philadelphia in the morning,
  You must telegraph for rooms at some Hotel.
You needn't try your luck at Epply's or the 'Buck,'
  Though the Father of his Country liked them well.
It is not the slightest use to inquire for Adam Goos,
  Or to ask where Pastor Meder has removed—so
You must treat as out-of-date the story I relate
  Of the Church in Philadelphia he loved so.

          He is gone, gone, gone with Martin Luther
          (Never say I didn't give you warning).
          In Seventeen Ninety-five he was (rest his soul!) alive,
          But he's not in Philadelphia this morning.

If you're off to Philadelphia this morning,
  And wish to prove the truth of what I say,
I pledge my word you'll find the pleasant land behind
  Unaltered since Red Jacket rode that way.
Still the pine-woods scent the noon; still the cat-bird sings his
    tune;
  Still Autumn sets the maple-forest blazing.
Still the grape-vine through the dusk flings her soul-compelling
    musk;
  Still the fire-flies in the corn make night amazing.

          They are there, there, there with Earth immortal
          (Citizens, I give you friendly warning).
          The things that truly last when men and times have
              passed,
          They are all in Pennsylvania this morning!

BROTHER SQUARE-TOES

IT WAS ALMOST THE END of their visit to the seaside. They had turned themselves out of doors while their trunks were being packed, and strolled over the Downs towards the dull evening sea. The tide was dead low under the chalk cliffs, and the little wrinkled waves grieved along the sands up the coast to New-haven and down the coast to long, grey Brighton, whose smoke trailed out across the Channel.

They walked to The Gap, where the cliff is only a few feet high. A windlass for hoisting shingle from the beach below stands at the edge of it. The Coastguard cottages are a little farther on, and an old ship's figurehead of a Turk in a turban stared at them over the wall.

'This time to-morrow we shall be at home, thank goodness,' said Una. 'I hate the sea!'

'I believe it's all right in the middle,' said Dan. 'The edges are the sorrowful parts.'

Cordery, the coastguard, came out of the cottage, levelled his telescope at some fishing-boats, shut it with a click and walked away. He grew smaller and smaller along the edge of the cliff, where neat piles of white chalk every few yards show the path even on the darkest night.

'Where's Cordery going?' said Una.

'Half-way to Newhaven,' said Dan. 'Then he'll meet the Newhaven coastguard and turn back. He says if coastguards were done away with, smuggling would start up at once.'

A voice on the beach under the cliff began to sing:—

'The moon she shined on Telscombe Tye—
On Telscombe Tye at night it was—
She saw the smugglers riding by,
A very pretty sight it was!'

Feet scrabbled on the flinty path. A dark, thin-faced man in very neat brown clothes and broad-toed shoes came up, followed by Puck.

'Three Dunkirk boats was standin' in!'

the man went on.

'Hssh!' said Puck. 'You'll shock these nice young people.'

'Oh! Shall I? *Mille pardons!*' He shrugged his shoulders almost up to his ears—spread his hands abroad, and jabbered in French. 'No comprenny?' he said. 'I'll give it you in Low German.' And he went off in another language, changing his voice and manner so completely that they hardly knew him for the same person. But his dark beady-brown eyes still twinkled merrily in his lean face, and the children felt that they did not suit the straight, plain, snuffy-brown coat, brown knee-breeches, and broad-brimmed hat. His hair was tied in a short pigtail which danced wickedly when he turned his head.

'Ha' done!' said Puck, laughing. 'Be one thing or t'other, Pharaoh—French or English or German—no great odds which.'

'Oh, but it is, though,' said Una quickly. 'We haven't begun German yet, and—and we're going back to our French next week.'

'Aren't you English?' said Dan. 'We heard you singing just now.'

'Aha! That was the Sussex side o' me. Dad he married a

French girl out o' Boulogne, and French she stayed till her dyin' day. She was an Aurette, of course. We Lees mostly marry Aurettes. Haven't you ever come across the saying:—

> 'Aurettes and Lees,
> Like as two peas.
> What they can't smuggle,
> They'll run over seas'?

'Then, are you a smuggler?' Una cried; and, 'Have you smuggled much?' said Dan.

Mr. Lee nodded solemnly.

'Mind you,' said he, 'I don't uphold smuggling for the generality o' mankind—mostly they can't make a do of it—but I was brought up to the trade, d'ye see, in a lawful line o' descent on'—he waved across the Channel—'on both sides the water. 'Twas all in the families, same as fiddling. The Aurettes used mostly to run the stuff across from Boulogne, and we Lees landed it here and ran it up to London Town, by the safest road.'

'Then where did you live?' said Una.

'You mustn't ever live too close to your business in *our* trade. We kept our little fishing smack at Shoreham, but otherwise we Lees was all honest cottager folk—at Warminghurst under Washington—Bramber way—on the old Penn estate.'

'Ah!' said Puck, squatted by the windlass. 'I remember a piece about the Lees at Warminghurst, I do:

> 'There was never a Lee to Warminghurst
> That wasn't a gipsy last and first.

I reckon that's truth, Pharaoh.'

Pharaoh laughed. 'Admettin' that's true,' he said, 'my gipsy blood must be.wore pretty thin, for I've made and kept a worldly fortune.'

'By smuggling?' Dan asked.

'No, in the tobacco trade.'

'You don't mean to say you gave up smuggling just to go and be a tobacconist!' Dan looked so disappointed they all had to laugh.

'I'm sorry; but there's all sorts of tobacconists,' Pharaoh replied. 'How far out, now, would you call that smack with the patch on her foresail?' He pointed to the fishing-boats.

'A scant mile,' said Puck with a quick look.

'Just about. It's seven fathom under her—clean sand. That was where Uncle Aurette used to sink his brandy kegs from Boulogne, and we fished 'em up and rowed 'em into The Gap here for the ponies to run inland. One thickish night in January of 'Ninety-three, Dad and Uncle Lot and me came over from Shoreham in the smack, and we found Uncle Aurette and the L'Estranges, my cousins, waiting for us in their lugger with New Year's presents from Mother's folk in Boulogne. I remember Aunt Cécile she'd sent me a fine new red knitted cap, which I put on then and there, for the French was having their Revolution in those days, and red caps was all the fashion. Uncle Aurette tells us that they had cut off their King Louis' head, and, moreover, the Brest forts had fired on an English man-o'-war. The news wasn't a week old.

' "That means war again, when we was only just getting used to the peace," says Dad. "Why can't King George's men and King Louis' men do on their uniforms and fight it out over our heads?"

' "Me too, I wish that," says Uncle Aurette. "But they'll be pressing better men than themselves to fight for 'em. The press-gangs are out already on our side. You look out for yours."

' "I'll have to bide ashore and grow cabbages for a while, after I've run this cargo; but I do wish"—Dad says, going over the lugger's side with our New Year presents under his arm and young L'Estrange holding the lantern—"I just *do* wish that those folk which make war so easy had to run one cargo a month all this winter. It 'ud show 'em what honest work means."

' "Well, I've warned ye," says Uncle Aurette. "I'll be slipping off now before your Revenue cutter comes. Give my love to Sister and take care o' the kegs. It's thicking to southward."

'I remember him waving to us and young Stephen L'Estrange blowing out the lantern. By the time we'd fished up the kegs the fog came down so thick Dad judged it risky for me to row 'em ashore, even though we could hear the ponies stamping on the beach. So he and Uncle Lot took the dinghy and left me in the smack playing on my fiddle to guide 'em back.

'Presently I heard guns. Two of 'em sounded mighty like Uncle Aurette's three-pounders. *He* didn't go naked about the seas after dark. Then come more, which I reckoned was Captain Giddens in the Revenue cutter. He was open-handed with his compliments, but he *would* lay his guns himself. I stopped fiddling to listen, and I heard a whole skyful o' French up in the fog—and a high bow come down on top o' the smack. I hadn't time to call or think. I remember the smack heeling over, and me standing on the gunwale pushing against the ship's side as if I hoped to bear her off. Then the square of an open port, with a lantern in it, slid by in front of my nose. I kicked back on our gunwale as it went under and slipped through that port into the French ship—me and my fiddle.'

'Gracious!' said Una. 'What an adventure!'

'Didn't anybody see you come in?' said Dan.

'There wasn't any one there. I'd made use of an orlop-deck port—that's the next deck below the gun-deck, which by rights should not have been open at all. The crew was standing by their guns up above. I rolled on to a pile of dunnage in the dark and I went to sleep. When I woke, men was talking all round me, telling each other their names and sorrows just like Dad told me pressed men used to talk in the last war. Pretty soon I made out they'd all been hove aboard together by the press-gangs, and left to sort 'emselves. The ship she was the *Embuscade*, a thirty-six-gun Republican frigate, Captain Jean Baptiste Bompard, two days out of Le Havre, going to the United States with a Republican French Ambassador of the name of Genêt. They had been up all night clearing for action on account of hearing guns in the fog. Uncle Aurette and Captain Giddens must have been passing the time o' day with each other off Newhaven, and the frigate had drifted past 'em. She never knew she'd run down our smack. Seeing so many aboard was total strangers to each other, I thought one more mightn't be noticed; so I put Aunt Cécile's red cap on the back of my head, and my hands in my pockets like the rest, and, as we French say, I circulated till I found the galley.

' "What! Here's one of 'em that isn't sick!" says a cook. "Take his breakfast to Citizen Bompard."

'I carried the tray to the cabin, but I didn't call this Bompard "Citizen." Oh no! "Mon Capitaine" was my little word, same as Uncle Aurette used to answer in King Louis' Navy. Bompard, he liked it. He took me on for cabin servant, and after that no one asked questions; and thus I got good victuals and light work all the way across to America. He talked a heap of politics, and so did his officers, and when this Ambassador Genêt got rid of his land-stomach and laid down the law after dinner, a rooks' parliament was nothing compared to their cabin. I learned to know most of the men which had worked the French Revolution, through waiting at table and hearing talk about 'em. One of our forecas'le six-pounders was called Danton and t'other Marat. I used to play the fiddle between 'em, sitting on the capstan. Day in and day out Bompard and Monsieur Genêt talked o' what France had done, and how the United States was going to join her to finish off the English in this war. Monsieur Genêt said he'd justabout make the United States fight for France. He was a rude common man. But I liked listening. I always helped drink any healths that was proposed—specially Citizen Danton's who'd cut off King Louis' head. An all-Englishman might have been shocked—but that's where my French blood saved me.

'It didn't save me from getting a dose of ship's fever though, the week before we put Monsieur Genêt ashore at Charleston; and what was left of me after bleeding and pills took the dumb horrors from living 'tween decks. The surgeon, Karaguen his name was, kept me down there to help him with his plasters—I was too weak to wait on Bompard. I don't remember much of any account for the next few weeks, till I smelled lilacs, and I looked out of the port, and we was moored to a wharf-edge and there was a town o' fine gardens and redbrick houses and all the green leaves o' God's world waiting for me outside.

' "What's this?" I said to the sick-bay man—old Pierre
Tiphaigne he was. "Philadelphia," says Pierre. "You've missed
it all. We're sailing next week."

'I just turned round and cried for longing to be amongst
the laylocks.

' "If that's your trouble," says old Pierre, "you go straight
ashore. None 'll hinder you. They're all gone mad on these
coasts—French and American together. 'Tisn't *my* notion o'
war." Pierre was an old King Louis man.

'My legs was pretty tottly, but I made shift to go on deck,
which it was like a fair. The frigate was crowded with fine
gentlemen and ladies pouring in and out. They sung and
they waved French flags, while Captain Bompard and his
officers—yes, and some of the men—speechified to all and
sundry about war with England. They shouted, "Down with
England!"—"Down with Washington!"—"Hurrah for France
and the Republic!" *I* couldn't make sense of it. I wanted to
get out from that crunch of swords and petticoats and sit in a
field. One of the gentlemen said to me, "Is that a genuine
cap o' Liberty you're wearing?" 'Twas Aunt Cécile's red one,
and pretty near wore out. "Oh yes!" I says, "straight from
France." "I'll give you a shilling for it," he says, and with
that money in my hand and my fiddle under my arm I
squeezed past the entry-port and went ashore. It was like a
dream—meadows, trees, flowers, birds, houses, and people
all different! I sat me down in a meadow and fiddled a bit,
and then I went in and out the streets, looking and smelling
and touching, like a little dog at a fair. Fine folk was setting
on the white stone doorsteps of their houses, and a girl
threw me a handful of laylock sprays, and when I said "Merci"
without thinking, she said she loved the French. They all was
the fashion in the city. I saw more tricolour flags in Philadelphia than ever I'd seen in Boulogne, and every one was

shouting for war with England. A crowd o' folk was cheering after our French Ambassador—that same Monsieur Genêt which we'd left at Charleston. He was a-horseback behaving as if the place belonged to him—and commanding all and sundry to fight the British. But I'd heard that before. I got into a long straight street as wide as the Broyle, where gentlemen was racing horses. I'm fond o' horses. Nobody hindered 'em, and a man told me it was called Race Street o' purpose for that. Then I followed some black niggers, which I'd never seen close before; but I left them to run after a great, proud, copper-faced man with feathers in his hair and a red blanket trailing behind him. A man told me he was a real Red Indian called Red Jacket, and I followed him into an alleyway off Race Street by Second Street, where there was a fiddle playing. I'm fond o' fiddling. The Indian stopped at a baker's shop—Conrad Gerhard's it was—and bought some sugary cakes. Hearing what the price was I was going to have some too, but the Indian asked me in English if I was hungry. "Oh yes!" I says. I must have looked a sore scrattel. He opens a door on to a staircase and leads the way up. We walked into a dirty little room full of flutes and fiddles and a fat man fiddling by the window, in a smell of cheese and medicines fit to knock you down. I *was* knocked down too, for the fat man jumped up and hit me a smack in the face. I fell against an old spinet covered with pill-boxes and the pills rolled about the floor. The Indian never moved an eyelid.

' "Pick up the pills! Pick up the pills!" the fat man screeches.

'I started picking 'em up—hundreds of 'em—meaning to run out under the Indian's arm, but I came on giddy all over and I sat down. The fat man went back to his fiddling.

' "Toby!" says the Indian after quite a while. "I brought the boy to be fed, not hit."

' "What?" says Toby, "I thought it was Gert Schwankfelder." He put down his fiddle and took a good look at me. "Himmel!" he says. "I have hit the wrong boy. It is not the new boy. Why are you not the new boy? Why are you not Gert Schwankfelder?"

' "I don't know," I said. "The gentleman in the pink blanket brought me."

'Says the Indian, "He is hungry, Toby. Christians always feed the hungry. So I bring him."

' "You should have said that first," said Toby. He pushed plates at me and the Indian put bread and pork on them, and a glass of Madeira wine. I told him I was off the French ship, which I had joined on account of my mother being French. That was true enough when you think of it, and besides I saw that the French was all the fashion in Philadelphia. Toby and the Indian whispered and I went on picking up the pills.

' "You like pills—eh?" says Toby.

' "No," I says. "I've seen our ship's doctor roll too many of 'em."

' "Ho!" he says, and he shoves two bottles at me. "What's those?"

' "Calomel," I says. "And t'other's senna."

' "Right," he says. "One week have I tried to teach Gert Schwankfelder the difference between them, yet he cannot tell. You like to fiddle?" he says. He'd just seen my kit on the floor.

' "Oh yes!" says I.

' "Oho!" he says. "What note is this?" drawing his bow acrost.

'He meant it for A, so I told him it was.

' "My brother," he says to the Indian. "I think this is the

hand of Providence! I warned that Gert if he went to play upon the wharves any more he would hear from me. Now look at this boy and say what you think."

'The Indian looked me over whole minutes—there was a musical clock on the wall and dolls came out and hopped while the hour struck. He looked me over all the while they did it.

' "Good," he says at last. "This boy is good."

' "Good, then," says Toby. "Now I shall play my fiddle and you shall sing your hymn, brother. Boy, go down to the bakery and tell them you are young Gert Schwankfelder that was. The horses are in Davy Jones's locker. If you ask any questions you shall hear from me."

'I left 'em singing hymns and I went down to old Conrad Gerhard. He wasn't at all surprised when I told him I was young Gert Schwankfelder that was. He knew Toby. His wife she walked me into the backyard without a word, and she washed me and she cut my hair to the edge of a basin, and she put me to bed, and oh! how I slept—how I slept in that little room behind the oven looking on the flower garden! I didn't know Toby went to the *Embuscade* that night and bought me off Dr. Karaguen for twelve dollars and a dozen bottles of Seneca Oil. Karaguen wanted a new lace to his coat, and he reckoned I hadn't long to live; so he put me down as "discharged sick." '

'I like Toby,' said Una.

'Who was he?' said Puck.

'Apothecary Tobias Hirte,' Pharaoh replied. 'One Hundred and Eighteen, Second Street—the famous Seneca Oil man, that lived half of every year among the Indians. But let me tell you my tale my own way, same as his brown mare used to go to Lebanon.'

'Then why did he keep her in Davy Jones's locker?' Dan asked.

'That was his joke. He kept her under David Jones's hat shop in the "Buck" tavern yard, and his Indian friends kept their ponies there when they visited him. I looked after the horses when I wasn't rolling pills on top of the old spinet, while he played his fiddle and Red Jacket sang hymns. I liked it. I had good victuals, light work, a suit o' clean clothes, a plenty music, and quiet, smiling German folk all around that let me sit in their gardens. My first Sunday, Toby took me to his church in Moravian Alley; and that was in a garden too. The women wore long-eared caps and handkerchiefs. They came in at one door and the men at another, and there was a brass chandeller you could see your face in, and a nigger-boy to blow the organ bellows. I carried Toby's fiddle, and he played pretty much as he chose all against the organ and the singing. He was the only one they let do it, for they was a simple-minded folk. They used to wash each other's feet up in the attic to keep 'emselves humble: which Lord knows they didn't need.'

'How very queer!' said Una.

Pharaoh's eyes twinkled. 'I've met many and seen much,' he said; 'but I haven't yet found any better or quieter or forbearinger people than the Brethren and Sistern of the Moravian Church in Philadelphia. Nor will I ever forget my first Sunday—the service was in English that week—with the smell of the flowers coming in from Pastor Meder's garden where the big peach tree is, and me looking at all the clean strangeness and thinking of 'tween decks on the *Embuscade* only six days ago. Being a boy, it seemed to me it had lasted for ever, and was going on for ever. But I didn't know Toby then. As soon as the dancing clock struck midnight that

Sunday—I was lying under the spinet—I heard Toby's fiddle. He'd just done his supper, which he always took late and heavy. "Gert," says he, "get the horses. Liberty and Independence for ever! The flowers appear upon the earth, and the time of the singing of birds is come. We are going to my country seat in Lebanon."

'I rubbed my eyes, and fetched 'em out of the "Buck" stables. Red Jacket was there saddling his, and when I'd packed the saddle-bags we three rode up Race Street to the Ferry by starlight. So we went travelling. It's a kindly, softly country there, back of Philadelphia among the German towns, Lancaster way. Little houses and bursting big barns, fat cattle, fat women, and all as peaceful as Heaven might be if they farmed there. Toby sold medicines out of his saddle-bags, and gave the French war-news to folk along the roads. Him and his long-hilted umberell was as well known as the stage-coaches. He took orders for that famous Seneca Oil which he had the secret of from Red Jacket's Indians, and he slept in friends' farmhouses, but he *would* shut all the windows; so Red Jacket and me slept outside. There's nothing to hurt except snakes—and they slip away quick enough if you thrash in the bushes.'

'I'd have liked that!' said Dan.

'I'd no fault to find with those days. In the cool o' the morning the cat-bird sings. He's something to listen to. And there's a smell of wild grape-vine growing in damp hollows which you drop into, after long rides in the heat, which is beyond compare for sweetness. So's the puffs out of the pine woods of afternoons. Come sundown, the frogs strike up, and later on the fireflies dance in the corn. Oh me, the fireflies in the corn! We were a week or ten days on the road, tacking from one place to another—such as Lancaster, Bethlehem-

Ephrata—"thou Bethlehem-Ephrata." No odds—I loved the going about. And so we jogged into dozy little Lebanon by the Blue Mountains, where Toby had a cottage and a garden of all fruits. He come north every year for this wonderful Seneca Oil the Seneca Indians made for him. They'd never sell to any one else, and he doctored 'em with von Swieten pills, which they valued more than their own oil. He could do what he chose with them, and, of course, he tried to make them Moravians. The Senecas are a seemly, quiet people, and they'd had trouble enough from white men—American and English—during the wars, to keep 'em in that walk. They lived on a Reservation by themselves away off by their lake. Toby took me up there, and they treated me as if I was their own blood brother. Red Jacket said the mark of my bare feet in the dust was just like an Indian's and my style of walking was similar. I know I took to their ways all over.'

'Maybe the gipsy drop in your blood helped you?' said Puck.

'Sometimes I think it did,' Pharaoh went on. 'Anyhow, Red Jacket and Cornplanter, the other Seneca chief, they let me be adopted into the tribe. It's only a compliment, of course, but Toby was angry when I showed up with my face painted. They gave me a side-name which means "Two Tongues," because, d'ye see, I talked French and English.

'They had their own opinions (*I've* heard 'em) about the French and the English, *and* the Americans. They'd suffered from all of 'em during the wars, and they only wished to be left alone. But they thought a heap of the President of the United States. Cornplanter had had dealings with him in some French wars out West when General Washington was only a lad. His being President afterwards made no odds to 'em. They always called him Big Hand, for he was a large-

fisted man, and he was all of their notion of a white chief.
Cornplanter 'ud sweep· his blanket round him, and after I'd
filled his pipe he'd begin—"In the old days, long ago, when
braves were many and blankets were few, Big Hand said——"
If Red Jacket agreed to the say-so he'd trickle a little smoke
out of the corners of his mouth. If he didn't, he'd blow
through his nostrils. Then Cornplanter 'ud stop and Red
Jacket 'ud take on. Red Jacket was the better talker of the
two. I've laid and listened to 'em for hours. Oh! they knew
General Washington well. Cornplanter used to meet him at
Epply's—the great dancing-place in the city before District
Marshal William Nichols bought it. They told me he was always glad to see 'em, and he'd hear 'em out to the end if
they had anything on their minds. They had a good deal in
those days. I came at it by degrees, after I was adopted into
the tribe. The talk up in Lebanon and everywhere else that
summer was about the French war with England and whether
the United States 'ud join in with France or make a peace
treaty with England. Toby wanted peace so as he could go
about the Reservation buying his oils. But most of the white
men wished for war, and they was angry because the President wouldn't give the sign for it. The newspaper said men
was burning Guy Fawkes images of General Washington and
yelling after him in the streets of Philadelphia. You'd have
been astonished what those two fine old chiefs knew of the
ins and outs of such matters. The little I've learned of politics
I picked up from Cornplanter and Red Jacket on the Reservation. Toby used to read the *Aurora* newspaper. He was what
they call a "Democrat," though our Church is against the
Brethren concerning themselves with politics.'

'I hate politics, too,' said Una, and Pharaoh laughed.

'I might ha' guessed it,' he said. 'But here's something that isn't politics. One hot evening late in August, Toby was reading the newspaper on the stoop and Red Jacket was smoking under a peach tree and I was fiddling. Of a sudden Toby drops his *Aurora*.

' "I am an oldish man, too fond of my own comforts," he says. "I will go to the Church which is in Philadelphia. My brother, lend me a spare pony. I must be there to-morrow night."

' "Good!" says Red Jacket, looking at the sun. "My brother shall be there. I will ride with him and bring back the ponies."

'I went to pack the saddle-bags. Toby had cured me of asking questions. He stopped my fiddling if I did. Besides, Indians don't ask questions much and I wanted to be like 'em.

'When the horses were ready I jumped up.

' "Get off," says Toby. "Stay and mind the cottage till I come back. The Lord has laid this on me, not on you. I wish He hadn't."

'He powders off down the Lancaster road, and I sat on the doorstep wondering after him. When I picked up the paper to wrap his fiddle-strings in, I spelled out a piece about the yellow fever being in Philadelphia so dreadful every one was running away. I was scared, for I was fond of Toby. We never said much to each other, but we fiddled together, and music's as good as talking to them that understand.'

'Did Toby die of yellow fever?' Una asked.

'Not him! There's justice left in the world still. He went down to the City and bled 'em well again in heaps. He sent back word by Red Jacket that, if there was war or he died, I was to bring the oils along to the City, but till then I was to go on working in the garden and Red Jacket was to see me do it. Down at heart all Indians reckon digging a squaw's business, and neither him nor Cornplanter, when he relieved watch, was a hard task-master. We hired a nigger-boy to do our work, and a lazy grinning runagate he was. When I found Toby didn't die the minute he reached town, why, boylike, I took him off my mind and went with my Indians again. Oh! those days up north at Canasedago, running races and gambling with the Senecas, or bee-hunting in the woods, or fishing in the lake.' Pharaoh sighed and looked across the water. 'But it's best,' he went on suddenly, 'after the first frostës. You roll out o' your blanket and find every leaf left green over night turned red and yellow, not by trees at a time, but hundreds and hundreds of miles of 'em, like sunsets splattered upside down. On one of such days—the maples was flaming scarlet and gold, and the sumach bushes were redder—Cornplanter and Red Jacket came out in full war-dress, making the very leaves look silly: feathered war-bonnets, yellow doeskin leggings, fringed and tasselled, red horse-blankets, and their bridles feathered and sheiled and beaded no bounds. I thought it was war against the British till I saw their faces weren't painted, and they only carried wrist-whips. Then I hummed "Yankee Doodle" at 'em. They told me they was going to visit Big Hand and find out for sure whether he meant to join the French in fighting the English or make a peace treaty with England. I reckon those two would ha' gone out on the warpath at a nod from Big Hand, but they knew well, if there was war 'twixt England and the United States, their tribe 'ud catch it from both parties same as in all the other wars. They asked me to come along and hold the ponies. That puzzled me, because they always put their ponies up at the "Buck" or Epply's when they went to see General Washington in the city, and horse-holding is a nigger's job. Besides, I wasn't exactly dressed for it.'

'D'you mean you were dressed like an Indian?' Dan demanded.

Pharaoh looked a little abashed. 'This didn't happen at Lebanon,' he said, 'but a bit farther north, on the Reservation; and at that particular moment of time, so far as blanket, hair-band, moccasins, and sunburn went, there wasn't much odds 'twix' me and a young Seneca buck. You may laugh'—he smoothed down his long-skirted brown coat—'but I told you I took to their ways all over. I said nothing, though I was bursting to let out the war-whoop like the young men had taught me.'

'No, and you don't let out one here, either,' said Puck before Dan could ask. 'Go on, Brother Square-toes.'

'We went on.' Pharaoh's narrow dark eyes gleamed and danced. 'We went on—forty, fifty miles a day, for days on end—we three braves. And how a great tall Indian a-horseback can carry his war-bonnet at a canter through thick timber without brushing a feather beats *me*! My silly head was banged often enough by low branches, but they slipped through like running elk. We had evening hymn-singing every night after they'd blown their pipe-smoke to the quarters of heaven. Where did we go? I'll tell you, but don't blame me if you're no wiser. We took the old war-trail from the end of the Lake along the East Susquehanna through the Nantego country, right down to Fort Shamokin on the Senachse river. We crossed the Juniata by Fort Granville, got into Shippensberg over the hills by the Ochwick trail, and then to Williams Ferry (it's a bad one). From Williams Ferry, across the Shanedore, over the Blue Mountains, through Ashby's Gap, and so south-east by south from there, till we found the President at the back of his own plantations. I'd hate to be trailed by Indians in earnest. They caught him like a partridge on a stump. After we'd left our ponies, we scouted forward through a woody piece, and, creeping slower and slower, at last if my moccasins even slipped Red Jacket 'ud turn and frown. I heard voices—Monsieur Genêt's for choice—long before I saw anything, and we pulled up at the edge of a clearing where some niggers in grey-and-red liveries were holding horses, and half-a-dozen gentlemen—but one was Genêt— were talking among felled timber. I fancy they'd come to see Genêt a piece on his road, for his portmantle was with him. I hid in between two logs as near to the company as I be to that old windlass there. I didn't need anybody to show me Big Hand. He stood up, very still, his legs a little apart, listening to Genêt, that French Ambassador, which never had more manners than a Bosham tinker. Genêt was as good as ordering him to declare war on England at once. I had heard that clack before on the *Embuscade*. He said he'd stir up the whole United States to have war with England, whether Big Hand liked it or not.

'Big Hand heard him out to the last end. I looked behind me, and my two chiefs had vanished like smoke. Says Big Hand, "That is very forcibly put, Monsieur Genêt——" "Citizen—citizen!" the fellow spits in. "*I*, at least, am a Republican!" "Citizen Genêt," he says, "you may be sure it will receive my fullest consideration." This seemed to take Citizen Genêt back a piece. He rode off grumbling, and never gave his nigger a penny. No gentleman!

'The others all assembled round Big Hand then, and, in their way, they said pretty much what Genêt had said. They put it to him, here was France and England at war, in a manner of speaking, right across the United States' stomach, and paying no regards to any one. The French was searching American ships on pretence they was helping England, but really for to steal the goods. The English was doing the same, only t'other way round, and besides searching, they was pressing American citizens into their Navy to help them fight France, on pretence that those Americans was lawful British subjects. His gentlemen put this very clear to Big Hand. It didn't look to *them*, they said, as though the United States trying to keep out of the fight was any advantage to *her*, because she only catched it from both French and English. They said that nine out of ten good Americans was crazy to fight the English then and there. They wouldn't say whether that was right or wrong; they only wanted Big Hand to turn it over in his mind. He did—for a while. I saw Red Jacket and Cornplanter watching him from the far side of the clearing, and how they had slipped round there was another mystery. Then Big Hand drew himself up, and he let his gentlemen have it.'

'Hit 'em?' Dan asked.

'No, nor yet was it what you might call swearing. He—he blasted 'em with his natural speech. He asked them half-a-dozen times over whether the United States had enough armed ships for any shape or sort of war with any one. He asked 'em, if they thought she *had* those ships, to *give* him those ships, and they looked on the ground, as if they expected to find 'em *there*. He put it to 'em whether, setting ships aside, their country—I reckon he gave 'em good reasons—whether the United States was ready or able to face a new big war; she having but so few years back wound up one against England, and being all holds full of her own troubles. As I said, the strong way he laid it all before 'em blasted 'em, and when he'd done it was like a still in the woods after a storm. A little man—but they all looked little— pipes up like a young rook in a blowed-down nest, "Never-

398

theless, General, it seems you will be compelled to fight England." Quick Big Hand wheels on him, "And is there anything in my past which makes you think I am averse to fighting Great Britain?"

'Everybody laughed except him. "Oh, General, you mistake us entirely!" they says. "I trust so," he says. "But I know my duty. We *must* have peace with England."

' "At any price?" says the man with the rook's voice.

' "At any price," says he, word by word. "Our ships will be searched—our citizens will be pressed, but——"

' "Then what about the Declaration of Independence?" says one.

' "Deal with facts, not fancies," says Big Hand. "The United States are in no position to fight England."

' "But think of public opinion," another one starts up. "The feeling in Philadelphia alone is at fever heat."

'He held up one of his big hands. "Gentlemen," he says—slow he spoke, but his voice carried far—"I have to think of our country. Let me assure you that the treaty with Great Britain will be made though every city in the Union burn me in effigy."

' "At any price?" the actor-like chap keeps on croaking.

' "The treaty must be made on Great Britain's own terms. What else can I do?"

'He turns his back on 'em and they looked at each other and slinked off to the horses, leaving him alone: and then I saw he was an old man. Then Red Jacket and Cornplanter rode down the clearing from the far end as though they had just chanced along. Back went Big Hand's shoulders, up went his head, and he stepped forward one single pace with a great deep Hough! so pleased he was. That was a statelified meeting to behold—three big men, and two of 'em looking like

399

jewelled images among the spattle of gay-coloured leaves. I
saw my chiefs' war-bonnets sinking together, down and down.
Then they made the sign which no Indian makes outside of
the Medicine Lodges—a sweep of the right hand just clear of
the dust and an inbend of the left knee at the same time,
and those proud eagle feathers almost touched his boot-top.'

'What did it mean?' said Dan.

'Mean!' Pharaoh cried. 'Why, it's what you—what we—it's
the Sachems' way of sprinkling the sacred corn-meal in front
of—oh! it's a piece of Indian compliment really, and it signifies
that you are a very big chief.

'Big Hand looked down on 'em. First he says quite softly,
"My brothers know it is not easy to be a chief." Then his voice
grew. "My children," says he, "what is in your minds?"

'Says Cornplanter, "We came to ask whether there will be
war with King George's men, but we have heard what our
Father has said to his chiefs. We will carry away that talk in
our hearts to tell to our people."

' "No," says Big Hand. "Leave all that talk behind—it was
between white men only—but take this message from *me* to
your people—'There will be no war.' "

'His gentlemen were waiting, so they didn't delay him; only
Cornplanter says, using his old side-name, "Big Hand, did
you see us among the timber just now?"

' "Surely," says he. "*You* taught me to look behind trees
when we were both young." And with that he cantered off.

'Neither of my chiefs spoke till we were back on our ponies
again and a half-hour along the home-trail. Then Cornplanter
says to Red Jacket, "We will have the Corn-dance this year.
There will be no war." And that was all there was to it.'

Pharaoh stood up as though he had finished.

'Yes,' said Puck, rising too. 'And what came out of it in the
long run?'

'Let me get at my story my own way,' was the answer. 'Look! it's later than I thought. That Shoreham smack's thinking of her supper.'

The children looked across the darkening Channel. A smack had hoisted a lantern and slowly moved west where Brighton pier lights ran out in a twinkling line. When they turned round The Gap was empty behind them.

'I expect they've packed our trunks by now,' said Dan. 'This time to-morrow we'll be home.'

IF——

If you can keep your head when all about you
    Are losing theirs and blaming it on you;
If you can trust yourself when all men doubt you,
    But make allowance for their doubting too;
If you can wait and not be tired by waiting,
    Or being lied about, don't deal in lies,
Or being hated, don't give way to hating,
    And yet don't look too good, nor talk too wise;

If you can dream—and not make dreams your master;
    If you can think—and not make thoughts your aim,
If you can meet with Triumph and Disaster
    And treat those two impostors just the same;
If you can bear to hear the truth you've spoken
    Twisted by knaves to make a trap for fools,
Or watch the things you gave your life to, broken,
    And stoop and build 'em up with worn-out tools;

If you can make one heap of all your winnings
    And risk it on one turn of pitch-and-toss,
And lose, and start again at your beginnings
    And never breathe a word about your loss;
If you can force your heart and nerve and sinew
    To serve your turn long after they are gone,
And so hold on when there is nothing in you
    Except the Will which says to them: 'Hold on!'

If you can talk with crowds and keep your virtue,
    Or walk with Kings—nor lose the common touch,

REWARDS AND FAIRIES

If neither foes nor loving friends can hurt you,
 If all men count with you, but none too much;
If you can fill the unforgiving minute
 With sixty seconds' worth of distance run,
Yours is the Earth and everything that's in it,
 And—which is more—you'll be a Man, my son!

'A PRIEST IN SPITE OF HIMSELF'

A ST. HELENA LULLABY

How far is St. Helena from a little child at play?
  What makes you want to wander there with all the world
    between?
Oh, Mother, call your son again or else he'll run away.
  (No one thinks of winter when the grass is green!)

How far is St. Helena from a fight in Paris street?
  I haven't time to answer now—the men are falling fast.
The guns begin to thunder, and the drums begin to beat.
  (If you take the first step you will take the last!)

How far is St. Helena from the field of Austerlitz?
  You couldn't hear me if I told—so loud the cannons roar.
But not so far for people who are living by their wits.
  ('Gay go up' means 'gay go down' the wide world o'er!)

How far is St. Helena from an Emperor of France?
  I cannot see—I cannot tell—the crowns they dazzle so.
The Kings sit down to dinner, and the Queens stand up to
    dance.
  (After open weather you may look for snow!)

How far is St. Helena from the Capes of Trafalgar?
  A longish way—a longish way—with ten year more to run.
It's South across the water underneath a setting star.
  (What you cannot finish you must leave undone!)

How far is St. Helena from the Beresina ice?
  An ill way—a chill way—the ice begins to crack.

REWARDS AND FAIRIES

But not so far for gentlemen who never took advice.
   (When you can't go forward you must e'en come back!)

How far is St. Helena from the field of Waterloo?
   A near way—a clear way—the ship will take you soon.
A pleasant place for gentlemen with little left to do.
   (Morning never tries you till the afternoon!)

How far from St. Helena to the Gate of Heaven's Grace?
   That no one knows—that no one knows—and no one ever
     will.
But fold your hands across your heart and cover up your face,
And after all your trapesings, child, lie still!

'A PRIEST IN SPITE OF HIMSELF'

THE DAY AFTER THEY CAME HOME from the seaside they set out on a tour of inspection to make sure everything was as they had left it. Soon they discovered that old Hobden had blocked their best hedge-gaps with stakes and thorn-bundles, and had trimmed up the hedges where the blackberries were setting.

'It can't be time for the gipsies to come along,' said Una. 'Why, it was summer only the other day!'

'There's smoke in Low Shaw!' said Dan, sniffing. 'Let's make sure!'

They crossed the fields towards the thin line of blue smoke that leaned above the hollow of Low Shaw which lies beside the King's Hill road. It used to be an old quarry till somebody planted it, and you can look straight down into it from the edge of Banky Meadow.

'I thought so,' Dan whispered, as they came up to the fence at the edge of the larches. A gipsy-van—not the showman's sort, but the old black kind, with little windows high up and a baby-gate across the door—was getting ready to leave. A man was harnessing the horses; an old woman crouched over the ashes of a fire made out of broken fence-rails; and a girl sat on the van-steps singing to a baby on her lap. A wise-looking, thin dog snuffed at a patch of fur on the ground till the old woman put it carefully in the middle of the fire. The girl reached back inside the van and tossed her a paper parcel. This was laid on the fire too, and they smelt singed feathers.

'Chicken feathers!' said Dan. 'I wonder if they are old Hobden's.'

Una sneezed. The dog growled and crawled to the girl's feet, the old woman fanned the fire with her hat, while the man led the horses up to the shafts. They all moved as quickly and quietly as snakes over moss.

'Ah!' said the girl. 'I'll teach you!' She beat the dog, who seemed to expect it.

'Don't do that,' Una called down. 'It wasn't his fault.'

'How do you know what I'm beating him for?' she answered.

'For not seeing us,' said Dan. 'He was standing right in the smoke, and the wind was wrong for his nose, anyhow.'

The girl stopped beating the dog, and the old woman fanned faster than ever.

'You've fanned some of your feathers out of the fire,' said Una. 'There's a tail-feather by that chestnut-tot.'

'What of it?' said the old woman, as she grabbed it.

'Oh, nothing!' said Dan. 'Only I've heard say that tail-feathers are as bad as the whole bird, sometimes.'

That was a saying of Hobden's about pheasants. Old Hobden always burned all feather and fur before he sat down to eat.

'Come on, mother,' the man whispered. The old woman climbed into the van, and the horses drew it out of the deep-rutted shaw on to the hard road.

The girl waved her hands and shouted something they could not catch.

'That was gipsy for "Thank you kindly, Brother and Sister,"' said Pharaoh Lee.

He was standing behind them, his fiddle under his arm.

'Gracious, you startled me!' said Una.

'*You* startled old Priscilla Savile,' Puck called from below them. 'Come and sit by their fire. She ought to have put it out before they left.'

They dropped down the ferny side of the shaw. Una raked the ashes together, Dan found a dead wormy oak branch that burns without flame, and they watched the smoke while Pharaoh played a curious wavery air.

'That's what the girl was humming to the baby,' said Una.

'I know it,' he nodded, and went on:—

> *'Ai Lumai, Lumai, Lumai! Luludia!*
> *Ai Luludia!'*

He passed from one odd tune to another, and quite forgot the children. At last Puck asked him to go on with his adventures in Philadelphia and among the Seneca Indians.

'I'm telling it,' he said, staring straight in front of him as he played. 'Can't you hear?'

'Maybe, but *they* can't. Tell it aloud,' said Puck.

Pharaoh shook himself, laid his fiddle beside him, and began:—

'I'd left Red Jacket and Cornplanter riding home with me after Big Hand had said that there wouldn't be any war. That's all there was to it. We believed Big Hand and we went home again—we three braves. When we reached Lebanon we found Toby at the cottage with his waistcoat a foot too big for him—so hard he had worked amongst the yellow-fever people. He beat me for running off with the Indians, but 'twas worth it—I was glad to see him,—and when we went back to Philadelphia for the winter, and I was told how he'd sacrificed himself over sick people in the yellow fever, I thought the world and all of him. No, I didn't neither. I'd thought that all along. That yellow fever must have been something dreadful. Even in December people had no more than begun to trinkle back to town. Whole houses stood empty and the niggers was robbing them out. But I can't call to mind that any of the Moravian Brethren had died. It seemed like they had just kept on with their own concerns, and the good Lord He'd just looked after 'em. That was the winter—yes, winter of 'Ninety-three—the Brethren bought a stove for the Church. Toby spoke in favour of it because the cold spoiled his fiddle hand, but many thought stove-heat not in the Bible, and there was yet a third party which always brought hickory coal foot-warmers to service and wouldn't speak either way. They ended by casting the Lot for it, which is like pitch-and-toss. After my summer with the Senecas, church-stoves didn't highly interest me, so I took to haunting round among the French *émigrés* which Philadelphia was full of. My French and my fiddling helped me there, d'ye see. They come over in shiploads from France, where, by what I made out, every one was killing every one else by any means, and they spread 'emselves about the city—mostly in Drinker's Alley and Elfrith's Alley—and they did odd jobs till times should mend. But whatever they stooped to, they were gentry and kept a cheerful countenance, and after an evening's fiddling at one of their poor little proud parties, the Brethren seemed old-fashioned. Pastor Meder and Brother Adam Goos didn't like my fiddling for hire, but Toby said it was lawful in me to earn my living by exercising my talents. He never let me be put upon.

'In February of 'Ninety-four—No, March it must have been, because a new Ambassador called Fauchet had come from France, with no more manners than Genêt the old one—in March, Red Jacket came in from the Reservation bringing news of all kind friends there. I showed him round the city, and we saw General Washington riding through a crowd of folk that shouted for war with England. They gave him quite rough music, but he looked 'twixt his horse's ears and made

out not to notice. His stirrup brished Red Jacket's elbow, and
Red Jacket whispered up, "My brother knows it is not easy
to be a chief?" Big Hand shot just one look at him and nodded.
Then there was a scuffle behind us over some one who wasn't
hooting at Washington loud enough to please the people. We
went away to be out of the fight. Indians won't risk being hit.'

'What do they do if they are?' Dan asked.

'Kill, of course. That's why they have such proper manners.
Well, then, coming home by Drinker's Alley to get a new
shirt which a French Vicomte's lady was washing to take the
stiff out of (I'm always choice in my body-linen) a lame Frenchman pushes a paper of buttons at us. He hadn't long landed
in the United States, and please would we buy. He sure-ly was
a pitiful scrattle—his coat half torn off, his face cut, but his
hands steady; so I knew it wasn't drink. He said his name was
Peringuey, and he'd been knocked about in the crowd round
the Stadt—Independence Hall. One thing leading to another
we took him up to Toby's rooms, same as Red Jacket had
taken me the year before. The compliments he paid to Toby's
Madeira wine fairly conquered the old man, for he opened
a second bottle and he told this Monsieur Peringuey all about
our great stove dispute in the Church. I remember Pastor
Meder and Brother Adam Goos dropped in, and although
they and Toby were direct opposite sides regarding stoves, yet
this Monsieur Peringuey he made 'em feel as if he thought
each one was in the right of it. He said he had been a clergy-
man before he had to leave France. He admired at Toby's
fiddling, and he asked if Red Jacket, sitting by the spinet, was
a simple Huron. Senecas aren't Hurons, they're Iroquois, of
course, and Toby told him so. Well, then, in due time he arose
and left in a style which made us feel he'd been favouring us,
instead of us feeding him. I've never seen that so strong be-

fore—in a man. We all talked him over but couldn't make
head or tail of him, and Red Jacket come out to walk with me
to the French quarter where I was due to fiddle at a party.
Passing Drinker's Alley again we saw a naked window with
a light in it, and there sat our button-selling Monsieur Peringuey throwing dice all alone, right hand against left.

'Says Red Jacket, keeping back in the dark, "Look at his
face!"

'I was looking. I protest to you I wasn't frightened like I
was when Big Hand talked to his gentlemen. I—I only looked,
and I only wondered that even those dead dumb dice 'ud dare
to fall different from what that face wished. It—it *was* a face!

' "He is bad," says Red Jacket. "But he is a great chief. The
French have sent away a great chief. I thought so when he told
us his lies. Now I know."

'I had to go on to the party, so I asked him to call round for
me afterwards and we'd have hymn-singing at Toby's as usual.

' "No," he says. "Tell Toby I am not Christian to-night. All
Indian." He had those fits sometimes. I wanted to know more
about Monsieur Peringuey, and the *émigré* party was the very
place to find out. It's neither here nor there, of course, but
those French *émigré* parties they almost make you cry. The
men that you bought fruit of in Market Street, the hairdressers
and fencing-masters and French teachers, they turn back again
by candlelight to what they used to be at home, and you catch
their real names. There wasn't much room in the wash-house,
so I sat on top of the copper and played 'em the tunes they
called for—"*Si le Roi m'avait donné*," and such nursery stuff.
They cried sometimes. It hurt me to take their money afterwards, indeed it did. And there I found out about Monsieur
Peringuey. He was a proper rogue too! None of 'em had a good
word for him except the Marquise that kept the French

boarding-house on Fourth Street. I made out that his real name was the Count Talleyrand de Périgord—a priest right enough, but sorely come down in the world. He'd been King Louis' Ambassador to England a year or two back, before the French had cut off King Louis' head; and, by what I heard, that head wasn't hardly more than hanging loose before he'd run back to Paris and prevailed on Danton, the very man which did the murder, to send him back to England again as Ambassador of the French Republic! That was too much for the English, so they kicked him out by Act of Parliament, and he'd fled to the Americas without money or friends or prospects. I'm telling you the talk in the wash-house. Some of 'em was laughing over it. Says the French Marquise, "My friends, you laugh too soon. That man will be on the winning side before any of us."

' "I did not know you were so fond of priests, Marquise," says the Vicomte. His lady did my washing, as I've told you.

' "I have my reasons," says the Marquise. "He sent my uncle and my two brothers to Heaven by the little door,"— that was one of the *émigré* names for the guillotine. "He will be on the winning side if it costs him the blood of every friend he has in the world."

' "Then what does he want here?" says one of 'em. "We have all lost our game."

' "My faith!" says the Marquise. "He will find out, if any one can, whether this *canaille* of a Washington means to help us to fight England. Genêt (that was my Ambassador in the *Embuscade*) has failed and gone off disgraced; Fauchet (he was the new man) hasn't done any better, but our Abbé will find out, and he will make his profit out of the news. Such a man does not fail."

' "He begins unluckily," says the Vicomte. "He was set upon

to-day in the street for not hooting your Washington." They all laughed again, and one remarks, "How does the poor devil keep himself?"

'He must have slipped in through the wash-house door, for he flits past me and joins 'em, cold as ice.

' "One does what one can," he says. "I sell buttons. And you, Marquise?"

' "I?"—she waves her poor white hands all burned—"I am a cook—a very bad one—at your service, Abbé. We were just talking about you."

'They didn't treat him like they talked of him. They backed off and stood still.

' "I have missed something, then," he says. "But I spent this last hour playing—only for buttons, Marquise—against a noble savage, the veritable Huron himself."

' "You had your usual luck, I hope?" she says.

' "Certainly," he says. "I cannot afford to lose even buttons in these days."

' "Then I suppose the child of nature does not know that your dice are usually loaded, Father Tout-à-tous," she continues. I don't know whether she meant to accuse him of cheating. He only bows.

' "Not yet, Mademoiselle Cunégonde," he says, and goes on to make himself agreeable to the rest of the company. And that was how I found out our Monsieur Peringuey was Count Charles Maurice Talleyrand de Périgord.'

Pharaoh stopped, but the children said nothing.

'You've heard of him?' said Pharaoh.

Una shook her head.

'Was Red Jacket the Indian he played dice with?' Dan asked.

'He was. Red Jacket told me the next time we met. I asked

if the lame man had cheated. Red Jacket said no—he had
played quite fair and was a master player. I allow Red Jacket
knew. I've seen him, on the Reservation, play himself out of
everything he had and in again. Then I told Red Jacket all
I'd heard at the party concerning Talleyrand.

' "I was right," he says. "I saw the man's war-face when he
thought he was alone. That is why I played him. I played him
face to face. He is a great chief. Do they say why he comes
here?"

' "They say he comes to find out if Big Hand makes war
against the English," I said.

'Red Jacket grunted. "Yes," he says. "He asked me that too.
If he had been a small chief I should have lied. But he is a
great chief. He knew I was a chief, so I told him the truth.
I told him what Big Hand said to Cornplanter and me in the
clearing—'There will be no war.' I could not see what he
thought. I could not see behind his face. But he is a great
chief. He will believe."

' "Will he believe that Big Hand can keep his people back
from war?" I said, thinking of the crowds that hooted Big
Hand whenever he rode out.

' "He is as bad as Big Hand is good, but he is not as strong
as Big Hand," says Red Jacket. "When he talks with Big Hand
he will feel this in his heart. The French have sent away a
great chief. Presently he will go back and make them afraid."

'Now wasn't that comical? The French woman that knew
him and owed all her losses to him; the Indian that picked
him up, cut and muddy on the street, and played dice with
him; they neither of 'em doubted that Talleyrand was something by himself—appearances notwithstanding.'

'And was he something by himself?' asked Una.

Pharaoh began to laugh, but stopped. 'The way *I* look at

it,' he said, 'Talleyrand was one of just three men in this world who are quite by themselves. Big Hand I put first, because I've seen him.'

'Ay,' said Puck. 'I'm sorry we lost him out of Old England. Who d'you put second?'

'Talleyrand: maybe because I've seen him too,' said Pharaoh.

'Who's third?' said Puck.

'Boney—even though I've seen him.'

'Whew!' said Puck. 'Every man has his own weights and measures, but that's queer reckoning.'

'Boney?' said Una. 'You don't mean you've ever met Napoleon Bonaparte?'

'There, I knew you wouldn't have patience with the rest of my tale after hearing that! But wait a minute. Talleyrand he come round to Hundred and Eighteen in a day or two to thank Toby for his kindness. I didn't mention the dice-playing, but I could see that Red Jacket's doings had made Talleyrand highly curious about Indians—though he *would* call him the Huron. Toby, as you may believe, was all holds full of knowledge concerning their manners and habits. He only needed a listener. The Brethren don't study Indians much till they join the Church, but Toby knew 'em wild. So evening after evening Talleyrand crossed his sound leg over his game one and Toby poured forth. Having been adopted into the Senecas I, naturally, kept still, but Toby 'ud call on me to back up some of his remarks, and by that means, and a habit he had of drawing you on in talk, Talleyrand saw I knew something of his noble savages too. Then he tried a trick. Coming back from an *émigré* party he turns into his little shop and puts it to me, laughing like, that I'd gone with the two chiefs on their visit to Big Hand. *I* hadn't told. Red Jacket hadn't told, and Toby, of course, didn't know. 'Twas just Talleyrand's guess. "Now,"

he says, "my English and Red Jacket's French was so bad that
I am not sure I got the rights of what the President really said
to the unsophisticated Huron. Do me the favour of telling it
again." I told him every word Red Jacket had told him and
not one word more. I had my suspicions, having just come
from an *émigré* party where the Marquise was hating and
praising him as usual.

' "Much obliged," he said. "But I couldn't gather from Red
Jacket exactly what the President said to Monsieur Genêt, or
to his American gentlemen after Monsieur Genêt had ridden
away."

'I saw Talleyrand was guessing again, for Red Jacket hadn't
told him a word about the white men's pow-wow.'

'Why hadn't he?' Puck asked.

'Because Red Jacket was a chief. He told Talleyrand what
the President had said to him and Cornplanter; but he didn't
repeat the talk, between the white men, that Big Hand ordered
him to leave behind.'

'Oh!' said Puck. 'I see. What did *you* do?'

'First I was going to make some sort of tale round it, but
Talleyrand was a chief too. So I said, "As soon as I get Red
Jacket's permission to tell that part of the tale, I'll be delighted
to refresh your memory, Abbé." What else could I have done?

' "Is that all?" he says, laughing. "Let me refresh your memory. In a month from now I can give you a hundred dollars
for your account of the conversation."

' "Make it five hundred, Abbé," I says.

' "Five, then," says he.

' "That will suit me admirably," I says. "Red Jacket will be
in town again by then, and the moment he gives me leave I'll
claim the money."

'He had a hard fight to be civil but he come out smiling.

' "Monsieur," he says, "I beg your pardon as sincerely as I envy the noble Huron your loyalty. Do me the honour to sit down while I explain."

'There wasn't another chair, so I sat on the button-box.

'He was a clever man. He had got hold of the gossip that the President meant to make a peace treaty with England at any cost. He had found out—from Genêt, I reckon, who was with the President on the day the two chiefs met him. He'd heard that Genêt had had a huff with the President and had ridden off leaving his business at loose ends. What he wanted—what he begged and blustered to know—was just the very words which the President had said to his gentlemen *after* Genêt had left, concerning the peace treaty with England. He put it to me that in helping him to those very words I'd be helping three great countries as well as mankind. The room was as bare as the palm of your hand, but I couldn't laugh at him.

' "I'm sorry," I says, when he wiped his forehead. "As soon as Red Jacket gives permission——"

' "You don't believe me, then?" he cuts in.

' "Not one little, little word, Abbé," I says; "except that you mean to be on the winning side. Remember, I've been fiddling to all your old friends for months."

'Well, then his temper fled him and he called me names.

' "Wait a minute, *ci-devant*," I says at last. "I *am* half English and half French, but I am not the half of a man. I will tell thee something the Indian told me. Has thee seen the President?"

' "Oh yes!" he sneers. "I had letters from the Lord Lansdowne to that estimable old man."

' "Then," I says, "thee will understand. The Red Skin said that when thee has met the President thee will feel in thy heart he is a stronger man than thee."

' "Go!" he whispers. "Before I kill thee, go."

'He looked like it. So I left him.'

'Why did he want to know so badly?' said Dan.

'The way I look at it is that if he *had* known for certain that Washington meant to make the peace treaty with England at any price, he'd ha' left old Fauchet fumbling about in Philadelphia while he went straight back to France and told old Danton—"It's no good your wasting time and hopes on the United States, because she won't fight on our side—that I've proof of!" Then Danton might have been grateful and given Talleyrand a job, because a whole mass of things hang on knowing for sure who's your friend and who's your enemy. Just think of us poor shop-keepers, for instance.'

'Did Red Jacket let you tell, when he came back?' Una asked.

'Of course not. He said, "When Cornplanter and I ask you what Big Hand said to the whites you can tell the Lame Chief. All that talk was left behind in the timber, as Big Hand ordered. Tell the Lame Chief there will be no war. He can go back to France with that word."

'Talleyrand and me hadn't met for a long time except at *émigré* parties. When I give him the message he just shook his head. He was sorting buttons in the shop.

' "I cannot return to France with nothing better than the word of an unsophisticated savage," he says.

' "Hasn't the President said anything to you?" I asked him.

' "He has said everything that one in his position ought to say, but—but if only I had what he said to his Cabinet after Genêt rode off I believe I could change Europe—the world, maybe."

' "I'm sorry," I says. "Maybe you'll do that without my help."

'He looked at me hard. "Either you have unusual observation for one so young, or you choose to be insolent," he says.

' "It was intended for a compliment," I says. "But no odds. We're off in a few days for our summer trip, and I've come to make my good-byes."

' "I go on my travels too," he says. "If ever we meet again you may be sure I will do my best to repay what I owe you."

' "Without malice, Abbé, I hope," I says.

' "None whatever," says he. "Give my respects to your adorable Dr. Pangloss" (that was one of his side-names for Toby) "and the Huron." I never *could* teach him the difference betwixt Hurons and Senecas.

'Then Sister Haga came in for a paper of what we call "pilly buttons," and that was the last I saw of Talleyrand in those parts.'

'But after that you met Napoleon, didn't you?' said Una.

'Wait just a little, dearie. After that, Toby and I went to Lebanon and the Reservation, and, being older and knowing better how to manage him, I enjoyed myself well that summer with fiddling and fun. When we came back, the Brethren got after Toby because I wasn't learning any lawful trade, and he had hard work to save me from being apprenticed to Helmbold and Geyer the printers. 'Twould have ruined our music together, indeed it would. And when we escaped that, old Mattes Roush, the leather-breeches maker round the corner, took a notion I was cut out for skin-dressing. But we were rescued. Along towards Christmas there comes a big sealed letter from the Bank saying that a Monsieur Talleyrand had put five hundred dollars—a hundred pounds—to my credit there to use as I pleased. There was a little note from him inside—he didn't give any address—to thank me for past kindnesses and my believing in his future, which he said was pretty cloudy at the time of writing. I wished Toby to share the money. *I* hadn't done more than bring Talleyrand up to Hundred and Eighteen. The kindnesses were Toby's. But Toby said, "No! Liberty and Independence for ever. I have all my wants, my son." So I gave him a set of new fiddle-strings, and the Brethren didn't advise us any more. Only Pastor Meder he preached about the deceitfulness of riches, and Brother Adam Goos said if there was war the English 'ud surely shoot down the Bank. *I* knew there wasn't going to be any war, but I drew the money out and on Red Jacket's advice I put it into horse-flesh, which I sold to Bob Bicknell for the Baltimore stage-coaches. That way, I doubled my money inside the twelve-month.'

'You gipsy! You proper gipsy!' Puck shouted.

'Why not? 'Twas fair buying and selling. Well, one thing leading to another, in a few years I had made the beginning of a worldly fortune and was in the tobacco trade.'

'Ah!' said Puck, suddenly. 'Might I inquire if you'd ever sent any news to your people in England—or in France?'

'O' course I had. I wrote regular every three months after I'd made money in the horse trade. We Lees don't like coming home empty-handed. If it's only a turnip or an egg, it's something. Oh yes, I wrote good and plenty to Uncle Aurette, and—Dad don't read very quickly—Uncle used to slip over Newhaven way and tell Dad what was going on in the tobacco trade.'

'I see—

> *'Aurettes and Lees—*
> *Like as two peas.*

Go on, Brother Square-toes,' said Puck. Pharaoh laughed and went on.

'Talleyrand he'd gone up in the world same as me. He'd sailed to France again, and was a great man in the Government there awhile, but they had to turn him out on account of some story about bribes from American shippers. All our poor *émigrés* said he was surely finished this time, but Red Jacket and me we didn't think it likely, not unless he was quite dead. Big Hand had made his peace treaty with Great Britain, just *as* he said he would, and there was a roaring trade 'twixt England and the United States for such as 'ud take the risk of being searched by British and French men-o'-war. Those two was fighting, and just *as* his gentlemen told Big Hand 'ud happen—the United States was catching it from both. If an English man-o'-war met an American ship he'd press half the best men out of her, and swear they was British subjects. Most of 'em was! If a Frenchman met her he'd, likely, have the cargo out of her, swearing it was meant to aid and comfort the English; and if a Spaniard or a Dutchman met her—they was hanging on to England's coat-tails too—Lord only knows what *they* wouldn't do! It came over me that what I wanted in my tobacco trade was a fast-sailing ship and a man who could be French, English, or American at a pinch. Luckily I could lay my hands on both articles. So along towards the end of September in the year 'Ninety-nine I sailed from Philadelphia with a hundred and eleven hogshead o' good Virginia tobacco, in the brig *Berthe Aurette*, named after Mother's maiden name, hoping 'twould bring me luck, which she didn't—and yet she did.'

'Where was you bound for?' Puck asked.

'Er—any port I found handiest. I didn't tell Toby or the Brethren. They don't understand the ins and outs of the tobacco trade.'

Puck coughed a small cough as he shifted a piece of wood with his bare foot.

'It's easy for you to sit and judge,' Pharaoh cried. 'But think o' what *we* had to put up with! We spread our wings and run across the broad Atlantic like a hen through a horse-fair. Even so, we was stopped by an English frigate, three days out. He sent a boat alongside and pressed seven able seamen. I remarked it was hard on honest traders, but the officer said they was fighting all creation and hadn't time to argue. The next English frigate we escaped with no more than a shot in our quarter. Then we was chased two days and a night by a French privateer, firing between squalls, and the dirty little English ten-gun brig which made him sheer off had the impudence to press another five of our men. That's how we reached to the chops of the Channel. Twelve good men pressed out of thirty-five; an eighteen-pound shot-hole close beside our rudder; our mainsail looking like spectacles where the Frenchman had hit us—and the Channel crawling with short-handed British cruisers. Put *that* in your pipe and smoke it next time you grumble at the price of tobacco!

'Well, then, to top it off, while we was trying to get at our leaks, a French lugger come swooping at us out o' the dusk. We warned him to keep away, but he fell aboard us, and up climbed his jabbering red-caps. We couldn't endure any more—indeed we couldn't. We went at 'em with all we could lay hands on. It didn't last long. They was fifty odd to our twenty-three. Pretty soon I heard the cutlasses thrown down and some one bellowed for the *sacré* captain.

' "Here I am!" I says. "I don't suppose it makes any odds to you thieves, but this is the United States brig *Berthe Aurette*."

' "My aunt!" the man says, laughing. "Why is she named that?"

' "Who's speaking?" I said. 'Twas too dark to see, but I thought I knew the voice.

' "Enseigne de Vaisseau Estèphe L'Estrange," he sings out, and then I was sure.

' "Oh!" I says. "It's all in the family, I suppose, but you *have* done a fine day's work, Stephen."

'He whips out the binnacle-light and holds it to my face. He was young L'Estrange, my full cousin, that I hadn't seen since the night the smack sank off Telscombe Tye—six years before.

' "Whew!" he says. "That's why she was named for Aunt Berthe, is it? What's your share in her, Pharaoh?"

' "Only half owner, but the cargo's mine."

' "That's bad," he says. "I'll do what I can, but you shouldn't have fought us."

' "Steve," I says, "you aren't ever going to report our little fall-out as a fight! Why, a Revenue cutter 'ud laugh at it!"

' "So'd I if I wasn't in the Republican Navy," he says. "But two of our men are dead, d'ye see, and I'm afraid I'll have to take you to the Prize Court at Le Havre."

' "Will they condemn my 'baccy?" I asks.

' "To the last ounce. But I was thinking more of the ship. She'd make a sweet little craft for the Navy if the Prize Court 'ud let me have her," he says.

'Then I knew there was no hope. I don't blame him—a man must consider his own interests—but nigh every dollar I had was in ship or cargo, and Steve kept on saying, "You shouldn't have fought us."

"Well, then, the lugger took us to Le Havre, and that being the one time we *did* want a British ship to rescue us, why, o' course we never saw one. My cousin spoke his best for us at the Prize Court. He owned he'd no right to rush alongside in the face o' the United States flag, but we couldn't get over those two men killed, d'ye see, and the Court condemned both ship and cargo. They was kind enough not to make us prisoners—only beggars—and young L'Estrange was given the *Berthe Aurette* to re-arm into the French Navy.

' "I'll take you round to Boulogne," he says. "Mother and the rest'll be glad to see you, and you can slip over to New-haven with Uncle Aurette. Or you can ship with me, like most o' your men, and take a turn at King George's loose trade. There's plenty pickings," he says.

'Crazy as I was, I couldn't help laughing.

' "I've had my allowance of pickings and stealings," I says. "Where are they taking my tobacco?" 'Twas being loaded on to a barge.

' "Up the Seine to be sold in Paris," he says. "Neither you nor I will ever touch a penny of that money."

' "Get me leave to go with it," I says. "I'll see if there's jus-tice to be gotten out of our American Ambassador."

' "There's not much justice in this world," he says, "without a Navy." But he got me leave to go with the barge and he gave me some money. That tobacco was all I had, and I fol-lowed it like a hound follows a snatched bone. Going up the river I fiddled a little to keep my spirits up, as well as to make friends with the guard. They was only doing their duty. Outside o' that they were the reasonablest o' God's creatures. They never even laughed at me. So we come to Paris, by river, along in November, which the French had christened Brumaire. They'd given new names to all the months, and after such an outrageous silly piece o' business as *that*, they wasn't likely to trouble 'emselves with my rights and wrongs. They didn't. The barge was laid up below Notre Dame church in charge of a caretaker, and he let me sleep aboard after I'd run about all day from office to office, seeking justice and fair dealing, and getting speeches concerning liberty. None heeded me. Looking back on it I can't rightly blame 'em. I'd no money, my clothes was filthy mucked; I hadn't changed my linen in weeks, and I'd no proof of my claims except the ship's papers, which, they said, I might have stolen. The thieves! The doorkeeper to the American Ambassador—for I never saw even the Secretary—he swore I spoke French a sight too well for an American citizen. Worse than that—I had spent my money, d'ye see, and I—I took to fiddling in the streets for my keep; and—and, a ship's captain with a fiddle under his arm—well, I *don't* blame 'em that they didn't believe me.

'I come back to the barge one day—late in this month Brumaire it was—fair beazled out. Old Maingon, the caretaker, he'd lit a fire in a bucket and was grilling a herring.

' "Courage, mon ami," he says. "Dinner is served."

' "I can't eat," I says. "I can't do any more. It's stronger than I am."

' "Bah!" he says. "Nothing's stronger than a man. Me, for example! Less than two years ago I was blown up in the *Orient* in Aboukir Bay, but I descended again and hit the water like a fairy. Look at me now," he says. He wasn't much to look at, for he'd only one leg and one eye, but the cheerfullest soul that ever trod shoe-leather. "That's worse than a hundred and eleven hogshead of 'baccy," he goes on. "You're young, too! What wouldn't I give to be young in France at this hour! There's nothing you couldn't do," he says. "The ball's at your feet—kick it!" he says. He kicks the old fire-bucket with his peg-leg. "General Buonaparte, for example!" he goes on. "That man's a babe compared to me, and see what he's done already. He's conquered Egypt and Austria and Italy—oh! half Europe!" he says, "and now he sails back to Paris, and he sails out to St. Cloud down the river here— *don't* stare at the river, you young fool!—and all in front of these pig-jobbing lawyers and citizens he makes himself Consul, which is as good as a King. He'll *be* King, too, in the next three turns of the capstan—King of France, England, and the world! Think o' that!" he shouts, "and eat your herring."

'I says something about Boney. If he hadn't been fighting England I shouldn't have lost my 'baccy—should I?

' "Young fellow," says Maingon, "you don't understand."

'We heard cheering. A carriage passed over the bridge with two in it.

' "That's the man himself," says Maingon. "He'll give 'em something to cheer for soon." He stands at the salute.

' "Who's t'other in black beside him?" I asks, fairly shaking all over.

' "Ah! he's the clever one. You'll hear of him before long. He's that scoundrel-bishop, Talleyrand."

' "It is!" I said, and up the steps I went with my fiddle, and run after the carriage calling, "Abbé, Abbé!"

'A soldier knocked the wind out of me with the back of his sword, but I had sense to keep on following till the carriage stopped—and there just was a crowd round the house-door! I must have been half-crazy else I wouldn't have struck up *"Si le Roi m'avait donné Paris la grande ville!"* I thought it might remind him.

' "That is a good omen!" he says to Boney sitting all hunched up; and he looks straight at me.

' "Abbé—oh, Abbé!" I says. "Don't you remember Toby and Hundred and Eighteen Second Street?"

'He said not a word. He just crooked his long white finger to the guard at the door while the carriage steps were let down, and I skipped into the house, and they slammed the door in the crowd's face.

' "You go there," says a soldier, and shoves me into an empty room, where I catched my first breath since I'd left the barge. Presently I heard plates rattling next door—there were only folding doors between—and a cork drawn. "I tell you," some one shouts with his mouth full, "it was all that sulky ass Sieyès' fault. Only my speech to the Five Hundred saved the situation."

' "Did it save your coat?" says Talleyrand. "I hear they tore it when they threw you out. Don't gasconade to me. You may be in the road of victory, but you aren't there yet."

'Then I guessed t'other man was Boney. He stamped about and swore at Talleyrand.

' "You forget yourself, Consul," says Talleyrand, "or rather you remember yourself—Corsican."

' "Pig!" says Boney, and worse.

' "Emperor!" says Talleyrand, but, the way he spoke, it sounded worst of all. Some one must have backed against the folding doors, for they flew open and showed me in the middle of the room. Boney whipped out his pistol before I could stand up. "General," says Talleyrand to him, "this gentleman has a habit of catching us canaille *en déshabillé*. Put that thing down."

'Boney laid it on the table, so I guessed which was master. Talleyrand takes my hand—"Charmed to see you again, Candide," he says. "How is the adorable Dr. Pangloss and the noble Huron?"

' "They were doing very well when I left," I said. "But I'm not."

' "Do *you* sell buttons now?" he says, and fills me a glass of wine off the table.

' "Madeira," says he. "Not so good as some I have drunk."

' "You mountebank!" Boney roars. "Turn that out." (He didn't even say "man," but Talleyrand, being gentle-born, just went on.)

' "Pheasant is not so good as pork," he says. "You will find some at that table if you will do me the honour to sit down. Pass him a clean plate, General." And, as true as I'm here, Boney slid a plate along just like a sulky child. He was a lanky-haired, yellow-skinned little man, as nervous as a cat—and as dangerous. I could feel that.

' "And now," said Talleyrand, crossing his game leg over his sound one, "will you tell me your story?"

'I was in a fluster, but I told him nearly everything from the time he left me the five hundred dollars in Philadelphia, up to my losing ship and cargo at Le Havre. Boney began by listening, but after a bit he dropped into his own thoughts and looked at the crowd sideways through the front-room curtains. Talleyrand called to him when I'd done.

' "Eh? What we need now," says Boney, "is peace for the next three or four years."

' "Quite so," says Talleyrand. "Meantime I want the Consul's order to the Prize Court at Le Havre to restore my friend here his ship."

' "Nonsense!" says Boney. "Give away an oak-built brig of two hundred and seven tons for sentiment? Certainly not! She must be armed into my Navy with ten—no, fourteen twelve-pounders and two long fours. Is she strong enough to bear a long twelve forward?"

'Now I could ha' sworn he'd paid no heed to my talk, but that wonderful head-piece of his seemingly skimmed off every word of it that was useful to him.

' "Ah, General!" says Talleyrand. "You are a magician—a magician without morals. But the brig is undoubtedly American, and we don't want to offend them more than we have."

' "Need anybody talk about the affair?" he says. He didn't

look at me, but I knew what was in his mind—just cold murder because I worried him; and he'd order it as easy as ordering his carriage.

' "You can't stop 'em," I said. "There's twenty-two other men besides me." I felt a little more 'ud set me screaming like a wired hare.

' "Undoubtedly American," Talleyrand goes on. "You would gain something if you returned the ship—with a message of fraternal good-will—published in the *Moniteur*" (that's a French paper like the Philadelphia *Aurora*).

' "A good idea!" Boney answers. "One could say much in a message."

' "It might be useful," says Talleyrand. "Shall I have the message prepared?" He wrote something in a little pocket ledger.

' "Yes—for me to embellish this evening. The *Moniteur* will publish it to-night."

' "Certainly. Sign, please," says Talleyrand, tearing the leaf out.

' "But that's the order to return the brig," says Boney. "Is that necessary? Why should I lose a good ship? Haven't I lost enough ships already?"

'Talleyrand didn't answer any of those questions. Then Boney sidled up to the table and jabs his pen into the ink. Then he shies at the paper again: "My signature alone is useless," he says. "You must have the other two Consuls as well. Sieyès and Roger Ducos must sign. We must preserve the Laws."

' "By the time my friend presents it," says Talleyrand, still looking out of window, "only one signature will be necessary."

'Boney smiles. "It's a swindle," says he, but he signed and pushed the paper across.

' "Give that to the President of the Prize Court at Le Havre," says Talleyrand, "and he will give you back your ship. I will settle for the cargo myself. You have told me how much it cost. What profit did you expect to make on it?"

'Well, then, as man to man, I was bound to warn him that I'd set out to run it into England without troubling the Revenue, and so I couldn't rightly set bounds to my profits.'

'I guessed that all along,' said Puck.

> *'There was never a Lee to Warminghurst—*
> *That wasn't a smuggler last and first.'*

The children laughed.

'It's comical enough now,' said Pharaoh. 'But I didn't laugh then. Says Talleyrand after a minute, "I am a bad accountant and I have several calculations on hand at present. Shall we say twice the cost of the cargo?"

'Say? I couldn't say a word. I sat choking and nodding like a China image while he wrote an order to his secretary to pay me, I won't say how much, because you wouldn't believe it.

' "Oh! Bless you, Abbé! God bless you!" I got it out at last.

' "Yes," he says, "I am a priest in spite of myself, but they call me Bishop now. Take this for my episcopal blessing," and he hands me the paper.

' "He stole all that money from me," says Boney over my shoulder. "A Bank of France is another of the things we must make. Are you mad?" he shouts at Talleyrand.

' "Quite," says Talleyrand, getting up. "But be calm. The disease will never attack you. It is called gratitude. This gentleman found me in the street and fed me when I was hungry."

' "I see; and he has made a fine scene of it and you have paid him, I suppose. Meantime, France waits."

' "Oh! poor France!" says Talleyrand. "Good-bye, Candide," he says to me. "By the way," he says, "have you yet got Red Jacket's permission to tell me what the President said to his Cabinet after Monsieur Genêt rode away?"

'I couldn't speak, I could only shake my head, and Boney— so impatient he was to go on with his doings—he ran at me and fair pushed me out of the room. And that was all there was to it.'

Pharaoh stood up and slid his fiddle into one of his big skirt-pockets as though it were a dead hare.

'Oh! but we want to know lots and lots more,' said Dan. 'How you got home—and what old Maingon said on the barge—and wasn't your cousin surprised when he had to give back the *Berthe Aurette*, and——'

'Tell us more about Toby!' cried Una.

'Yes, and Red Jacket,' said Dan.

'Won't you tell us any more?' they both pleaded.

Puck kicked the oak branch on the fire, till it sent up a column of smoke that made them sneeze. When they had finished the Shaw was empty except for old Hobden stamping through the larches.

'They gipsies have took two,' he said. 'My black pullet and my liddle gingy-speckled cockrel.'

'I thought so,' said Dan, picking up one tail-feather that the old woman had overlooked.

'Which way did they go? Which way did the runagates go?' said Hobden.

'Hobby!' said Una. 'Would you like it if we told Keeper Ridley all your goings and comings?'

'POOR HONEST MEN'

Your jar of Virginny
Will cost you a guinea,
Which you reckon too much by five shilling or ten;
But light your churchwarden
And judge it accordin'
When I've told you the troubles of poor honest men.

From the Capes of the Delaware,
As you are well aware,
We sail with tobacco for England—but then
Our own British cruisers,
They watch us come through, sirs,
And they press half a score of us poor honest men.

Or if by quick sailing
(Thick weather prevailing)
We leave them behind (as we do now and then)
We are sure of a gun from
Each frigate we run from,
Which is often destruction to poor honest men!

Broadsides the Atlantic
We tumble short-handed,
With shot-holes to plug and new canvas to bend,
And off the Azores,
Dutch, Dons and Monsieurs
Are waiting to terrify poor honest men!

REWARDS AND FAIRIES

Napoleon's embargo
Is laid on all cargo
Which comfort or aid to King George may intend;
And since roll, twist and leaf,
Of all comforts is chief,
They try for to steal it from poor honest men!

With no heart for fight,
We take refuge in flight,
But fire as we run, our retreat to defend,
Until our stern-chasers
Cut up her fore-braces,
And she flies off the wind from us poor honest men!

'Twix' the Forties and Fifties,
South-eastward the drift is,
And so, when we think we are making Land's End,
Alas, it is Ushant
With half the King's Navy,
Blockading French ports against poor honest men!

But they may not quit station
(Which is our salvation),
So swiftly we stand to the Nor'ard again;
And finding the tail of
A homeward-bound convoy,
We slip past the Scillies like poor honest men.

'Twix' the Lizard and Dover,
We hand our stuff over,
Though I may not inform how we do it, nor when;
But a light on each quarter

'POOR HONEST MEN'

Low down on the water
Is well understanded by poor honest men.

Even then we have dangers
From meddlesome strangers,
Who spy on our business and are not content
To take a smooth answer,
Except with a handspike . . .
And they say they are murdered by poor honest men!

To be drowned or be shot
Is our natural lot,
Why should we, moreover, be hanged in the end—
After all our great pains
For to dangle in chains,
As though we were smugglers, not poor honest men?

THE CONVERSION OF ST. WILFRID

EDDI'S SERVICE

Eddi, priest of St. Wilfrid
  In the chapel at Manhood End,
Ordered a midnight service
  For such as cared to attend.

But the Saxons were keeping Christmas,
  And the night was stormy as well.
Nobody came to service
  Though Eddi rang the bell.

'Wicked weather for walking,'
  Said Eddi of Manhood End.
'But I must go on with the service
  For such as care to attend.'

The altar candles were lighted,—
  An old marsh donkey came,
Bold as a guest invited,
  And stared at the guttering flame.

The storm beat on at the windows,
  The water splashed on the floor,
And a wet yoke-weary bullock
  Pushed in through the open door.

'How do I know what is greatest,
  How do I know what is least?
That is My Father's business,'
  Said Eddi, Wilfrid's priest.

'But, three are gathered together—
  Listen to me and attend.
I bring good news, my brethren!'
  Said Eddi, of Manhood End.

And he told the Ox of a manger
  And a stall in Bethlehem,
And he spoke to the Ass of a Rider
  That rode to Jerusalem.

They steamed and dripped in the chancel,
  They listened and never stirred,
While, just as though they were Bishops,
  Eddi preached them The Word.

Till the gale blew off on the marshes
  And the windows showed the day,
And the Ox and the Ass together
  Wheeled and clattered away.

And when the Saxons mocked him,
  Said Eddi of Manhood End,
'I dare not shut His chapel
  On such as care to attend.'

THE CONVERSION OF ST. WILFRID

THEY HAD BOUGHT PEPPERMINTS up at the village, and were coming home past little St. Barnabas' Church, when they saw Jimmy Kidbrooke, the carpenter's baby, kicking at the churchyard gate, with a shaving in his mouth and the tears running down his cheeks.

Una pulled out the shaving and put in a peppermint. Jimmy said he was looking for his grand-daddy—he never seemed to take much notice of his father—so they went up between the old graves, under the leaf-dropping limes, to the porch, where Jim trotted in, looked about the empty Church, and screamed like a gate-hinge.

Young Sam Kidbrooke's voice came from the bell-tower, and made them jump.

'Why, Jimmy,' he called, 'what are you doin' here? Fetch him, Father!'

Old Mr. Kidbrooke stumped downstairs, jerked Jimmy on to his shoulder, stared at the children beneath his brass spectacles, and stumped back again. They laughed: it was so exactly like Mr. Kidbrooke.

'It's all right,' Una called up the stairs. 'We found him, Sam. Does his mother know?'

'He's come off by himself. She'll be justabout crazy,' Sam answered.

'Then I'll run down street and tell her.' Una darted off.

'Thank you, Miss Una. Would you like to see how we're mendin' the bell-beams, Mus' Dan?'

Dan hopped up, and saw young Sam lying on his stomach in

443

a most delightful place among beams and ropes, close to the five great bells. Old Mr. Kidbrooke on the floor beneath was planing a piece of wood, and Jimmy was eating the shavings as fast as they came away. He never looked at Jimmy; Jimmy never stopped eating; and the broad gilt-bobbed pendulum of the Church clock never stopped swinging across the white-washed wall of the tower.

Dan winked through the sawdust that fell on his upturned face. 'Ring a bell,' he called.

'I mustn't do that, but I'll buzz one of 'em a bit for you,' said Sam. He pounded on the sound-bow of the biggest bell, and waked a hollow groaning boom that ran up and down the tower like creepy feelings down your back. Just when it almost began to hurt, it died away in a hurry of beautiful sorrowful cries, like a wine-glass rubbed with a wet finger. The pendulum clanked—one loud clank to each silent swing.

Dan heard Una return from Mrs. Kidbrooke's, and ran down to fetch her. She was standing by the font staring at some one who kneeled at the Altar-rail.

'Is that the Lady who practises the organ?' she whispered.

'No. She's gone into the organ-place. Besides, she wears black,' Dan replied.

The figure rose and came down the nave. It was a white-haired man in a long white gown with a sort of scarf looped low on the neck, one end hanging over his shoulder. His loose long sleeves were embroidered with gold, and a deep strip of gold embroidery waved and sparkled round the hem of his gown.

'Go and meet him,' said Puck's voice behind the font. 'It's only Wilfrid.'

'Wilfrid who?' said Dan. 'You come along too.'

'Wilfrid—Saint of Sussex, and Archbishop of York. *I* shall

wait till he asks me.' He waved them forward. Their feet squeaked on the old grave-slabs in the centre aisle. The Archbishop raised one hand with a pink ring on it, and said something in Latin. He was very handsome, and his thin face looked almost as silvery as his thin circle of hair.

'Are you alone?' he asked.

'Puck's here, of course,' said Una. 'Do you know him?'

'I know him better now than I used to.' He beckoned over Dan's shoulder, and spoke again in Latin. Puck pattered forward, holding himself as straight as an arrow. The Archbishop smiled.

'Be welcome,' said he. 'Be very welcome.'

'Welcome to you also, O Prince of the Church,' Puck replied. The Archbishop bowed his head and passed on, till he glimmered like a white moth in the shadow by the font.

'He does look awfully princely,' said Una. 'Isn't he coming back?'

'Oh yes. He's only looking over the Church. He's very fond of churches,' said Puck. 'What's that?'

The Lady who practises the organ was speaking to the blower-boy behind the organ-screen. 'We can't very well talk here,' Puck whispered. 'Let's go to Panama Corner.'

He led them to the end of the south aisle, where there is a slab of iron which says in queer, long-tailed letters: *Orate p. annema Jhone Coline.* The children always called it Panama Corner.

The Archbishop moved slowly about the little Church, peering at the old memorial tablets and the new glass windows. The Lady who practises the organ began to pull out stops and rustle hymnbooks behind the screen.

'I hope she'll do all the soft lacey tunes—like treacle on porridge,' said Una.

'I like the trumpety ones best,' said Dan. 'Oh, look at Wilfrid! He's trying to shut the Altar-gates!'

'Tell him he mustn't,' said Puck, quite seriously.

'He can't, anyhow,' Dan muttered, and tiptoed out of Panama Corner while the Archbishop patted and patted at the carved gates that always sprang open again beneath his hand.

'That's no use, sir,' Dan whispered. 'Old Mr. Kidbrooke says Altar-gates are just *the* one pair of gates which no man can shut. He made 'em so himself.'

The Archbishop's blue eyes twinkled. Dan saw that he knew all about it.

'I beg your pardon,' Dan stammered—very angry with Puck.

'Yes, I know! He made them so Himself.' The Archbishop smiled, and crossed to Panama Corner, where Una dragged up a certain padded arm-chair for him to sit on.

The organ played softly. 'What does that music say?' he asked.

Una dropped into the chant without thinking: ' "O all ye works of the Lord, bless ye the Lord; praise him and magnify him for ever." We call it the Noah's Ark, because it's all lists of things—beasts and birds and whales, you know.'

'Whales?' said the Archbishop quickly.

'Yes—"O ye whales, and all that move in the waters," ' Una hummed—' "Bless ye the Lord." It sounds like a wave turning over, doesn't it?'

'Holy Father,' said Puck with a demure face, 'is a little seal also "one who moves in the water"?'

'Eh? Oh yes—yess!' he laughed. 'A seal moves wonderfully in the waters. Do the seal come to my island still?'

Puck shook his head. 'All those little islands have been swept away.'

'Very possible. The tides ran fiercely down there. Do you know the land of the Sea-calf, maiden?'

'No—but we've seen seals—at Brighton.'

'The Archbishop is thinking of a little farther down the coast. He means Seal's Eye—Selsey—down Chichester way—where he converted the South Saxons,' Puck explained.

'Yes—yess; if the South Saxons did not convert me,' said the Archbishop, smiling. 'The first time I was wrecked was on that coast. As our ship took ground and we tried to push her off, an old fat fellow of a seal, I remember, reared breast-high out of the water, and scratched his head with his flipper as if he were saying: "What *does* that excited person with the pole think he is doing?" I was very wet and miserable, but I could not help laughing, till the natives came down and attacked us.'

'What did you do?' Dan asked.

'One couldn't very well go back to France, so one tried to make them go back to the shore. All the South Saxons are born wreckers, like my own Northumbrian folk. I was bringing over a few things for my old Church at York, and some of the natives laid hands on them, and—and I'm afraid I lost my temper.'

'It is said—' Puck's voice was wickedly meek—'that there was a great fight.'

'Eh, but I must ha' been a silly lad.' Wilfrid spoke with a sudden thick burr in his voice. He coughed, and took up his silvery tones again. 'There was no fight really. My men thumped a few of them, but the tide rose half an hour before its time, with a strong wind, and we backed off. What I wanted to say, though, was, that the seas about us were full of sleek seals watching the scuffle. My good Eddi—my chaplain—insisted that they were demons. Yes—yess! That was my first acquaintance with the South Saxons and their seals.'

'But not the only time you were wrecked, was it?' said Dan.

'Alas, no! On sea and land my life seems to have been one long shipwreck.' He looked at the Jhone Coline slab as old Hobden sometimes looks into the fire. 'Ah, well!'

'But did you ever have any more adventures among the seals?' said Una, after a little.

'Oh, the seals! I beg your pardon. They are the important things. Yes—yess! I went back to the South Saxons after twelve —fifteen—years. No, I did not come by water, but overland from my own Northumbria, to see what I could do. It's little one *can* do with that class of native except make them stop killing each other and themselves——'

'Why did they kill themselves?' Una asked, her chin in her hand.

'Because they were heathen. When they grew tired of life (as if *they* were the only people!) they would jump into the sea. They called it going to Wotan. It wasn't want of food always —by any means. A man would tell you that he felt grey in the heart, or a woman would say that she saw nothing but long days in front of her; and they'd saunter away to the mud-flats and—that would be the end of them, poor souls, unless one headed them off! One had to run quick, but one can't allow people to lay hands on themselves because they happen to feel grey. Yes—yess! Extraordinary people, the South Saxons. Disheartening, sometimes. . . . What does that say now?' The organ had changed tune again.

'Only a hymn for next Sunday,' said Una. ' "The Church's One Foundation." Go on, please, about running over the mud. I should like to have seen you.'

'I dare say you would, and I really *could* run in those days. Ethelwalch the King gave me some five or six muddy parishes by the sea, and the first time my good Eddi and I rode there we saw a man slouching along the slob, among the seals at Manhood End. My good Eddi disliked seals—but he swallowed his objections and ran like a hare.'

'Why?' said Dan.

'For the same reason that I did. We thought it was one of our people going to drown himself. As a matter of fact, Eddi and I were nearly drowned in the pools before we overtook him. To cut a long story short, we found ourselves very muddy, very breathless, being quietly made fun of in good Latin by a very well-spoken person. No—he'd no idea of going to Wotan. He was fishing on his own beaches, and he showed us the beacons and turf-heaps that divided his lands from the Church property. He took us to his own house, gave us a good dinner, some more than good wine, sent a guide with us into Chichester, and became one of my best and most refreshing friends. He was a Meon by descent, from the west edge of the kingdom; a scholar educated, curiously enough, at Lyons, my old school; had travelled the world over, even to Rome, and was a brilliant talker. We found we had scores of acquaintances in common. It seemed he was a small chief under King Ethelwalch, and I fancy the King was somewhat afraid of him. The South Saxons mistrust a man who talks too well. Ah! *Now,* I've left out the very point of my story. He kept a great grey-muzzled old dog-seal that he had brought up from a pup. He called it Padda—after one of my clergy. It *was* rather like fat, honest old Padda. The creature followed him everywhere, and nearly knocked down my good Eddi when we first met him. Eddi loathed it. It used to sniff at his thin legs and cough at him. I can't say I ever took much notice of it (I was not fond of animals), till one day Eddi came to me with a circumstantial account of some witchcraft that Meon worked. He would tell the seal to go down to the beach the last thing at night, and bring him word of the weather. When it came back, Meon might say to his slaves, "Padda thinks we shall have wind to-morrow. Haul up the boats!" I spoke to Meon casually about the story, and he laughed.

'He told me he could judge by the look of the creature's coat and the way it sniffed what weather was brewing. Quite possible. One need not put down everything one does not understand to the work of bad spirits—or good ones, for that matter.' He nodded towards Puck, who nodded gaily in return.

'I say so,' he went on, 'because to a certain extent I have been made a victim of that habit of mind. Some while after I was settled at Selsey, King Ethelwalch and Queen Ebba ordered their people to be baptized. I fear I'm too old to believe that a whole nation can change its heart at the King's command, and I had a shrewd suspicion that their real motive was to get a good harvest. No rain had fallen for two or three years, but as soon as we had finished baptizing, it fell heavily, and they all said it was a miracle.'

'And was it?' Dan asked.

'Everything in life is a miracle, but'—the Archbishop twisted the heavy ring on his finger—'I should be slow—ve-ry slow should I be—to assume that a certain sort of miracle happens whenever lazy and improvident people say they are going to turn over a new leaf if they are paid for it. My friend Meon had sent his slaves to the font, but he had not come himself, so the next time I rode over—to return a manuscript—I took the liberty of asking why. He was perfectly open about it. He looked on the King's action as a heathen attempt to curry favour with the Christians' God through me the Archbishop, and he would have none of it. "My dear man," I said, "admitting that that is the case, surely you, as an educated person, don't believe in Wotan and all the other hobgoblins any more than Padda here?" The old seal was hunched up on his ox-hide behind his master's chair.

' "Even if I don't," he said, "why should I insult the memory of my fathers' Gods? I have sent you a hundred and three of my rascals to christen. Isn't that enough?"

' "By no means," I answered. "I want *you*."

' "He wants us! What do you think of that, Padda?" He pulled the seal's whiskers till it threw back its head and roared, and he pretended to interpret. "No! Padda says he won't be baptized yet awhile. He says you'll stay to dinner and come fishing with me to-morrow, because you're overworked and need a rest."

' "I wish you'd keep yoh brute in its proper place," I said, and Eddi, my chaplain, agreed.

' "I do," said Meon. "I keep him just next my heart. He can't tell a lie, and he doesn't know how to love any one except me. It 'ud be the same if I were dying on a mud-bank, wouldn't it, Padda?"

' "Augh! Augh!" said Padda, and put up his head to be scratched.

'Then Meon began to tease Eddi: "Padda says, if Eddi saw his Archbishop dying on a mud-bank Eddi would tuck up his gown and run. Padda knows Eddi can run too! Padda came into Wittering Church last Sunday—all wet—to hear the music, and Eddi ran out."

'My good Eddi rubbed his hands and his shins together, and flushed. "Padda is a child of the Devil, who is the father of lies!" he cried, and begged my pardon for having spoken. I forgave him.

' "Yes. You are just about stupid enough for a musician," said Meon. "But here he is. Sing a hymn to him, and see if he can stand it. You'll find my small harp beside the fireplace."

'Eddi, who is really an excellent musician, played and sang for quite half an hour. Padda shuffled off his ox-hide, hunched himself on his flippers before him, and listened with his head thrown back. Yes—yess! A rather funny sight! Meon tried not to laugh, and asked Eddi if he were satisfied.

'It takes some time to get an idea out of my good Eddi's head. He looked at me.

' "Do you want to sprinkle him with holy water, and see if he flies up the chimney? Why not baptize him?" said Meon.

'Eddi was really shocked. I thought it was bad taste myself.

' "That's not fair," said Meon. "You call him a demon and a familiar spirit because he loves his master and likes music, and when I offer you a chance to prove it you won't take it. Look here! I'll make a bargain. I'll be baptized if you'll baptize Padda too. He's more of a man than most of my slaves."

' "One doesn't bargain—or joke—about these matters," I said. He was going altogether too far.

' "Quite right," said Meon; "I shouldn't like any one to joke about Padda. Padda, go down to the beach and bring us to-morrow's weather!"

'My good Eddi must have been a little overtired with his day's work. "I am a servant of the Church," he cried. "My business is to save souls, not to enter into fellowships and understandings with accursed beasts."

' "Have it your own narrow way," said Meon. "Padda, you needn't go." The old fellow flounced back to his ox-hide at once.

' "Man could learn obedience at least from that creature," said Eddi, a little ashamed of himself. Christians should not curse.

' "Don't begin to apologise just when I am beginning to like you," said Meon. "We'll leave Padda behind to-morrow—out

452

of respect to your feelings. Now let's go to supper. We must be up early to-morrow for the whiting."

'The next was a beautiful crisp autumn morning—a weather-breeder, if I had taken the trouble to think; but it's refreshing to escape from kings and converts for half a day. We three went by ourselves in Meon's smallest boat, and we got on the whiting near an old wreck, a mile or so off shore. Meon knew the marks to a yard, and the fish were keen. Yes—yess! A perfect morning's fishing! If a Bishop can't be a fisherman, who can?' He twiddled his ring again. 'We stayed there a little too long, and while we were getting up our stone, down came the fog. After some discussion, we decided to row for the land. The ebb was just beginning to make round the point, and sent us all ways at once like a coracle.'

'Selsey Bill,' said Puck under his breath. 'The tides run something furious there.'

'I believe you,' said the Archbishop. 'Meon and I have spent a good many evenings arguing as to where exactly we drifted. All I know is we found ourselves in a little rocky cove that had sprung up round us out of the fog, and a swell lifted the boat on to a ledge, and she broke up beneath our feet. We had just time to shuffle through the weed before the next wave. The sea was rising.

' "It's rather a pity we didn't let Padda go down to the beach last night," said Meon. "He might have warned us this was coming."

' "Better fall into the hands of God than the hands of demons," said Eddi, and his teeth chattered as he prayed. A nor'-west breeze had just got up—distinctly cool.

' "Save what you can of the boat," said Meon; "we may need it," and we had to drench ourselves again, fishing out stray planks.'

'What for?' said Dan.

'For firewood. We did not know when we should get off. Eddi had flint and steel, and we found dry fuel in the old gulls' nests and lit a fire. It smoked abominably, and we guarded it with boat-planks up-ended between the rocks. One gets used to that sort of thing if one travels. Unluckily I'm not so strong as I was. I fear I must have been a trouble to my friends. It was blowing a full gale before midnight. Eddi wrung out his cloak, and tried to wrap me in it, but I ordered him on his obedience to keep it. However, he held me in his arms all the first night, and Meon begged his pardon for what he'd said the night before—about Eddi running away if he found me on a sandbank, you remember.

' "You are right in half your prophecy," said Eddi. "I have tucked up my gown, at any rate." (The wind had blown it over his head.) "Now let us thank God for His mercies."

' "Hum!" said Meon. "If this gale lasts, we stand a very fair chance of dying of starvation."

' "If it be God's will that we live, God will provide," said Eddi. "At least help me to sing to Him." The wind almost whipped the words out of his mouth, but he braced himself against a rock and sang psalms.

'I'm glad I never concealed my opinion—from myself—that Eddi was a better man than I. Yet I have worked hard in my time—very hard! Yes—yess! So the morning and the evening were our second day on that islet. There was rain-water in the rock-pools, and, as a Churchman, I knew how to fast, but I admit we were hungry. Meon fed our fire chip by chip to eke it out, and they made me sit over it, the dear fellows, when I was too weak to object. Meon held me in his arms the second night, just like a child. My good Eddi was a little out of his senses, and imagined himself teaching a York choir to sing. Even so, he was beautifully patient with them.

'I heard Meon whisper, "If this keeps up we shall go to our Gods. I wonder what Wotan will say to me. He must know I don't believe in him. On the other hand, I can't do what Ethelwalch finds so easy—curry favour with your God at the last minute, in the hope of being saved—as you call it. How do you advise, Bishop?"

' "My dear man," I said, "if that is your honest belief, I take it upon myself to say you had far better not curry favour with any God. But if it's only your Jutish pride that holds you back, lift me up, and I'll baptize you even now."

' "Lie still," said Meon. "I could judge better if I were in my own hall. But to desert one's fathers' Gods—even if one doesn't believe in them—in the middle of a gale, isn't quite— What would you do yourself?"

'I was lying in his arms, kept alive by the warmth of his big, steady heart. It did not seem to me the time or the place for subtle arguments, so I answered, "No, I certainly should not desert my God." I don't see even now what else I could have said.

' "Thank you. I'll remember that, if I live," said Meon, and I must have drifted back to my dreams about Northumbria and beautiful France, for it was broad daylight when I heard him calling on Wotan in that high, shaking heathen yell that I detest so.

' "Lie quiet. I'm giving Wotan his chance," he said. Our dear Eddi ambled up, still beating time to his imaginary choir.

' "Yes. Call on your Gods," he cried, "and see what gifts they will send you. They are gone on a journey, or they are hunting."

'I assure you the words were not out of his mouth when old Padda shot from the top of a cold wrinkled swell, drove himself over the weedy ledge, and landed fair in our laps with a rock-cod between his teeth. I could not help smiling at Eddi's face. "A miracle! A miracle!" he cried, and kneeled down to clean the cod.

'"You've been a long time winding us, my son," said Meon. "Now fish—fish for all our lives. We're starving, Padda."

'The old fellow flung himself quivering like a salmon backward into the boil of the currents round the rocks, and Meon said, "We're safe. I'll send him to fetch help when this wind drops. Eat and be thankful."

'I never tasted anything so good as those rock-codlings we took from Padda's mouth and half roasted over the fire. Between his plunges Padda would hunch up and purr over Meon with the tears running down his face. I never knew before that seals could weep for joy—as I have wept.

'"Surely," said Eddi, with his mouth full, "God has made the seal the loveliest of His creatures in the water. Look how Padda breasts the current! He stands up against it like a rock; now watch the chain of bubbles where he dives; and now— there is his wise head under that rock-ledge! Oh, a blessing be on thee, my little brother Padda!"

'"You *said* he was a child of the Devil!" Meon laughed.

'"There I sinned," poor Eddi answered. "Call him here, and I will ask his pardon. God sent him out of the storm to humble me, a fool."

'"I won't ask you to enter into fellowships and understandings with any accursed brute," said Meon, rather unkindly. "Shall we say he was sent to our Bishop as the ravens were sent to your prophet Elijah?"

'"Doubtless that is so," said Eddi. "I will write it so if I live to get home."

'"No—no!" I said. "Let us three poor men kneel and thank God for His mercies."

'We kneeled, and old Padda shuffled up and thrust his head

under Meon's elbows. I laid my hand upon it and blessed him. So did Eddi.

' "And now, my son," I said to Meon, "shall I baptize thee?"

' "Not yet," said he. "Wait till we are well ashore and at home. No God in any Heaven shall say that I came to him or left him because I was wet and cold. I will send Padda to my people for a boat. Is that witchcraft, Eddi?"

' "Why, no. Surely Padda will go and pull them to the beach by the skirts of their gowns as he pulled me in Wittering Church to ask me to sing. Only then I was afraid, and did not understand," said Eddi.

' "You are understanding now," said Meon, and at a wave of his arm off went Padda to the mainland, making a wake like a war-boat till we lost him in the rain. Meon's people could not bring a boat across for some hours; even so it was ticklish work among the rocks in that tideway. But they hoisted me aboard, too stiff to move, and Padda swam behind us, barking and turning somersaults all the way to Manhood End!'

'Good old Padda!' murmured Dan.

'When we were quite rested and re-clothed, and his people had been summoned—not an hour before—Meon offered himself to be baptized.'

'Was Padda baptized too?' Una asked.

'No, that was only Meon's joke. But he sat blinking on his ox-hide in the middle of the hall. When Eddi (who thought I wasn't looking) made a little cross in holy water on his wet muzzle, he kissed Eddi's hand. A week before Eddi wouldn't have touched him. *That* was a miracle, if you like! But seriously, I was more glad than I can tell you to get Meon. A rare and splendid soul that never looked back—never looked back!' The Archbishop half closed his eyes.

'But, sir,' said Puck, most respectfully, 'haven't you left out what Meon said afterwards?' Before the Bishop could speak he turned to the children and went on: 'Meon called all his fishers and ploughmen and herdsmen into the hall and he said: "Listen, men! Two days ago I asked our Bishop whether it was fair for a man to desert his fathers' Gods in a time of danger. Our Bishop said it was not fair. You needn't shout like that, because you are all Christians now. My red war-boat's crew will remember how near we all were to death when Padda fetched them over to the Bishop's islet. You can tell your mates that even in that place, at that time, hanging on the wet, weedy edge of death, our Bishop, a Christian, counselled me, a heathen, to stand by my fathers' Gods. I tell you now that a faith which takes care that every man shall keep faith, even though he may save his soul by breaking faith, is the faith for a man to believe in. So I believe in the Christian God, and in Wilfrid His Bishop, and in the Church that Wilfrid rules. You have been baptized once by the King's orders. I shall not have you baptized again; but if I find any more old women being sent to Wotan, or any girls dancing on the sly before Balder, or any men talking about Thun or Lok or the rest, I will teach you with my own hands how to keep faith with the Christian God. Go out quietly; you'll find a couple of beefs on the beach." Then of course they shouted "Hurrah!" which meant "Thor help us!" and—I think you laughed, sir?'

'I think you remember it all too well,' said the Archbishop, smiling. 'It was a joyful day for me. I had learned a great deal on that rock where Padda found us. Yes—yess! One should deal kindly with all the creatures of God, and gently with their masters. But one learns late.'

He rose, and his gold-embroidered sleeves rustled thickly.

The organ clacked and took deep breaths.

'Wait a minute,' Dan whispered. 'She's going to do the

trumpety one. It takes all the wind you can pump. It's in Latin, sir.'

'There is no other tongue,' the Archbishop answered.

'It's not a real hymn,' Una explained. 'She does it as a treat after her exercises. She isn't a real organist, you know. She just comes down here sometimes, from the Albert Hall.'

'Oh, what a miracle of a voice!' said the Archbishop.

It rang out suddenly from a dark arch of lonely noises— every word spoken to the very end:—

> 'Dies Irae, dies illa,
> Solvet soeclum in favilla,
> Teste David cum Sibylla.'

The Archbishop caught his breath and moved forward.
The music carried on by itself a while.

'Now it's calling all the light out of the windows,' Una whispered to Dan.

'I think it's more like a horse neighing in battle,' he whispered back. The voice cried:—

> 'Tuba mirum spargens sonum
> Per sepulchra regionum.'

Deeper and deeper the organ dived down, but far below its deepest note they heard Puck's voice joining in the last line:—

> 'Coget omnes ante thronum.'

As they looked in wonder, for it sounded like the dull jar of one of the very pillars shifting, the little fellow turned and went out through the south door.

'Now's the sorrowful part, but it's very beautiful.' Una found herself speaking to the empty chair in front of her.

'What are you doing that for?' Dan said behind her. 'You spoke so politely too.'

'I don't know . . . I thought . . .' said Una. 'Funny!'

' 'Tisn't. It's the part you like best,' Dan grunted.

The music had turned soft—full of little sounds that chased each other on wings across the broad gentle flood of the main tune. But the voice was ten times lovelier than the music.

> *'Recordare Jesu pie,*
> *Quod sum causa Tuae viae,*
> *Ne me perdas illâ die!'*

There was no more. They moved out into the centre aisle.

' 'That you?' the Lady called as she shut the lid. 'I thought I heard you, and I played it on purpose.'

'Thank you awfully,' said Dan. 'We hoped you would, so we waited. Come on, Una, it's pretty nearly dinner-time.'

SONG OF THE RED WAR-BOAT

Shove off from the wharf-edge! Steady!
    Watch for a smooth Give way!
If she feels the lop already
    She'll stand on her head in the bay.
It's ebb—it's dusk—it's blowing,
    The shoals are a mile of white,
But (snatch her along!) we're going
    To find our master to-night.

        For we hold that in all disaster·
            Of shipwreck, storm, or sword,
        A man must stand by his master
            When once he has pledged his word!

Raging seas have we rowed in,
    But we seldom saw them thus;
Our master is angry with Odin—
    Odin is angry with us!
Heavy odds have we taken,
    But never before such odds.
The Gods know they are forsaken,
    We must risk the wrath of the Gods!

Over the crest she flies from,
    Into its hollow she drops,
Crouches and clears her eyes from
    The wind-torn breaker-tops,
Ere out on the shrieking shoulder
    Of a hill-high surge she drives.

REWARDS AND FAIRIES

Meet her! Meet her and hold her!
Pull for your scoundrel lives!

The thunders bellow and clamour
The harm that they mean to do;
There goes Thor's Own Hammer
Cracking the dark in two!
Close! But the blow has missed her,
Here comes the wind of the blow!
Row or the squall 'll twist her
Broadside on to it!—Row!

Hearken, Thor of the Thunder!
We are not here for a jest—
For wager, warfare, or plunder,
Or to put your power to test.
This work is none of our wishing—
We would stay at home if we might—
But our master is wrecked out fishing,
We go to find him to-night.

For we hold that in all disaster—
As the Gods Themselves have said—
A man must stand by his master
Till one of the two is dead.

That is our way of thinking,
Now you can do as you will,
While we try to save her from sinking,
And hold her head to it still.
Bale her and keep her moving,
Or she'll break her back in the trough . . .

SONG OF THE RED WAR-BOAT

Who said the weather's improving,
  And the swells are taking off?
    .   .   .   .   .

Sodden, and chafed and aching,
  Gone in the loins and knees—
No matter—the day is breaking,
  And there's far less weight to the seas!
Up mast, and finish baling—
  In oars, and out with the mead—
The rest will be two-reef sailing . . .
  That was a night indeed!

But we hold that in all disaster
  (And faith, we have found it true!)
If only you stand by your master,
  The Gods will stand by you!

A DOCTOR OF MEDICINE

AN ASTROLOGER'S SONG

To the Heavens above us
  Oh, look and behold
The Planets that love us
  All harnessed in gold!
What chariots, what horses,
  Against us shall bide
While the Stars in their courses
  Do fight on our side?

All thought, all desires,
  That are under the sun,
Are one with their fires,
  As we also are one;
All matter, all spirit,
  All fashion, all frame,
Receive and inherit
  Their strength from the same.

(Oh, man that deniest
  All power save thine own,
Their power in the highest
  Is mightily shown.
Not less in the lowest
  That power is made clear.
Oh, man, if thou knowest,
  What treasure is here!)

Earth quakes in her throes
  And we wonder for why!

REWARDS AND FAIRIES

But the blind planet knows
  When her ruler is nigh;
And, attuned since Creation,
  To perfect accord,
She thrills in her station
  And yearns to her Lord.

The waters have risen,
  The springs are unbound—
The floods break their prison,
  And ravin around.
No rampart withstands 'em,
  Their fury will last,
Till the Sign that commands 'em
  Sinks low or swings past.

Through abysses unproven,
  And gulfs beyond thought,
Our portion is woven,
  Our burden is brought.
Yet They that prepare it,
  Whose Nature we share,
Make us who must bear it
  Well able to bear.

Though terrors o'ertake us
  We'll not be afraid,
No Power can unmake us
  Save that which has made.
Nor yet beyond reason
  Nor hope shall we fall—
All things have their season,
  And Mercy crowns all.

AN ASTROLOGER'S SONG

Then, doubt not, ye fearful—
The Eternal is King—
Up, heart, and be cheerful,
And lustily sing:—
What chariots, what horses,
    Against us shall bide
While the Stars in their courses
    Do fight on our side?

A DOCTOR OF MEDICINE

THEY WERE PLAYING HIDE-AND-SEEK with bicycle lamps after tea. Dan had hung his lamp on the apple tree at the end of the hellebore bed in the walled garden, and was crouched by the gooseberry bushes ready to dash off when Una should spy him. He saw her lamp come into the garden and disappear as she hid it under her cloak. While he listened for her footsteps, somebody (they both thought it was Phillips the gardener) coughed in the corner of the herb-beds.

'All right,' Una shouted across the asparagus; 'we aren't hurting your old beds, Phippsey!'

She flashed her lantern towards the spot, and in its circle of light they saw a Guy Fawkes-looking man in a black cloak and a steeple-crowned hat, walking down the path beside Puck. They ran to meet him, and the man said something to them about *rooms* in their head. After a time they understood he was warning them not to catch colds.

'You've a bit of a cold yourself, haven't you?' said Una, for he ended all his sentences with a consequential cough. Puck laughed.

'Child,' the man answered, 'if it hath pleased Heaven to afflict me with an infirmity——'

'Nay, nay,' Puck struck in, 'the maid spoke out of kindness. *I* know that half your cough is but a catch to trick the vulgar; and that's a pity. There's honesty enough in you, Nick, without rasping and hawking.'

'Good people'—the man shrugged his lean shoulders—'the vulgar crowd love not truth unadorned. Wherefore we philos-

471

ophers must needs dress her to catch their eye or—ahem!—
their ear.'

'And what d'you think of *that*?' said Puck solemnly to Dan.
'I don't know,' he answered. 'It sounds like lessons.'

'Ah—well! There have been worse men than Nick Culpeper
to take lessons from. Now, where can we sit that's not indoors?'

'In the hay-mow, next to old Middenboro,' Dan suggested.
'*He* doesn't mind.'

'Eh?' Mr. Culpeper was stooping over the pale hellebore
blooms by the light of Una's lamp. 'Does Master Middenboro
need my poor services, then?'

'Save him, no!' said Puck. 'He is but a horse—next door to
an ass, as you'll see presently. Come!'

Their shadows jumped and slid on the fruit-tree walls.
They filed out of the garden by the snoring pig-pound and
the crooning hen-house, to the shed where Middenboro the
old lawn-mower pony lives. His friendly eyes showed green in
the light as they set their lamps down on the chickens' drinking-trough outside, and pushed past to the hay-mow. Mr. Culpeper stooped at the door.

'Mind where you lie,' said Dan. 'This hay's full of hedge-
brishings.'

'In! in!' said Puck. 'You've lain in fouler places than this,
Nick. Ah! Let us keep touch with the stars!' He kicked open
the top of the half-door, and pointed to the clear sky. 'There
be the planets you conjure with! What does your wisdom
make of that wandering and variable star behind those apple
boughs?'

The children smiled. A bicycle that they knew well was
being walked down the steep lane.

'Where?' Mr. Culpeper leaned forward quickly. 'That?
Some countryman's lantern.'

'Wrong, Nick,' said Puck. ' 'Tis a singular bright star in Virgo, declining towards the house of Aquarius the water-carrier, who hath lately been afflicted by Gemini. Aren't I right, Una?'

Mr. Culpeper snorted contemptuously.

'No. It's the village nurse going down to the Mill about some fresh twins that came there last week. Nurse,' Una called, as the light stopped on the flat, 'when can I see the Morris twins? And how are they?'

'Next Sunday, perhaps. Doing beautifully,' the Nurse called back, and with a *ping-ping-ping* of the bell brushed round the corner.

'Her uncle's a vetinary surgeon near Banbury,' Una explained, 'and if you ring her bell at night, it rings right beside her bed—not downstairs at all. Then she jumps up—she always keeps a pair of dry boots in the fender, you know—and goes anywhere she's wanted. We help her bicycle through gaps sometimes. Most of her babies do beautifully. She told us so herself.'

'I doubt not, then, that she reads in my books,' said Mr. Culpeper quietly. 'Twins at the Mill!' he muttered half aloud. ' "And again He sayeth, Return, ye children of men." '

'Are you a doctor or a rector?' Una asked, and Puck with a shout turned head over heels in the hay. But Mr. Culpeper was quite serious. He told them that he was a physician-astrologer—a doctor who knew all about the stars as well as all about herbs for medicine. He said that the sun, the moon, and five Planets, called Jupiter, Mars, Mercury, Saturn, and Venus, governed everybody and everything in the world. They all lived in Houses—he mapped out some of them against the dark with a busy forefinger—and they moved from House to House like pieces at draughts; and they went loving and hating each other all over the skies. If you knew their likes and dislikes, he said, you could make them cure your patient and hurt your enemy, and find out the secret causes of things. He talked of these five Planets as though they belonged to him, or as though he were playing long games against them. The children burrowed in the hay up to their chins, and looked out over the half-door at the solemn, star-powdered sky till they seemed to be falling upside down into it, while Mr. Culpeper talked about 'trines' and 'oppositions' and 'conjunctions' and 'sympathies' and 'antipathies' in a tone that just matched things.

A rat ran between Middenboro's feet, and the old pony stamped.

'Mid hates rats,' said Dan, and passed him over a lock of hay. 'I wonder why.'

'Divine Astrology tells us,' said Mr. Culpeper. 'The horse, being a martial beast that beareth man to battle, belongs naturally to the red planet Mars—the Lord of War. I would show you him, but he's too near his setting. Rats and mice, doing their businesses by night, come under the dominion of our Lady the Moon. Now between Mars and Luna, the one red, t'other white, the one hot, t'other cold and so forth, stands, as I have told you, a natural antipathy, or, as you say, hatred. Which antipathy their creatures do inherit. Whence, good people, you may both see and hear your cattle stamp in their stalls for the self-same causes as decree the passages of the stars across the unalterable face of Heaven! Ahem!'

Puck lay along chewing a leaf. They felt him shake with laughter, and Mr. Culpeper sat up stiffly.

'I myself,' said he, 'have saved men's lives, and not a few neither, by observing at the proper time—there is a time, mark you, for all things under the sun—by observing, I say, so small a beast as a rat in conjunction with so great a matter as this dread arch above us.' He swept his hand across the sky. 'Yet there are those,' he went on sourly, 'who have years without knowledge.'

'Right,' said Puck. 'No fool like an old fool.'

Mr. Culpeper wrapped his cloak round him and sat still while the children stared at the Great Bear on the hill-top.

'Give him time,' Puck whispered behind his hand. 'He turns like a timber-tug—all of a piece.'

'Ahem!' Mr. Culpeper said suddenly. 'I'll prove it to you. When I was physician to Saye's Horse, and fought the King— or rather the man Charles Stuart—in Oxfordshire (I had *my* learning at Cambridge), the plague was very hot all around us. I saw it at close hands. He who says I am ignorant of the plague, for example, is altogether beside the bridge.'

'We grant it,' said Puck solemnly. 'But why talk of the plague this rare night?'

'To prove my argument. This Oxfordshire plague, good people, being generated among rivers and ditches, was of a werish, watery nature. Therefore it was curable by drenching the patient in cold water, and laying him in wet cloths; or at least, so I cured some of them. Mark this. It bears on what shall come after.'

'Mark also, Nick,' said Puck, 'that we are not your College of Physicians, but only a lad and a lass and a poor lubberkin. Therefore be plain, old Hyssop on the Wall!'

'To be plain and in order with you, I was shot in the chest while gathering of betony from a brookside near Thame, and was took by the King's men before their Colonel, one Blagg or Bragge, whom I warned honestly that I had spent the week past among our plague-stricken. He flung me off into a cow-shed, much like this here, to die, as I supposed; but one of their priests crept in by night and dressed my wound. He was a Sussex man like myself.'

'Who was that?' said Puck suddenly. 'Zack Tutshom?'

'No, Jack Marget,' said Mr. Culpeper.

'Jack Marget of New College? The little merry man that stammered so? Why a plague was stuttering Jack at Oxford then?' said Puck.

'He had come out of Sussex in hope of being made a Bishop when the King should have conquered the rebels, as he styled us Parliament men. His College had lent the King some monies too, which they never got again, no more than simple Jack got his bishopric. When we met he had had a bitter bellyful of King's promises, and wished to return to his wife and babes. This came about beyond expectation, for, so soon as I could stand of my wound, the man Blagge made excuse that I had been among the plague, and Jack had been tending me, to thrust us both out from their camp. The King had done with Jack now that Jack's College had lent the money, and Blagge's physician could not abide me because I would not sit silent and see him butcher the sick. (He was a College of Physicians man!) So Blagge, I say, thrust us both out, with many vile words, for a pair of pestilent, prating, pragmatical rascals.'

'Ha! Called *you* pragmatical, Nick?' Puck started up. 'High time Oliver came to purge the land! How did you and honest Jack fare next?'

'We were in some sort constrained to each other's company. I was for going to my house in Spitalfields, he would go to his parish in Sussex; but the plague was broke out and spreading through Wiltshire, Berkshire, and Hampshire, and he was so mad distracted to think that it might even then be among his folk at home that I bore him company. He had comforted me in my distress. I could not have done less; and I remembered that I had a cousin at Great Wigsell, near by Jack's parish. Thus we footed it from Oxford, cassock and buff coat together, resolute to leave wars on the left side henceforth; and either through our mean appearances, or the plague making men less cruel, we were not hindered. To be sure, they put us in the stocks one half-day for rogues and vagabonds at a village under St. Leonard's forest, where, as I have heard, nightingales never sing; but the constable very honestly gave me back my Astrological Almanac, which I carry with me.' Mr. Culpeper tapped his thin chest. 'I dressed a whitlow on his thumb. So we went forward.

'Not to trouble you with impertinences, we fetched over against Jack Marget's parish in a storm of rain about the day's end. Here our roads divided, for I would have gone on to my cousin at Great Wigsell, but while Jack was pointing me out his steeple, we saw a man lying drunk, as he conceived, athwart the road. He said it would be one Hebden, a parishioner, and till then a man of good life; and he accused himself bitterly for an unfaithful shepherd, that had left his flock to follow princes. But I saw it was the plague, and not the beginnings of it neither. They had set out the plague-stone, and the man's head lay on it.'

'What's a plague-stone?' Dan whispered.

'When the plague is so hot in a village that the neighbours shut the roads against 'em, people set a hollowed stone, pot, or pan, where such as would purchase victual from outside may lay money and the paper of their wants, and depart. Those that would sell come later—what will a man not do for gain?—snatch the money forth, and leave in exchange such goods as their conscience reckons fair value. I saw a silver groat in the water, and the man's list of what he would buy was rain-pulped in his wet hand.

' "My wife! Oh, my wife and babes!" says Jack of a sudden, and makes uphill—I with him.

'A woman peers out from behind a barn, crying out that

the village is stricken with the plague, and that for our lives' sake we must avoid it.

' "Sweetheart!" says Jack. "Must I avoid thee?" and she leaps at him and says the babes are safe. She was his wife.

'When he had thanked God, even to tears, he tells me this was not the welcome he had intended, and presses me to flee the place while I was clean.

' "Nay! The Lord do so to me and more also if I desert thee now," I said. "These affairs are, under God's leave, in some fashion my strength."

' "Oh, sir," she says, "are you a physician? We have none."

' "Then, good people," said I, "I must e'en justify myself to you by my works."

' "Look—look ye," stammers Jack, "I took you all this time for a crazy Roundhead preacher." He laughs, and she, and then I—all three together in the rain are overtook by an unreasonable gust or clap of laughter, which none the less eased us. We call it in medicine the Hysterical Passion. So I went home with 'em.'

'Why did you not go on to your cousin at Great Wigsell, Nick?' Puck suggested. ' 'Tis barely seven mile up the road.'

'But the plague was here,' Mr. Culpeper answered, and pointed up the hill. 'What else could I have done?'

'What were the parson's children called?' said Una.

'Elizabeth, Alison, Stephen, and Charles—a babe. I scarce saw them at first, for I separated to live with their father in a cart-lodge. The mother we put—forced—into the house with her babes. She had done enough.

'And now, good people, give me leave to be particular in this case. The plague was worst on the north side of the street, for lack, as I showed 'em, of sunshine; which, proceeding from the *primum mobile*, or source of life (I speak astrologically),

478

is cleansing and purifying in the highest degree. The plague was hot too by the corn-chandler's, where they sell forage to the carters; extreme hot in both Mills, along the river, and scatteringly in other places, *except,* mark you, at the smithy. Mark here, that all forges and smith-shops belong to Mars, even as corn and meat and wine shops acknowledge Venus for their mistress. There was no plague in the smithy at Munday's Lane——'

'Munday's Lane? You mean our village? I thought so when you talked about the two Mills,' cried Dan. 'Where did we put the plague-stone? I'd like to have seen it.'

'Then look at it now,' said Puck, and pointed to the chickens' drinking-trough where they had set their bicycle lamps. It was a rough-oblong stone pan, rather like a small kitchen sink, which Phillips, who never wastes anything, had found in a ditch and had used for his precious hens.

'That?' said Dan and Una, and stared, and stared, and stared.

Mr. Culpeper made impatient noises in his throat and went on.

'I am at these pains to be particular, good people, because I would have you follow, so far as you may, the operations of my mind. That plague which I told you I had handled outside Wallingford in Oxfordshire was of a watery nature, conformable to the brookish riverine country it bred in, and curable, as I have said, by drenching in water. This plague of ours here, for all that it flourished along watercourses— every soul at both Mills died of it,—could not be so handled. Which brought me to a stand. Ahem!'

'And your sick people in the meantime?' Puck demanded.

'We persuaded them on the north side of the street to lie out in Hitheram's field. Where the plague had taken one, or at most two, in a house, folk would not shift for fear of thieves in their absence. They cast away their lives to die among their goods.'

'Human nature,' said Puck. 'I've seen it time and again. How did your sick do in the fields?'

'They died not near so thick as those that kept within doors, and even then they died more out of distraction and melancholy than plague. But I confess, good people, I could not in any sort master the sickness, or come at a glimmer of its nature or governance. To be brief, I was flat bewildered at the brute malignity of the disease, and so—did what I should have done before—dismissed all conjectures and apprehensions that had grown up within me, chose a good hour by my Almanac, clapped my vinegar-cloth to my face, and entered some empty houses, resigned to wait upon the stars for guidance.'

'At night? Were you not horribly frightened?' said Puck.

'I dared to hope that the God who hath made man so nobly curious to search out His mysteries might not destroy a devout seeker. In due time—there is a time, as I have said, for everything under the sun—I spied a whitish rat, very puffed and scabby, which sat beneath the dormer of an attic through which shined our Lady the Moon. Whilst I looked on him— and her—she was moving towards old cold Saturn, her ancient ally—the rat creeped languishingly into her light, and there, before my eyes, died. Presently his mate or companion came out, laid him down beside there, and in like fashion died too. Later—an hour or less to midnight—a third rat did e'en the same; always choosing the moonlight to die in. This threw me into an amaze, since, as we know, the moonlight is favourable, not hurtful, to the creatures of the Moon; and Saturn, being friends with her, as you would say, was hourly strengthening her evil influence. Yet these three rats had been stricken dead in very moonlight. I leaned out of the window to see which of Heaven's host might be on our side, and there beheld I good trusty Mars, very red and heated, bustling about his setting. I straddled the roof to see better.

'Jack Marget came up street going to comfort our sick in Hitheram's field. A tile slipped under my foot.

'Says he, heavily enough, "Watchman, what of the night?"

' "Heart up, Jack," says I. "Methinks there's one fighting for us that, like a fool, I've forgot all this summer." My meaning was naturally the planet Mars.

' "Pray to Him then," says he. "I forgot Him too this summer."

'He meant God, whom he always bitterly accused himself of having forgotten up in Oxfordshire, among the King's men. I called down that he had made amends enough for his sin by his work among the sick, but he said he would not believe so till the plague was lifted from 'em. He was at his strength's end—more from melancholy than any just cause. I have seen this before among priests and over-cheerful men. I drenched him then and there with a half-cup of waters, which I do not say cure the plague, but are excellent against heaviness of the spirits.'

'What were they?' said Dan.

'White brandy rectified, camphor, cardamoms, ginger, two sorts of pepper, and aniseed.'

'Whew!' said Puck. 'Waters you call 'em!'

'Jack coughed on it valiantly, and went downhill with me. I was for the Lower Mill in the valley, to note the aspect of the Heavens. My mind had already shadowed forth the reason, if not the remedy, for our troubles, but I would not impart it to the vulgar till I was satisfied. That practice may be perfect, judgment ought to be sound, and to make judgment sound is required an exquisite knowledge. Ahem! I left Jack and his lantern among the sick in Hitheram's field. He still maintained the prayers of the so-called Church, which were rightly forbidden by Cromwell.'

'You should have told your cousin at Wigsell,' said Puck, 'and Jack would have been fined for it, and you'd have had half the money. How did you come so to fail in your duty, Nick?'

Mr. Culpeper laughed—his only laugh that evening—and the children jumped at the loud neigh of it.

'We were not fearful of *men's* judgment in those days, he answered. 'Now mark me closely, good people, for what follows will be to you, though not to me, remarkable. When I reached the empty Mill, old Saturn, low down in the House of the Fishes, threatened the Sun's rising-place. Our Lady the Moon was moving towards the help of him (understand, I speak astrologically). I looked abroad upon the high Heavens, and I prayed the Maker of 'em for guidance. Now Mars sparklingly withdrew himself below the sky. On the instant of his departure, which I noted, a bright star or vapour leaped forth above his head (as though he had heaved up his sword), and broke all about in fire. The cocks crowed midnight through the valley, and I sat me down by the mill-wheel, chewing spearmint (though that's an herb of Venus), and calling myself all the asses' heads in the world! 'Twas plain enough *now*!"

'What was plain?' said Una.

'The true cause and cure of the plague. Mars, good fellow, had fought for us to the uttermost. Faint though he had been in the Heavens, and this had made me overlook him in my computations, he more than any of the other planets had kept the Heavens—which is to say, had been visible some part of each night wellnigh throughout the year. Therefore his fierce and cleansing influence, warring against the Moon, had stretched out to kill those three rats under my nose, and under the nose of their natural mistress, the Moon. I had known Mars lean half across Heaven to deal our Lady the Moon some shrewd blow from under his shield, but I had never before seen his strength displayed so effectual.'

'I don't understand a bit. Do you mean Mars killed the rats because he hated the Moon?' said Una.

'*That* is as plain as the pikestaff with which Blagge's men pushed me forth,' Mr. Culpeper answered. 'I'll prove it. Why had the plague not broken out at the blacksmith's shop in Munday's Lane? Because, as I've shown you, forges and smithies belong naturally to Mars, and, for his honour's sake, Mars 'ud keep 'em clean from the creatures of the Moon. But was it like, think you, that he'd come down and rat-catch in general for lazy, ungrateful mankind? That were working a willing horse to death. So, then, you can see that the meaning of the blazing star above him when he set was simply this: "Destroy and burn the creatures of the Moon, for they are at the root of your trouble. And thus, having shown you a taste of my power, good people, adieu." '

'Did Mars really say all that?' Una whispered.

'Yes, and twice so much as that to any one who had ears to hear. Briefly, he enlightened me that the plague was spread by the creatures of the Moon. The Moon, our Lady of Ill-aspect, was the offender. My own poor wits showed me that I, Nick Culpeper, had the people in my charge, God's good providence aiding me, and no time to lose neither.

'I posted up the hill, and broke into Hitheram's field amongst 'em all at prayers.

' "Eureka, good people!" I cried, and cast down a dead mill-rat which I'd found. "Here's your true enemy, revealed at last by the stars."

' "Nay, but I'm praying," says Jack. His face was as white as washed silver.

' "There's a time for everything under the sun," says I. "If you would stay the plague, take and kill your rats."

' "Oh, mad, stark mad!" says he, and wrings his hands.

'A fellow lay in the ditch beside him, who bellows that he'd as soon die mad hunting rats as be preached to death on a cold fallow. They laughed round him at this, but Jack Marget falls on his knees, and very presumptuously petitions that he may be appointed to die to save the rest of his people. This was enough to thrust 'em back into their melancholy.

' "You are an unfaithful shepherd, Jack," I says. "Take a bat" (which we call a stick in Sussex) "and kill a rat if you die before sunrise. 'Twill save your people."

' "Aye, aye. Take a bat and kill a rat," he says ten times over, like a child, which moved 'em to ungovernable motions of that hysterical passion before mentioned, so that they laughed all, and at least warmed their chill bloods at that very hour—one o'clock or a little after—when the fires of life burn lowest. Truly there is a time for everything; and the physician must work with it—ahem!—or miss his cure. To be brief with you, I persuaded 'em, sick or sound, to have at the whole generation of rats throughout the village. And there's a reason for all things too, though the wise physician need not blab 'em all. *Imprimis,* or firstly, the mere sport of it, which lasted ten days, drew 'em most markedly out of their melancholy. I'd defy sorrowful Job himself to lament or scratch while he's routing rats from a rick. *Secundo,* or secondly, the vehement act and operation of this chase or war opened their skins to generous transpiration—more vulgarly, sweated 'em handsomely; and this further drew off their black bile—the mother of sickness. Thirdly, when we came to burn the bodies of the rats, I sprinkled sulphur on the faggots, whereby the onlookers were as handsomely suffumigated. This I could not have compassed if I had made it a mere physician's business; they'd have thought it some conjuration. Yet more, we cleansed, limed, and burned out a hundred foul poke-holes, sinks, slews, and corners of unvisited filth in and about the houses in the village, and by good fortune (mark here that Mars was in opposition to Venus) burned the corn-chandler's shop to the ground. Mars loves not Venus. Will Noakes the saddler dropped his lantern on a truss of straw while he was rat-hunting there.'

'Had ye given Will any of that gentle cordial of yours, Nick, by any chance?' said Puck.

'A glass—or two glasses—not more. But as I would say, in fine, when we had killed the rats, I took ash, slag and charcoal from the smithy, and burnt earth from the brickyard (I reason that a brickyard belongs to Mars), and rammed it with iron crowbars into the rat-runs and buries, and beneath all the house floors. The Creatures of the Moon hate all that Mars hath used for his own clean ends. For example—rats bite not iron.'

'And how did poor stuttering Jack endure it?' said Puck.

'He sweated out his melancholy through his skin, and catched a loose cough, which I cured with electuaries, according to art. It is noteworthy, were I speaking among my equals, that the venom of the plague translated, or turned itself into, and evaporated, or went away as, a very heavy hoarseness and thickness of the head, throat, and chest. (Observe from my books which planets govern these portions of man's body, and

your darkness, good people, shall be illuminated—ahem!)
None the less, the plague, *qua* plague, ceased and took off (for
we only lost three more, and two of 'em had it already on 'em)
from the morning of the day that Mars enlightened me by the
Lower Mill.' He coughed—almost trumpeted—triumphantly.

'It is proved,' he jerked out. 'I say I have proved my conten-
tion, which is, that by Divine Astrology and humble search
into the veritable causes of things—at the proper time—the
sons of wisdom may combat even the plague.'

'H'm!' Puck replied. 'For my own part I hold that a simple
soul——'

'Mine?—simple, forsooth?' said Mr. Culpeper.

'A very simple soul, a high courage tempered with sound
and stubborn conceit, is stronger than all the stars in their
courses. So I confess truly that you saved the village, Nick.'

'I stubborn? I stiff-necked? I ascribed all my poor success,
under God's good providence, to Divine Astrology. Not to me
the glory! You talk as that dear weeping ass Jack Marget
preached before I went back to my work in Red Lion House,
Spitalfields.'

'Oh! Stammering Jack preached, did he? They say he loses
his stammer in the pulpit.'

'And his wits with it. He delivered a most idolatrous dis-
course when the plague was stayed. He took for his text: "The
wise man that delivered the city." I could have given him a
better, such as: "There is a time for——" '

'But what made you go to church to hear him?' Puck interrupted. 'Wail Attersole was your lawfully appointed preacher,
and a dull dog he was!'

Mr. Culpeper wriggled uneasily.

'The vulgar,' said he, 'the old crones and—ahem!—the children, Alison and the others, they dragged me to the House of

Rimmon by the hand. I was in two minds to inform on Jack for maintaining the mummeries of the falsely-called Church, which, I'll prove to you, are founded merely on ancient fables——'

'Stick to your herbs and planets,' said Puck, laughing. 'You should have told the magistrates, Nick, and had Jack fined. Again, why did you neglect your plain duty?'

'Because—because I was kneeling, and praying, and weeping with the rest of 'em at the Altar-rails. In medicine this is called the Hysterical Passion. It may be—it may be.'

'That's as may be,' said Puck. They heard him turn the hay. 'Why, your hay is half hedge-brishings,' he said. 'You don't expect a horse to thrive on oak and ash and thorn leaves, do you?'

Ping-ping-ping went the bicycle bell round the corner. Nurse was coming back from the Mill.

'Is it all right?' Una called.

'All quite right,' Nurse called back. 'They're to be christened next Sunday.'

'What? What?' They both leaned forward across the half-door. It could not have been properly fastened, for it opened, and tilted them out with hay and leaves sticking all over them.

'Come on! We must get those two twins' names,' said Una, and they charged uphill shouting over the hedge, till Nurse slowed up and told them.

When they returned, old Middenboro had got out of his stall, and they spent a lively ten minutes chasing him in again by starlight.

'OUR FATHERS OF OLD'

Excellent herbs had our fathers of old—
　Excellent herbs to ease their pain—
Alexanders and Marigold,
　Eyebright, Orris, and Elecampane,
Basil, Rocket, Valerian, Rue,
　(Almost singing themselves they run)
Vervain, Dittany, Call-me-to-you—
　Cowslip, Melilot, Rose of the Sun.
　　Anything green that grew out of the mould
　　Was an excellent herb to our fathers of old.

Wonderful tales had our fathers of old—
　Wonderful tales of the herbs and the stars—
The Sun was Lord of the Marigold,
　Basil and Rocket belonged to Mars.
Pat as a sum in division it goes—
　(Every plant had a star bespoke)—
Who but Venus should govern the Rose?
　Who but Jupiter own the Oak?
　　Simply and gravely the facts are told
　　In the wonderful books of our fathers of old.

Wonderful little, when all is said,
　Wonderful little our fathers knew.
Half their remedies cured you dead—
　Most of their teaching was quite untrue—
'Look at the stars when a patient is ill,
　(Dirt has nothing to do with disease),

Bleed and blister as much as you will,
  Blister and bleed him as oft as you please.'
    Whence enormous and manifold
      Errors were made by our fathers of old.

Yet when the sickness was sore in the land,
  And neither planet nor herb assuaged,
They took their lives in their lancet-hand
  And, oh, what a wonderful war they waged!
Yes, when the crosses were chalked on the door—
  Yes, when the terrible dead-cart rolled,
Excellent courage our fathers bore—
  Excellent heart had our fathers of old.
    None too learned, but nobly bold,
      Into the fight went our fathers of old.

If it be certain, as Galen says,
  And sage Hippocrates holds as much—
'That those afflicted by doubts and dismays
  Are mightily helped by a dead man's touch,'
Then, be good to us, stars above!
  Then, be good to us, herbs below!
We are afflicted by what we can prove;
  We are distracted by what we know—
      So—ah, so!
    Down from your Heaven or up from your mould.
    Send us the hearts of our fathers of old!

SIMPLE SIMON

THE THOUSANDTH MAN

One man in a thousand, Solomon says,
  Will stick more close than a brother.
And it's worth while seeking him half your days
  If you find him before the other.
Nine hundred and ninety-nine depend
  On what the world sees in you,
But the Thousandth Man will stand your friend
  With the whole round world agin you.

'Tis neither promise nor prayer nor show
  Will settle the finding for 'ee.
Nine hundred and ninety-nine of 'em go
  By your looks or your acts or your glory.
But if he finds you and you find him,
  The rest of the world don't matter;
For the Thousandth Man will sink or swim
  With you in any water.

You can use his purse with no more shame
  Than he uses yours for his spendings;
And laugh and mention it just the same
  As though there had been no lendings.
Nine hundred and ninety-nine of 'em call
  For silver and gold in their dealings;
But the Thousandth Man he's worth 'em all,
  Because you can show him your feelings!

His wrong's your wrong, and his right's your right,
  In season or out of season.

REWARDS AND FAIRIES

Stand up and back it in all men's sight—
With that for your only reason!
Nine hundred and ninety-nine can't bide
The shame or mocking or laughter,
But the Thousandth Man will stand by your side
To the gallows-foot—and after!

SIMPLE SIMON

CATTIWOW CAME DOWN THE STEEP LANE with his five-horse timber-tug. He stopped by the woodlump at the back gate to take off the brakes. His real name was Brabon, but the first time the children met him, years and years ago, he told them he was 'carting wood,' and it sounded so exactly like 'catti-wow' that they never called him anything else.

'Hi!' Una shouted from the top of the woodlump, where they had been watching the lane. 'What are you doing? Why weren't we told?'

'They've just sent for me,' Cattiwow answered. 'There's a middlin' big log sticked in the dirt at Rabbit Shaw, and'—he flicked his whip back along the line—'so they've sent for us all.'

Dan and Una threw themselves off the woodlump almost under black Sailor's nose. Cattiwow never let them ride the big beam that makes the body of the timber-tug, but they hung on behind while their teeth thuttered.

The Wood road beyond the brook climbs at once into the woods, and you see all the horses' backs rising, one above another, like moving stairs. Cattiwow strode ahead in his sackcloth woodman's petticoat, belted at the waist with a leather strap; and when he turned and grinned, his red lips showed under his sackcloth-coloured beard. His cap was sack-cloth too, with a flap behind, to keep twigs and bark out of his neck. He navigated the tug among pools of heather-water that splashed in their faces, and through clumps of young birches that slashed at their legs, and when they hit an old toadstooled stump, they never knew whether it would give way in showers of rotten wood, or jar them back again.

At the top of Rabbit Shaw half-a-dozen men and a team of horses stood round a forty-foot oak log in a muddy hollow. The ground about was poached and stoached with sliding hoof-marks, and a wave of dirt was driven up in front of the butt.

'What did you want to bury her for this way?' said Cattiwow. He took his broad-axe and went up the log tapping it.

'She's sticked fast,' said 'Bunny' Lewknor, who managed the other team.

Cattiwow unfastened the five wise horses from the tug. They cocked their ears forward, looked, and shook themselves.

'I believe Sailor knows,' Dan whispered to Una.

'He do,' said a man behind them. He was dressed in flour sacks like the others, and he leaned on his broad-axe, but the children, who knew all the wood-gangs, knew he was a stranger. In his size and oily hairiness he might have been Bunny Lewknor's brother, except that his brown eyes were as soft as a spaniel's, and his rounded black beard, beginning close up under them, reminded Una of the walrus in 'The Walrus and the Carpenter.'

'Don't he justabout know?' he said shyly, and shifted from one foot to the other.

'Yes. "What Cattiwow can't get out of the woods must have roots growing to her"'—Dan had heard old Hobden say this a few days before.

At that minute Puck pranced up, picking his way through the pools of black water in the ling.

'Look *out!*' cried Una, jumping forward. 'He'll see you, Puck!'

'Me and Mus' Robin are pretty middlin' well acquainted,'

the man answered with a smile that made them forget all
about walruses.

'This is Simon Cheyneys,' Puck began, and cleared his
throat. 'Shipbuilder of Rye Port; burgess of the said town,
and the only——'

'Oh, look! Look ye! That's a knowing one,' said the man.
Cattiwow had fastened his team to the thin end of the log,
and was moving them about with his whip till they stood at
right angles to it, heading downhill. Then he grunted. The
horses took the strain, beginning with Sailor next the log,
like a tug-of-war team, and dropped almost to their knees.
The log shifted a nail's breadth in the clinging dirt, with
the noise of a giant's kiss.

'You're getting her!' Simon Cheyneys slapped his knee.
'Hing on! Hing on, lads, or she'll master ye! Ah!'

Sailor's left hind hoof had slipped on a heather-tuft. One
of the men whipped off his sack apron and spread it down.
They saw Sailor feel for it, and recover. Still the log hung,
and the team grunted in despair.

'Hai!' shouted Cattiwow, and brought his dreadful whip
twice across Sailor's loins with the crack of a shot-gun. The
horse almost screamed as he pulled that extra last ounce
which he did not know was in him. The thin end of the log
left the dirt and rasped on dry gravel. The butt ground round
like a buffalo in his wallow. Quick as an axe-cut, Lewknor
snapped on his five horses, and sliding, trampling, jingling,
and snorting, they had the whole thing out on the heather.

'Dat's the very first time I've knowed you lay into Sailor—
to hurt him,' said Lewknor.

'It is,' said Cattiwow, and passed his hand over the two
wheals. 'But I'd ha' laid my own brother open at that pinch.
Now we'll twitch her down the hill a piece—she lies just
about right—and get her home by the low road. My team'll
do it, Bunny; you bring the tug along. Mind out!'

He spoke to the horses, who tightened the chains. The great log half rolled over, and slowly drew itself out of sight downhill, followed by the wood-gang and the timber-tug. In half a minute there was nothing to see but the deserted hollow of the torn-up dirt, the birch undergrowth still shaking, and the water draining back into the hoof-prints.

'Ye heard him?' Simon Cheyneys asked. 'He cherished his horse, but he'd ha' laid him open in that pinch.'

'Not for his own advantage,' said Puck quickly. ' 'Twas only to shift the log.'

'I reckon every man born of woman has his log to shift in the world—if so be you're hintin' at any o' Frankie's doings. *He* never hit beyond reason or without reason,' said Simon.

'*I* never said a word against Frankie,' Puck retorted, with a wink at the children. 'An' if I did, do it lie in your mouth to contest my say-so, seeing how you——'

'Why don't it lie in my mouth, seeing I was the first which knowed Frankie for all he was?' The burly sack-clad man puffed down at cool little Puck.

'Yes, and the first which set out to poison him—Frankie— on the high seas——'

Simon's angry face changed to a sheepish grin. He waggled his immense hands, but Puck stood off and laughed mercilessly.

'But let me tell you, Mus' Robin,' he pleaded.

'I've heard the tale. Tell the children here. Look, Dan! Look, Una!'—Puck's straight brown finger levelled like an arrow. 'There's the only man that ever tried to poison Sir Francis Drake!'

'Oh, Mus' Robin! 'Tidn't fair. You've the 'vantage of us all in your upbringin's by hundreds o' years. Stands to nature you know all the tales against every one.'

He turned his soft eyes so helplessly on Una that she cried, 'Stop ragging him, Puck! You know he didn't really.'

'I do. But why are you so sure, little maid?'

'Because—because he doesn't look like it,' said Una stoutly.

'I thank you,' said Simon to Una. 'I—I was always trustable-like with children if you let me alone, you double handful o' mischief!' He pretended to heave up his axe on Puck; and then his shyness overtook him afresh.

'Where did you know Sir Francis Drake?' said Dan, not liking being called a child.

'At Rye Port, to be sure,' said Simon, and seeing Dan's bewilderment, repeated it.

'Yes, but look here,' said Dan. ' "Drake he was a Devon man." The song says so.'

' "*And* ruled the Devon seas," ' Una went on. 'That's what I was thinking—if you don't mind.'

Simon Cheyneys seemed to mind very much indeed, for he swelled in silence while Puck laughed.

'Hutt!' he burst out at last, 'I've heard that talk too. If you listen to them West Country folk, you'll listen to a pack o' lies. I believe Frankie was born somewhere out west among the Shires, but his father had to run for it when Frankie was a baby, because the neighbours was wishful to kill him, d'ye see? He run to Chatham, old Parson Drake did, an' Frankie was brought up in a old hulks of a ship moored in the Medway river, same as it might ha' been the Rother. Brought up *at* sea, you might say, before he could walk *on* land—nigh Chatham in Kent. And ain't Kent back-door to Sussex? And don't that make Frankie Sussex? O' course it do. Devon man! Bah! Those West Country boats they're always fishin' in other folks' water.'

'I beg your pardon,' said Dan. 'I'm sorry.'

'No call to be sorry. You've been misled. I met Frankie at Rye Port when my Uncle, that was the shipbuilder there, pushed me off his wharf-edge on to Frankie's ship. Frankie had put in from Chatham with his rudder splutted, and a man's arm—Moon's that 'ud be—broken at the tiller. "Take this boy aboard an' drown him," says my Uncle, "and I'll mend your rudder-piece for love." '

'What did your Uncle want you drowned for?' said Una.

'That was only his fashion of say-so, same as Mus' Robin. I'd a foolishness in my head that ships could be builded out of iron. Yes—iron ships! I'd made me a liddle toy one of iron plates beat out thin—and she floated a wonder! But my Uncle, bein' a burgess of Rye, and a shipbuilder, he 'prenticed me to Frankie in the fetchin' trade, to cure this foolishness.'

'What was the fetchin' trade?' Dan interrupted.

'Fetchin' poor Flemishers and Dutchmen out o' the Low Countries into England. The King o' Spain, d'ye see, he was burnin' 'em in those parts, for to make 'em Papishers, so Frankie he fetched 'em away to *our* parts, and a risky trade it was. His master wouldn't never touch it while he lived, but he left his ship to Frankie when he died, and Frankie turned her into this fetchin' trade. Outrageous cruel hard work—on besom-black nights bulting back and forth off they Dutch roads with shoals on all sides, and having to hark out for the *frish-frish-frish*-like of a Spanish galliwopses' oars creepin' up on ye. Frankie 'ud have the tiller and Moon he'd peer forth at the bows, our lantern under his skirts, till the boat we was lookin' for 'ud blurt up out o' the dark, and we'd lay hold and haul aboard whoever 'twas—man, woman, or babe—an' round we'd go again, the wind bewling like a kite in our riggin's, and they'd drop into the hold and praise God for happy deliverance till they was all sick.

'I had nigh a year at it, an' we must have fetched off—oh, a hundred pore folk, I reckon. Outrageous bold, too, Frankie growed to be. Outrageous cunnin' he was. Once we was as near as nothin' nipped by a tall ship off Tergoes Sands in a snowstorm. She had the wind of us, and spooned straight before it, shootin' all bow guns. Frankie fled inshore smack for the beach, till he was atop of the first breakers. Then he hove his anchor out, which nigh tore our bows off, but it twitched us round end-for-end into the wind, d'ye see, an' we clawed off them sands like a drunk man rubbin' along a tavern bench. When we could see, the Spanisher was laid flat along in the breakers with the snows whitening on his wet belly. He thought he could go where Frankie went.'

'What happened to the crew?' said Una.

'We didn't stop,' Simon answered. 'There was a very liddle new baby in our hold, and the mother she wanted to get to some dry bed middlin' quick. We runned into Dover, and said nothing.'

'Was Sir Francis Drake very much pleased?'

'Heart alive, maid, he'd no head to his name in those days. He was just a outrageous, valiant, crop-haired, tutt-mouthed boy, roarin' up an' down the narrer seas, with his beard not yet quilled out. He made a laughing-stock of everything all day, and he'd hold our lives in the bight of his arm all the besom-black night among they Dutch sands; and we'd ha' jumped overside to behove him any one time, all of us.'

'Then why did you try to poison him?' Una asked wickedly, and Simon hung his head like a shy child.

'Oh, that was when he set me to make a pudden, for because our cook was hurted. *I* done my uttermost, but she all fetched adrift like in the bag, an' the more I biled the bits of her, the less she favoured any fashion o' pudden. Moon he chawed and chammed his piece, and Frankie chawed and chammed his'n, and—no words to it—he took me by the ear an' walked me out over the bow-end, an' him an' Moon hove the pudden at me on the bowsprit gub by gub, something cruel hard!' Simon rubbed his hairy cheek.

' "Nex' time you bring me anything," says Frankie, "you bring me cannon-shot an' I'll know what I'm getting." But as for poisonin'——' He stopped, the children laughed so.

'Of course you didn't,' said Una. 'Oh, Simon, we *do* like you!'

'I was always likeable with children.' His smile crinkled up through the hair round his eyes. 'Simple Simon they used to call me through our yard gates.'

'Did Sir Francis mock you?' Dan asked.

'Ah, no. He was gentle-born. Laugh he did—he was always laughing—but not so as to hurt a feather. An' I loved 'en. I loved 'en before England knew 'en, or Queen Bess she broke his heart.'

'But he hadn't really done anything when you knew him, had he?' Una insisted. 'Armadas and those things, I mean.'

Simon pointed to the scars and scrapes left by Cattiwow's great log. 'You tell me that that good ship's timber never done nothing against winds and weathers since her upspring-ing, and I'll confess ye that young Frankie never done nothing neither. Nothing? He adventured and suffered and made shift on they Dutch sands *as* much in any one month as ever he had occasion for to do in a half-year on the high seas after-wards. An' what was his tools? A coaster boat—a liddle box o' walty plankin' an' some few fathom feeble rope held to-gether an' made able by *him* sole. He drawed our spirits up in our bodies same as a chimney-towel draws a fire. 'Twas *in* him, and it comed out all times and shapes.'

'I wonder did he ever 'magine what he was going to be? Tell himself stories about it?' said Dan with a flush.

'I expect so. We mostly do—even when we're grown. But bein' Frankie, he took good care to find out beforehand what his fortune might be. Had I rightly ought to tell 'em this piece?' Simon turned to Puck, who nodded.

'My Mother, she was just a fair woman, but my Aunt, her sister, she had gifts by inheritance laid up in her,' Simon began.

'Oh, that'll never do,' cried Puck, for the children stared blankly. 'Do you remember what Robin promised to the Widow Whitgift so long as her blood and get lasted?'[1]

'Yes. There was always to be one of them that could see farther through a millstone than most,' Dan answered promptly.

'Well, Simon's Aunt's mother,' said Puck slowly, 'married the Widow's blind son on the Marsh, and Simon's Aunt was the one chosen to see farthest through millstones. Do you understand?'

'That was what I was gettin' at,' said Simon, 'but you're so desperate quick. My Aunt she knew what was comin' to people. My Uncle being a burgess of Rye, he counted all such things odious, and my Aunt she couldn't be got to practise her gifts hardly at all, because it hurted her head for a week afterwards; but when Frankie heard she had 'em, he was all for nothin' till she foretold on him—till she looked in his hand to tell his fortune, d'ye see? One time we was at Rye he come aboard with my other shirt and some apples, and he fair beazled the life out of her about it.

' "Oh, you'll be twice wed, and die childless," she says, and pushes his hand away.

[1] See 'Dymchurch Flit' in *Puck of Pook's Hill*.

503

' "That's the woman's part," he says. "What'll come to me
—to me?" an' he thrusts it back under her nose.

' "Gold—gold, past belief or counting," she says. "Let go o'
me, lad."

' "Sink the gold!" he says. "What'll I *do*, mother?" He
coaxed her like no woman could well withstand. I've seen
him with 'em—even when they were seasick.

' "If you *will* have it," she says at last, "you shall have it.
You'll do a many things, and eating and drinking with a
dead man beyond the world's end will be the least of them.
For you'll open a road from the East unto the West, and back
again, and you'll bury your heart with your best friend by
that roadside, and the road you open none shall shut so long
as you're let lie quiet in your grave."[1]

' "And if I'm not?" he says.

' "Why, then," she says, "Sim's iron ships will be sailing on
dry land. Now ha' done with this foolishness. Where's Sim's
shirt?"

'He couldn't fetch no more out of her, and when we come
up from the cabin, he stood mazed-like by the tiller, playing
with a apple.

' "My Sorrow!" says my Aunt; "d'ye see that? The great
world lying in his hand, liddle and round like a apple."

' "Why, 'tis one you gived him," I says.

' "To be sure," she says. " 'Tis just a apple," and she went
ashore with her hand to her head. It always hurted her to
show her gifts.

'Him and me puzzled over that talk plenty. It sticked in his
mind quite extravagant. The very next time we slipped out

[1] The old lady's prophecy is in a fair way to come true, for now the
Panama Canal is finished, one end of it opens into the very bay where Sir
Francis Drake was buried. So ships are taken through the Canal, and the
road round Cape Horn which Sir Francis opened is very little used.

for some fetchin' trade, we met Mus' Stenning's boat over by Calais sands; and he warned us that the Spanishers had shut down all their Dutch ports against us English, and their galliwopses was out picking up our boats like flies off hogs' backs. Mus' Stenning he runs for Shoreham, but Frankie held on a piece, knowin' that Mus' Stenning was jealous of our good trade. Over by Dunkirk a great gor-bellied Spanisher, with the Cross on his sails, came rampin' at us. We left him. We left him all they bare seas to conquest in.

' "Looks like this road was going to be shut pretty soon," says Frankie, humourin' her at the tiller. 'I'll have to open that other one your Aunt foretold of."

' "The Spanisher's crowdin' down on us middlin' quick," I says.

' "No odds," says Frankie, "he'll have the inshore tide against him. Did your Aunt say I was to lie quiet in my grave for ever?"

' "Till my iron ships sailed dry land," I says.

' "That's foolishness," he says. "Who cares where Frankie Drake makes a hole in the water now or twenty years from now?"

'The Spanisher kept muckin' on more and more canvas. I told him so.

' "He's feelin' the tide," was all he says. "If he was among Tergoes Sands with this wind, we'd be picking his bones proper. I'd give my heart to have all their tall ships there some night before a north gale, and me to windward. There'd be gold in my hands then. Did your Aunt say she saw the world settin' in my hand, Sim?"

' "Yes, but 'twas a apple," says I, and he laughed like he always did at me. "Do you ever feel minded to jump overside and be done with everything?" he asks after a while.

' "No. What water comes aboard is too wet as 'tis," I says. "The Spanisher's going about."

' "I told you," says he, never looking back. "He'll give us the Pope's Blessing as he swings. Come down off that rail. There's no knowin' where stray shots may hit." So I came down off the rail, and leaned against it, and the Spanisher he ruffled round in the wind, and his port-lids opened all red inside.

' "Now what'll happen to my road if they don't let me lie quiet in my grave?" he says. "Does your Aunt mean there's two roads to be found and kept open—or what does she mean? I don't like that talk about t'other road. D'you believe in your iron ships, Sim?"

'He knowed I did, so I only nodded, and he nodded back again.

' "Anybody but me 'ud call you a fool, Sim," he says. "Lie down. Here comes the Pope's Blessing!"

'The Spanisher gave us his broadside as he went about. They all fell short except one that smack-smooth hit the rail behind my back, an' I felt most won'erful cold.

' "Be you hit anywhere to signify?" he says. "Come over to me."

' "O Lord, Mus' Drake," I says, "my legs won't move," and that was the last I spoke for months.'

'Why? What had happened?' cried Dan and Una together.

'The rail had jarred me in here like.' Simon reached behind him clumsily. 'From my shoulders down I didn't act no shape. Frankie carried me piggy-back to my Aunt's house, and I lay bed-rid and tongue-tied while she rubbed me day and night, month in and month out. She had faith in rubbing with the hands. P'rhaps she put some of her gifts into it, too. Last of all, something loosed itself in my pore back, and lo! I was whole restored again, but kitten-feeble.

' "Where's Frankie?" I says, thinking I'd been a longish while abed.

' "Down-wind amongst the Dons—months ago," says my Aunt.

' "When can I go after 'en?" I says.

' "Your duty's to your town and trade now," says she. "Your Uncle he died last Michaelmas and he've left you and me the yard. So no more iron ships, mind ye."

' "What?" I says. "And you the only one that beleft in 'em!"

' "Maybe I do still," she says, "but I'm a woman before I'm a Whitgift, and wooden ships is what England needs us to build. I lay it on ye to do so."

'That's why I've never teched iron since that day—not to build a toy ship of. I've never even drawed a draft of one for my pleasure of evenings.' Simon smiled down on them all.

'Whitgift blood is terrible resolute—on the she-side,' said Puck.

'Didn't you ever see Sir Francis Drake again?' Dan asked.

'With one thing and another, and my being made a burgess of Rye, I never clapped eyes on him for the next twenty years. Oh, I had the news of his mighty doings the world over. They was the very same bold, cunning shifts and passes he'd worked with beforetimes off they Dutch sands, but, naturally, folk took more note of them. When Queen Bess made him knight, he sent my Aunt a dried orange stuffed with spiceries to smell to. She cried outrageous on it. She blamed herself for her foretellings, having set him on his won'erful road; but I reckon he'd ha' gone that way all withstanding. Curious how close she foretelled it! The world in his hand like an apple, an' he burying his best friend, Mus' Doughty——'

'Never mind for Mus' Doughty,' Puck interrupted. 'Tell us where you met Sir Francis next.'

'Oh, ha! That was the year I was made a burgess of Rye—

the same year which King Philip sent his ships to take England without Frankie's leave.'

'The Armada!' said Dan contentedly. 'I was hoping that would come.'

'*I* knowed Frankie would never let 'em smell London smoke, but plenty good men in Rye was two-three minded about the upshot. 'Twas the noise of the gun-fire tarrified us. The wind favoured it our way from off behind the Isle of Wight. It made a mutter like, which growed and growed, and by the end of a week women was shruckin' in the streets. They *they* come slidderin' past Fairlight in a great smoky pat vambrished with red gun-fire, and our ships flyin' forth and duckin' in again. The smoke-pat sliddered over to the French shore, so I knowed Frankie was edgin' the Spanishers toward they Dutch sands where he was master. I says to my Aunt, "The smoke's thinnin' out. I lay Frankie's just about scrapin' his hold for a few last rounds shot. 'Tis time for me to go."

' "Never in them clothes," she says. "Do on the doublet I bought you to be made burgess in, and don't you shame this day."

'So I mucked it on, and my chain, and my stiffed Dutch breeches and all.

' "I be comin', too," she says from her chamber, and forth she come pavisandin' like a peacock—stuff, ruff, stomacher and all. She was a notable woman.'

'But how did you go? You haven't told us,' said Una.

'In my own ship—but half-share was my Aunt's. In the *Antony of Rye*, to be sure; and not empty-handed. I'd been loadin' her for three days with the pick of our yard. We was ballasted on cannon-shot of all three sizes; and iron rods and straps for his carpenters; and a nice passel of clean three-inch oak planking and hide breech-ropes for his cannon, and gubs of good oakum, and bolts o' canvas, and all the sound rope in the yard. What else could I ha' done? *I* knowed what he'd need most after a week's such work. I'm a shipbuilder, little maid.

'We'd a fair slant o' wind off Dungeness, and we crept on till it fell light airs and puffed out. The Spanishers was all in a huddle over by Calais, and our ships was strawed about mending 'emselves like dogs lickin' bites. Now and then a Spanisher would fire from a low port, and the ball 'ud troll across the flat swells, but both sides was finished fightin' for that tide.

'The first ship we foreslowed on, her breast-works was crushed in, an' men was shorin' 'em up. She said nothing. The next was a black pinnace, his pumps clackin' middling quick, and he said nothing. But the third, mending shot-holes, he spoke out plenty. I asked him where Mus' Drake might be, and a shiny-suited man on the poop looked down into us, and saw what we carried.

' "Lay alongside you!" he says. "We'll take that all."

' " 'Tis for Mus' Drake," I says, keeping away lest his size should lee the wind out of my sails.

' "Hi! Ho! Hither! We're Lord High Admiral of England! Come alongside, or we'll hang ye," he says.

' 'Twas none of my affairs who he was if he wasn't Frankie, and while he talked so hot I slipped behind a green-painted ship with her topsides splintered. We was all in the middest of 'em then.

' "Hi! Hoi!" the green ship says. "Come alongside, honest man, and I'll buy your load. I'm Fenner that fought the seven Portugals—clean out of shot or bullets. Frankie knows me."

' "Ay, but I don't," I says, and I slacked nothing.

'He was a masterpiece. Seein' I was for goin' on, he hails a

Bridport hoy beyond us and shouts, "George! Oh, George!
Wing that duck. He's fat!" An' true as we're all here, that
squatty Bridport boat rounds to acrost our bows, intendin' to
stop us by means o' shooting.

'My Aunt looks over our rail. "George," she says, "you finish
with your enemies afore you begin on your friends."

'Him that was laying the liddle swivel-gun at us sweeps off
his hat an' calls her Queen Bess, and asks if she was selling
liquor to pore dry sailors. My Aunt answered him quite a
piece. She was a notable woman.

'Then *he* come up—his long pennant trailing overside—
his waistcloths and netting tore all to pieces where the Spanishers had grappled, and his sides black-smeared with their
gun-blasts like candle-smoke in a bottle. We hooked on to a
lower port and hung.

' "Oh, Mus' Drake! Mus' Drake!" I calls up.

'He stood on the great anchor cathead, his shirt open to
the middle, and his face shining like the sun.

' "Why, Sim!" he says. Just like that—after twenty year!
"Sim," he says, "what brings you?"

' "Pudden," I says, not knowing whether to laugh or cry.
"You told me to bring cannon-shot next time, an' I've brought
'em."

'He saw we had. He ripped out a fathom and a half o'
brimstone Spanish, and he swung down on our rail, and he
kissed me before all his fine young captains. His men was
swarming out of the lower ports ready to unload us. When
he saw how I'd considered all his likely wants, he kissed me
again.

' "Here's a friend that sticketh closer than a brother!" he
says. "Mistress," he says to my Aunt, "all you foretold on me
was true. I've opened that road from the East to the West,
and I've buried my heart beside it."

' "I know," she says. "That's why I be come."

' "But ye never foretold this"; he points to both they great fleets.

' "This don't seem to me to make much odds compared to what happens *to* a man," she says. "Do it?"

' "Certain sure a man forgets to remember when he's proper mucked up with work. Sim," he says to me, "we must shift every living Spanisher round Dunkirk corner on to our Dutch sands before morning. The wind'll come out of the North after this calm—same as it used—and then they're our meat."

' "Amen," says I. "I've brought you what I could scutchel up of odds and ends. Be you hit anywhere to signify?"

' "Oh, our folk'll attend to all that when we've time," he says. He turns to talk to my Aunt, while his men flew the stuff out of our hold. I think I saw old Moon amongst 'em, but we was too busy to more than nod like. Yet the Spanishers was going to prayers with their bells and candles before we'd cleaned out the *Antony*. Twenty-two ton o' useful stuff I'd fetched him.

' "Now, Sim," says my Aunt, "no more devouring of Mus' Drake's time. He's sending us home in the Bridport hoy. I want to speak to them young springalds again."

' "But here's our ship all ready and swept," I says.

' "Swep' an' garnished," says Frankie. "I'm going to fill her with devils in the likeness o' pitch and sulphur. We must shift the Dons round Dunkirk corner, and if shot can't do it, we'll send down fire-ships."

' "I've given him my share of the *Antony*," says my Aunt. "What do you reckon to do about yours?"

' "She offered it," said Frankie, laughing.

' "She wouldn't have if I'd overheerd her," I says; "because I'd have offered my share first." Then I told him how the *Antony's* sails was best trimmed to drive before the wind, and seeing he was full of occupations we went acrost to that Bridport hoy, and left him.

'But Frankie was gentle-born, d'ye see, and that sort they never overlook any folks' dues.

'When the hoy passed under his stern, he stood bare-headed on the poop same as if my Aunt had been his Queen, and his musicianers played "Mary Ambree" on their silver trumpets quite a long while. Heart alive, little maid! I never meaned to make you look sorrowful——'

Bunny Lewknor in his sackcloth petticoats burst through the birch scrub wiping his forehead.

'We've got the stick to rights now! She've been a whole hatful o' trouble. You come an' ride her home, Mus' Dan and Miss Una!'

They found the proud wood-gang at the foot of the slope, with the log double-chained on the tug.

'Cattiwow, what are you going to do with it?' said Dan, as they straddled the thin part.

'She's going down to Rye to make a keel for a Lowestoft fishin'-boat, I've heard. Hold tight!'

Cattiwow cracked his whip, and the great log dipped and tilted, and leaned and dipped again, exactly like a stately ship upon the high seas.

FRANKIE'S TRADE

Old Horn to All Atlantic said:—
    (A-hay O! To me O!)
'Now where did Frankie learn his trade?
For he ran me down with a three-reef mains'le.'
    (All round the Horn!)

Atlantic answered:—'Not from me!
You'd better ask the cold North Sea,
For he ran me down under all plain canvas.'
    (All round the Horn!)

The North Sea answered:—'He's my man,
For he came to me when he began—
Frankie Drake in an open coaster.
    (All round the Sands!)

'I caught him young and I used him sore,
So you never shall startle Frankie more,
Without capsizing Earth and her waters.
    (All round the Sands!)

'I did not favour him at all,
I made him pull and I made him haul—
And stand his trick with the common sailors.
    (All round the Sands!)

'I froze him stiff and I fogged him blind,
And kicked him home with his road to find
By what he could see of a three-day snow-storm.
    (All round the Sands!)

REWARDS AND FAIRIES

'I learned him his trade o' winter nights,
'Twixt Mardyk Fort and Dunkirk lights
On a five-knot tide with the forts a-firing
    (All round the Sands!)

'Before his beard began to shoot,
I showed him the length of the Spaniard's foot—
And I reckon he clapped the boot on it later.
    (All round the Sands!)

'If there's a risk which you can make
That's worse than he was used to take
Nigh every week in the way of his business;
    (All round the Sands!)

'If there's a trick that you can try
Which he hasn't met in time gone by,
Not once or twice, but ten times over;
    (All round the Sands!)

'If you can teach him aught that's new,
    (A-hay O! To me O!)
I'll give you Bruges and Niewport too,
And the ten tall churches that stand between 'em.'
    Storm along, my gallant Captains!
    (All round the Horn!)

THE TREE OF JUSTICE

THE BALLAD OF MINEPIT SHAW

About the time that taverns shut
  And men can buy no beer,
Two lads went up by the keepers' hut
  To steal Lord Pelham's deer.

Night and the liquor was in their heads—
  They laughed and talked no bounds,
Till they waked the keepers on their beds,
  And the keepers loosed the hounds.

They had killed a hart, they had killed a hind,
  Ready to carry away,
When they heard a whimper down the wind
  And they heard a bloodhound bay.

They took and ran across the fern,
  Their crossbows in their hand,
Till they met a man with a green lantern
  That called and bade 'em stand.

'What are you doing, O Flesh and Blood,
  And what's your foolish will,
That you must break into Minepit Wood
  And wake the Folk of the Hill?'

'Oh, we've broke into Lord Pelham's park,
  And killed Lord Pelham's deer,
And if ever you heard a little dog bark
  You'll know why we come here!'

REWARDS AND FAIRIES

'We ask you let us go our way,
   As fast as we can flee,
For if ever you heard a bloodhound bay,
   You'll know how pressed we be.'

'Oh, lay your crossbows on the bank
   And drop the knife from your hand,
And though the hounds are at your flank
   I'll save you where you stand!'

They laid their crossbows on the bank,
   They threw their knives in the wood,
And the ground before them opened and sank
   And saved 'em where they stood.

'Oh, what's the roaring in our ears
   That strikes us well-nigh dumb?'
'Oh, that is just how things appears
   According as they come.'

'What are the stars before our eyes
   That strike us well-nigh blind?'
'Oh, that is just how things arise
   According as you find.'

'And why's our bed so hard to the bones
   Excepting where it's cold?'
'Oh, that's because it is precious stones
   Excepting where 'tis gold.

'Think it over as you stand,
   For I tell you without fail,

THE BALLAD OF MINEPIT SHAW

If you haven't got into Fairyland
  You're not in Lewes Gaol.'

All night long they thought of it,
  And, come the dawn, they saw
They'd tumbled into a great old pit,
  At the bottom of Minepit Shaw.

And the keepers' hound had followed 'em close
  And broke her neck in the fall;
So they picked up their knives and their cross-bows
  And buried the dog. That's all.

But whether the man was a poacher too
  Or a Pharisee so bold—
I reckon there's more things told than are true,
  And more things true than are told.

THE TREE OF JUSTICE

IT WAS A WARM, dark winter day with the Sou'-West wind singing through Dallington Forest, and the woods below the Beacon. The children set out after dinner to find old Hobden, who had a three months' job in the Rough at the back of Pound's Wood. He had promised to get them a dormouse in its nest. The bright leaf still clung to the beech coppice; the long chestnut leaves lay orange on the ground, and the rides were speckled with scarlet-lipped sprouting acorns. They worked their way by their own short cuts to the edge of Pound's Wood, and heard a horse's feet just as they came to the beech where Ridley the keeper hangs up the vermin. The poor little fluffy bodies dangled from the branches—some perfectly good, but most of them dried to twisted strips.

'Three more owls,' said Dan, counting. 'Two stoats, four jays, and a kestrel. That's ten since last week. Ridley's a beast.'

'In my time this sort of tree bore heavier fruit.' Sir Richard Dalyngridge[1] reined up his grey horse, Swallow, in the ride behind them. 'What play do you make?' he asked.

'Nothing, sir. We're looking for old Hobden,' Dan replied. 'He promised to get us a sleeper.'

'Sleeper? A *dormeuse*, do you say?'

'Yes, a dormouse, sir.'

'I understand. I passed a woodman on the low grounds. Come!'

He wheeled up the ride again, and pointed through an

[1] This is the Norman knight they met the year before in *Puck of Pook's Hill*. See 'Young Men at the Manor,' 'The Knights of the Joyous Venture,' and 'Old Men at Pevensey,' in that book.

opening to the patch of beech-stubs, chestnut, hazel, and birch that old Hobden would turn into firewood, hop-poles, pea-boughs, and house-faggots before spring. The old man was as busy as a beaver.

Something laughed beneath a thorn, and Puck stole out, his finger on his lip.

'Look!' he whispered. 'Along between the spindle-trees. Ridley has been there this half-hour.'

The children followed his point, and saw Ridley the keeper in an old dry ditch, watching Hobden as a cat watches a mouse.

'Huhh!' cried Una. 'Hobden always 'tends to his wires before breakfast. He puts his rabbits into the faggots he's allowed to take home. He'll tell us about 'em to-morrow.'

'We had the same breed in my day,' Sir Richard replied, and moved off quietly, Puck at his bridle, the children on either side between the close-trimmed beech stuff.

'What did you do to them?' said Dan, as they repassed Ridley's terrible tree.

'That!' Sir Richard jerked his head toward the dangling owls.

'Not he!' said Puck. 'There was never enough brute Norman in you to hang a man for taking a buck.'

'I—I cannot abide to hear their widows screech. But why am I on horseback while you are afoot?' He dismounted lightly, tapped Swallow on the chest, so that the wise thing backed instead of turning in the narrow ride, and put himself at the head of the little procession. He walked as though all the woods belonged to him. 'I have often told my friends,' he went on, 'that Red William the King was not the only Norman found dead in a forest while he hunted.'

'D'you mean William Rufus?' said Dan.

'Yes,' said Puck, kicking a clump of red toad-stools off a dead log.

'For example, there was a knight new from Normandy,' Sir Richard went on, 'to whom Henry our King granted a manor in Kent near by. He chose to hang his forester's son the day before a deer-hunt that he gave to pleasure the King.'

'Now when would that be?' said Puck, and scratched an ear thoughtfully.

'The summer of the year King Henry broke his brother Robert of Normandy at Tenchebrai fight. Our ships were even then at Pevensey loading for the war.'

'What happened to the knight?' Dan asked.

'They found him pinned to an ash, three arrows through his leather coat. *I* should have worn mail that day.'

'And did you see him all bloody?' Dan continued.

'Nay, I was with De Aquila at Pevensey, counting horse-shoes, and arrow-sheaves, and ale-barrels into the holds of the ships. The army only waited for our King to lead them against Robert in Normandy, but he sent word to De Aquila that he would hunt with him here before he set out for France.'

'Why did the King want to hunt so particularly?' Una demanded.

'If he had gone straight to France after the Kentish knight was killed, men would have said he feared being slain like the knight. It was his duty to show himself debonair to his English people as it was De Aquila's duty to see that he took no harm while he did it. But it was a great burden! De Aquila, Hugh, and I ceased work on the ships, and scoured all the Honour of the Eagle—all De Aquila's lands—to make a fit, and, above all, a safe sport for our King. Look!'

The ride twisted, and came out on the top of Pound's Hill Wood. Sir Richard pointed to the swells of beautiful, dappled

Dallington, that showed like a woodcock's breast up the valley. 'Ye know the forest?' said he.

'You ought to see the bluebells there in Spring!' said Una.

'I have seen,' said Sir Richard, gazing, and stretched out his hand. 'Hugh's work and mine was first to move the deer gently from all parts into Dallington yonder, and there to hold them till the King came. Next, we must choose some three hundred beaters to drive the deer to the stands within bowshot of the King. Here was our trouble! In the mellay of a deer-drive a Saxon peasant and a Norman King may come over-close to each other. The conquered do not love their conquerors all at once. So we needed sure men, for whom their village or kindred would answer in life, cattle, and land if any harm come to the King. Ye see?'

'If one of the beaters shot the King,' said Puck, 'Sir Richard wanted to be able to punish that man's village. Then the village would take care to send a good man.'

'So! So it was. But, lest our work should be too easy, the King had done such a dread justice over at Salehurst, for the killing of the Kentish knight (twenty-six men he hanged, as I heard), that our folk were half mad with fear before we began. It is easier to dig out a badger gone to earth than a Saxon gone dumb-sullen. And atop of their misery the old rumour waked that Harold the Saxon was alive and would bring them deliverance from us Normans. This has happened every autumn since Santlache fight.'

'But King Harold was killed at Hastings,' said Una.

'So it was said, and so it was believed by us Normans, but our Saxons always believed he would come again. *That* rumour did not make our work any more easy.'

Sir Richard strode on down the far slope of the wood, where the trees thin out. It was fascinating to watch how he managed his long spurs among the lumps of blackened ling.

'But we did it!' he said. 'After all, a woman is as good as a man to beat the woods; and the mere word that deer are afoot makes cripples and crones young again. De Aquila laughed when Hugh told him over the list of beaters. Half were women; and many of the rest were clerks—Saxon and Norman priests.

'Hugh and I had not time to laugh for eight days, till De Aquila, as Lord of Pevensey, met our King and led him to the first shooting-stand—by the Mill on the edge of the forest. Hugh and I—it was no work for hot heads or heavy hands— lay with our beaters on the skirts of Dallington to watch both them and the deer. When De Aquila's great horn blew we went forward, a line half a league long. Oh, to see the fat clerks, their gowns tucked up, puffing and roaring, and the sober millers dusting the undergrowth with their staves; and, like as not, between them a Saxon wench, hand in hand with her man, shrilling like a kite as she ran, and leaping high through the fern, all for joy of the sport.'

'*Ah! How! Ah! How! How-ah! Sa-how-ah!*' Puck bellowed without warning, and Swallow bounded forward, ears cocked, and nostrils cracking.

'*Hal-lal-lal-lal-la-hai-ie!*' Sir Richard answered in a high clear shout.

The two voices joined in swooping circles of sound, and a heron rose out of a red osier-bed below them, circling as though he kept time to the outcry. Swallow quivered and swished his glorious tail. They stopped together on the same note.

A hoarse shout answered them across the bare woods.

'That's old Hobden,' said Una.

'Small blame to him. It is in his blood,' said Puck. 'Did your beaters cry so, Sir Richard?'

'My faith, they forgot all else. (Steady, Swallow, steady!) They forgot where the King and his people waited to shoot.

They followed the deer to the very edge of the open till the first flight of wild arrows from the stands flew fair over them.

'I cried, " 'Ware shot! 'Ware shot!" and a knot of young knights new from Normandy, that had strayed away from the Grand Stand, turned about, and in mere sport loosed off at our line shouting: " 'Ware Santlache arrows! 'Ware Santlache arrows!" A jest, I grant you, but too sharp. One of our beaters answered in Saxon: " 'Ware New Forest arrows! 'Ware Red William's arrow!" so I judged it time to end the jests, and when the boys saw my old mail gown (for, to shoot with strangers *I* count the same as war), they ceased shooting. So *that* was smoothed over, and we gave our beaters ale to wash down their anger. They were excusable! We—they had sweated to show our guests good sport, and our reward was a flight of hunting-arrows which no man loves, and worse, a churl's jibe over hard-fought, fair-lost Hastings fight. So, before the next beat, Hugh and I assembled and called the beaters over by name, to steady them. The greater part we knew, but among the Netherfield men I saw an old, old man, in the dress of a pilgrim.

'The Clerk of Netherfield said he was well known by repute for twenty years as a witless man that journeyed without rest to all the shrines of England. The old man sits, Saxon fashion, head between fists. We Normans rest the chin on the left palm.

' "Who answers for him?" said I. "If he fails in his duty, who will pay his fine?"

' "Who will pay my fine?" the pilgrim said. "I have asked that of all the Saints in England these forty years, less three months and nine days! They have not answered!" When he lifted his thin face I saw he was one-eyed, and frail as a rush.

' "Nay, but, Father," I said, "to whom hast thou commended

thyself?" He shook his head, so I spoke in Saxon: "Whose man
art thou?"

' "I think I have a writing from Rahere, the King's Jester,"
said he after a while. "I am, as I suppose, Rahere's man."

'He pulled a writing from his scrip, and Hugh, coming up,
read it.

'It set out that the pilgrim was Rahere's man, and that
Rahere was the King's Jester. There was Latin writ at the back.

' "What a plague conjuration's here?" said Hugh, turning it
over. "*Pum-quum-sum oc-occ.* Magic?"

' "Black Magic," said the Clerk of Netherfield (he had been
a monk at Battle). "They say Rahere is more of a priest than
a fool and more of a wizard than either. Here's Rahere's name
writ, and there's Rahere's red cockscomb mark drawn below
for such as cannot read." He looked slyly at me.

' "Then read it," said I, "and show thy learning." He was a
vain little man, and he gave it us after much mouthing.

' "The charm, which I think is from Virgilius the Sorcerer,
says: 'When thou art once dead, and Minos' (which is a heathen
judge) 'has doomed thee, neither cunning, nor speechcraft, nor
good works will restore thee!' A terrible thing! It denies any
mercy to a man's soul!"

' "Does it serve?" said the pilgrim, plucking at Hugh's cloak.
"Oh, man of the King's blood, does it cover me?"

'Hugh was of Earl Godwin's blood, and all Sussex knew it,
though no Saxon dared call him kingly in a Norman's hearing.
There can be but one King.

' "It serves," said Hugh. "But the day will be long and hot.
Better rest here. We go forward now."

' "No, I will keep with thee, my kinsman," he answered like
a child. He was indeed childish through great age.

'The line had not moved a bowshot when De Aquila's great

horn blew for a halt, and soon young Fulke—our false Fulke's son—yes, the imp that lit the straw in Pevensey Castle[1]—came thundering up a woodway.

' "Uncle," said he (though he was a man grown, he called me Uncle), "those young Norman fools who shot at you this morn are saying that your beaters cried treason against the King. It has come to Harry's long ears, and he bids you give account of it. There are heavy fines in his eye, but I am with you to the hilt, Uncle!"

'When the boy had fled back, Hugh said to me: "It was Rahere's witless man that cried, ' 'Ware Red William's arrow!' I heard him, and so did the Clerk of Netherfield."

' "Then Rahere must answer to the King for his man," said I. "Keep him by you till I send," and I hastened down.

'The King was with De Aquila in the Grand Stand above Welansford down in the valley yonder. His Court—knights and dames—lay glittering on the edge of the glade. I made my homage, and Henry took it coldly.

' "How came your beaters to shout threats against me?" said he.

' "The tale has grown," I answered. "One old witless man cried out, ' 'Ware Red William's arrow,' when the young knights shot at our line. We had two beaters hit."

' "I will do justice on that man," he answered. "Who is his master?"

' "He is Rahere's man," said I.

' "Rahere's?" said Henry. "Has my fool a fool?"

'I heard the bells jingle at the back of the stand, and a red leg waved over it; then a black one. So, very slowly, Rahere the King's Jester straddled the edge of the planks, and looked down on us, rubbing his chin. Loose-knit, with cropped hair, and a

1 See 'Old Men at Pevensey' in *Puck of Pook's Hill.*

sad priest's face, under his cockscomb cap, that he could twist like a strip of wet leather. His eyes were hollow-set.

' "Nay, nay, Brother," said he. "If I suffer you to keep your fool, you must e'en suffer me to keep mine."

'This he delivered slowly into the King's angry face! My faith, a King's Jester must be bolder than lions!

' "Now we will judge the matter," said Rahere. "Let these two brave knights go hang my fool because he warned King Henry against running after Saxon deer through woods full of Saxons. 'Faith, Brother, if *thy* Brother, Red William, now among the Saints as we hope, had been timely warned against a certain arrow in New Forest, one fool of us four would not be crowned fool of England this morning. Therefore, hang the fool's fool, knights!"

'Mark the fool's cunning! Rahere had himself given us order to hang the man. No king dare confirm a fool's command to such a great baron as De Aquila; and the helpless King knew it.

' "What? No hanging?" said Rahere, after a silence. "A' God's Gracious Name, kill something, then! Go forward with the hunt!"

'He splits his face ear to ear in a yawn like a fish-pond. "Henry," says he, "the next time I sleep, do not pester me with thy fooleries." Then he throws himself out of sight behind the back of the stand.

'I have seen courage with mirth in De Aquila and Hugh, but stark mad courage of Rahere's sort I had never even guessed at.'

'What did the King say?' cried Dan.

'He had opened his mouth to speak, when young Fulke, who had come into the stand with us, laughed, and, boy-like, once begun, could not check himself. He kneeled on the instant for pardon, but fell sideways, crying: "His legs! Oh, his long, waving red legs as he went backward!"

'Like a storm breaking, our grave King laughed,—stamped and reeled with laughter till the stand shook. So, like a storm, this strange thing passed!

'He wiped his eyes, and signed to De Aquila to let the drive come on.

'When the deer broke, we were pleased that the King shot from the shelter of the stand, and did not ride out after the hurt beasts as Red William would have done. Most vilely his knights and barons shot!

'De Aquila kept me beside him, and I saw no more of Hugh till evening. We two had a little hut of boughs by the camp, where I went to wash me before the great supper, and in the dusk I heard Hugh on the couch.

' "Wearied, Hugh?" said I.

' "A little," he says. "I have driven Saxon deer all day for a Norman King, and there is enough of Earl Godwin's blood left in me to sicken at the work. Wait awhile with the torch."

'I waited then, and I thought I heard him sob.'

'Poor Hugh! Was he so tired?' said Una. 'Hobden says beating is hard work sometimes.'

'I think this tale is getting like the woods,' said Dan, 'darker and twistier every minute.'

Sir Richard had walked as he talked, and though the children thought they knew the woods well enough, they felt a little lost.

'A dark tale enough,' says Sir Richard, 'but the end was not all black. When we had washed, we went to wait on the King at meat in the great pavilion. Just before the trumpets blew for the Entry—all the guests upstanding—long Rahere comes posturing up to Hugh, and strikes him with his bauble-bladder.

' "Here's a heavy heart for a joyous meal!" he says. "But each man must have his black hour or where would be the merit of laughing? Take a fool's advice, and sit it out with my man. I'll make a jest to excuse you to the King if he remember to ask for you. That's more than I would do for Archbishop Anselm."

'Hugh looked at him heavy-eyed. "Rahere?" said he. "The King's Jester? Oh, Saints, what punishment for my King!" and smites his hands together.

' "Go—go fight it out in the dark," says Rahere, "and thy Saxon Saints reward thee for thy pity to my fool." He pushed him from the pavilion, and Hugh lurched away like one drunk.'

'But why?' said Una. 'I don't understand.'

'Ah, why indeed? Live you long enough, maiden, and you shall know the meaning of many whys.' Sir Richard smiled. 'I wondered too, but it was my duty to wait on the King at the High Table in all that glitter and stir.

'He spoke me his thanks for the sport I had helped show him, and he had learned from De Aquila enough of my folk and my castle in Normandy to graciously feign that he knew and had loved my brother there. (This, also, is part of a king's work.) Many great men sat at the High Table—chosen by the King for their wits, not for their birth. I have forgotten their names, and their faces I only saw that one night. But'—Sir Richard turned in his stride—'but Rahere, flaming in black and scarlet among our guests, the hollow of his dark cheek flushed with wine—long, laughing Rahere, and the stricken sadness of his face when he was not twisting it about—Rahere I shall never forget.

'At the King's outgoing De Aquila bade me follow him, with his great bishops and two great barons, to the little pavilion.

We had devised jugglers and dances for the Court's sport; but
Henry loved to talk gravely with grave men, and De Aquila
had told him of my travels to the world's end. We had a fire
of applewood, sweet as incense,—and the curtains at the door
being looped up, we could hear the music and see the lights
shining on mail and dresses.

'Rahere lay behind the King's chair. The questions he darted
forth at me were as shrewd as the flames. I was telling of our
fight with the apes, as ye called them, at the world's end.[1]

' "But where is the Saxon knight that went with you?" said
Henry. "He must confirm these miracles."

' "He is busy," said Rahere, "confirming a new miracle."

' "Enough miracles for to-day," said the King. "Rahere, you
have saved your long neck. Fetch the Saxon knight."

' "Pest on it," said Rahere. "Who would be a King's Jester?
I'll bring him, Brother, if you'll see that none of your home-
brewed bishops taste my wine while I am away." So he jingled
forth between the men-at-arms at the door.

'Henry had made many bishops in England without
the Pope's leave. I know not the rights of the matter, but
only Rahere dared jest about it. We waited on the King's next
word.

' "I think Rahere is jealous of you," said he, smiling, to
Nigel of Ely. He was one bishop; and William of Exeter, the
other—Wal-wist the Saxons called him—laughed long. "Rahere
is a priest at heart. Shall I make him a bishop, De Aquila?"
says the King.

' "There might be worse," said our Lord of Pevensey. "Rahere would never do what Anselm has done."

'This Anselm, Archbishop of Canterbury, had gone off rag-

[1] See 'The Knights of the Joyous Venture' in *Puck of Pook's Hill*.

ing to the Pope at Rome, because Henry would make bishops without *his* leave either. I knew not the rights of it, but De Aquila did, and the King laughed.

' "Anselm means no harm. He should have been a monk, not a bishop," said the King. "I'll never quarrel with Anselm or his Pope till they quarrel with my England. If we can keep the King's peace till my son comes to rule, no man will lightly quarrel with our England."

' "Amen," said De Aquila. "But the King's peace ends when the King dies."

'That is true. The King's peace dies with the King. The custom then is that all laws are outlaw, and men do what they will till the new King is chosen.

' "I will amend that," said the King hotly. "I will have it so that though King, son, and grandson were all slain in one day, *still* the King's peace should hold over all England! What is a man that his mere death must upheave a people? We must have the Law."

' "Truth," said William of Exeter; but that he would have said to any word of the King.

'The two great barons behind said nothing. This teaching was clean against their stomachs, for when the King's peace ends, the great barons go to war and increase their lands. At that instant we heard Rahere's voice returning, in a scurril Saxon rhyme against William of Exeter:—

> *"Well wist Wal-wist where lay his fortune*
> *When that he fawned on the King for his crozier,"*

and amid our laughter he burst in, with one arm round Hugh, and one round the old pilgrim of Netherfield.

' "Here is your knight, Brother," said he, "and for the better disport of the company, here is my fool. Hold up, Saxon Samson, the gates of Gaza are clean carried away!"

'Hugh broke loose, white and sick, and staggered to my side; the old man blinked upon the company.

'We looked at the King, but he smiled.

' "Rahere promised he would show me some sport after supper to cover his morning's offence," said he to De Aquila. "So this is thy man, Rahere?"

' "Even so," said Rahere. "My man he has been, and my protection he has taken, ever since I found him under the gallows at Stamford Bridge telling the kites atop of it that he was—Harold of England!"

'There was a great silence upon these last strange words, and Hugh hid his face on my shoulder, woman-fashion.

' "It is most cruel true," he whispered to me. "The old man proved it to me at the beat after you left, and again in our hut even now. It is Harold, my King!"

'De Aquila crept forward. He walked about the man and swallowed.

' "Bones of the Saints!" said he, staring.

' "Many a stray shot goes too well home," said Rahere.

'The old man flinched as at an arrow. "Why do you hurt me still?" he said in Saxon. "It was on some bones of some Saints that I promised I would give my England to the Great Duke." He turns on us all crying, shrilly: "Thanes, he had caught me at Rouen—a lifetime ago. If I had not promised, I should have lain there all my life. What else could I have done? I have lain in a strait prison all my life none the less. There is no need to throw stones at me." He guarded his face with his arms, and shivered.

' "Now his madness will strike him down," said Rahere.

"Cast out the evil spirit, one of you new bishops."

'Said William of Exeter: "Harold was slain at Santlache fight. All the world knows it."

' "I think this man must have forgotten," said Rahere. "Be comforted, Father. Thou was well slain at Hastings forty years gone, less three months and nine days. Tell the King."

'The man uncovered his face. "I thought they would stone me," he said. "I did not know I spoke before a King." He came to his full towering height—no mean man, but frail beyond belief.

'The King turned to the tables, and held him out his own cup of wine. The old man drank, and beckoned behind him, and, before all the Normans, my Hugh bore away the empty cup, Saxon-fashion, upon the knee.

' "It is Harold!" said De Aquila. "His own stiff-necked blood kneels to serve him."

' "Be it so," said Henry. "Sit, then, thou that hast been Harold of England."

'The madman sat, and hard, dark Henry looked at him between half-shut eyes. We others stared like oxen, all but De Aquila, who watched Rahere as I have seen him watch a far sail on the sea.

'The wine and the warmth cast the old man into a dream. His white head bowed; his hands hung. His eye indeed was opened, but the mind was shut. When he stretched his feet, they were scurfed and road-cut like a slave's.

' "Ah, Rahere," cried Hugh, "why hast thou shown him thus? Better have let him die than shame him—and me!"

' "Shame thee?" said the King. "Would any baron of mine kneel to me if I were witless, discrowned, and alone, and Harold had my throne?"

' "No," said Rahere. "I am the sole fool that might do it,

Brother, unless"—he pointed at De Aquila, whom he had only met that day—"yonder tough Norman crab kept me company. But, Sir Hugh, I did not mean to shame him. He hath been somewhat punished through, maybe, little fault of his own."

' "Yet he lied to my Father, the Conqueror," said the King, and the old man flinched in his sleep.

' "Maybe," said Rahere, "but thy Brother Robert, whose throat we purpose soon to slit with our own hands——"

' "Hutt!" said the King, laughing. "I'll keep Robert at my table for a life's guest when I catch him. Robert means no harm. It is all his cursed barons."

' "None the less," said Rahere, "Robert may say that thou hast not always spoken the stark truth to him about England. I should not hang too many men on *that* bough, Brother."

' "And it is certain," said Hugh, "that"—he pointed to the old man—"Harold was forced to make his promise to the Great Duke."

' "Very strongly forced," said De Aquila. He had never any pride in the Duke William's dealings with Harold before Hastings. Yet, as he said, one cannot build a house all of straight sticks.

' "No matter how he was forced," said Henry, "England was promised to my Father William by Edward the Confessor. Is it not so?" William of Exeter nodded. "Harold confirmed that promise to my Father on the bones of the Saints. Afterwards he broke his oath and would have taken England by the strong hand."

' "Oh! Là! Là!" Rahere rolled up his eyes like a girl. "That ever England should be taken by the strong hand!"

'Seeing that Red William and Henry after him had each in just that fashion snatched England from Robert of Normandy, we others knew not where to look. But De Aquila saved us quickly.

' "Promise kept or promise broken," he said, "Harold came near enough to breaking us Normans at Santlache."

' "Was it so close a fight, then?" said Henry.

' "A hair would have turned it either way," De Aquila answered. "His house-carles stood like rocks against rain. Where wast thou, Hugh, in it?"

' "Among Godwin's folk beneath the Golden Dragon till your front gave back, and we broke our ranks to follow," said Hugh.

' "But I bade you stand! I bade you stand! I knew it was all a deceit!" Harold had waked, and leaned forward as one crying from the grave.

' "Ah, now we see how the traitor himself was betrayed!" said William of Exeter, and looked for a smile from the King.

' "I made thee Bishop to preach at *my* bidding," said Henry; and turning to Harold, "Tell us here how thy people fought us?" said he. "Their sons serve me now against my Brother Robert!"

'The old man shook his head cunningly. "Na—Na—Na!" he cried. "I know better. Every time I tell my tale men stone me. But, Thanes, I will tell you a greater thing. Listen!" He told us how many paces it was from some Saxon Saint's shrine to another shrine, and how many more back to the Abbey of the Battle.

' "Ay," said he. "I have trodden it too often to be out even ten paces. I move very swiftly. Harold of Norway knows that, and so does Tostig my brother. They lie at ease at Stamford Bridge, and from Stamford Bridge to the Battle Abbey it is——" he muttered over many numbers and forgot us.

' "Ay," said De Aquila, all in a muse. "That man broke Harold of Norway at Stamford Bridge, and came near to breaking us at Santlache—all within one month."

' "But how did he come alive from Santlache fight?" asked the King. "Ask him! Hast thou heard it, Rahere?"

' "Never. He says he has been stoned too often for telling the tale. But he can count you off Saxon and Norman shrines till daylight," said Rahere, and the old man nodded proudly.

' "My faith!" said Henry after a while. "I think even my Father the Great Duke would pity if he could see him."

' "How if he *does* see?" said Rahere.

'Hugh covered his face with his sound hand. "Ah, why hast thou shamed him?" he cried again to Rahere.

' "No—no," says the old man, reaching to pluck at Rahere's cape. "I am Rahere's man. None stone me now," and he played with the bells on the scollops of it.

' "How if he had been brought to me when you found him?" said the King to Rahere.

' "You would have held him prisoner again—as the Great Duke did," Rahere answered.

' "True," said our King. "He is nothing except his name. Yet that name might have been used by stronger men to trouble my England. Yes. I must have made him my life's guest—as I shall make Robert."

' "I knew it," said Rahere. "But while this man wandered mad by the wayside, none cared what he called himself."

' "I learned to cease talking before the stones flew," says the old man, and Hugh groaned.

' "Ye have heard!" said Rahere. "Witless, landless, nameless, and, but for my protection, masterless, he can still make shift to bide his doom under the open sky."

' "Then wherefore didst thou bring him here for a mock and a shame?" cried Hugh, beside himself with woe.

' "A right mock and a just shame!" said William of Exeter.

' "Not to me," said Nigel of Ely. "I see and I tremble, but I neither mock nor judge."

' "Well spoken, Ely." Rahere falls into the pure fool again. "I'll pray for thee when I turn monk. Thou hast given thy blessing on a war between two most Christian brothers." He meant the war forward 'twixt Henry and Robert of Normandy. "I charge you, Brother," he says, wheeling on the King, "dost thou mock my fool?"

'The King shook his head, and so then did smooth William of Exeter.

' "De Aquila, dost thou mock him?" Rahere jingled from one to another, and the old man smiled.

' "By the Bones of the Saints, not I," said our Lord of Pevensey. "I know how dooms near he broke us at Santlache."

' "Sir Hugh, you are excused the question. But you, valiant, loyal, honourable, and devout barons, Lords of Man's Justice in your own bounds, do *you* mock my fool?"

'He shook his bauble in the very faces of those two barons whose names I have forgotten. "Na—Na!" they said, and waved him back foolishly enough.

'He hies him across to staring, nodding Harold, and speaks from behind his chair.

' "No man mocks thee. Who here judges this man? Henry of England—Nigel—De Aquila! On your souls, swift with the answer!" he cried.

'None answered. We were all—the King not least—overborne by that terrible scarlet-and-black wizard-jester.

' "Well for your souls," he said, wiping his brow. Next, shrill like a woman: "Oh, come to me!" and Hugh ran forward to hold Harold, that had slidden down in the chair.

' "Hearken," said Rahere, his arm round Harold's neck. "The King—his bishops—the knights—all the world's crazy chessboard neither mock nor judge thee. Take that comfort with thee, Harold of England!"

'Hugh heaved the old man up and he smiled.

' "Good comfort," said Harold. "Tell me again! I have been somewhat punished——"

'Rahere hallooed it once more into his ear as the head rolled. We heard him sigh, and Nigel of Ely stood forth, praying aloud.

' "Out! I will have no Norman!" Harold said as clearly as I speak now, and he refuged himself on Hugh's sound shoulder, and stretched out, and lay all still.'

'Dead?' said Una, turning up a white face in the dusk.

'That was his good fortune. To die in the King's presence, and on the breast of the most gentlest, truest knight of his own house. Some of us envied him,' said Sir Richard, and fell back to take Swallow's bridle.

'Turn left here,' Puck called ahead of them from under an oak. They ducked down a narrow path through close ash plantation.

The children hurried forward, but cutting a corner charged full-breast into the thorn-faggot that old Hobden was carrying home on his back.

'My! My!' said he. 'Have you scratted your face, Miss Una?'

'Sorry! It's all right,' said Una, rubbing her nose. 'How many rabbits did you get to-day?'

'That's tellin's,' the old man grinned as he re-hoisted his faggot. 'I reckon Mus' Ridley he've got rheumatism along o' lyin' in the dik to see I didn't snap up any. Think o' that now!'

They laughed a good deal while he told them the tale.

'An' just as he crawled away I heard some one hollerin' to the hounds in our woods,' said he. 'Didn't you hear? You must ha' been asleep sure-ly.'

'Oh, what about the sleeper you promised to show us?' Dan
cried.

' 'Ere he be—house an' all!' Hobden dived into the prickly
heart of the faggot and took out a dormouse's wonderfully
woven nest of grass and leaves. His blunt fingers parted it as if
it had been precious lace, and tilting it toward the last of the
light he showed the little, red, furry chap curled up inside, his
tail between his eyes that were shut for their winter sleep.

'Let's take him home. Don't breathe on him,' said Una. 'It'll
make him warm and he'll wake up and die straight off. Won't
he, Hobby?'

'Dat's a heap better by my reckonin' than wakin' up and
findin' himself in a cage for life. No! We'll lay him into the
bottom o' this hedge. Dat's jus' right! No more trouble for him
till come Spring. An' now we'll go home.'

A CAROL

Our Lord Who did the Ox command
   To kneel to Judah's King,
He binds His frost upon the land
   To ripen it for Spring—
To ripen it for Spring, good sirs,
   According to His word;
Which well must be as ye can see—
   And who shall judge the Lord?

When we poor fenmen skate the ice
   Or shiver on the wold,
We hear the cry of a single tree
   That breaks her heart in the cold—
That breaks her heart in the cold, good sirs,
   And rendeth by the board;
Which well must be as ye can see—
   And who shall judge the Lord?

Her wood is crazed and little worth
   Excepting as to burn,
That we may warm and make our mirth
   Until the Spring return—
Until the Spring return, good sirs,
   When people walk abroad;
Which well must be as ye can see—
   And who shall judge the Lord?

God bless the master of this house,
   And all that sleep therein!

REWARDS AND FAIRIES

And guard the fens from pirate folk,
And keep us all from sin,
To walk in honesty, good sirs,
Of thought and deed and word!
Which shall befriend our latter end—
And who shall judge the Lord?

THE END